BIG LEAGUE BALDERDASH

Tall Tales of Dandies, Thugs & Cheats Who Forged Our National Pastime

An American Flim-Flam Series

~

Written and Illustrated by
Tracy Tomkowiak

Copyright © 2013 by Tracy Tomkowiak

All rights reserved. No part of this book may be reproduced in any form or by any electronic or mechanical means, including information storage and retrieval systems, without written permission from the author, except in the case of a reviewer, who may quote brief passages embodied in critical articles or in a review.

This is a work of fiction. Names, characters, places, and incidents either are the product of the author's imagination or are used fictitiously, and any resemblance to actual persons, living or dead, events, or locales is entirely coincidental.

Edition: November 2013

Special thanks to Chris Bittler | badideabooks.com

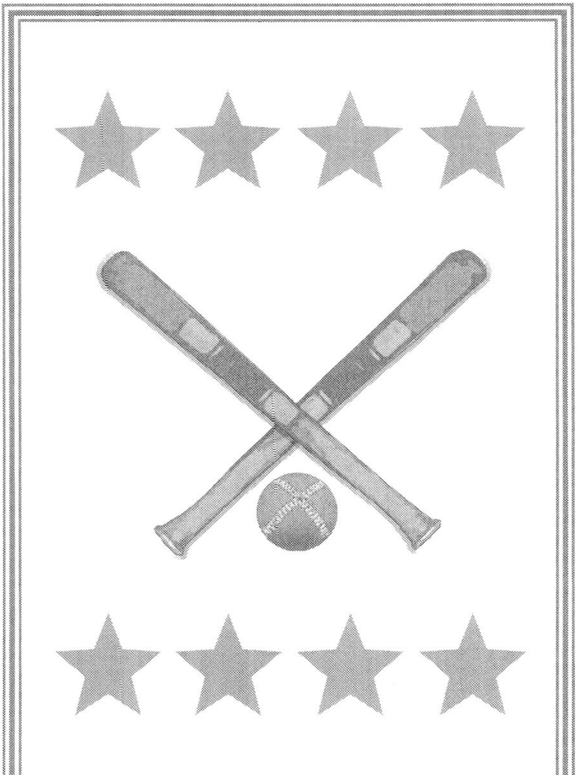

"This great game of Base-Ball—with all its glory and magnificence—has enraptured the masses in such a convincing manner, all the while continuing to advance as a pure, wholesome form of entertainment. I quiver to think what it will be like in the next few years, let alone the next century."

— Grantham Ford Wentworth,
outfielder, New York Elites, 1875

CONTENTS

Prelude **DOGGED DAYS** (1887) 1

I. **A LEDE OFF FIRST** (1976) 5
II. **A BOODLER'S GRAB** (1857) 27
III. **CODFISH ARISTOCRACY** (1857-1860) 53
IV. **PENNY FARTHING ARCADE** (1860-1865) 79
    a. *Daisy Cutter* (J.E. Tunney) 87
    b. *"A Muffin Who Couldn't Stir Your Stumps"* (Everitt Townsend) . . 89
V. **HULLABALOO ALABASTER** (1868-1873) 94
    a. *Smart as a Steel Trap Snapdragon* (W.H. Pierce) 102
    b. *Uncle Charley Comes to Towne* (Alexander Bookeward) . . 106
    c. *Catawump* (Royal Duff Ferguson) 108
    d. *Splendiferous Whitewash* (Grantham Ford Wentworth) . . 109
VI. **SHOESTRING HUZZAH!** (1874-1881) 117
    a. *Difficult Cheese* (Clifford "The Mule" Grumsley) 126
    b. *Chin Music to Soften the Senses* (Tip Bullinger) 131
    c. *Dew-Drop Whimsy* (Kermit Givers) 133
    d. *Yakker* (Ralph Sweek) 135
    e. *Whiffed on Anti-Fogmatic* (Flynt Doyle) 140
VII. **SCHNOCKERD** (1879-1883) 155
    a. *Split-Fingered Muckler* (Mac Aintree) 170
    b. *Caught Looking Like a Dilly-Dob* (Jim Purfidies) . . . 174
    c. *Soaplock Stinger* (Hughie O'Hallarhan) 183
    d. *Bodacious Pluck* (Larry Digby) 188
    e. *Rhubarb* (Sorley McGrady) 196
VIII. **STRETCH TIME** (1882-1887) 209
    a. *Duck Snorts & Greasy Doorknobs* (Paddy Duggins) . . 209
    b. *Melancholy Opine* (Creepy Crowley) 212
    c. *'Tween Killing* (Bill Whalen and "Doc" Abercrombie) . . 216
    d. *Slanticular* (William "Twitchy Bill" Connell) 219
    e. *Bilious Brushback* (George Williamson) 222
    f. *Phenomenal* (Mike Fowler) 224
    g. *"Where'd All the Fungo?"* (Baltimore Federals) 228
    h. *Monkey* (Mr. Buggles, Detroit's Mascot) 232

IX. **A Cut-Plug Can of Corn** (1883-1893) 237
   a. *Horsehide Indiscriminate* (Philo Grogan) 244
   b. *Tree-Fingers* (Stacks Bittner) 246
   c. *Cork Tip of the Hat* (Gus Johnson) 248
   d. *Mustard Skedaddle* (Holly McBride) 255
   e. *Gallknipper* (Russell "Red" Cheatham) 258
   f. *Effervescent Elixirol* (Frank Horgan) 265
   g. *A Febrile Hankering* (George Malone) 271

X. **Gummer of the Century** (1893) 285

Epilogue **Honey Fuggle Tailpiece** (1976) 347

BUSH LEAGUE

H. Recker p. Pittsburgh

Wm. S. Heche & Sons

Cigarettes

PRELUDE

DOGGED DAYS
(1887)

Hap "Sliver" Moss punches the ball through the infield, a clean base hit to right. The willowy player for the Scranton club busts it down the line, thinking two all the way.

He rounds first, eyes fixed on second base. But before he hits his stride, a flash of something enters the corner of his eye and then...BLAM! An explosion of searing pain seizes his mouth, dropping him to the ground.

"Goddamn you again, Mullansky!" Chester Deevers, Scranton's player-manager, leaps off the bench and races out to the infield toward Philadelphia's first baseman.

Bill "Spit" Mullansky, gnawing on a giant wad of tobacco, discharges a cord of brown extract. Directly below him, Moss writhes in pain, moaning.

Deevers slams his body into Mullansky's, knocking his own cap off. "You no-good-fer-nothin' sleazebag! That's the third time you blatantly hit one of my men, right square in the chops! What're got to say about this one?"

Both men are caked in dirt, dust and sweat. Their prominent mustaches recede into a thicket of three-day old whiskers. Their breath reeks of something scraped from the bottom of a forgotten compost tank.

Mullansky juts his face an inch from Deevers' and curls his lips. "Eat shit, old man."

That does it for Deevers. He lashes out at his bitter adversary. "You hog's tit of a human being! You flea-bitten mutt! You…*skuzzlebug!*"

Mullansky cheerily enjoys the blistering abuse, not moving an inch, until Deevers mentions his infamous transgression in '82.

"What did you say, Deevers?"

"You heard me, Spit. You take your chicanery too far and what does it get you? A broken skull!"

"Why you dried up, sorry-ass leather poke—"

A vicious exchange of invective follows until the umpire tries to butt in. "You two pipe down and get—"

Still riveted on Deevers, Mullansky buries his fist in the officiator's chest and shoves him to the ground, where he lands squarely on his ass and doesn't get up.

They continue their verbal tussling. Dust blows everywhere. The scorching midday sun has not let up. Everyone wants the game to end and either go home or to the saloon. Mercifully, only a couple dozen people are left in the rickety stands, trying to find a spot of shade.

"What are you gonna do about my guy?" Deevers points down at Moss, covered in dirt and gushing blood, his front teeth missing.

"That spindly little crotch hair got in my way. I was just getting in position to catch the throw back in from right."

"That's the second time you nailed this poor bastard. The first time was a nut-buster!"

"Whaddy'a want me to say? I guess he's unlucky."

"Unlucky, my ass! You'll do anything to stop anyone from getting past first, this side of bashing their knees in with a bat for crissakes!"

"What are you sayin' Deevers?"

"I'm saying you'll go as far as necessary to get your way without getting your head cracked open."

"Are you calling me a *shecoonery artist?*"

"If the shoe fits…"

"You got some nerve calling me that, Deevers. How many times have I caught you pulling a Blind Man's Logroll or a Dogcatcher's Pair-O-Pants?"

Deevers crosses his arms. "I don't know what the hell you're talkin' about."

"Come off it, dustbag. You're just as rotten as the next guy!"

Both men stare at each other until Philadelphia's pitcher approaches them. "Gimme the goddamned ball, Spit."

Mullansky points to the pitcher's flask tucked in between his shirt and belt. "A drink first."

He gives him the flask and he takes a quick snort. He gags. "Jesus Christ, Ed. This is water!"

"What?" The pitcher shrugs his shoulders. "It's already the sixth inning, Spit. You expect anything else?"

Deevers turns Mullansky around. "You have to give the runner an open path to the bases."

"Says who?"

"The rulebook."

"Rulebook?" Mullansky lets out a laugh. "What rulebook? Show me this goddamned basepath."

The umpire raises his hand and is about to interject before Mullansky takes his foot and slams him back down in the dirt.

They survey the infield between first and second base. Deevers draws an imaginary line with his hands, pointing between the bases. "See? You interfered with my guy."

"Bullshit. It's anyone's space while the play is going on. I got there first. Tough shit."

Deevers calls out another Scranton player to help Moss get on his feet and escort him back to the bench.

"Thuckin' cock-thucker!" Blood flies out of Moss' mouth and hits Mullansky in the chest. They jaw at each other all the way to the other end of the infield.

Mullansky backs up, accidentally trips over the umpire. "Somebody get this piece of shit outta here!"

Deevers bends down to retrieve his cap and tie his shoes next to first base. Just as he bounces up from his crouch, without anybody looking, he gives the bag a quick nudge several inches closer to home plate before returning to the bench. ∎

I.
———

A Lede Off First
(1976)

With a jet roar flush of the toilet and the slam of the opened stall door, Jack Mullen propels himself out of the men's room and into the foyer of the *Chicago Daily Times*. During his mid-morning ritual, an angle to a story abruptly manifests. Now he's got to get upstairs and get it down on paper before it disappears.

The Splendid Summer of 1976 has turned into a long and dreadful stretch of baseball for both the North and South Side teams and Mullen's been searching for something to stir up for readers of his column. There's nothing more repugnant than a pair of awful teams steaming like a pile of horse shit in the middle of a hot, humid summer. To make matters worse, no one from either team has supplied a good quote, controversy or newsworthy item during this stretch.

Wearing his trademark plaid trilby and pursing an extinguished plastic-tipped Black & Mild, Mullen heads for the elevator, hoping to avoid any chatty passerby.

Too late. "Hey, Jack! What the hell was Marshall doing leaving Reuschel in for so damn long?"

Always the blatherer, Mullen usually can't resist breaking out into one of his famed rapturous orations—talking about anything from last night's slugfest to Bridgeport saloon politics. But this time, he dodges the opportunity. "Had to leave him in. Bullpen's horrendous this year."

At the elevator, he pushes the button with one hand holding a cup of coffee, the other his briefcase, and the morning edition tucked underneath his arm.

The eighth floor sports desk is an open sea of cluttered desks, papers, trash cans, wall fans and a hodgepodge of old Underwoods and boxy word processors.

He drops in his chair and lands the briefcase next to his file cabinet. He reaches for a notepad among the stacks of old newspapers, Styrofoam cups, pens, pencils, and weeks-old debris.

He flips open the notepad and pulls out his ballpoint pen from his shirt pocket. He scribbles down the words: "What's that smell? Crosstown rivals aim to outdo each other in the rotten department. Who will kill off its fans first?"

Injecting some humor. It's the only way to go, right? Can't spend the rest of summer ripping and criticizing. No one gives a crap anymore. Both teams so bad, apathy is seeping in.

The attendance slide has gained momentum. Just the other day at Comiskey, Mullen saw a fan from the upper deck heckle Terry Forster as he gave up another run and Forster heard every word of him, clear as a bell.

At Wrigley, the thing to do on a weekend when they're in town is to bring the Sunday papers to the park, get a ticket, and spend the afternoon basking leisurely in the sunshine, spreading each section out among the empty seats.

Mullen leans back in his chair, thinking where to go next. Counting on a stream of playful hyperbole, he can't imagine anything humorous that can alleviate the stench that suspends over the city. He's stuck.

The beat writer two desks down hangs up the phone and drops his head down into a small piece of paper, scratching down some words.

"Hey, Chuck. Got anything more on that Rosello injury?"

Chuck lifts his head up. "They're not saying anything, but I bet they DL him on Friday. I'm hearing from my guy they're gonna call up that infielder from the minors once again. Give him another shot."

"The golden-arm kid who can sling it across the diamond? He's still down there? I thought they traded him?"

"They're giving him another try. See if he straightened out enough to do something with the bat. Just don't ask him to slide going into second. Don't want to rip that dime bag he's carrying in his back pocket."

"Didn't they put a stop to that?"

The beat writer twists in his chair. "Everybody knows except old man P.K. He thinks that's pixie dust he's got back there."

Mullen returns to his notepad: "Ankle-biters coming up to the big leagues — either they have no clue or they don't care."

He puts his pen and notepad down and reaches for the phone. He dials, stops, and hangs up. Then he picks it up again and dials another number.

"Frank, Jack here. Whaddy'a got on that Rick Monday deal? Is it gonna go through? You think Salty's gonna pull the trigger now or wait till the offseason? No one's talking."

Mullen engages for several minutes and hangs up. He makes several more calls. After the last call, Mullen tosses the notepad and pen onto the desk and sits back, scratching his knuckles. It's the middle of summer and even the rumor mill has dried up.

The phone rings. "Sports desk. Mullen." It's his editor. "Yeah, yeah. I'll be right there."

In his office, his editor lights up a cigarette. "The lede, Jack.

What's your angle going to be for your next column?"

"Stanley, for the love of Odd McIntyre, I'm working on it."

His editor empties his ashtray in the trashcan. "What's the problem? Both teams suck and you're plum out of anything fresh to say?"

Mullen grumbles something.

"I never thought I'd see the day when Jack Mullen runs out of opinions." He sighs. "Well, your biting sarcasm can make a comeback by answering readers' letters. I'm just saying."

Mullen's face flushes with red. "I'd rather peek up the garb of Sister Francine of Mount Carmel."

"You mean Pete from Brookfield or Testy Dave from the Northwest Side doesn't do anything for you?"

Mullen crosses his arms. "Or the wonderful Wally Czernecki. Haven't heard from him lately since he got my desk number. Maybe retirement wasn't his thing and went back to the post office. Y'know, he makes more sense the more drunk he is."

"Maybe we should get him in here and help with the column twice a week."

"Yeah, you can do that but it'll cost you a fridge full of Old Styles. At least with me, all you had to do was buy me the chicken Vesuvio at Fritzel's every year."

"It wasn't the chicken, Jack."

"Ah, Fritzel's. The good, old days. Let's see. There was me, Whitey McClendon, Frankie Young, Phil Conklin. The old crew that came from the *Trib*."

"Jack…"

"Of course now it's O'Rourke's and Riccardo's in Old Town. Can't say I know all the new faces."

"Jack, the column. What are you going to give me today?"

"I wonder whatever happened to that little German fellow who would come into the place with his pockets stuffed with letters to the editor."

"Jack, I need something soon. If you can't get an angle, find me."

"Or that lady friend of Al Baumgartner's. She had one helluva—"

"This morning, Jack. Get back to me. No fooling."

Mullen stares at his desk and the stockpiles of papers and notes. *Maybe there's something in there I can use after all*, he thinks. *Stir something up in the head.* He starts randomly sifting through the stacks.

Finally, he reaches for the stack of letters and quickly fans through the familiar names on the return addresses. *God not again*, he says to himself, mulling over the possibility of answering reader letters.

Near the bottom of the stack, Mullen pulls out a clasp envelope with the return address of Milburn, Illinois. *Not familiar with this one.* The last name is printed in uppercase letters: W.A. FOOTE. The envelope itself is carefully sealed with Scotch tape and he feels the stiffness of two pieces of cardboard protecting its contents. He bypasses the tape and slices through the top with his pocketknife.

Three things come out: a typed letter, a Photostat of two sides to a vintage baseball card and a newspaper clipping. The picture on the baseball card is of a kid that looks to be no more than a teenager with his cap around his eyes, a blast of freckles and the biggest set of ears one could imagine. Under the picture is the line "C. FOOTE, INFIELDER." Mullen squints at the other side of the card listing the player's stats: played 1891 to 1912, career batting average of .241, 504 stolen bases, great fielding percentage. *Never heard of this guy*, he thinks.

Mullen opens up the letter dated April 21 and starts reading:

```
Dear Mr. Mullen,
We are great fans of your column even though
we have to get it from the local library since
we're all the way downstate. Your baseball
```

acumen is superb and that's why we are writing to tell you about recent events and our grandfather who is about to turn a hundred and one. As you can see from the baseball card copy, Charlie "Fleet" Foote played ball as a young man around the turn of the century and had quite a lengthy career before heading out to the Midwest to start a family and business. Our grandfather has always been — and still is — a treasure trove of stories from the days when baseball was just starting out. We could listen to him for hours tell us stories of the odd and funny things that happened along with the people and players back in those days—stories that are virtually unheard of today. The gentleman in the newspaper clipping played against Pop in what could be called the very first World Series back in the 1890s and once we got this article we decided to write to someone like you and ask if you'd be interested in interviewing our grandfather before it's too late. Like we said, all the stories from Pop are stories we've never come across in newspapers, magazines or books. If you're like us who love the game of baseball and appreciate the history behind it, we don't think there's a better source out there than our grandfather who's more than happy to share his stories.

William Foote, D.D.S.
Phone Number and Address on next page.

The newspaper clipping is a single column folded in half with a paper clip holding it together with a note reading, "This man played with my grandfather—briefly—in 1893." The clipping headline starts out in bold, seriffed text: "Nineteenth century ballplayer dies. 'Goat' of first-ever World Series."

According to the article, the man who died was a former player named Gerald Wheatley who figured in the outcome in the first championship matchup between the two existing leagues in the majors, dubbed as the precursor to the World Series.

The article goes on to say that Wheatley, pitching for the National Frontier League, gave up the winning run in the decisive last game of the series. Fans never forgave him and he never returned to the majors after that. He stayed in the Midwest and died in Springfield at the age of 104.

"Hey Chuck. Have you ever heard of an old-time baseball player by the name of Foote? Let's see...Charlie "Fleet" Foote?"

"What, he play in the '50s or '60s?"

"No, the nineteenth century, early twentieth. Says here he played more than twenty years in the big leagues."

Chuck rolls his chair to Mullen's desk and looks at the Photostat.

"And the guy is still alive, somewhere downstate. A grandson wrote a letter. Says he played with this other guy." He hands Chuck the newspaper clipping.

"Hmm... Wheatley. That sounds kind of familiar," Chuck adjusts his glasses. "Wait a sec."

Chuck pulls out a yellowed paperback, The Encyclopedia of Baseball Players, and flips through.

"Yeah, Wheatley. Gerald Wheatley. Pitcher. Played one game, 1893. Known for being the 'Goat from Terre Haute', single-handedly giving away the championship to the rival American Association League. Hounded and ridiculed for years."

"Died this year, according to this clipping. Christ, where'd they dig up these old codgers? A hundred years old..."

"Plays in the big leagues for one game and goes down in the history books as the world's biggest schmuck the rest of his life.

Stuff of baseball legend. Haven't you heard of him?" Chuck asks.

"Yeah, maybe. But I don't know, kid," Mullen says. "That was even before my time when guys like Ted Lyons and Luke Appling roamed the diamond. Hell, the 1800s. Them's the bygone days BEFORE the bygone days. I'd have to dig up my own grandpop to find out what those days were like."

"You should brush up on your history, Jack. People were playing this game for more than a hundred years. Lots of stories there, I'm sure. Why don't you contact this guy, Foote? Could be something there for you."

Mullen shakes his head. "Who cares about what happened way back then? Readers want to hear what happened today and what might happen tomorrow. Besides, who's to say this old man is telling the truth? Could be nothing but a bunch of fantasy tales coming out of his senile brain."

"It's worth a call, ain't it? You're looking for a new angle, right? Maybe the old guy's really got some stories there? You can always get them checked out."

"How?"

"Archives downstairs. Start there."

The Archives and Collections Department is located below street level and contains all things related to the newspaper since its inception. Mullen arrives at the foyer and descends down three flights of stairs to the lower level where a sign-in book awaits him. As soon as he opens the door a waft of musty staleness hits him.

The room is darkened and packed with rows and rows of shelves reaching up toward the ceiling. At the other end is a warmly lit enclosure that looks like a cage with green metal mesh surrounding an opening with a counter.

He walks up. The counter contains a yellow legal pad, a mug filled with pens with rubber Abe Lincoln toppers, and a makeshift lost-and-found box with trinkets inside.

"Help you?" Behind the counter, a man sits on a stool eating a sandwich.

"Archives, huh? In my day, they used to call it the Morgue." Mullen buttresses his arms against the countertop.

The man remains seated, chewing slowly while eyeing the columnist behind a pair of bifocals.

"I couldn't find an intern, so I thought I'd drop in and see first hand how you guys make do with the past."

"What are you looking for in particular?" The man asks in between bites. He wears a heavy woolen cardigan with his name stitched on the front.

"Ah, yes, Leonid."

"That's Leonard. And typically I get phone calls or order requests. I haven't been getting any guests lately. And you are —"

"I'm Jack Mullen."

"— looking for something?"

"Been covering both sides of town for twenty-three years. Senior baseball columnist since '62. Syd Feeney Award winner in '66 and in '69 for that three-part piece on the miracles of artificial turf. You heard the name right? I coined the phrase 'Go-Go Sox'."

Leonard puts his sandwich down and takes a bite out of a pickle. "I know who you are Mr. Mullen. I pretty much know everything about this newspaper since the very first edition."

"Since the first?" Mullen mocks astonishment. "That was a hundred years ago. You don't look that old. You remind me of John Cazale." He notices dark hairs protruding from Leonard's nostrils.

"Eighty-three."

"Get out of here. You don't look a day over forty."

"I meant the age of the newspaper."

"Oh, yeah. How many editions does that make?"

"Nearing twenty-six thousand."

"Lemme' guess. You know every damned one by heart."

"You can say that, but don't go calling me a genius. I take the

Ravenswood every day. But I do take the business of the past very seriously."

"Right. Say, what was the price of a tie bar at Wieboldt's in '56, like this one here?" He pinches his own in the middle of his torso. "Know that one by heart?"

Leonard doesn't respond. He finishes his sandwich.

Mullen looks him over, trying to get a read on him. "Look, Leonard. I need someone to do a little exhuming on my part. I don't suppose you can dig up some gold for me?"

"Depends, Mr. Mullen. How far down do you want to go?"

Mullen gives him the story of the letter and clipping. "What I need is some solid fact-checking. I want to know whether or not this old gray hair's telling the truth and not making it up."

Leonard gives him a befuddled look. "Why would a man that age be making up stories? What would he have to lie about?"

"Senility could be messing up this old timey's mind. Living in his own world of make believe."

Leonard picks at his teeth. "Or he could look at you and think, 'Man, I got me a sucker this time,' and off he goes with some real doozies."

"I want to make sure this stuff checks out before I go further. Can you help me?" He pulls out the letter and newspaper clipping and hands it to Leonard.

Leonard looks it over and let's out a breath. "Baseball series, 1893. Wheatley. Yep, I think I can help you out Mr. Mullen. That's a good year."

"What do you mean?"

"The *Times* started publishing in 1893 and was the first in the city to promote sports in a big way. Shecky Montgomery, Harold Loomis. Those guys really put it on the map. You should thank them for your career."

"I'm the luckiest man on the face of the—"

"Anyway, yes, I've got something. Be right back." Leonard ducks away and disappears in a back room.

Mullen waits, playing with a toy plastic hula girl out of the lost-and-found box. After several minutes, Leonard re-appears with a small white box. "Microfilm."

Leonard escorts Mullen to a small room with a desktop reader, loads a roll, and begins twirling until an image pops on the screen. "Is this what you had in mind?"

Mullen plants his hands on his knees and nods with approval. "Uh-huh."

On the front page, circa October, 1893, the headline reads: "WORLD'S" SERIES WINNER! An illustration depicts a cheering crowd with a victorious baseball player sitting on their shoulders. Above the player is the word "Champion." In the corner of the illustration is a shot of another player looking lost and forlorn with an arrow pointing at it with the word "Goat."

"Local player's gaffe costs game," Mullen reads the subhead. "That's him, this Wheatley fellow. Can you get me a printout of this?"

Mullen stashes the printout of the front page in his shirt pocket. "What about the other guy, Foote. What can you get me on him?"

"Foote may take a little longer, but I'll get you something."

"Like what, his shoe size? The name of his first sweetheart?"

"If that's what you want, sure. I can find anything. I just need to look in the right places."

"How about looking on those shelves? I bet you even got the bones to some of the past publishers stuffed somewhere in those boxes."

"Not quite. But if it's not there, then it's up here." Leonard points to his head. "I have a good memory. I can find stuff no one else can. Stuff that's been buried and long-forgotten."

"An infinite well of minutiae waiting to be tapped. I should get you in the sports trivia contest at Schulien's Tap. You can really clean house there."

"I don't drink."

Mullen scratches something on a piece of paper. "If you get anything on this Foote fellow, here's my extension. If he checks out I'll decide whether to call this grandson of his, before I shore it up with my editor."

"Sure thing, Mr. Mullen. And by the way…"

"Yeah?"

"I'm fifty-six and it was Trace and Jagiello who came up with the nickname."

"What?"

"'Go-Go White Sox'. They wrote the fight song with that tag and you made it famous by sprinkling it in your columns. But you weren't the one to come up with the original phrase."

Mullen turns and mutters under his breath, "Pissant."

"Stanley, for the millionth time, no. I'll go back on the beat before I answer any more stinking letters."

Stanley downs his water and crushes the paper cone cup. "That gets me to my next point."

Mullen's ire is up, judging by his swollen carotid pressed up against his collar. "What might that be?"

Stanley re-adjusts his rolled-up sleeves and rubs his hand over is mouth. "Did you get a hold of that grandson?"

"Yeah, I did. Brief conversation. Told him it was a nice story and left it at that."

"And that's that?"

"Jesus Christ, Stan. What'd you want me to say? Who gives a royal shit about some wrinkled old worm who played ball a hundred years ago? Yeah, he might have some stories to tell but no one's gonna want to read about 'em."

"That's where you come in, Jack. If these stories have any legs you'll be able to put your own narrative stamp on them."

Mullen shakes his head. His face becomes redder. "What's this all about, anyway? Let's get down to business, Stan. This ain't about some old fossil desperate to tell his story before he croaks. This is about me being gently nudged out of my sphere by some hip executive editor up on the twelfth floor. Well, I'll tell you, to hell with it. My place is in the press box for good or bad. That's my reputation."

"No one's pushing you out of here, Jack. But let's face it. Your columns have become stale and I'm starting to hear about it. I just thought it might do you good to get a different angle on something. It might do you some good."

"Stanley, for God's sakes, run the goddamn piece I did on the Almonte kid again until I come up with something else. Don't send me to the sticks chasing a dead end story."

"Just for two weeks, that's all. We need something fresh here and you're going on assignment until you get a good feature."

"You want me to come up with a fresh evergreen by interviewing a hundred-year-old relic who may or may not be mentally confused?"

Stanley rests his arms on his desk and leans forward. "I called the grandson myself and checked the story. He swears the old man's telling the truth."

Mullen's cornered. "If I don't like what I hear, I'm turning right back. Story or no story. And if this crazy coot's full'a beans I'm pinning this one on you, Stan."

"As always," Stan smiles. "Now let's get down to real business." He reaches down and opens the desk file cabinet, pulling out a half-empty bottle of Jim Beam and two rocks glasses.

The air conditioning unit kicks on and wakens Mullen from an early afternoon doze. The curtains to the motel room are closed and he lies atop the made bed with an ashtray sitting next to him. He checks his watch: 2:47. The first interview is at three.

The drive down from the city took longer than expected, and with the air out on his Olds, he's already bushed. He rolls his body off the bed and plants his feet on the floor. He checks the address one more time against the map. *These small hick towns, he thinks to himself, you can be anywhere in under five minutes.*

He slips his loafers back on and grabs his things — a notepad and his reel-to-reel recorder. He dons his hat and looks at himself in the mirror one last time before departing.

The town is quiet and dusty. A dog scampers across the street. Several turns and Mullen stops at the end of a block. A row of single-story apartments stands in front of him. Clasping the paper with the address on it, he can't spot a number through his windshield. He parks and gets out.

He walks slowly down the sidewalk until he finally reaches the address. The door inside is open. He steps up to the screen door and looks at the paper one last time. The sun's glare prevents him from seeing much inside. He hears a voice but can't make out the words because of a train rumbling in the distance.

"Mr. Mullen?" A man appears at the doorway. "So glad to see you." He swings open the screen door and extends his arm for a handshake. Jack immediately notices the man's comb-over and pockmarked complexion.

"It really is a pleasure, sir. You don't know how much this means to our family. A baseball writer from the big city's finally going to meet Pop."

"Are you William?"

"Yes, sir. And please, call me Bill."

"Jack. It's a pleasure." He tries to pull his hand back but can't release it from the other man's grip.

Bill steps into the sunshine. Shorter than Jack, he gleams a toothy smile and a set of familiar-looking ears.

"How was the drive down? The directions I gave you were fine? Fairly easy to get down here if you took 57."

"No problems, Bill. Happy to be here. It's nice to get out of the city once in a while and visit Smalltown, U.S.A."

"Well, we'd like to think we have a wholesome little community here, though things have changed quite a bit since they closed down the last of the coal mines a few years back. But we're managing just fine. Did you see our new community center out on the main strip?"

"Ah, no."

"Oh, that's too bad, because we just received a new—"

"Um, say Bill. You're granddad's here, right?"

"Sure is, Jack. We've been waiting for you. This is Pop's place. Why don't we step inside and—"

"Let me get my stuff out of the car first."

"I'll help you."

They walk back to the car and Jack unlocks the trunk.

"Like I said, Mr. Mullen—I mean Jack—we're so glad to have you take the time to visit our town and conduct an interview with our granddad. We were going to mention it in the newspaper but it'll have to wait, I guess. He's considered a local legend around here, though he hasn't been getting out lately."

Jack lifts the reel-to-reel out of the trunk and drops it into Bill's arms. "Hold onto that, will you?" He takes his notepad and closes the trunk.

"Y'know, Bill, I never really heard of your grandfather until I read your letter. Seems like he had a pretty good career. When did he stop playing?"

"Nineteen-twelve was his last season. He tore up his leg sliding into third and wasn't the same after that. He already had twenty seasons under his belt, starting when he was a teenager. If it weren't for the injury, he would've played a few more seasons. He loved the game so much. It was the only thing he knew."

"What'd he do after that?"

"Like I told your editor, Pop packed up his things and moved out here from the East. Opened up a feed and hardware store in Murphysboro. He fell in love with the area after he played in the World Series."

"Not THE World Series."

"No, no. Not the official one, but definitely its forefather. Pop played at a time when the game was taking its shape into what we recognize it as today, playing with the likes of Philo Grogan, Stacks Bittner, Frank Horgan."

"Who?"

"You know, the legends."

They stand face to face in front of the screen door. Mullen pulls out a fresh Black & Mild from his shirt pocket and eyes Bill. "Pardon me for sounding a bit ill-mannered but I had my reservations about doing this in the first place. I mean, I thought I had my baseball history down and some of these names that get mentioned—"

"You got them checked out, right? Your editor mentioned something. He said you were concerned. Mr Mullen, I can assure you Pop wouldn't—"

"I hope you understand."

"Well, it's a common thing to hear. People think that baseball history began when the Babe started smashing home runs for New York in the '20s. They don't take into account the sixty-odd years prior to that—a stretch of history no one seems to know much about. Pops's one of the last links to that time. Just give him the chance."

Mullen hesitates. "Your granddad, he's up for this?"

Bill smiles and peeks inside the apartment. "Only one way to find out."

The tiny living room is cramped with decades-old furniture. Toward the back Mullen spots a kitchen and another door he suspects is a bathroom or bedroom. The air is stuffy with dust floating in the streams of sunlight. As he looks around he notices only a couple of baseball-related items: a tiny pennant on the wall with its letters faded out and a ball encased in a clear box on a credenza.

"Pop," Bill raises his voice. "Our visitor from the city's arrived."

Sunken in the chair is a frail framework of skin and bones with a layer of heavy clothes fit for a hobo. His face is like a tattered leather-bound book with a wisp of snow-white hair that pokes up past the top of the chair cushion.

"Jack, meet Charles 'Fleet' Foote, one of the very best fielding shortstops to ever play the game."

"How do you do?" Jack extends his hand, pulling out his cigarillo with his other.

The wrinkled Foote stares off into space past Jack and Bill.

"Pop? Pop?"

Pop finally raises his head to make eye contact. A string of drool escapes his mouth and drips down in his lap. The old man attempts to raise his arm but fails in the first try. He tries two more times before making it all the way up. Mullen glances at Bill before carefully receiving the shriveled hand.

"It's my pleasure, Mr. Foote. I'm glad we have this opportunity."

The old man's head droops slightly to the side. His eyes are clouded with an emptiness matched by the number of teeth left in his open mouth.

While still cradling the shrunken hand, Mullen hears the distinct sound of liquid discharging in the old man's pants. Mullen releases his hold and turns away. "Jesus Christ," he mutters under his breath.

"Pop, what the hell?"

The stagnant air of the room is quickly suffused with the pungent odor of urine.

"You'll have to excuse us, Mr. Mullen. I don't know what's gotten to Pop. He's never done this before."

"Never?" Jack takes a couple steps back and pulls his handkerchief out of his back pocket.

Suddenly a feathery wheeze comes out of Pop's mouth and gains momentum, turning into a guffaw. "I got 'im! Billy, did 'ya see that! You should'a seen the look on this poor bastard's face. Ha! I've been saving this up all day. I got 'ya, you sonofabitch!"

"Pop!" Bill reaches for the nearest crocheted blanket and stuffs it into his grandfather's lap. "I'm sorry about this Mr. Mullen. Really, I never—"

"I gotta say that was one heck of an introduction." Mullen's voice is muffled through the handkerchief.

Bill keeps apologizing as he works Pop off the cushion. "We got to get you in the bathroom and get you cleaned up. Pop, how could you in front of our guest?"

"For chrissakes, it's not like the first time I ever pissed myself. Lighten up. Whatever happened to good, old-fashioned shenanigans? I'm sure it takes a truckload to offend this guy. Ain't I right, fella?"

Bill leads Pop into the bathroom. "Make yourself at home, Jack. There's fresh iced tea in the fridge or if you want a beer you'll have to ask Pop where he hid the last six-pack."

The door closes and Mullen sets up the recorder on the coffee table. He puts his unlit cigarillo in his shirt pocket and switches to his pen and notepad. "OK—He's not dead. Don't dilly-dally. Get to the stories. Find out what he really knows."

After a few minutes both men return to the living room and Bill assists the old man into another chair, facing Jack.

"Gentlemen, if you don't mind I'd like to get started," Mullen says. "Are we all comfy and nice?"

Bill looks down at Pop. "Are you ready with this or are you scheming to do something else?"

"Give me a minute and maybe I'll shit out a bunny rabbit."

Bill turns to Jack. "Are you sure you don't want anything before you get started, Jack? If not, he's all yours. I'll be over here sopping up this cushion."

Mullen presses a button and the reels start turning. He moves the microphone stand to the edge of the coffee table.

"Okay, Mr. Foote," Mullen adjusts his glasses and gets ready to write on the pad.

"Call me something else other than 'mister,' unless you plan on selling me a car."

"How about Charles, then?"

Pop shrugs his shoulders.

"Or how about Fleet? When did you get that nickname?"

"Oh, well, let's see." Pop tilts his head back and mulls over the question. "I got in the majors in '91 and already had it, so probably a couple of years before when I was in the minors."

"The minors? How old were you? You mustn't have been more than fifteen."

Pop laughs. "A scrap of a kid who could barely read or write and already had enough working in the mills back East. First time I picked up a baseball, it was like trying on a pair of perfectly tailored trousers. A real fit."

"And how did you learn to play so well?"

"Back in my time, if you were a kid in some steel town you weren't afforded much play time. Work by the time you were able to lift a bundle over your head, and do it until your body wore out. Me, I was lucky to get Sunday mornings off. I was supposed to be at church. Instead, I snuck off to the open field behind the rail yard and played with the local boys. Lucky to get my hands on one of those beat-up, lemon-peel baseballs. Y'know, those lumpy, brown things with the seams all come loose."

"You must have been a natural."

"A natural? Shoot, I wish it were the case. I must have eaten so much dirt in my first year playing, getting knocked around the diamond. But I stuck with it and soon got the hang of it and never looked back. I left town soon after that and joined some barnstorming circuits."

"The vagabond life at fourteen, fifteen."

Pop shrugs. "Even back then, I played with some real tough joes looking to do something other than break their backs working in a factory or field. You see, baseball was their escape. If you were good enough to reach the big leagues, you actually got paid well to play a game. A frickin' game! So there was real motive to get in and play like hell to stay in."

"Real competitive?"

"Sure, but that wasn't always the case. Long before I came around, the game was more like a field day, a picnic for the hoity-toity looking to get a breath of fresh air and some exercise. By the time I arrived, it had already changed. Teams were trying to beat your brains in something fierce. Cheating, fighting, blood spilled. Even the hecklers in the stands got into it."

Bill interrupts. "Yeah, Pop. Tell him about them time that little Napoleon-type went after that nut coming out of the stands during the World Series."

"Mr. Foote, I wanted to get into that, the 'World's Series.' Your grandson said you played in the very first one in 1893. Wasn't the first one actually in 1903?"

"That's right. What we played in was an exhibition match between the two major leagues. Nothing yet formalized. But, boy, that sure made an impression."

"What were the two leagues?"

Pop's eyes widen. "Okay, listen up, mister sportswriter. There were two top guys who basically owned each league and they couldn't stand each other. A pretty intense rivalry, each one thinking they knew what was good for the sport better than the other one. Well, that started a pretty big pissing match that led to the Series, to see who was better than the other.

"Who were these guys again?"

"In the very beginning there was Mr. Sterne, a rich and powerful industrialist back East who really got the game off the ground and popularized it. Then along came the fat beer heir from Milwaukee, Mr. Schnockerd."

"*Schnockerd?* You gotta be kidding me? How do you spell that?"

"Y'see, Sterne was a real stickler for formality. Wanted things done in a certain way, real stiff and proper. And baseball was his baby. He didn't want anybody messing with it. So, when Schnockerd came around and got hold of it with his head full of ideas, this led to a colossal clash. All hell broke loose."

"Schnockerd? Sterne? What are their first names?"

Pop brings his hands together up to his chest. "You really don't know? Not even a clue? My grandson warned me you thought this was fishy."

Mullen puts his pen and notepad down. "I guess I need a new history lesson, the real story."

"Or I could be bullshitting you just for kicks."

"I'll get it checked it out. Do my homework."

"Do that on you own time, sonny. I never had much to do with homework or libraries or whatever else you think it takes to get to the facts. A man and his word is all that it should take. Especially for an old goat like me."

"I'm all ears."

"Yeah, me too. Where do you want to start?"

"Why don't we start at the beginning? Can you do that?"

"When I entered the league?"

"Can you go farther than that? I want to hear this business about these two owners."

"You want it all?" Pop sinks back in his chair. "Fair enough. But I'm warning you. I can't tell my stories without my Schlitz and a few naps in between. So settle in and keep that handkerchief up to your nose."

Mullen opens the door to his darkened motel room and nearly trips over himself lugging in the recorder. He plops it down on the bed, shuts the door and turns on the desk lamp. He sits down and picks up the phone. He flips open his notepad and dials.

"Stanley, Jack here. I know it's late. I just got back to the room and I need a favor." He listens. "Yeah, the old man started talking. It went well, to say the least. Got a pen? I want to give you a few names for you to check on downstairs."

Mullen waits. "Okay, Stan, ready? First name is Sterne, J.B. Spelled S-T-E-R-N…"

II.

A Boodler's Grab
(1857)

A plume of smoke weaves its way through the valley of freshly tapped virgin forest and the exhale of a steam whistle announces the coming of the *General Stockton*, prize of the Hinkley 4-4-0 class. Behind the engine and its tender is a lone passenger car—the ornate, private coach of J. Barron Sterne.

The engine slows once it enters the clearing and makes its stop before the sawmill and cluster of timber rafts in the water. Another blast of steam and the coach door swings open.

A youthful-looking Sterne steps out and lands on the ground. Exquisitely dressed in a velvet black regency tailcoat, double-breasted vest, silk tie, top hat and cane, Sterne puffs out his chest, taking in the dewy morning air.

Another figure pops out of the coach, donning his top hat, veiling his mouth with a silk handkerchief—Sterne's business confidant and associate H.H. Niedler.

"Henry," Sterne clenches his lapels with both hands, "another fine day to behold the vast terrain in front of us, a continent

J. Barron Sterne - "The Governor" 1893

of infinite resources and unlimited potential, barely grazed by the human hand, awaits us. Over mountains and waterways, we arrive, inviting the red lady of possibility to kneel down in front of us with her arms wide open. What unforeseen bounty will she bequeath us?"

Niedler pats his forehead with the handkerchief and straightens his tie. "Nicely spoken, J.B. Was that Herman Melville?"

"No. My own words, thank you very much."

"Keeping with the florid language, this timbering operation is owned by our very own Lord Boston Adversary with the Twitchy Eyelids. He's got the land and river access for the next hundred miles."

"Yes, but we secured the rail rights. Let's see what's out here before we decide to take it all. Perhaps there's something else waiting for us to confiscate. My intuition is bristling with aplomb. I can feel it."

Along the river's bank a door to a shed opens and a stocky figure steps out.

"We're being greeted," Niedler says. "Let's temper your enthusiasm. Right now we're just executives with the rail line. That's all."

The figure comes into view wearing a derby, a red-striped work shirt and a pair of minuscule spectacles. He struggles uphill, waving his left arm, until he reaches the level ground of the tracks.

"Who the hell are you two boys, all dressed up lookin' like a couple of Jack-a-Dandies?"

Sterne smiles. "I beg your pardon, little man?"

The man, whose face is flushed with pink hostility, flares his eyes. "I got a bunch of goddamned logs jammed at the end of the flume that can't make water and my river pigs ain't doin' a goddamned thing to dislodge 'em. Nothin's gettin' done this morning, and by the looks of you I don't need any more distractions. I got me a logjam!"

"Log-jam?"

"That's right. And those axmen up the mountainside are gonna be choppin' down fresh white oaks soon after breakfast and someone's got to get up there and tell 'em we got a big mess down here."

"Is there something we can do?"

The man looks them over. "Just who in hell are you, anyway? Nobody's come down this rail track since it was laid. You ain't agents with the company, I know that."

"The company?" Niedler asks. "Do you mean the Ehrland & Overton Timber Company?"

"Of course, E&O. Who else would be down in these parts? They got all this land and the river to boot. Say, what are you, a couple of snoops?"

"Allow me to introduce us," Sterne doffs his hat, "my name is Sterne and this is my associate, Henry Huntington Niedler. We are related to the ownership of this rail line, part of the executive office learning the usefulness of this branch. Your cordiality and kindness would be most welcome as we journey along our newly laid tracks."

"I don't have time, like I said—"

"Yes, it's understandable. We don't want to burden you with our presence, but like I said, perhaps we can help you as we make an unscheduled stop."

"You want to help? I need somebody to get up that god-dammned mountainside and tell that bull to stop production until my pigs can fix this mess. I don't suppose you can do that?"

Niedler begins to speak but Sterne interrupts him. "We'd be delighted to help, mister…?"

"Shawkey. Lester P. Shawkey. I'm waterway foreman, sawmill manager, clerk, you name it."

Sterne offers his hand to Shawkey and looks into his eyes. "If you give us just a few precious moments of your time, Mr. Niedler and I will trek up that mountainside and contact whoever's in charge up there."

Shawkey's eyes shift between Sterne and Niedler. "You're putting me on, ain't you? You're willing to climb up that side for what? Out of kindness? Judging by your costumes and your passenger car, you've never even seen the side of a mountain let alone—"

"I just ask for a brief moment of your time, Mr. Shawkey. Perhaps we can continue this conversation in your outbuilding over there over some freshly brewed coffee?"

Shawkey's suspicion subsides as he fixes his eyes into Sterne's, whose practice of persuasive facial expression is put to test once again.

"A brilliant move, extracting the names of the E&O execs who were down here taking a look at our line," Niedler says to Sterne as they take measure of the mountainside. "We now know who to conduct business with without interference from the Boston people."

"Yes. Sometimes it's much easier to get what you want by stepping down the ladder and dealing with simpletons like these."

Niedler covers his mouth with his handkerchief. "You're not really going to hike up this mountain, are you J.B.?"

"I keep my word. I said we would climb up this mountain and contact the man in charge in exchange for some basic information. It can't be more than a thousand yards."

"Uphill in this attire? If I knew we were going hiking I would have packed for something more suitable. This twill will never survive the climb."

"Or you could wait in the coach while I complete our clandestine operation to see what is out here worth taking. Are you with me?"

Niedler hesitates, then nods.

"Good. He said to follow this jerry-built plankway until it leads to the camp."

The mountainside is covered in a canopy of white pines and the landscape is dotted with woodsmen, felled trees, oxen, and tools. The air is filled with a cacophony of thwacking axes, rasping saws, rattling chains, hoots and hollers.

Sterne and Niedler maneuver along the plank walkway until they enter the view of the camp. Both men stop in the middle of the noise and activity. Sterne plants his cane and examines the site.

Suddenly all the sounds and movement halt and all eyes fixate on the two dapper gentlemen—everyone from the cattle wranglers to the fellers positioned on their springboards high atop the trees.

The silence is quickly broken by a croakish-throated laugh among the group, triggering a wave of other laughs and howls until the entire camp is roaring with shrieks and catcalls.

After the laughter subsides, one of the camp workers approaches Sterne, covered in a thick film of sweat and dirt. "Ballroom ain't built yet, gents. We're still at phase one. Yer' gonna have to wait," he busts out laughing.

"If this were my property, my good man, I would have threshed every bit of raw material out of it by now and not only would there be a ballroom on top of your scant existence but an entire estate. Now, where is your logger boss? We have a message to give him."

A large, burly man in suspenders, puffing on a cigar, stomps in front of the onlookers. "Just what in the hell is goin' on here?"

He yells loud enough for all to hear. "Get goin' or you'll all be licking your boots for supper!"

The men quickly return to their tasks. The boss swings himself around to face the young gentlemen, his hairy belly protruding from his shirt and bits of something dangling from his black, bristly beard.

"Excuse us," Sterne politely proceeds. "You must be the camp foreman. We have an urgent message."

The man studies Sterne and Niedler. "You're not E&O men."

"Why don't you think we're with your company?" Niedler asks.

"For one thing, you're half their age and decked out plenty better. If I had my druthers, I'd say you're a couple of fancy-schmancy sightseers from Dudes-ville."

"Not quite. We're here, in part, to deliver a message from the gentleman down by the river. He says he has incurred a 'log-jam', and that you must cease activities until all things are clear."

The boss turns back toward the men. "Anybody know about this? Has anybody from the mill shown up this morning? Where is Horton?"

"Horton's gone over the ridge for some game, Cuddy."

"Goddammned Shawkey. A pygmy can't muddle up an operation more than this imbecile!" The logger boss straightens his body and begins barking out new orders to send a gang of men to go down to the spillway and straighten things out, sending the camp into disarray. He disappears into the chaos.

Sterne and Niedler advance along the plank walkway and scrutinize the camp unnoticed. They reach a shack with a sign posted on the door with scratchy lettering: O. CUTHBERT: FOREMAN. Sterne opens the door.

The shack is small, dark and grimy. In front of them is a table scattered with papers and topographic maps. Sterne sifts through the pile until he finds a correspondence journal. He fingers through the pages. "Our Boston Adversary is getting ambitious," Sterne says. "He's thinking of purchasing another ten-thousand hectares."

"If that's the case, then maybe we should strike now," Niedler says.

"Not until we know for sure what it is we're dealing with out here."

"The rail line passes right through the remaining tract. If we beat him to the punch, he'd be forced to cede his assets to us and we'd have total control of this valley."

"I'm not completely convinced, Henry. We may have to dig a little more."

"What is there to dig? We've been out here in this god-awful terrain for more than two weeks. I think we've seen enough."

The door abruptly slams open and a massive, rotund figure blocks the sunlight from entering the hovel. They see the small, red glow of a burning cigar and realize it's the logger boss. As the ash grows brighter, they see his eyes aflame with fury. Niedler stands back from the table and crouches down onto a stool. Sterne lays the journal down.

"You boys again! What the hell are you doin' in here, with my papers?" He snarls and the cigar ash burns brighter.

Sterne and Niedler stay silent.

Suddenly the ferocity in the boss' eyes vanishes. "Mind if I squeeze in and join you? I almost forgot about you two, with all that commotion out there." He shuts the door, grabs a stool and plops down.

"You sure whipped them along, didn't you?" asks Niedler.

"Yeah, I sure did," he begins to laugh. "That ol' trick in the book never gets old. Put the fear of God in them, they'll work harder, yes sir. But in truth I'm just another old soft leather bumpkin looking to get by. Say, care for some whiskey?"

"Don't mind if we do, Mr. Cuthbert," Sterne says.

"Call me Cuddy." The logger boss pulls out a bottle and three glasses.

"No thank you," Niedler says.

"What's wrong? Your friend don't like fire-brand whiskey?"

"A non-imbiber and a little claustrophobic, I'm afraid." Sterne replies.

"Shoot, just a taster won't kill you. Seems like you boys have come a long way and need a refreshment. Have one on me and we'll get to know each other, tell me what you two gents are doing out here in the wilderness." He pours into all three glasses. "By the way, I didn't get your boys' name."

"I'm Sterne and this is Niedler."

"Need'ler, huh? Which one of you is the older one?"

"I'm the older one but is still the junior partner," Niedler says.

"Older but junior?" the logger boss shakes his head. "Okay, I'm game. Down the hatch."

Cuddy slugs his drink down and eyes his two friends. "What's the matter? Come on now, have a drink."

Sterne looks at Niedler. "Just once, Henry," he urges.

Niedler shakes his head.

Sterne leans closer toward Niedler and says, in a calm, gentle manner, "Shadrach and Toplitz."

The words jolt Niedler. His eyes flare and he takes a deep breath through his nostrils. "Very well. If you must insist!" He snaps up the glass and downs the contents. His face clenches and he makes a gagging sound. "I shouldn't have done that."

"Shat-Rack and Toe-Plitts?" Cuddy shrugs his shoulders and pours another round. "Where are you two from?"

"New York."

"*New York?* My God, that's sure a long ways away. What made you come out this far? There's nothing out here but stuff we're trying to chop down."

"Do you still think we are a couple of vacationers off on some far-flung excursion?"

Cuddy throws another shot down and makes a guttural sound. "Hell, what else could you be? You're too young to be E&O big shots, and by the way you're dressed up, I'd say you're a couple of highfalutin country ramblers bent on seeing what's on offer of God's green earth. Ain't I right?"

"In one respect, you're exactly right."

"Shoot, ain't nothin' here but hilly land, trees, dirt, water and plenty of sweaty timbermen earning a little wage so they can spend it on some amusement."

"Not much amusement up here, I would venture to guess."

"They could go down to the nearest town, but that's half a day away. They're pretty good at staying amused on their days off, when they're not drinking and gambling." Cuddy points to Sterne's and Niedler's glasses before he pours himself another one.

Niedler waves him off. The effects of the airless, cramped compartment mixed with a shot of whiskey has turned him into a sweating wreck.

"Well, Henry, one more?" Sterne asks.

Niedler wipes his brow with his ever-present handkerchief.

"Maybe you two drifters should stick around and see what it's like to work hard and live hard off this mountainside," the boss inquires. He pushes Niedler's glass closer to him.

Niedler's eyes become like saucers. He waves his hand more vociferously.

"What do you say, H.H.?" Sterne looks at his confidant. "Do we two wayfarers have the fortitude to endure what this mountain's got to offer?"

Niedler finally gives in. He takes a deep breath and knocks the whiskey down in one quick motion.

"'Atta boy!" Cuthbert bellows.

Suddenly Niedler's face turns red and sweat begins to pour off his forehead. He leaps up from his stool, grabs his throat with both hands and makes a retching sound.

"Henry?"

He propels forward, thrusting the papers off the table. Then he darts outside and bolts away, screaming at the top of his lungs.

Daylight has almost ended and the fellers and peelers put their instruments down and head toward the mess hall for dinner after a long day.

Sterne walks back into camp and encounters Cuddy.

"Have you found your friend yet?"

"No. Some of your buckers along the skid road thought they saw him running into the outskirts, ripping off his jacket and vest."

"Well, he seems like a reasonable fellow. I'm sure he'll turn up."

"He's a good colleague and partner. I can't afford anything to happen to him. He's too valuable an asset for me to lose, you see."

"Maybe I can scare up a couple of men with some lanterns and go looking after dinner."

"That would help my conscience, to say the least."

"Good, in the meantime let's head over to the mess before my boys eat everything in sight."

To Sterne's surprise the mess hall contains a tidy display of benches with tablecloths, tin plates, cutlery, and heaping bowls and dishes of steaming food waiting to be demolished. The room quickly fills up and the clanking of dinnerware is joined with the sounds of rough-and-tumble banter as the men dive into hash, stews, baked beans, greens, corn on the cob and assortment of roasted meats.

"They eat like this all the time?" Sterne sits down next to Cuddy and begins loading his plate.

"Can't expect to have your men giving you an honest day's effort without giving them the fuel to do it. It starts with the belly. Look how jovial I am." Cuddy pats his stomach.

"Duly noted."

"What business are you in, Sterne?" Cuddy casually asks. "Or do you just wander around all the time?"

Sterne pokes at his plate with his fork. "Mergers and acquisitions."

"What do you mean by 'merge'?"

"Take what's on your plate," Sterne illustrates his point. "Normally you'd see your mashed potatoes alone on one side, your green beans on another. But what we do is put the green beans atop your potatoes and add a slosh of gravy over them. Then maybe a piece of cornbread as an added bonus. We enhance things and make them more tempting for consumption. Understand?"

"Hell, I sure do. That sounds delicious. Maybe I'll have you help out in the kitchen." Before Cuddy asks more questions, he loses himself in the giant plate of food in front of him.

After dinner, Cuddy rounds up some men to go look for Niedler. "Why don't you wait with us until my boys return. I'll show you the rest of the camp," he offers.

"Do I have a choice?" Sterne says. "I'm not leaving without my trusted adviser and it's already too dark to venture down the mountainside."

"Fair enough."

The bunkhouse is a dark, fetid ramshackle capable of jamming up to forty men and their belongings. Sterne peeks his head in and is astonished to see so much stuff densely packed together: half-naked men drying their wet, woolen clothing over cast iron stoves, kerosene lamps, stacks of trunks and footlockers, bed rolls, an improvised wooden table used to play cards on, hats and overalls hanging from nails on the wall, mice scurrying, an intense odor combining sweat, smoke and rot.

Cuddy smacks his hand on Sterne's shoulder. "Luxurious, ain't it?"

"I thought my coach was a bit cramped."

"Whaddy'a say we fix you up a bunk?"

"I'd sooner hire one of your men to take me down to the waterway."

"You can sleep with me in my own sleeping quarters. There's

an extra cot. Fresh blankets. No lice, guaranteed. However, I snore as loud as a good saw man teething through a northern red oak."

"I'll take that under consideration."

Sitting around a campfire, waiting for the search party to return, Sterne befriends a loggerman.

"I worked as a whaler before this," a man named Skaggs continues, "off Sag Harbor, some years ago. You think this is dangerous work? Imagine getting pulled through a choppy cove by a hooked bowhead in a rickety vessel that's already lost two of your crew. I came out here to take it easy. The only hazard is getting pummeled by a racing log veering down the greased skid road."

"And the pay?" Sterne asks.

"Decent, actually. Best pay you can get out here. If they shut this operation down, then forget it. You might as well take a steamer back home and lose a month's pay. Nobody wants to do that. They know if they muck it up here — poor performance, fighting, drunkenness — they're done for. It's a long way home and for most there's nothing to go back home to."

Sterne sits quietly.

"What are you doing out here in these parts, anyway?" Skaggs asks.

"You can say we're scouting," Sterne says. "Keeping our eyes open for the next opportunity."

Skaggs slurps some coffee out of a tin cup and shoots a line of liquid into the fire. "Hell, out here, a man with some ingenuity and capital can do a lot. Turn beaver shit into an enterprise."

Sterne changes the subject. "What do you do for entertainment around here when not felling trees?"

"Basically go nuts. Cuddy gives us Sundays off and that means only one thing."

"Tomorrow's Sunday. Are you heading into town?"

"Shit no. They don't even have a respectable bawdy house. We stay up here and keep occupied."

"Cards? Drinking?"

"Ever hear of 'Ball the Jack?'"

Sterne gives him an odd look.

"It's our version of Rounders. Y'know, the kids game."

Suddenly Cuddy enters the circle with two men. "Looks like your friend Need'ler has left camp. We can't find him and these two saw him going down the same plank pathway as the one you came up on."

"Is that right?" Sterne asks the two men. They nod in compliance.

"Must've gone back down to the waterway," Cuddy says.

"Back down to the coach." He looks at Cuddy. "I'll meet up with him in the morning. Looks like you'll be getting a bunkmate after all."

Sunlight peeks through the mist and trees. Cuddy sits up on his cot, snaps on his suspenders and opens the door. He sees Sterne sitting on a bench next to a washbasin.

"You're up early. The breakfast bell hasn't even rung yet."

"I've been up for some time, thinking about heading down."

"I'm sure your friend is down there. Want me to send someone down, make you feel better?"

Sterne adjusts his tie. "I could use a little coffee. You were right about your snoring."

Cuddy laughs. "What you need is a hearty breakfast to get you going. No work today. The boys usually get their game in after breakfast."

"Ball the Jack?"

"Why don't you stick around and catch a little of it? In the meantime I'll make sure your man is found and taken care of. Whaddy'a say?"

The men are full from a load of freshly prepared eggs, oats, bacon, coffee, pudding and hot cakes. Sterne and Cuddy follow them to an open field stripped of trees and watch as each lay claim to a spot to limber up.

Someone pulls a round object out of a canvas bag.

"What is that?" Sterne asks Cuddy.

"That's the ball."

"That is a ball?" Sterne takes a closer look.

"It's the best they could do for around here. A piece of ox hide wrapped around a rolled-up sock with a lump of gypsum inside. It travels pretty far. Of course, when they take a good whack at it sometimes the stitches come loose and the ball gets a little lopsided."

"They 'whack' it?"

"Sure, you'll see. The hafts to their axes make for good whacking. Bat that ball pretty far."

Sterne pays close attention. The men finish loosening up and begin tossing the ball around, flicking it from one to the other, testing their reflexes and catching agility.

After several moments they split into two groups of about eight or nine. One group stays in the field and the other huddle off to the side. The group on the field spreads out.

Someone pulls out three burlap sacks filled with something and lays them down in the field at equal distances from each other.

"Stations," Cuddy remarks.

"What?" Sterne asks.

"Stations. Y'know, railroad lingo. Once the ball's whacked,

they travel from station to station until they arrive back at the roundhouse or homestead."

"I see. So the object of this game is to hit the ball and run from station to station until they arrive back home. Sounds very simplistic. When do they switch sides?"

"They take turns. Either they rack up a set of 'outs' or they just get plain bored and switch sides."

"Outs?"

"The 'whacker' is 'out' if anyone catches the ball before it hits the ground. Or you can throw him out by hitting him with the ball before he reaches the first station."

Sterne rubs his chin. "A game this rudimentary, where's the strategy or entertainment? How could it compete against a game like chess?"

"Well, just being outside in the air and sunshine sure beats holing yourself up in the bunkhouse."

"I guess I'll just have to see for myself."

The game begins when one of the men picks up the ball and stands on top of a tree stump, waiting to deliver the ball to the whacker several yards away.

The whacker stands in a patch of dirt. He spits in his hands, rubs them together, and lifts his haft up to his shoulders. The 'deliverer' lifts his arms in the air, bends his back, and lunges forward, chucking the ball.

The whacker strikes the ball and pops it up. One of the men in the field, a 'tender', plays it off a bounce and throws it toward the whacker running to the first station. The ball misses his target and the runner safely reaches the sack.

The second whacker pounds the ball past the stump, forcing another 'tender' to make a throw at the runner. He plunks him on the back before reaching the sack for an out. The first whacker makes it to the second station.

Other whackers take their turn either making outs or reaching to safety, pushing the line forward until their fellow axmen reach the homestead.

Sterne and Cuddy watch the game under the shade of a pine tree. Cuddy pulls out a tin from his pocket. "Nuts?"

Sterne, engrossed in the action, doesn't turn his head. "No, I wouldn't call it that."

"I meant do you want some nuts?"

"I've never seen anything like it before. Grown men in the act of organized play. Something so unconventional, yet somehow appealing."

Cuddy tosses a nut in his mouth. "Not bad for being a kiddie game, but they changed it up a bit."

Sterne closely observes the display of bodies in motion—running, chasing, throwing, catching, swinging and smacking. "What synergy. Quite enchanting."

They pause the game and switch sides. The tenders become the whackers. A young man steps up to the dirt patch with his haft.

"Who is that?" Sterne asks, jolted by the youngster's appearance.

"Oh, that's Redcorn."

The young man sports a boyish face and a lean, strapping body. He rolls up his sleeves, revealing a pair of muscular forearms. He whirls his haft. The ball leaves the deliverer's hands and Redcorn blasts it to the outer field, sending the tenders chasing back toward a stand of pitch pines. It crashes down into a cluster of branches.

Redcorn races to the first station and doesn't stop. He wheels around to the next station, then the next, and, picking up speed, barrels headlong to the roundhouse. He slides in headfirst.

His fellow whackers jump up and holler. "A full circuit! With a head-in! He does it again!" A crowd gathers around the dirt patch to congratulate Redcorn, who pops up in a cloud of dirt, glistening with sweat.

"Amazing." Sterne is awestruck by the young man's physique and athleticism. "Such classical lines and graceful movement. He's like a bronze Greek statue. Simply breathtaking."

"Yeah, that boy's got some serious country-strong in him."

The ball comes back looking like an egg with the stitches torn. They stop the game to make repairs.

"Tell me more about this Redcorn. Who is he?"

"Him? He's just a kid. Hasn't been here long."

Sterne can't keep his eyes off him. "Did you just see what he did?"

"Oh, that? He does it all the time. They keep telling him to lay off but he never listens. He likes showing off."

Sterne gets up. "Excuse me for a minute."

He approaches the boy taking a drink of water out of a bucket.

"A really intriguing game, I must say." Sterne gets his attention.

"Yup." Redcorn glances at Sterne and slurps down a ladleful of water. Then he scoops up another and splashes it on his face.

"This is the first time I ever laid my eyes on this 'Ball the Jack.' Quite charming. And you play with exception."

Redcorn wipes his face and neck with his handkerchief.

He reaches out his hand. "My name is Sterne. I'm from the East. I'm a businessman. How do you do?"

Redcorn clamps down on it. "Name's Owen. Nice to meet you."

"I must say I'm highly impressed. I didn't know a game—a child's game to say the least—can be so captivating. Where are you from, Owen?"

"Well, my family's a bunch of Quakers and as I got older I didn't square up with them right, so I took off. Now here I am bucking trees for a living."

"I see. And you've been playing this game for a while?"

"I guess. There's nothin' much else to do when we get a day off. I don't drink or gamble. Playing the game seems about the best thing I can do around here except stripping bark off pines."

Sterne gleefully observes Owen. "This may sound abrupt, Owen, but I seldom dawdle when I see a potential golden opportunity. How would you like to work for me, back East?"

Owen drops the ladle. "Me? Gosh, Mister Sterne. I'm just a timberin' hand making a little money here. What could I do with you back East?"

"My specialty back home is finding value in things nobody else does and transforming them into a commodity everyone wants. This game of yours has piqued my entrepreneurial interest. And you, Owen. You're a precious metal that isn't discovered very often."

"What do you mean?"

"Owen, I want you to come back East and play this game for me."

Redcorn looks at Sterne from the corner of his eyes. "You want me to go with you to play 'Ball the Jack?'"

"Yes."

An incredulous look crosses his face.

"I see something in you that I rarely ever see. You are the perfect embodiment for what I've been searching for all this time."

"What's that?"

"Unblemished purity. Promise. A new ideal introduced to this country."

Redcorn flushes with embarrassment. He hesitates. "Excuse me for saying this, mister, but I—"

Sterne lifts his finger in front of Redcorn's face. "I will be right back to continue this conversation. Don't go away."

Niedler is sprawled out on the Louis XVI Revival sofa in the passenger coach with a damp towel on his forehead. The door opens and Sterne jumps in.

"Oh, thank God," Niedler says. "You're back. Edmonds says he's ready. We can get out of this infernal place and return home."

"You're a pathetic shambles, Henry. What became of you?"

"You saw it. I drank that incendiary concoction. And then the walls started closing in. I was in trouble, so I fled. Though I'm not sure how I made it down."

"Well, at least you appear to be in one piece. Always good to see my closest associate fit and ready for the next venture."

"No more ventures for me, thank you. I'm ready to get back home and soak in my copper-plated bathtub."

"Not yet. I have something to tell you. I saw a vision, right before my eyes, Henry. A manifestation of enthralling simplicity. I must have it, I tell you!"

Niedler sits up and removes the towel.

"I was treated by the loggermen to a game called Ball the Jack. No more than a child's game but played by these men of brawn and sinew. Very rudimentary — a crude ball is hit with an ax handle and once struck the participant rounds a set of stations until they reach the original starting point."

"A child's game?"

"I wasn't intrigued until I saw them physically engaged. I tell you, Henry, there is something to this. I've never seen anything like it."

"All for striking a ball and running around?" Niedler massages his temples.

"That's just the surface. But deep down there's truly something else there — unsullied, flawless, pristine."

"What do you want to do with this game?"

"Make it ours, of course. Then we'll take it back and tout it amongst our peers. We'll present a new endeavor — men playing a game, employing the benefits of exercise, out in the fresh, open air, forming bonds and kinship. It can be the makings of something revolutionary."

Niedler drops his shoulders. "You're back on this again?"

"This is the one, Henry. Finally, something that can be weaved into the cultural grain of this country. And it's ours. Imagine the legacy!"

Niedler studies him. "We went over this before. We should stick to what we do well. And that's the business of—"

"This time I finally found it. I saw it with my own eyes."

He edges himself off the sofa. "Fine. What is it going to take to get us out of this godforsaken terrain and back into our homes and comfortable beds?"

"I want you to draw up a standardized contract. I'm going to make him sign away the rights to that game and give us full authority."

"Who?"

"That fat, bulbous man who fed you that repulsive liquid."

"Very well."

"Also, I need you to draw another one for a personal services contract. We'll have to make room for a third passenger."

Cuddy empties his whiskey glass and leans back in his stool. "You want me to sign what?" His eyes are cloudy.

"A contract that relinquishes all rights to the game 'Ball and Jack.'"

Cuddy's face is a jumble of confusion. "Rights to what? It's just a game they were playing, that's all. If you want to play it, then be my guest."

"You don't understand. This contract calls for you to cease and desist all associations with the game—you can't play it, can't divulge the rules, can't even call it by name."

"You're serious?"

"I want this game, Mr. Cuthbert. My proprietary right to do as I see fit with it with no outside meddling, you see."

Cuddy sits up and plants his feet on the ground. "I don't see how you can own a game like this. It's like trying to own the air we breathe. How are you going control something like this?"

"That will be my business."

"Good luck with that. You can try the scare tactics but that only lasts a little while until someone else comes along with a fresh take on things and before you know it you're knocked off your pedestal."

"Are you going to comply with my wishes, or do I have to resort to my own scare tactics?"

Cuddy fills his glass again. "It don't matter to me one way or another if I sign this piece of paper. But the boy. That's a different story."

"He'll come around. I have a way of convincing people."

Sterne steps into the bunkhouse with contract in hand and weaves his way through the airless, cramped quarters until he spots his target. Owen Redcorn lies in his top bunk with one arm under his pillow and the other holding a dime novel. He drops the rag onto his chest and sees Sterne.

"What do you want Mr. Sterne?"

"I think you know. Let's cut to the point, shall we?" He lifts up the contract.

"What is that?"

"This is what we call a personal services contract. By signing this, you can join me back East in New York and play this game under my sponsorship. You will be taken care of wholeheartedly, I guarantee it."

Redcorn sits up. "You're actually going to pay me to play Ball and Jack?"

Sterne hands him the contract. "Everything will be provided for—salary, lodging, meals, personal needs. In return you play the game the way I witnessed this morning and do everything you can to be the ambassador to this soon-to-be American pastime."

Redcorn swings himself off the bunk. "I'm sorry, Mr. Sterne." He hands him the contract.

"Sorry for what?"

"I can't read this."

"I know, there may be a lot of complex language but I can sit with you and explain it all line by line."

"No, I mean I don't know how to read anything."

"What was it you were looking at just a minute ago?"

"I was looking at the pictures. I can read a few words here and there and get an idea of what's going on. But this contract. How would I know what I'd be getting into?"

Sterne drops his head. "If you had any idea who I am back where I come from you would know the amount of resources I have at my disposal. You would be treated extraordinarily well and if this game takes off there would be no telling the amount of fame and riches coming your way."

Redcorn shoves his thumbs through the belt loops of his trousers.

"Remember what I said about transforming an unknown raw material into a valued commodity? This game has the potential to be the next great American institution. I have that capability to make it happen. Especially if you were its personification." Sterne pulls out a gold-nibbed fountain pen from his pocket. "Sign it."

"I can't Mr. Sterne. You don't understand." Redcorn pushes his way past Sterne and walks out the door.

Sterne follows Redcorn through the camp. "What don't I understand?"

Redcorn stops. "I don't want riches or fame or anything else like that, Mr. Sterne. Where you come from you may think those things are worth something, but out here, I like rising at the crack of dawn and working all day, sweating and grinding it out day after day. It's who I am."

"You would rather break your back for a mere pittance than engage in a game you love to play?"

"It's all I know. I don't know anything about being someone's ambassador."

"All you have to do is play the game and I'll provide the rest. I'll build this from the ground up. That's all I ask."

Redcorn shakes his head. "Sorry." He turns around and keeps walking.

"Goddamned simpletons!" Sterne follows him briskly across the camp and passes Cuthbert's shack. Sterne stops and rushes in. "Get Redcorn to sign the contract or else you'll be paying for it in other ways!"

Cuthbert, thoroughly drunk from the whiskey, makes a sloshing sound from his mouth. "I got three of diamonds!"

"I will deal with you later!" Sterne dashes out, running briskly across the camp until he finds Redcorn at the upper terminus of the log flume. "Stop!" He sees Redcorn picking up a small wooden contraption that looks like an animal trough.

"What do you want from me? I'm just a loggerman, nothing else. Now stay away!" He plunks the wooden contraption into the flume, forcing water to splash up.

"You idiot! You don't know what you're throwing away. Your name can be etched in the history books. A chance for immortality!"

Redcorn, to Sterne's astonishment, jumps into the makeshift vessel and squats down. "I don't care about immortality. Who wants to live forever?" Then he pushes himself off with a piece of lumber and drifts forward until the trough picks up speed and hurtles down the mountainside, disappearing around a bend.

"Redcorn!" Sterne freezes, his heart pounding. He sees another trough lying on its side and picks it up. He drops it in the water and hops in. He gives it a nudge and begins moving forward, the trough swaying side to side, until it reaches the sharp decline and barrels down the mountainside at full speed.

Sterne clutches the sides of the trough, crashing against the sides of the flume, terrified of flying over the side with every sharp turn. Air flies in his face. Trees zoom by.

Suddenly, the treeline opens up and Sterne sees the spillway. The final leg of the flume is a straight drop. Sterne ducks his head and zooms down, crashing into the cold water.

Completely drenched, he trudges to the water's edge and flops down. He searches the spillway. Redcorn's nowhere in sight.

He hears a voice coming from behind him. "Goddamn it! How many times do I have to tell you not to be doin' that?" Sterne turns and sees an approaching Lester Shawkey.

"Oh, it's you again," Shawkey says.

"Where did he go?" Sterne asks.

"Where'd who go?"

"Redcorn!"

"I don't know. I just heard you guys plunge into the water and I dashed over here to yell at you hooligans. What the hell made you do that?"

"Redcorn. He's the one. He can't get away from me. Go find him!"

"What'd he do, steal somethin' from you?"

"I won't take this lightly. No one rejects my overtures. You simpletons won't get the last laugh. I will make sure of it. J. Barron Sterne always wins out in the end. Don't forget that! I always win in the end!" ■

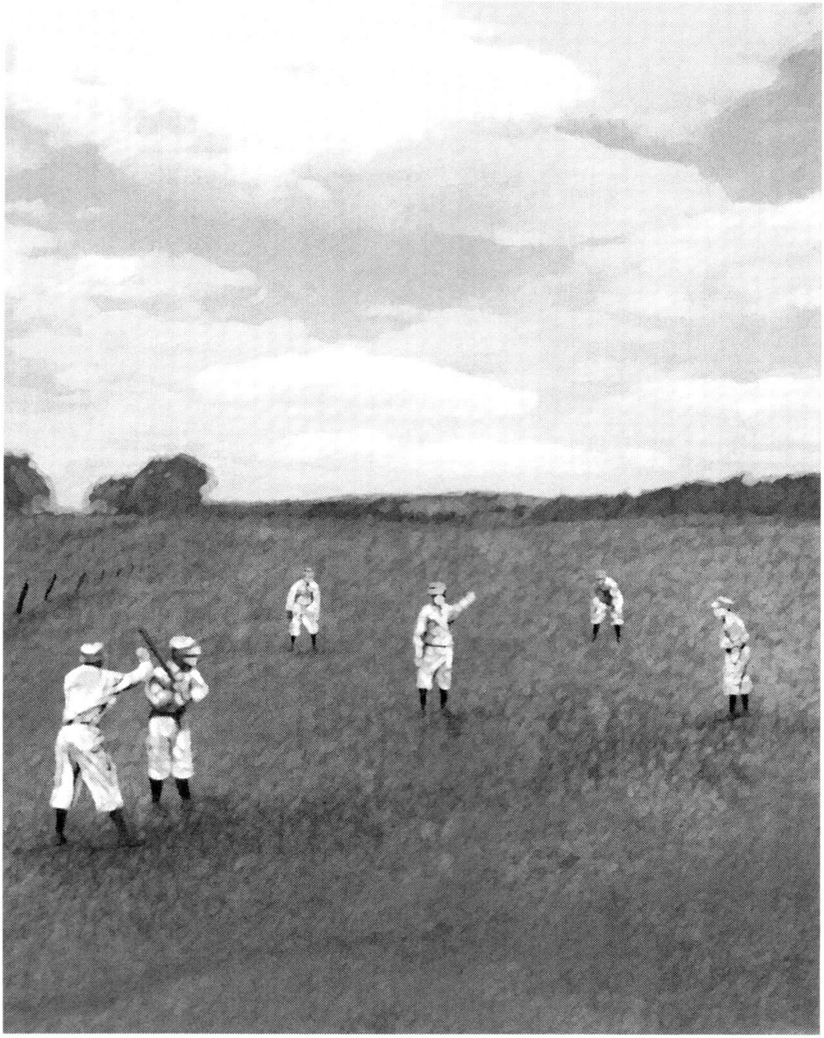

III.

Codfish Aristocracy
(1857-1860)

A mid-morning rain briefly halts the bustle on the corner of Amity and Broadway. Shafts of sunlight finally break through the cloud cover and bathe the main thoroughfare with golden light all the way down to the Battery public walk. Men and women return to their routine of strolling and scurrying along shops, rowhouses, churches and manors.

J.B. Sterne steps out of his residence and waits for his coachman to swing around the block. Wrapped in a wool frock coat and cravat, Sterne unbuttons himself and hands the coachman his umbrella before hopping into the brougham for his commute to the office.

The distance from his Washington Square brownstone to his second-floor office on Pine in the financial district affords him time to read the morning edition, gather his thoughts and take in the ever-expanding scenery of a burgeoning Manhattan. What was once a pastoral setting of fields, cows and farmhouses has quickly transformed itself, in a manner of a few decades, into a booming center of commerce and capitalism. Like many other mornings, Sterne marvels at the spectacle of progress through his window and wonders if there can be any end in sight.

Twelve Pine Street is a modest three-story building with a sign in front reading "Sterne & Asscoc." Upstairs, H.H. Niedler toils at his desk in the single-room office, poring over record books and financial statements. Sterne enters and hangs up his coat and hat. He looks across at his associate. "Well, Henry, what can you tell me?"

Niedler remains facedown in a multitude of papers. "Nothing is official yet but I'd say by the end of the week you'll be the sole owner of the Ehrland & Overton Timber Company and the next ten-thousand hectares slated to be acquired. The entire run through the valley will be ours all the way to the junction point with the main trunk line. A lucrative grab, to say the least."

"And our Lord Boston Adversary with the Twitchy Eyelids?"

"Blind-sided. Had no idea until it was too late. Stealth worked to perfection."

Sterne sits at his desk and leans back.

Niedler lifts his head. "Long time coming on this one, wouldn't you say? When did he snatch away that copper mine out of our hands? Three years?"

"Two years, eight months."

"A long time of planning. Waiting until the day comes when the ripened melon bursts and what comes out? The delicious taste of retaliation."

"Just another business deal, Henry. Nothing more."

"Right. What are you planning to do with the assets once you gain possession? The mill? The lumbering camp?"

Sterne leans further back in his chair and looks at the ceiling, his fingers interlocked over his midriff. "Liquidate it all. Start over."

"Not a wise decision for such a business deal, J.B., considering these reports show they've been profitable for fourteen straight months. If we tear it down and start over that would mean we won't be seeing anything out of it for at least two years. We should be taking full advantage of the rail line."

Sterne sits up and shoots Niedler a familiar glare of dagger eyes. Niedler relents. "An immediate dismantling it shall be. I'll insert the necessary verbiage in the final paperwork."

"Anything else?"

"One more thing." Niedler shuffles a few things on his desk and hands Sterne a periodical. "*The Wall Street Gazette's* done another piece about you. This one makes it number six. You're becoming a regular darling."

Sterne reads it.

> "Not since the time of Alexander has there been a sweep over a continent of such swift and methodical nature at such a budding age than that of the brilliant and astute J. Barron Sterne. By the age of twenty-eight, Sterne has amassed a fortune in holdings and investments spanning the country's exploding economic landscape that includes railroads, steamships, real estate, mines, finance, and steel—making him the youngest to be deemed a "Captain of Industry" or "Champion of Capitalism."
>
> Born in humble obscurity, the youthful Sterne achieved early success with a series of investments in the stock exchange—primarily gold and copper futures—during which time he was suspected of "cornering the market" for each commodity. His standing as an emerging entrepreneur escalated with every deal thereafter, mixing an unparalleled amount of boldness and vision with a keen sense of market acumen and, what has been described by his closest associates as "statistical analytics

through objective metrics"—a turn of phrase not recognized within the prudent Wall Street echelon of speculators and capitalists.

Renowned for his intense desire for privacy, Mr. Sterne grants very few personal interviews, employing instead a small staff to handle public correspondence. Given how little information Sterne and Associates imparts, rumors abound as to his next business venture, not to mention his personal dealings.

His rising status within the ranks of the business hierarchy will be closely monitored, as will his attempts to fit within the older and exclusive social stratum of New York's upper classes. To be sure, if the year 1857 and its precedents are any indication, J. Barron Sterne will reach near-immortality in the future through sheer force and cunning, much like the King of Macedon did two millennia ago. We will have to wait and see what his next great achievement will be prior to running out of worlds to conquer."

Sterne pushes the paper aside.

"Why don't you just grant them an interview already, J.B.? Everyone's dying to know who J.B. Sterne is. What are you going to do about it?"

"As I've always done, send you to do it."

Niedler smirks. "I'm not the one about to convert two blocks of upper Fifth Avenue into his private stately home. Regardless of what you think, you're in their neighborhood now and you can't sneer at these old patrician families any longer. If they're going to let you play amongst them you need to be accessible."

Sterne snorts. "Same can go for them as well. These old lines of wealth don't like the up-and-comers outside of their tight circle. I'm a threat to them. A parvenu."

"How are you a threat?"

"Look at us, Henry. What took these men decades to cultivate, I did in under ten years. Do you think they're about to let me in their little coterie without some sort of snooty backlash?"

"Hell, the way you're going, in five years they'll be the ones begging to enter into your circle," Niedler quips.

"I wouldn't waste my time if it weren't for this." Sterne taps lightly on a rolled-up piece of vellum on his desk.

"What is that? Your little project again?"

"Little project?" Sterne clears his desk and unrolls the vellum, unveiling a jumble of sketches and scrawls. "The Game, Henry. I'll use them to get the Game off the ground. These men have influence, if nothing else. With the right twist of the arm the Game will reach a threshold and soon be a commonplace sight in every city and township."

In the middle of the vellum sheet is a diagram in the shape of a diamond. The words, "Ball Delivery Zone" are written inside. The rest of the surface is filled with words and phrases, lists and notes. Some of them are underlined, others scratched over or crossed out.

Sterne, bent over with his arms pillared against the desk, looks like a draftsman examining his latest batch of schematics. "This is what I saw that Sunday morning on the mountain. I believe I have it, Henry. It's really close, with some modifications on my part. But the core essence is there."

Niedler looks closer. "Sorry, J.B., I can't make it out."

Sterne rips the vellum off the desk and pins it to the wall. The late-morning sun shines its rays warmly against the work. "A game of deceptively simple nature but ripe with unexpected outcome." He points to the diamond. "Your main playing area, but there will be players roving the outer field. At the center is the dispenser who'll deliver the ball to this quarter," he points to the bottom of the diamond, "where a striker will wield a club and hit the ball, who, in turn, will march to the first station, or base, if he's not snuffed out."

"*Snuffed out?*" Niedler asks.

"There are two ways for the striker running to the base to be declared snuffed out. One is if the ball is caught on the fly without it hitting the ground first. Or two, if the fielder throws the ball at the runner and hits him before he reaches the base. Almost exact from what I witnessed."

Niedler inspects the wall for some time. "In effect, you have a ball dispenser who serves the ball to a player looking to strike it. Very cricket-like to me."

"Striking similarities, but there are distinct differences, such as the bases and the act of circumnavigating them."

"Differences?"

"Yes," Sterne says. "There has to be a reason why to circle these said bases. In cricket, you can score virtually anytime you make contact with the ball. In my game, you have to successfully round all four bases before you garner a *tally point*. That's the strategy I'm betting on."

Niedler pauses one more time. "Do you think it will catch on? You're talking about well-healed, grown men whose idea of recreation is a game of Whist while nursing a brandy. What makes you think you'll get them out in the open air playing a child's game?"

Sterne smiles. "I will use my persuasive techniques once again."

"And what are you going to call this newly-hatched game of yours?"

Sterne raises his hand to his chin. "'Ball the Jack' is a little too vague for my tastes, wouldn't you say?"

"How about something with a little more character and whimsy, such as 'Rounding Willies' or simply 'The Runs.'"

Sterne glares at Niedler once again. "No, something simplistic and distinctive. Something that tells you what the game is before you even see it." Sterne thinks for a moment before picking up a stick of graphite and writes in large, bold letters underneath the diamond drawing: Bases and Ball."

Niedler tilts his head to one side. "I can't say it's fanciful or catchy, but it does make sense."

Thaddeus Snodgrass holds the match flame close to Sterne's cigar as he takes his initial draw, carefully observing any reaction from the young magnate. "Nice and easy. Let the smoke waft around. Savor the flavors and aromas. That's it. Now gently exhale. Allow the smoke to escape on its own." His voice is calm and soothing. "What do you think?"

Sterne takes a deep breath and examines the cigar. His face reveals slight approval.

"The Old Excelsior Gentlemen's Club has got the finest humidor in the city. The best hand-rolled cigars straight from Havana. If it's perfection you want out of the finer things in life, you've joined the right association. No expense is spared. Take a look at this chair you're sitting in. Imported llama leather. The wood you see from floor to ceiling? African mahogany. The only thing more refined under this roof is the Madeira selection and the blood running through the veins of our established members."

Sterne stops examining the cigar and his eyelids narrow. Snodgrass quickly adds, "Of course its more recent members are just as blue-blooded as the club's founding successors. The Excelsior Club does not discriminate when it comes to selecting the best our society offers."

Sterne notices a clamminess come over Snodgrass' skin. Even

his wiry red hair, brushed over to one side, appears overtaken by a dewy sheen.

"So, dear boy, welcome aboard. The club is honored to have your name in its Grand Register. The Great Wunderkind himself!"

"Thank you, Tad, but please spare me with the epithet. Anyway, it couldn't have happened without your expeditiousness. If not for you, I'd still be an outsider."

"Nonsense! You underestimate your sparkling prestige. Any club worth its salt would have been champing at the bit to allow you in."

Sterne returns to his cigar.

Snodgrass lights up his own cigar and blows an assertive puff straight up the air. "My compliments to you for finally giving the old house a try. You've been a subject of conversation throughout these drawing rooms for some time and now we have our very own chance to rub shoulders with the man who's skyrocketed to prominence like no other. We're eager to know what is exactly buzzing around in that little head of yours, dear boy. You're finally all ours, come now!"

Sterne looks around the room and sees men more than twice his age with silver, wispy muttonchops and double-breasted waistcoats with pocket watches streamed across their bellies, sunken in their massive chairs, hobnobbing quietly, looking exceptionally dull and stodgy.

"How long have you been a member of this club, Tad?" Sterne asks.

"About fifteen years. Father was the one who brought me in when I was just a couple of years older than you. Now I'm champion backgammon player three years running."

"Impressive. And what other modes of entertainment can I find lurking around?"

"The usual card and board games, but that's not where the real entertainment lies, I'm afraid."

"Oh?" Sterne coyly answers.

Snodgrass smiles, revealing a gap tooth. He leans closer to Sterne, making a rubbing sound against the leather of the chair. He lifts his hand and twirls it in a circular motion. "It lies in the space between us. The game has no name, but everyone in this building knows what the objective is: to fill that space with mutually coveted information that benefits both parties."

Sterne puts his lips to his cigar. Snodgrass inches closer.

"Now I could be blunt and ask you point blank, 'What is the system you're using to pull down a percentage on returns of which most of us in this room can only be so lucky?' But that wouldn't be the gentlemanly way of doings things. I shan't be so blunt. I'd have to engage you in a long series of semantics and subtleties, I'm afraid, and how boring would that be?" Snodgrass' smile widens.

Sterne taps his cigar into an ashtray and looks around the room. "I thought brusqueness is an intolerable offense in this club, especially on matters of personal business. It says so in the rules of conduct. What would the founding members have to say about that?"

"They'd say, 'Piss on the rules. If wealth is to be made, share it with your fellow members.' If you haven't been told yet, J.B., you're now part of an exclusive brotherhood that is concerned with only one thing."

"What is that?"

"Creating wealth and finding ways to create more. We all know you have a certain knack for this and we're all dying to get our hands on your little secret. If one member has a course to more prosperity, the others must know about it. It's our right and privilege."

"This 'secret' of mine? If I managed to explain it to you, how would I know it stays within these walls?"

Snodgrass snickers. "Why on earth would we want to share it with the rest of the world? Sensitive information needs to be in the hands of a select few who know what to do with it."

Sterne pushes the cigar into the ashtray and wipes his hands. "I've got a 'secret' all right."

"Yes?" Snodgrass perks up.

"But I'm not sure it's fit for ears such as those," he points to the silver-haired men sitting across the room. "I need someone closer to my age who's willing to invest in the concept, someone who will put in the physical work to get this thing off the ground."

"Yes! What is it?" Snodgrass' knees nearly touch Sterne's.

Sterne reaches for his coat pocket and pulls out a piece of the vellum cut from the original roll. He unfolds it, revealing the diamond diagram and the words BASES AND BALL boldly written underneath.

Snodgrass stares at the vellum. His piqued expression lessens, unable to make any meaning of the diagram. "What is it?"

"My latest business venture. A certain start-up I'm particularly fond of. It just needs an infusion of assets. Namely, able-bodied men. Can you help me get this off the ground?"

Snodgrass keeps staring at the diagram.

"Thaddeus, are you with me?"

"It'll do." Sterne waves his hand, continuing his inspection of the crude lot near Houston Street.

Niedler teeters along, pushing a wheelbarrow, picking up rocks and stones and keeping his handkerchief close to his mouth. "Best I could find on such short notice. These open plots are quickly disappearing, especially east of the Harlem line."

"It'll be a tight fit if we keep our distance from that lovely open cesspool you got over there behind the strikers' area."

"It could be worse. It could be a breezy day with the wind

blowing in the wrong direction. Instead, we have clear skies and sunshine. A perfect day to launch your grand endeavor."

Sterne eyes the diamond one more time, examining the straight, fine lines of dirt dug out from under the grass, leading to the burlap sacks of flour serving as bases. He squats down close to the ground. "The distance is short from one base to the next. I can tell. The distance is too short!"

Niedler concedes, "I moved them up five feet, to eight-five feet."

"You did what?" Sterne jumps to his feet. "This is outrageous! How dare you go against my schematics! Do you know how many times I had that distance tested out? Exactly ninety feet yielded a fifty-four percent success rate of reaching base. Move it back!"

Niedler straightens up. "Your calculations were based on a swift-legged runner. Not exactly the calling card of our crew."

Suddenly a carriage rattles up and Snodgrass steps out. "Gentlemen! What a fine day to fill our lungs with invigorating fresh air!" His face radiates exhilaration.

Niedler leans into Sterne and whispers, "Did you finally have to bribe him to go along with you?"

"Not exactly. I sort of hinted at taking over his entire industry if he didn't agree to help me assemble a promising crew of players."

Snodgrass walks up and extends handshakes.

"Where are my players, Tad? I can't wait to see them take the field and play my game. How soon?"

Snodgrass flips open his timepiece and peeks at it, then tucks it back in his vest pocket. "Almost, my dear good man. In a few minutes, we will begin laying the groundwork to another road paved toward prosperity. But first, we celebrate." He pulls out a bottle of champagne and proposes a toast. "On the cusp of your new enterprise, may it last a thousand years and be just as fruitful then as it will be going forward. To J. Barron Sterne, a man whose vision and aspiration can never be replaced!"

The three men sip their glasses in the middle of the diamond before a caravan arrives and delivers Sterne's much-anticipated players. A dozen men get out, dressed in an assortment of peculiar attire.

"There, there! Your men have arrived!"

"My goodness," Niedler gapes, "we've got a real hodgepodge here."

Some are dressed casually wearing ivory cotton shirts and dark trousers held by suspenders. Others are dressed in tweed waistcoats and neckties. The last to arrive is a pair of men dressed in hunting attire with black mid-calf boots, scarlet coats and leather gauntlets.

"Ah, yes, the Gaffney twins. Gentlemen!" Snodgrass welcomes them.

"All they need is a riding crop and we got ourselves a foxhunt," Niedler quips.

Snodgrass gathers the men inside the diamond. "If you will, please, gentlemen. Allow me to make the formal introductions. It is my great honor to introduce you to the man whom you are all most familiar with by now. The man whose budding concept you are about to turn into reality, Mr. J. Barron Sterne!"

"Ah, yes," says one of the pair of hunting gear-clad men, "the fine gentleman with the most fantastic idea to allow grown, mature men to frolic about in an open field, chasing a tiny sphere around. My name is Charles H. Gaffney and this is my brother Charles W. Gaffney, of the Gaffney & Sons Shoe Manufacturing empire. We are the sporting men of the family and we hear from Mr. Snodgrass that you have a new, exciting brand of recreation you're eager to inaugurate."

"That's correct," Sterne says. "You will be the first to participate in a game meant to bring men of affluence like yourselves out of their cramped offices and dark, smoky social clubs and get them into airy fields such as this one and enjoy the fruits of leisurely activity. I call it Bases and Ball."

Charles W. Gaffney chimes in. "Mr. Snodgrass gave us a

briefing on the subject. His unbridled enthusiasm convinced us to take a leap of faith but I am afraid my experience in leisurely activity, especially one having to do with a spheroid object and prancing around a field without a mount, is a little, shall we say, limited?" He turns to his brother. "Mmmm, yes, a somewhat unconventional activity. Almost bizarre, don't you agree?" They begin debating the merits of open-air exercise before turning the conversation into a prattling exchange in claptrap.

"Gentlemen," Sterne interrupts, "my red-clad daredevils, pay attention. Your friend here, Mr. Snodgrass, has assured me wholeheartedly that each and every one of you is not only fit and firmly established in physical activities but that you are all enthusiastic to partake in this brand-new recreation. Are you ready to indulge yourselves? Let's begin with a simple practice."

Niedler starts pulling out a set of booklets from a trunk and hands one to each player. "'Bases and Ball: Etiquette and Playing Regulations.' What kind of etiquette are we talking about?"

"Everything you need to know about this game is inside these pages—what it is and how to play it—written by yours truly and subject to revision. As you'll see, the concept is simple. What has Mr. Snodgrass explained to you so far?"

"He said it was a game very similar to cricket, that we needn't worry too much about the details."

"Yes, a ball is thrown and a striker attempts to make contact with it, but that's where the similarities end."

One of the Gaffney twins leans forward and peers at the strikers' area. "I do not see a set of wickets."

"That's because there aren't any. Instead, we have bases." He points at each sack of flour. "Once the ball is struck you must run to the first base and reach safely without getting 'snuffed out.' You get enough players to reach safely, starting from the first base and all the way around, and your team is awarded a tally point. Am I clear? It is all written clearly in the handbook."

Gaffney tugs at his chin and scans around the diamond.

"Running around a set of 'bases?' Oh my, and not even in clockwise fashion! Truly befuddling!"

"It's all in the book. I've laid it out in a most precise manner. But now, since this is our very first practice session, I want to keep things extremely elementary. Mr Niedler?"

"Yes. Before we get into the details of the game itself, we must first limber up, get the body warm and pliable. Gentlemen, allow me to show you some maneuvers I picked up while at university on the rowing club." Niedler shows the group stretching exercises and soon the diamond is filled with men bent over twisting, contorting, lunging, thrusting and extending in a jumble of moans and grumbles.

Niedler then lines them along the base path. Sterne bends pulls out a dark, round object.

"Ah, yes, at last!" Charles W. cries out, "The sphere itself!"

"Ball. It is called a ball." Sterne balances the ball on the tips of his fingers and slowly displays it to everyone. "Custom made, the only one of its kind, per my specifications — dark leather, hand-stitched, cork and yarn stuffing. Promised not to come loose or become deformed. In your hands is the most essential part of the game. Please familiarize yourself with it."

"I say, a rather odd sort of specimen, wouldn't you agree?" Gaffney comments to his brother.

"Yes, indeed. The quality of leather is most striking. Is it Spanish? And the stitches, what an exquisite pattern! Such artisanship!"

Sterne continues. "There are three things you do with this: throw it, catch it, strike it. That's what you'll be practicing from here on out. Another important aspect is running the bases. Let's work on that first."

Starting at the batters' area, Sterne sends each one off to the first base as fast as they can run, making a mad dash before collapsing to the ground, writhing and gasping for breath.

"Reconsidering moving the bases up another five feet?" Niedler asks Sterne.

Snodgrass speaks up. "They may not be a herd of gazelles just yet, but give them a stretch and they'll be well-winded quarter horses in no time!"

Sterne spreads the players out and gives them the ball to toss around. They watch as they slowly, awkwardly, pass it around, looking as if they're not entirely sure how to achieve the simple task.

Niedler grows impatient. "My god, my eyes are starting to ache. Even I know what to do with a ball!"

"I beg your pardon," Snodgrass says, "but this is totally new to them. Allow them some time to get acquainted with the finer points of the game." He peeks at Sterne, watching the players carefully.

Niedler steps closer to Snodgrass. "It's becoming plainly obvious that these men you selected have no real natural ability. We asked for men with an athletic countenance. So far, none is present."

Snodgrass turns red. "These men are of vigorous and hardy stock. I would challenge you to find better bodies more suited for your newfangled game."

"Our request was very specific," Niedler carries on. "We wanted strapping young sporting types adept enough to throw a ball and run a short distance without keeling over. Instead, it appears we have acquired an inept troupe of gentry who think they're on their way to a fox chase. Shame on you, sir, for trying to pull the wool over our eyes. Such amateurship!"

"You scoundrel!" Snodgrass struggles to stay calm. "How dare you accuse me—"

"Gentlemen! Enough!" Sterne gets in between them. "This adolescent exchange must cease. Incendiary remarks will not help us get to where we need to be. Clearly, there is plenty of work to do but I didn't expect to master anything right from the start. Judging from what I see, we will have to double our efforts. But I can assure you I will not lower my expectations. I won't accept anything less than near-perfection for what this game deserves. If it takes twice as long—ten times as long—I am determined to establish this game the proper way, under the existing requirements, with men willing to do whatever it takes. Now, who is with me?" He stares at both men, then turns to the players on the field. They all stand silently.

Sterne walks over to the trunk and pulls out a batting club. "Now is the time to learn how this works." He hands it to Niedler.

"What?"

"Show them how this works."

"I-I can't do that. I've never seen it done before."

"But you were with me when I drafted the pages on the very subject. Surely you know more about it than anybody else here except me."

"All in theory, but never practiced in the flesh."

"You'll be the first on this playing field. Who knows, perhaps you are a natural at this and don't even know it. Show them how to brandish this club."

Niedler takes the club from Sterne's hands and walks into the batters' area. He lifts the oversized club and, misjudging its heft, slings it over his head and drops it behind him. He lifts it again but drops it one more time, clutching his fingers.

"Now what?" Sterne says.

"Splinter!"

"Good God. Put your gloves back on."

Niedler puts his gloves on and lifts the club. After a moment, he settles in and gets comfortable, wielding the club with enough confidence to start taking half swings. He loosens his wrists and sways his hips, handling the club freely.

"Now take a full swing with all your might!" Sterne commands.

Niedler swings the club in one whirlwind motion and corkscrews himself into the ground, collapsing face first into the dirt. A cloud of dust rises.

"That may have been too strong a word," Sterne says to the players. "Always maintain your balance during the follow-through."

Niedler picks himself up, his clothes smeared with dirt.

"Now it's time to see the ball in action." He tosses it to Snodgrass. "You are the dispenser."

"Me? I've never—"

"Be the first to show your finely selected group of sporting men how it's done."

A reluctant Snodgrass takes the ball and enters the delivery zone. He removes his coat and rolls up his sleeves. Sweating profusely, his red, wiry hair sticks out in all directions. He looks at Sterne, completely bewildered.

"A nice trajectory into the batters' area," Sterne gestures with his arm, "so the striker can meet wood to leather."

Snodgrass paces, wipes his face, and peeks at the players watching him. He clears his throat. "Right."

Niedler, waiting for Snodgrass to make his delivery, starts to tremble.

Snodgrass grips the ball tightly and faces him. He cocks his arm back and flings the ball as hard as he can. It sails across the diamond and smacks Niedler on the side of the head, ricocheting away. He drops to the ground.

The players rush in and surround Niedler, sprawled out in the dirt.

"Is he dead?" Charles H. Gaffney cringes. "My heavens, that sphere is a deadly weapon! Get this man a silk handkerchief!"

Sterne squats down and gently taps Niedler on the cheeks.

Niedler lets out a raspy moan.

Sterne gets close and whispers, "Shadrach and Toplitz, Shadrach and Toplitz,"

Niedler's eyes flare open.

Sterne repeats himself.

"I say, what is this 'Shadrach and Toplitz' business?" Gaffney inquires.

Suddenly, Niedler shoots up. "Shadrach! Toplitz! Noooo!"

"Thank God, the man is alive!"

They help him get to his feet and dust him off. As soon as his senses return, Niedler breaks free and charges Snodgrass, chasing him around the entire field.

Sterne gets more enthusiastic with each practice session, watching his players grow more comfortable with the game, coalescing into a functional unit. Soon, the sounds of playful banter ring around the field.

Charles H. Gaffney receives the ball back from his brother and steps inside the dispenser's zone. "That last delivery was my best so far — right where the striker needed it to make optimum contact."

"You are a fine dispenser of that sphere, indeed!" Charles W. praises. "No one else could place it in a more prime spot than you. Look how far it went!"

"Yes, they are certainly getting their hacks in. But no time for bragging!" Gaffney continues his generous delivery.

A striker steps in and calls for a ball down low near his knees. "That's where I've been most successful. Can you oblige?"

"I will do my best, good man." Gaffney sets himself and winds his arms. The throw is high. Nevertheless, the striker swings and pops the ball up directly behind them.

It drifts back and lands in the open cesspool.

The entire team stops what they are doing and surrounds the pit, looking at the only ball they have sitting in the middle of fetid sewage and muck.

"Oh, how revolting!" Both Gaffneys pull out their handkerchiefs.

"Yes, a most foul ball if you've ever seen one. The foulest ball, indeed!"

They turn toward Sterne. "What do we do now?"

"That's the only custom ball we have. I can only get one made at a time. We need to be careful not to lose these valuable objects. Unless we have a brave soul among us." He looks around. More than half the players are bent over, gagging and retching. "Then I'd say practice is cancelled until further notice. Until I can get another ball constructed."

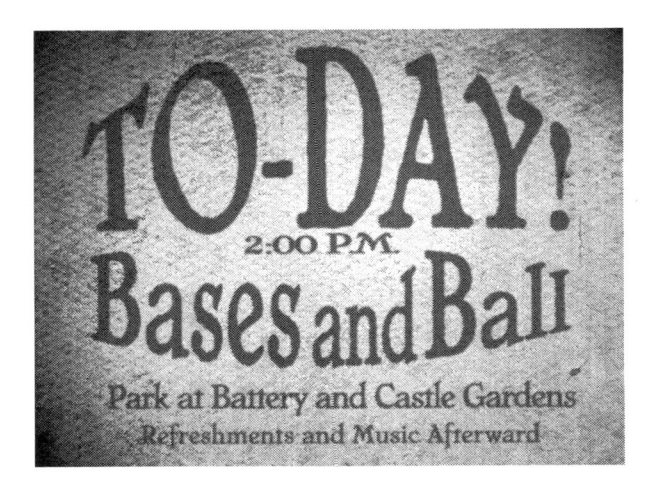

TO-DAY!
2:00 P.M.
Bases and Ball
Park at Battery and Castle Gardens
Refreshments and Music Afterward

On this third Sunday of June, *The Wall Street Gazette* announces an event sponsored by the exceptionally accomplished and brilliant Captain of Industry, J. Barron Sterne, who has agreed to give his very first interview to discuss his latest undertaking.

On a breathtaking afternoon in Battery Park, awash in sunshine and cotton clouds, Sterne is impeccably dressed in regent silver from his top hat down to his spats. Known for his elusiveness and taciturn demeanor, Sterne is beaming today with a striking assertiveness and conviction.

This latest of Sterne's ventures, though, is not associated with finance or industry. It is an outdoor game to be played by men.

What was his motivation? "My game, called Bases and Ball, is a variation of a typical bat and ball game, intended to inspire men to get out of their offices or social clubs and get some exercise and fresh air, stimulate their vitals and participate in a cooperative, team-inspired exhibition."

The concept is deceptively simple, he explains. The objective is to hit the ball and round the stations, or bases, and earn a tally point with each successful full circuit, The opposing team, manning positions throughout the 'diamond' and beyond, have to 'snuff out' that effort.

Will your new game, we asked, strike an inquisitive chord among the folks out taking a leisurely walk along the waterfront? "I intend to create a common recreational activity played and embraced by all Americans—a national game—sewn into the social fabric and lasting for many generations to come."

Judging by his facial expression, Sterne is totally sincere and believes what he says. The campaign to make his game a national fixture begins with a small gathering of these Sunday strollers.

At the stroke of 2:00 p.m. the game commences without any formal procedures or introduction. The players, dressed in leisurely attire, shake hands and split into two factions—one team takes to the diamond and spreads out on the playing field. The other team huddles along the base path and waits to take turns striking.

In the middle of the diamond, a player pitches the

ball in the direction of the striker. Some balls are hit in the air and caught in the bellies of the outer fielders. Other balls are struck on the ground and an inner fielder races to pick the ball up and throw at the runner, 'snuffing' him out before he reaches the first base. Sometimes the runner reaches safely, either on account the inner fielder misses him with the ball or the outer fielder fails to catch it. After each member of the striking team takes a turn hitting the ball and completes a few circuits around the bases, garnering tally points, the fielding team steps off the diamond and takes to their clubs.

On one occasion, the ball dispenser steps outside his designated zone and approaches the current striker and apologizes to him for not locating the ball exactly where the striker wanted it.

It is visually striking to see a bunch of grown men at play. Smiles and jocularity abound, but also an air of solemnity as they try to play the game the way Sterne envisions it, all the while growing more comfortable with the act of managing a small sphere.

Evidently, the players are still addressing their foibles and Sterne will have to accept the fact that it will take time for his game to reach a level of performance that he deems acceptable for the onlookers. For now, they are intent on basking in the sunshine and casually observing Sterne's creation in motion.

The good-natured display of gentlemanly interplay is interrupted when a certain striker waves his club at an incoming pitch and sends the diminutive sphere high and deep into the sky, out of the park, crashing into a second-story window on the corner of Battery Place and Broadway. The players, along with

Mr. Sterne, stand rooted to the spot, as that was the only ball in their possession on this momentous occasion.

Across the street, a Mrs. Hagginswine, aged eighty-years, steps out of her residence carrying the well-travelled ball and is met by an apologetic Sterne. He pleads for the ball—explaining to the matron that it's still the only custom-made sphere in their possession. He promises to pay to fix her window.

The woman lifts her finger in front of the young magnate's face and delivers a scolding before slipping the ball behind her hooped skirt and stepping back inside. She turns to say a few more unkind words, waving the ball for everyone to see, before slamming the door.

Sterne, unable to carry on, is forced to halt the event and postpone the festivities until another ball is produced. He will have to wait another day to showcase his latest venture.

For the rest of the summer, Sterne sends out his players to perform in front of the sun-bathed spectators on their afternoon strolls. With each exhibition the crowd, sprinkled with straw hats and parasols, casts its gaze a little while longer on the players.

But Sterne does not stay still. He leans on his Old Excelsior Gentlemen's Club friends to spread the word that a new form of recreation is sweeping the city in exchange for being in Sterne's good graces.

Besides playing at the Battery on weekends, he mobilizes his trusted lieutenant Niedler to find other open plots of land in the city and transform them into suitable playing fields.

A new set of eyes take notice of his new enterprise and soon people start asking if they can not only watch as spectators but also join in playing. These people are from a different stratum, skilled working-class men looking for a respite between their day and domestic toils — merchants, clerks, doctors, lawyers, tradesmen and craftsmen — seeking a brief moment to roll up their sleeves and join in a gathering of diversion and camaraderie.

To satisfy their enthusiasm, Sterne offers them a copy of his rulebook and sends them off to play at any vacant field. After some time, it becomes apparent that they never read the book and play in a disorderly manner that does not resemble Sterne's game at all. Also, in the absence of a custom-made ball, expensive to procure, they improvise one in any which way, from rolled-up stockings to ivory billiard balls.

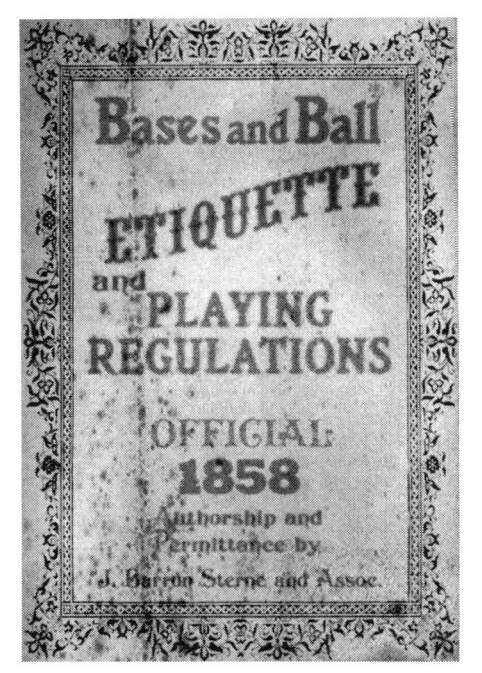

While he appreciates their admiration for the game, he can't come to terms with their disregard of the prerequisites he demands if they are to play. As the summer ends and a brief fall makes way for winter, Sterne goes to work modifying his rulebook, hoping to add new sets of rules that will be followed.

Huddled in their modest office, Sterne and Niedler add the rule of three "outs" ending an "inning" and the designation of permanent fielding positions. These rules are meant to standardize the game and eliminate some of the disorderliness hat has become prevalent on the field.

But the overriding problem of making sure the players follow the rules is still a concern. Sterne wants the game to spread but does not want to sacrifice its original integrity. Order and conformity becomes a central issue.

Leading up to the spring months, Sterne gets an idea. He floats the proposition to the players that if they pay a small fee and promise Sterne they'll play by the rules in his rulebook, they'll get a set of custom-made balls and premium maple clubs. He waits for an answer. A month before spring arrives, the players agree.

It's a shrewd gamble that pays off.

The city men get off work in the early evening and head to the fields to catch a few innings of throwing, catching, running and striking. Sterne manages to preserve the basic elements of his game while earning a small amount of money.

For that summer, and a couple more after that, Bases and Ball flourishes under this agreement.

More and more working-class men find the game enticing and ask Sterne to be brought into the fold and the game spreads outward and away from the city. Happily handing out his rulebook, Sterne watches as his game is taken up by butchers, coopers, shoemakers, blacksmiths and tailors. These men from their particular trades proudly form teams, calling themselves "guilds," and play each other to much fanfare and growing spectatorship.

One day in their office, on a hot summer day, Niedler hands Sterne a newspaper with a headline reading: FIRST OFFICIALLY RECOGNIZED CLUB FOR THE SPORT BASES-AND-BALL.

The newspaper reports that a small band of glass blowers from Bushwick has dubbed itself the first-ever "officially recognized" guild and demanded some sort of recognition. Sterne is beside himself. What makes them "official" to begin with, and why is there no mention of Sterne?

The Bushwick Glass Blowers Guild prove their "legitimacy" by playing every Saturday and Wednesday evening and attracting a small but devoted following of spectators. They promote themselves by printing a pamphlet they call a "program" that lists game schedules and biographical information on the players.

Sterne, though irritated, relishes the publicity the Bushwick guild draws and decides to do the same, promising to shift the attention back on his own team and into the game's original hands.

While things are pleasantly underway, one event threatens the entire endeavor: the Civil War. Sterne watches, disheartened and helpless as his best and youngest sportsmen go off to war, leaving him with a game no one can play well and no one has the appetite to watch.

There remains, however, the faction of players who were there in the beginning—the wealthy, established gentlemen from the social clubs who were drafted into the war but had the means to buy substitutes to take their place.

Faced with this setback, Sterne is forced to accept the reality that his game has to survive as a gentleman's leisure sport played by a privileged few, watched by the upper-class nobility, while the rest of the country is mired in the horrors of warfare.

Sterne must wait to further advance his vision of the game. ■

IV.

PENNY FARTHING ARCADE
(1860-1865)

While far to the west and south the country is ripped by cannon fire and drenched in blood, the bucolic fields of Schenectady are blanketed by blue skies and intermittent clouds—perfect to take in a day's game of Bases and Ball.

Men, women and children, all buttoned up and well-shaded, lazily settle down in their familiar spots in the meadow and watch their sportsmen begin their warm-up routines. A diamond has already been carved out with white canvas sacks filled with sawdust serving as appropriate bases.

Underneath the largest of the oak trees, tables with white tablecloths display refreshments: silver punch bowls filled with cider, bottles of champagne and an endless spread of wild game, cheeses, cherries, currants, mulberries, baskets of walnuts and chestnuts, and desserts including cobblers and crisps.

Another table holds a trophy given after each outing to a particular player who demonstrates outstanding skills and manners in the eyes of his fellow teammates and opposing ballplayers.

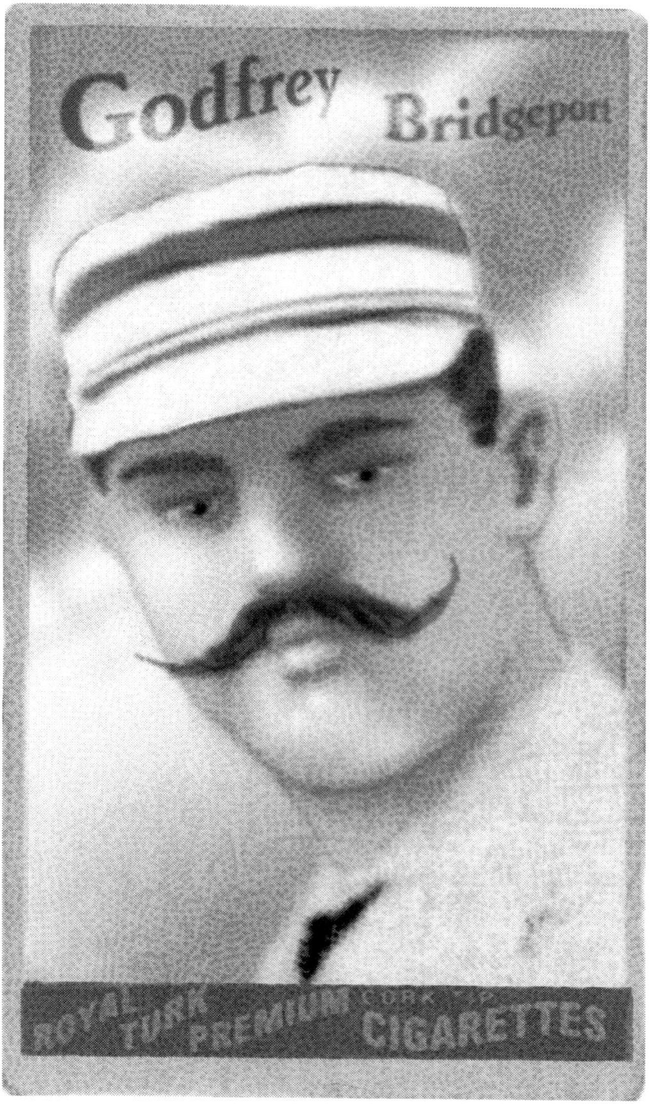
Godfrey
Bridgeport
ROYAL TURK PREMIUM
CIGARETTES

Courtesy and gamesmanship—how well you treat your opponent and how well you look during your particular performance—trumps everything else, including the main objective highlighted in the rulebook: scoring tallies. Actually winning the game is frowned down by these folks, for fear of embarrassing the opposing club.

After warming up, the game gets underway with an exchange of handshakes in the middle of the diamond and a tip of caps to the ladies in attendance. Then the official game arbitrator steps in the playing field wearing a dark suit and felt derby. This man is responsible for monitoring the actions of the players and presiding over the integrity of the game. Above all else, the match is going to be a proper display of sportsmanship.

What follows is a spectacle of vanity in an effort to fashion the perfect throw, catch, strike of the ball, even trot to first base. A routine ball hit to an inner fielder is met with pretentious glee, with the athlete leaping in the path of the ball and squatting down so far as to almost touch the ground with his buttocks, then bouncing up like a ballet artist and finishing the throw to the first baseman, who does his best impersonation of a classical marble pose.

Another ground ball, however, causes a slight awkward moment for the inner fielder, forcing him to his left too quickly. In his urgency, he trips over himself and lands in a spot of dirt, soiling his uniform. The runner, safe at the base, argues that he accidentally hit the ball too hard, precipitating the embarrassing outcome for the fielder. Turning to the arbitrator, the runner demands to be called out. The arbitrator, praising the runner's sportsmanship, grants him his wish and postpones the game until the fielder can change out of his dirtied attire and into clean replacements.

The game continues with both clubs scoring a number of tallies until the later innings when one of the clubs has a one-tally advantage. To even things up, the pitcher of the leading club deliberately slows his deliveries down in the attempt to curry more hits for his opponents. But they run out of innings.

They request the arbitrator to extend the game on the trailing club's behalf to get another round of at-bats. Citing their generosity, the arbitrator obliges.

The next go-around, the defenders allow a couple of baserunners by feigning dropped balls and outstretched arms. The next striker pops the ball up in the outer field. The defender positions himself underneath, lifting his arms up to shield his eyes from the sun, which is actually hiding behind a billowy cloud.

The ball harmlessly drops in front of him, allowing the baserunners to safely return home, evening the score.

As a result, the game ends in a fitting tie. Satisfied with their performances, the players congregate under the oak tree and spend the rest of the afternoon mingling and rubbing elbows, feasting and chatting.

Finally, in ceremonious fashion, the arbitrator presents the trophy to the most outstanding player. Scanning his pocketbook with a pencil, the arbitrator checks off a name and stuffs it back in his coat pocket. Then he lifts the trophy and says, "I hereby declare Mr. Wickersham today's recipient of the Sportsman's Trophy for his elegant striking technique and for his gracious decision to wisely hold the ball and not throw out the runner at the third base, potentially preventing a dreadful collision. That decision led to the opposing club's first tally point. A most courteous and exemplary sporting effort. Three cheers!"

A round of applause follows pops of champagne corks.

J.B. Sterne is in a quandary. His game is off and running, even during the volatile years of the war, but those who are able to participate in it are men of means not necessarily interested in competing or learning the nuances that make the game interesting. They aren't even keen on getting dirty. They want to be involved in Sterne's endeavor, but simply aren't the athletic types Sterne envisioned.

He has no choice but to let them play it their way, even if they aren't one hundred percent faithful to his rulebook. He needs men willing to keep playing until the war is over and the younger, more robust players return home.

As the game proliferates up and down the Northeast Coast — as far north as New England and as far south as Philadelphia — Sterne looks for ways to further enhance his growing enterprise. His first act is to improve its name. Bases and Ball is shortened and simply becomes Base-Ball.

Another improvement is in the area of publicity. As much as Base-Ball has spread into big cities and smaller towns, he knows more could be done to publicize his game. The answer comes in the form of the influx of daily periodicals and weekly magazines devoted to the evolving world of gentlemen's leisure activities.

Another industry trying to do the same is the growing tobacco market with its numerous brands of pipe, chewing and cigar products. Tobacco companies are eager to find new markets as a new product is coming into fruition: a finely cut tobacco mince wrapped in paper called the cigarette. Sterne has an idea. Why not integrate the tobacco industry with Base-Ball and market them together? The plan has far-reaching implications, immersing both in the worlds of advertising and media as a joint entity. One unique promotional tool to come out of this partnership is the tobacco card.

Sterne travels around the country to view firsthand who is partaking in the game and how they are playing it. He knows that it is still in its infancy and needs plenty of seasoning. He actively seeks individuals who can inject some character and allure into the game beyond the stuffy and stiff image embodied by his current players.

One such figure is Reginald Fairfax Darlington IV, a man whose admirable dignity and strong principles captivate Sterne so much that he is inspired to fuse many of Darlington's standards into a code of conduct.

Born in an affluent family of public servants in the town of Warwick, Rhode Island, Darlington's family can trace its roots back to the days of Colonial America. His paternal great-grandfather, the first Reginald Fairfax Darlington, was a member of the Sons of Liberty and a ferocious combatant against the tyranny of the British Crown, culminating in the Gaspée Affair of 1772. While studying to be a lawyer and working as a financial broker, Darlington the Fourth becomes enchanted with the game of Base-Ball when it rolls into Providence in the summer of 1864 and soon finds himself playing an inner field position because of his steady hands and quick footwork.

Sterne takes notice of the inner fielder's skills and approaches him about coming back to New York to upgrade his original club. Darlington turns him down, however, citing his career path and eventual entrance into Rhode Island politics. Sensing the man's honor and fervor, Sterne does not put up much of a fight but gets to know him well during his stay. A rabid Anglophobe, Darlington hates the comparisons of cricket with Base-Ball and suggests to Sterne ways to "Americanize" the game by adding patriotic elements such as singing the national anthem, "Hail, Columbia," before every game and prominently displaying the United States flag at every venue.

A fierce proponent of formality, Darlington shares with Sterne his admiration of the regulations set forward in the rulebook and encourages him to enforce its principles.

He even recommends some of his own rules, including adding a strict dress code requiring that each team sport identical uniforms for every contest, preferably ones including neckwear and stiff collars.

Though his hatred toward anything British is unmatched, Darlington holds to the core belief that a game such as Base-Ball should be held to the highest standard if it is to be truly considered a national game and only those capable of demonstrating proper reverence for it should be allowed to participate in it — a wink toward the idea of keeping Base-Ball an exclusive gentlemen's sport.

Taking these ideas back to New York, Sterne goes about amending the rulebook while refashioning his own ball club to meet these new expectations. He wants players of impeccable character and deftness to re-establish his club in Manhattan as the heart and center of Base-Ball. He calls them his New York Elites.

P.E. Hickamore   K.S. Knox   C.Y. Polk   J.B. Sterne (Owner)   T. Baggersdyne
C.F. Nichols   J.D. McGrew   U.N. Byrdsley   J.E. Tunney   O.Q. Mulrooney

NEW YORK BASE-BALL CLUB, 1863

Through his travels, Sterne seeks out the players best suited to his brand of superior Base-Ball and convinces them to join his club. Still having trouble finding players with natural athleticism who are willing to play competitive ball, Sterne focuses on players committed to teamwork and a level of performance appealing enough to the growing profusion of spectators.

Seeking the best venue for a ballpark in an already dense Manhattan, Sterne has an enormous stroke of good luck when the city begins construction on a public park in the heart of the city. Sitting on more than eight hundred acres of swampy terrain, the future Central Park will be transformed into a majestic reserve of trees, gardens, walking paths, bridges, ponds and lakes.

Jumping at the prospect of securing a suitable home for his upgraded Elites, Sterne uses his persuasive powers to convince the park commissioners to include a permanent playing field and diamond in the Greensward Plan. When they initially balk at the idea, Sterne pledges to guarantee up to half of the total cost of the entire park, which turns out to be more than two and a half million dollars.

Work begins to construct grounds for the playing field and diamond between 61st and 66th Streets near the intersection of Broadway and Eighth Avenue. As summer quickly approaches and the ball grounds are not close to completion, Sterne hands over another quarter million dollars and lands access to the most modern steam-powered construction equipment available.

With record speed, the ball grounds for Sterne's Elites are finished, just in time to start the new season and give Sterne the opportunity to trot out his new and improved club in front of the city's well-to-do, nestled in an artificial pastoral paradise.

Daisy Cutter

Jeremiah Ezekiel Tunney was anything but athletic. Tall and delicately built, he looked more like a bookish scholar apt to be surrounded by stacks of hardbound volumes than an athlete kicking up dirt in a Base-Ball diamond.

Raised in a hardworking and strict Methodist family, Tunney received his formal education before setting off on a life dedicated to service and missionary work. One day, before jumping on a train bound for Buffalo, Tunney stopped to see a friend pitch in a game of Base-Ball.

After three innings, his friend, fatigued and dehydrated, implored his Methodist friend to continue where he left off.

Tunney, never shy to help out a friend in need, picked up the ball and immediately began delivering perfectly placed pitches for the strikers to put into play.

It happened to be the day Sterne was in attendance scouting players for his own club. Sterne noticed right away the lanky pitcher's demeanor and quick study. Before jumping on the train for Buffalo, Sterne had a deal in place with him to play ball for his Elites.

For the next few summers, Tunney was the epitome of Sterne's vision of Elite Base-Ball—grasping the broader essence of the game and recognizing its subtle nuances all the while exuding a serene confidence. Soon, Tunney was a regular recipient of the Sportsman's Trophy for his politeness and manners toward the opponent as well as his graceful deference toward the arbitrator.

Unfortunately, Tunney did not possess a hardy physique or dexterity. He regularly failed to hit or run out balls to the first base, oftentimes slowed by pulled muscles or swollen joints. Nevertheless, Tunney kept pushing himself and never surrendered to his fragility.

One day, however, the end came. He was lucky enough to get a hit when a ball floated down in between the inner fielder and outer fielder. Deciding to stretch the hit into a double, Tunney rounded the first base and tried to accelerate when his lower half crumpled from under him like a pair of axles breaking off a wagon bed. Tunney shattered both his ankles.

They never healed properly and made walking, much less running, an ordeal for him the rest of his life. Forced out of the game prematurely, Tunney finally took that train to Buffalo and became a minister and holistic health practitioner.

"A Muffin Who Couldn't Stir Your Stumps"

Quite possibly the worst player to ever don a Base-Ball uniform and play the game, Everitt Townsend, for all practical purposes, had a Base-Ball IQ no higher than a field mouse.

By all accounts, Townsend was a sharp man who found his way to the diamond through his chummy connections with The Old Excelsior club, but had no conception whatsoever of the basic fundamentals of the game.

A successful investment banker and accomplished yachtsman, Townsend, nevertheless, could not comprehend even the most rudimentary tasks—he literally could not hit, catch or throw the ball.

When throwing, the ball would invariably do one of two things: fall harmlessly at his feet or trace an unpredictable yet inevitable path into someone's face.

His outfield defense consisted of standing immobile, arm fully extended and hand splayed open as if the ball would land on its own in his palm. Players and spectators fled whenever he stepped in the batters' circle for fear of his club being launched in the air.

Yet he managed somehow to stay with his Stuyvesant Heights club for three seasons, during that time recording his first and only base hit.

The lone achievement came when an errant pitch sailed inside and accidentally struck Townsend's club and the ball trickled down the third base path. Dumbfounded by the unexpected contact, Townsend dropped his club and raced down the line—on the third base side.

At first, the official arbitrator ruled him out, but the opposing team, perhaps in an act of charity, pleaded with the arbitrator to overrule himself and award Townsend the hit, arguing that he would have been safe if he had ran to the correct base. Townsend was awarded the base in what has been historically designated as the first-ever bunt single.

"This game is outpacing my best efforts to properly govern its progress." An irritated Sterne gazes out his second floor office window. The gaslights take their effect both inside and out.

Niedler, seated at his desk, hunches over his usual stacks of papers and ledgers.

"The rulebooks are required reading, but I'm afraid no one is reading them," Sterne laments. "Each club in each town and city is playing the way as they see fit and the principles of this game have been ignored. I can't have this, Henry."

Niedler lifts his face up and stares silently at Sterne.

"Here, listen to this." Sterne pulls out a letter from his pocket and begins reading. "From a Mister Dundee in Worcester, Massachusetts. It reads, 'Dear Sir, your permission for us to organize a club and play this newly devised game of Base-Ball is a welcome addition to our town and for our men seeking an innocent respite from their daily routines. As it happens , the men are quite successful reaching the bases and registering an exorbitant amount of tally points as to be near impossible for our field official to keep track. So we rectified this thorny issue by *adding an extra base*, therefore providing ample time for our man to record our advances around the *pentagon*."

Sterne slams the letter down. "THE PENTAGON!"

Niedler realizes the moment has arrived. He closes his ledger, leans back in his chair, and detaches his shirt collar. "I had warned you this would happen."

His eyes burning red and jugular vein pumping against his collar, Sterne snaps his head. "What?"

"You're starting to realize your precious little titmouse wants to leave your nest and take flight, but you keep pinching its wings."

"What do you expect me to do, let it go? I can't. I won't!"

"In the name of progress, isn't your personal stamp on the game already firmly established?"

"Not by a longshot. I won't give in and see this dissolve into chaotic ruin. If the rulebooks won't be complied with, then I'll have to step up my efforts to make sure the game is not compromised."

"So you want the game to proliferate but you still want absolute control of its progress?"

A vicious look comes to Sterne's eyes.

Niedler lets out a sigh. "Then there is only one way to do it and that is to treat it more like a business and apply a business model to it. It can no longer be just a game, I'm afraid."

"God, how I rued this day. Suppose it ruins it?"

"You can't expect to see it expand across the country without relinquishing your misgivings about its inevitable transformation. What if they want something different?"

"I'm open to improvements, but its core values must remain firmly grounded. I'll guard against any threat to the essence of the game."

"Which is?"

"The exact thing I saw the first time I laid eyes on this game—an innocence and purity that transcended everything else. If I could have one legacy above all others, it's the accomplishment of nationalizing this game while preserving those qualities."

Niedler doesn't say anything.

"What?" Sterne stares at him, detecting derision.

"Nothing."

He drops his head and closes his eyes. "Okay, Henry. What do you have in mind?"

Niedler leans forward. "What happens every time you seize a new property and its assets? You install a board of directors to make sure things get done."

Sterne's face scrunches. "A board of directors overseeing Base-Ball?"

"A group of hand-selected individuals supervising each club, making sure they play by your rules and managing all profits."

"Profits? Where do profits come in?"

"That leads me to my next point. If you want your fellow board members protecting the sanctity of the game, you're going to want them have a stake in the business side. That's where revenue comes in. They'll be motivated to preserve your romantic notion while making money in the process."

"Selling the rights to play this game isn't exactly high profit."

"But why stop there? What about the spectators?"

Sterne's face reddens. "What about them?"

"Shouldn't they be charged for watching the game?"

His vein starts to churn. "You expect me to charge these people an admittance fee? Are you crazy?"

"They will no longer be attendees, but patrons."

Sterne buries his face in his hands.

Niedler unearths a folder tucked in his desk with comprehensive notes written over the years that justify his reasoning. "I figured a reasonable charge in the beginning won't cause a stir. But by the third year we'll raise the price annually by a nominal percentage as long as we maintain a growth margin of…"

Sterne peeks through his fingers, watching his associate pull out charts and graphs. ■

SPORTSMAN'S
DAILY
EDITION VOL. 4
JUNE 1865
HINDOO CIGARETTES
Base-Ball

V.

Hullabaloo Alabaster
(1868-1873)

The aroma of coffee mingles with the scent of freshly cut carnations neatly arranged along the banquet tables of the suite. The seventh floor of the newly built Grand Hotel on Broadway radiates a warm, golden brilliance from the morning's rays, complementing the porcelain floor vases and Persian carpets.

The double doors swing open and well-dressed men of different ages pour in and converge upon the banquet spread. During their interlude, the men chitchat about business while nibbling on their pastries and muffins.

H.H. Niedler strolls in sporting a bow-tie and monogrammed blazer. He quickly addresses the group. "Gentlemen, if I may, the Governor is delayed and so asked me to begin the meeting in his absence. We have Eloise, our stenographer, here to record the entire discussion. So if you please take your seats, we'll commence our fourth annual owners meeting."

A set of chairs and tables covered in fine linen create a U-shape in the middle of the room. The gentlemen sit down with their coffees and tarts. Niedler sits next to an empty parson chair in the middle.

"I want to thank you all for making it to today's occasion. Some of you are coming from cities far away and I appreciate your efforts to attend. As you can see, our sporting enterprise is growing at such a brisk pace that we now have a total of eighteen represented clubs in three different leagues as far west as Cincinnati and the expansion continues as we speak. The allure of Base-Ball is truly sweeping the nation, finding its rightful place in the country's bosom, and gaining momentum. As the game continues its march into every city and every town, appealing to the hearts and minds of men, women and children, Base-Ball will become the next great American institution and each and every one of you will stand to gain from it!"

Mild applause breaks out around the tables.

Niedler pours himself a glass of water. "As we prepare for the coming season we will address matters such as the new rules additions including the *six-pitch walk* and stipulating a *foot-high dirt mound* in the pitcher's zone, which we think will be a benefit for hitters, according to our early analyses. But first, I think we should start off by addressing the latest developments in some of our newer venues, namely the concept of raised rows of planked seating for our paying spectators—"

A slight stir occurs around the tables.

"—which will improve their viewing experience as well as potentially adding an ten to fifteen percent more spectators in the park per game, which could amount, per our analyses—"

More stirring, a few coughs and a clearing of the throat.

Niedler continues, oblivious to the growing rustle of his attendees. Finally, someone coughs loud enough to jolt him out of his discourse.

"Mister Snodgrass? Is there something you wish to ask?"

Thaddeus Snodgrass, already coated with a film of perspiration, his jowly skin pushed up by his stiff collar, puckers his face before speaking. "Excuse me for the interruption, Chairman Niedler," his voice is whiny and nasally, "but it is my opinion of the group that we should address more pressing issues."

"Such as…"

"Such as?" He wriggles in his seat. "Such as the most distressing issue facing all of us seated here today—the growing calls for player compensation." An eruption of harrumphs.

Niedler puts his hand up. "It was my intention to leave this issue unaddressed until the Governor was present and we could properly—"

"I think we must address this matter of extreme importance now *and* after the Governor has arrived. These vile demands have to be immediately extinguished!" The harrumphs grow louder.

"Mister Snodgrass. Mister Snodgrass! If you wish to proceed with this matter, on behalf of your fellow owners—"

"These players are demanding remuneration, as if they believe they are actually employed in a trade or occupation. A gross absurdity!"

Niedler attempts to get a word in but Snodgrass keeps fulminating. The longer he goes the more incensed he gets. The folds of his skin turn salmon-tinged and his ear lobes and helixes turn a shade redder. His thinning, wiry red hair stands up on his head. "It's these wretched little *boonswogglers* who think they can come tearing into our leagues, making a disgrace out of everything—spitting, cursing and treating the ball as if it were a ten-cent whore! They're making a mockery out of our operation and then have the ballocks to demand a wage! Preposterous!"

Niedler asserts himself. "These men you refer to as boonswogglers are bringing a welcomed energy to the game not seen since before the war started."

"Pismires, each and every one of them! They should go back to their hovels and weave the hairs on their scrotum together for amusement. How dare they think they can crawl out of their dirt holes and commingle with our most professional ballers, who are setting shining examples each and every day!"

"They've raised the level of competition, you must admit that."

"All the while committing a travesty, showing utter disdain for the proper manner of playing the game. Even *he*, the Governor, must not appreciate the brand of Base-Ball these players are representing. It's revolting!"

Niedler looks down at his notes. "The issue of discussion at present is the likelihood of compensating the players for performance related to that day's game. If any such measure is implemented, as you know, it must be unanimously approved by the owners first."

The growing uproar around the room turns into shouts.

"If the idea is to line the pockets of these scoundrels and, in doing so, prevent us from maximizing our revenue share," Snodgrass hisses, "then a great offense will occur which I simply cannot allow. I will do everything in my power to make sure these malcontents get thrown out of our leagues, much less get one cent. I, and my fellow colleagues, stand united in this front and will not be superseded by *his Governorship* once again!"

"Is this another demonstration of hyperbole or should I take this threat of usurpation seriously this time, Thaddeus Snodgrass?" A familiar voice comes from behind. Everyone jerks around to see the Governor standing in the doorway. The room immediately silences.

Snodgrass stands with his hands clenched and drives them into the table. "Call it what you will, J. Barron Sterne, but if you grant wages to those malcontents—for playing a game—then you will be doing a terrible disservice to your colleagues here. You will have to answer to each and every one of us who are protecting your best interests of the game." His face becomes a steam boiler with the pressure gauge flitting upward.

"Is that right?" Sterne steps into the suite and casually removes his deerskin gloves, wedging his walking stick in the pit of his elbow. He doffs his stovepipe, all the while wearing a devious smirk.

"What do you find so amusing?" Snodgrass asks.

"Your rhetoric has always been amusing. The only thing more

amusing is your remarkable shortsightedness."

"Beg your pardon? Shortsighted?"

"You have a skewed perspective when it comes to what are the best interests of the game."

"My only perspective is the one that we all share here today, and that is from a business standpoint. Having us share our revenue with these wretches is not good business, from whatever skewed perspective you care to be in."

"Ah yes, revenues. Is that all that matters?"

Snodgrass snaps to attention and thrusts upward his top half. "Indubitably."

"I'm afraid you're mistaken. They must be paid, all of them."

"Pismires!" The pressure of his boiler face spikes.

"The way I see it, these men—outliers from a lower rung on the ladder, wretches and ants in your vocabulary—are setting the standard for the way the game is to be played ever since they returned from the war. They possess skills and a hunger that enlivens the game, and it's no coincidence attendance has flourished since they have come back to society."

"They don't have one ounce of the gravitas our most experienced ballers have."

"I can do with less gravitas and more interest in scoring tallies and making a game out of it. You can only preen and prance so much. The spirit of competition—that's what is driving revenues."

"How can you side with these wretches?"

"As long as they continue to play hard, run, throw, hit—we'll refine their character to match the principles set by our more cultivated players, who, in turn, can learn a thing or two about real competition."

"Bosh! You'll never be able to do that. These dregs will never live up to our principles of dignity and honor. It's not in their nature to play that way. As soon as you give them a salary you'll be changing the game forever and you'll live to regret it. I'm prepared to do anything to prevent this from happening, as long as I have a stake in the matter."

"Let's face it, Tad. You could not care less about any such principles of the game other than how it affects your pocketbook. You'll do anything to prevent a reduction in your revenue coffers even if it meant threatening the long-term health of the game. That's my definition of shortsightedness."

The steam pressure causes Snodgrass's face to quiver. His skin turns fuchsia and his hair spikes out even further. "Slanderous!"

"You'll do anything to make sure nothing gets between you and maximized profits." Sterne continues. "Long-term be damned. Such as the time when your coal mining workforce went on strike and you threatened them with armed force to get back to work."

"You fiendish, sadistic—"

"And the only way out of your mess was through the help of some mediators that were quickly summoned by whom?"

"—*pettifilcher!*"

The boiler finally bursts and jets of steam blast out of his ears and nostrils. His stiff collar pops and flies out. His mouth opens wide and emits a deep, loud roar that shakes his flabby skin. Snodgrass flips one of the tables over and stomps out of the suite. Something crashes, followed by the sound of a door slamming. Then silence.

Sterne issues a quick exhale of breath and smiles at Niedler. "Right. Shall we vote then? All in favor of player salaries—"

Niedler looks up at the Governor. "We'll need all votes to make this official. One just left."

"I don't think that will be a problem," he says, looking around the tables and seeing the other owners slowly raising their hands. "Eloise, my dearest lady, may I see the transcript? The slightest little adjustment needs to be made on behalf of the Governorship."

The deafening *bonng-bonnnng!* of the university clock tower does not stop the men and adolescent boys from racing to the top of the observatory and squeezing every last inch of themselves onto the terrace to get a bird's-eye view of the season's opening day.

Below, elm trees adorned with bunting surround the lush green commons. Around the diamond, players from both clubs fraternize with each other, leaning on their bats. Men in bowlers with their sleeves rolled up congregate on the perimeter to speculate on the day's events, nodding their heads and twiddling with their mustaches. Several dainty women in touring hats claim a spot on one of the rows of planks behind the batter's box and nestle down on small velvet cushions. They pull out their lorgnettes and cling to their programs, sitting transfixed, backs arched, waiting for the contest to begin. Children in white chase each other on the grass playing a game of tag. The onlookers without a ticket are forced to climb trees and snatch a view from behind the stands.

The giddy anticipation grows as more and more people flock to the grounds to see for the first time the town's very own ballclub—men in ash gray uniforms ready to play a game of nine-on-nine against the neighboring club from across the river.

They wait to see their players square up on pitches and drive the ball deep into the outfield, catch fly balls on the run, dig hard for the first base, scoop up ground balls on one knee, run from the second base to the home plate and slide safely under the tag and, finally, converge at the end of the contest with rounds of celebration, ciders and lemonade.

The festive air is punctuated by the distant sound of a steam whistle and a brass band in full swing, growing louder and louder until it suddenly appears from behind a row of hedges. Playing the jovial tune "Mockingbird Quickstep," it marches onto the outfield grass behind the conductor wagging his baton. The band crescendos and halts at the top of the diamond to roaring applause.

Both clubs assemble on opposite sides of the band in rows of three. A photographer and his assistant scurries onto the field to set up their equipment. A rotund man in spats and tails steps into view accompanied by the umpiring official balancing a ball on his fingertips as if it were an egg. A banner is draped in front with the words "Northampton Professional Ball Players. Inaugural Season. 1872."

The photographer signals that he is ready but the rotund man interrupts him and delivers a rambling speech about civic pride and the virtues of the game. Finally, he ends his speech and everyone bunches together, chins up and chests out. The photographer ducks under his hood and removed the lens cap.

The lone tintype will be mounted to a card with the studio's name embossed in cursive lettering and a gold-stamped border. It will hang in the university's athletics department display case, tucked between the school's championship rugby team and the young women's croquet auxiliary. There the proud faces will remain for the next hundred years, suffocating in stale air, cracking and fading into obscurity.

Smart as a Steel Trap Snapdragon

The passage of time failed to unlock a great mystery. Why did W.H. Pierce, a man possessing a first-rate mind and thirst for wealth—destined to be propelled into the upper echelons of affluence as a Captain of Industry—suddenly change course and enter the big leagues, only to flounder as a scuffling infielder? Over the years, no one could give a straight answer. Pierce himself was asked many times and always dodged the question. Even in extreme old age, sick and penniless, he preferred to boast about the many innovations he introduced in the game that enhanced the sport like no one before him.

J.B. Sterne, perhaps the only other person with direct knowledge, was never asked, at least publicly. That didn't seem unusual given Sterne's penchant for throwing up brick walls whenever approached with personal questions. But it was no secret that Sterne coveted men of intellect to play his game and Pierce was certainly one of them.

Others have speculated over the years that Pierce was a victim of J.B Sterne's crushing gauntlet of corporate might, that he went face to face against the master in a business skirmish and lost everything he had. And perhaps the only way to pay back his debts was through forced participation in Sterne's beloved game.

Levi Whiteman Horatio Pierce was a brash and exceptionally astute young man coming out of Harvard Law School with two other degrees under his belt and a gold-laden cache of Wall Street connections. Intent on becoming a corporate attorney, Pierce was quickly groomed to be an eventual heir to one of the emerging giants in the steel industry. Somewhere along the way he encountered Sterne and, either by choice or coercion, found himself playing Base-Ball and getting his breeches tattered.

As if that wasn't surprising enough, Pierce signed the very first binding contract between a player and an owner to an astonishing ten-year deal worth a mere pittance compared to that of even moderately-skilled veterans. Some have suggested that this was proof that Sterne had conquered his rival in whatever business clash they had had and this was the last thrust of the sword into the heart of the defeated Pierce.

Three years into the deal, however, Pierce had proven to be a less-than-mediocre player, unable to hit the ball on a consistent basis or field his position with even a modicum of skill.

He decided to find a way to break his deal with the Governor. Honing his skills as a brilliant lawyer, he presented his case to Sterne, hoping to convince the great man to grant him his release from the seven years remaining on his contract. Sterne rebuked him and threatened to send him to one of the dustbin towns beyond the Appalachians looking to establish their own club.

Unable to break his contract and yet unwilling to flee Sterne's authority, Pierce hunkered down to face the remaining years of his deal and conjured up ways to make the time bearable. It was around this time that something happened between Pierce and Sterne that changed the course of the game.

Pierce, always a keen observer of detail and possessor of what would later be termed micromanagement skills, began offering ideas to augment the pace and competitiveness of the game, something Sterne had been desperately seeking for years.

The ambition to score more runs than the opponent finally became widespread. But the problem remained: how to make it happen. One solution involved introducing offense-friendly regulations to Sterne's rulebook. The other involved the use of in-game strategies that took advantage of what was going on during that day's game.

Sterne, knowing full well the magnitude of Pierce's intellectual prowess, encouraged him to innovate. He was rewarded with a plethora of ideas that pushed Sterne to rewrite the rulebook seven times, effectively transforming the game from a sleepy, carefree, frolicking picnic into a competitive game of tactics, skill, risk and reward.

Some of Pierce's innovations emphasized base-running and the need to advance runners into scoring position. Bunting became a common practice, as did the sacrificial fly out. Stealing bases, under certain conditions, was allowed as long as the opposing team was given proper forewarning.

The batting lineup, before a fixed arrangement, became fluid. For the first time, the athletes on the team most capable of getting on base batted first. Then the batters with the most skill in driving in runs batted next, no matter what position they played on the field.

The walk, a free pass for the hitter if the pitcher missed the strike zone, went down to four pitches per plate appearance. If the pitcher mistakenly hit the batter in his lower half—his hips or legs—the batter was awarded a base. If he was struck anywhere above his waist, the batter was awarded *two bases*.

But it was not all about offense. Defense was also emphasized under Pierce's suggestions. A standardized set of positions were finally established with a total of three outfield positions, a player manning each base, the pitcher and catcher, and finally an extra infielder guarding the middle of the diamond later to be called the shortstop.

Pitching was no longer a service for the hitter. Instead of providing what the opposing batter wanted — a ball perfectly placed over the plate for the batter to crush — the pitcher tried to get the batter out with a number of strategically placed and newly devised pitches.

Whether or not Sterne willfully enslaved Pierce into the world of Base-Ball will probably never be determined. What's most obvious was Sterne was successful in unleashing Pierce's superior intellect for the benefit of the game and advancing Sterne's vision of the way it should be played. With Pierce's innovations, the game received a much-needed boost of sophistication, requiring clubs to be more competitive while retaining a high level of dignity and respect for each opposing club.

One other innovation credited to Pierce was the creation of the field manager. When he was no longer athletic enough to play the game himself, Pierce invented the role of a manager who stayed on the sidelines and directed his club on strategic matters such as hitting, base-running, fielding, pitching and scoring.

Pierce finally settled into his own and managed his club not only through the rest of his contract but for many years afterward, eventually becoming the manager for the game's preeminent club, the New York Elites, and staying in the game for the remainder of his working life.

Uncle Charley Comes to Towne

Alexander Bookeward had a penchant for reciting classical works—from Plutarch and Ovid to Chaucer and Milton—while manning his station at first base, to the annoyance of everyone on the infield. He also rambled off the Pythagorean theorem, quotes from 17th-century philosophers and historic names and dates that soon earned him the nickname "Booke-worm."

His flashes of trivia were nothing but a product of sheer boredom while he passed the time in between plays. Though a very good first baseman capable of scooping up throws bounced in the dirt or snagging errant throws above his head, Base-Ball was just not his cup of tea. It was not in his blood. It was not the one, continuous thought at the forefront of his mind every day. It was not his beginning, middle or end.

Alexander Bookeward was, in fact, just a schoolteacher who dreamed big of escaping the one-room schoolhouse with its potbelly stove and inattentive pupils and trekking across the country in search of America's emerging heritage. Base-Ball seemed like a good place to start.

Once he won a job as a first sacker in the town of Springfield, Massachusetts, he played so well that the club's owner refused to let him wander off and kept giving him pay raises to stay.

But the game did not surge through his veins as it did so many of his club-mates, who would have done anything—legal or otherwise—to avoid returning to the mines, factories and fields from which they had escaped.

Luckily for Bookeward, the game came easily and he did not

spend even one extra minute practicing or honing his skills. He preferred reading Lord Tennyson under a Sycamore tree leading up to the first pitch. This nonchalant manner rubbed the rest of the club the wrong way and soon they brushed him off as an intellectual popinjay with his head in the clouds.

One day he overheard his club's pitchers jawing during their pre-game practice, vowing to subdue their opponents with a superior arsenal of pitches. Noticing their tendency to throw harder with every pitch, Bookeward laid his book down and strolled over to the playing field.

He mentioned to them they should try to ease up on the hard stuff and put a spin on the ball to intensify the Magnus effect.

The hurlers responded with blank stares.

Before they kicked him off the field, Bookeward explained to them that the Magnus effect was nothing more than the interaction of the ball in trajectory with the surrounding air. He noted that if one tried to make the ball spin when it left one's hand one could do some impressive tricks with it — sure enough to deceive the batters and get them out.

Bookeward picked up a ball and showed them what he was talking about. He stepped up on the mound and delivered a pitch, letting the ball roll off his fingers. It spun like a top whizzing through the air, darting and diving down right in front of the squatting receiver.

There, Bookeward said, a physics lesson for you!

Speechless and thunderstruck, the pitchers urged him to do it again and again and every time the ball fluttered and danced like a hummingbird in flight.

The one-time schoolteacher, whose only ambition was to travel across the country, made it as far as the next four counties before he had seen enough. He settled down in a quiet farming community and taught up-and-coming pitchers the art of the breaking ball.

Catawump

The name "Royal" Duff Ferguson had nothing to do with noble peerage and certainly nothing to do with the man's backside. "Royal" had everything to do with his preferred choice of whisky from his native country of Scotland.

Ferguson worked on the docks of the western terminus of the Erie Canal in Buffalo and dreamed of becoming a ballplayer since he landed in the States. Unfortunately, the nearest club was seventy-five miles away in Rochester. The best he could do was play sandlot games on his off days and wait for his opportunity to arrive.

Central Wharf was a constant tumult of activity, loading and unloading goods, commodities, foodstuffs, immigrants, animals and belongings on their westward passage. Ferguson, broad-shouldered and thick as an oak, moved his fair share.

On what seemed like another typical day, Ferguson went to work on a load of cargo in a ship's hold. What he didn't know was the hold contained crates and crates of a new explosive material called TNT and no one had the sense to stamp a warning on the crates. While getting to work on the cargo, a cigar-chomping longshoremen accidentally dropped some ash into the hold. That's all it took for the entire lot to go up.

The explosion flattened the entire dock and waterfront block. It also shot Ferguson up high in the air. He finally came down, about a quarter-mile away, and fell through the roof of a dairy plant, landing in a vat of buttermilk.

Miraculously, he survived, his only injuries burns to his body and temporary blindness. For six months, Ferguson was laid up and in the process became a local celebrity for his improbable feat in avoiding death.

Then, that summer, a traveling caravan of players from back East stopped in town for a series of exhibition games against the town's best ballplayers. Once Ferguson got word, there was no stopping him despite his condition. Half-blind, wrapped in bandages from head to toes, he jumped out of bed, grabbed his bat, and ran to the municipal park.

"Royal" Duff Ferguson played three games and managed seven hits, four doubles and a ringing line drive into center field that won the final game of the series. Impressed with his talents and unprecedented determination, the players invited Duff to join them back East once he healed up and regained all his vision.

His dream to become a big leaguer finally came true and he went on to have a very productive career, playing six seasons in the Passaic County Gentlemen's League before succumbing to a bee sting at the age of thirty-two.

Years later, back in Buffalo, they finally managed to get their very own ball club. In remembrance of their hometown folk hero, they nicknamed their club The Buttered-Scotch Royals.

Splendiferous Whitewash

J. B. Sterne had been on a quest since the very beginning to find the one ballplayer who fully personified his vision of Base-Ball. Someone savvy enough to play the game the right way with plenty of natural instincts and dexterity. Someone who could impose a commanding presence yet radiate chivalric sophistication. A leader capable of setting a precedent. A transcendent figure for the masses. A hero. An icon.

If that one ballplayer wasn't out there, Sterne declared, he was determined to manufacture him.

Time and circumstance yielded an unexpected result. Grantham Ford Wentworth, an unheralded outfielder playing for the Bridgeport, Connecticut, club and one-time sewing machine manufacturer, caught the attention of Sterne and wound up turning both their fortunes around.

Wentworth was a backup reserve player who barely made an

appearance during the regular season. On the very last day he stepped in to play for a teammate who was nursing a sprained ankle. Luckily for him, the Governor was in attendance and he witnessed Wentworth go three for four with a couple of hard-hit balls in the gap and some impressive outfield catches. Without even meeting the young man, he sent a contract down to Wentworth after the game and he became Sterne's property the next season.

Signed to be another backup coming off the bench, Wentworth got his big break when the starting outfielder came down with typhoid, opening up a spot for the up-and-comer. In his first week playing for the Elites in front of swarming crowds on the grounds of Central Park, Wentworth collected ten hits including three game-winning tallies, all the while saving games with spectacular catches.

Rising from the depths of obscurity, Wentworth became an immediate sensation and stirred the attention of his boss with his masterful play and self-confidence, not to mention his striking appearance, charming wit and knack for captivating the spectators.

For every at-bat, Wentworth displayed a disciplined approach of the strike zone and belted pitches with authoritative deft. On the basepaths, he galloped around the circuit as if he owned them. In the outfield, his feet covered more ground than anybody before him. As impressive as he was with the bat and his defense, Wentworth remained humble and deferential to his teammates. They quickly grew so enamored with him that they designated him "Captain of the New York Elites Team."

His trajectory clear and obvious, Sterne went to work and promoted his outfielder all over the city as the best and brightest the game had yet offered. Word spread quickly and soon huge throngs of people from all over converged upon the grounds to watch a game played by Sterne's New York Elites and witness the budding celebrity become the very first super-star to emerge in the game.

His meteoric rise to fame led newspapers and magazines to fight for an interview. His likeness started appearing on posters and billboards hawking everything from menswear and toiletries to baking goods and quack remedies. Fervid admirers tracked his whereabouts in the city.

As far as Wentworth had gone, so had the Elites, to the delight of Sterne. Throughout the country where Base-Ball was prevalent, the Elites had sewn a reputation as the best of the best, led by their swarthy, impeccable captain. He, in turn, touted their renown so well that Wentworth had stitched a felt letter "E" on the front of their caps as a sort of badge of pride.

On every road trip, news of the Elites' arrival at the train station sent hundreds of people flocking to catch a glimpse of the larger-than-life figures clad in three-piece suits and felt derbies. They surged upon Wentworth as he made his way to the hotel, requesting autographs and personal favors.

Wentworth went along with all of it and the glory and riches that followed for years never seemed to affect his day-to-day playing duties, even when his lifestyle became increasingly more lavish. While his reputation in and around the ball yards continued to portray him as a good-natured, dedicated purist, his appetite for expensive hotel suites, cigars, delicacies, liquor and, especially, women reached unparalleled proportions. Whispers circulated that Wentworth was a frequent guest at the best-known brothels and parlors each town and city had to offer.

His insatiable appetite for both the princely life and hard play on the diamond became unsustainable and his body soon deteriorated. He started striking out, dropping balls, getting thrown out at the plate by several feet. But he kept on and his standing as the best ballplayer in the world remained intact. Eventually, though, the superstar's luster was fading—and fast.

Deep down Wentworth knew his time was coming to an end. He privately yearned to walk away from the game before his talents dwindled to nothing. But there was a problem. His drawing card was still strong despite his declining performance and Sterne wanted nothing to do with any talk of Wentworth walking away. To him, Wentworth was his making and he did as he pleased with his creation for as long as he wished, especially if his winning formula kept producing dividends.

And so, the once-invincible king of Base-Ball was now little but an oddity on display, his once svelte, robust body now a broken down, syphilitic ramshackle.

Despite Sterne's efforts to prop up his prized treasure, it finally became obvious that Wentworth was just a shadow of his former self. He quickly descended into being a parody of what he had once been. Knowledgeable spectators found it painful to watch him wince in agony every time he swung and missed, sad to watch him haul his creaky body down the line to first base, embarrassing to watch him fall over himself trying to make a routine catch in right field.

Forced to play every day, whispers of criticism began to be heard that Wentworth was clinging to past glories and was too vain to admit his days of glory were gone. The truth was he begged Sterne for his release but the Governor steadfastly refused.

There weren't going to be any farewell ceremonies for Wentworth. No chance to hang up his uniform and emblazoned cap in one final, symbolic gesture. No honors or tributes. No handing off the reigns to the next generation of ballplayers.

Sterne was determined that his valued possession was not going to leave the center stage after all he had done to secure his lucrative masquerade. He was determined to keep him playing forever or until he crumpled dead on the playing field.

Dudley Livingston Dorfmann, all legs and elbows at six-feet five inches and a slight one hundred and sixty pounds, circles the mound, fretting over what's about to happen. With a runner on first and the game all tied up, the befuddled pitcher dithers, fighting against himself not to blow it.

He removes his cap, wipes the sweat off his brow, and fixes it neatly back on his head. He adjusts his tie. He examines the ball in his hand and rubs it down with his palm.

His Reading, Pennsylvania, club, rarely in such a predicament, had built its reputation on solid pitching and timely hitting, stymieing their opponent for several innings before breaking the game open with several runs and coasting to the win.

But the Allentown crew, their chief rival for several years with a lineup of former miners, railroaders and roustabouts, is not politely given in.

Instead of allowing Dorfmann to dictate the game with his command of pitches, they force him to throw an unbelievable number of pitches to get through seven innings. The stubborn Allentown batters foul off pitches and run the count up before drawing a walk or lining a base hit.

On the mound, the weary Dorfmann eyes the runner on first. Higgs McShea stares back at him, standing on the base with his hands on his knees and his mouth bulging with chaw.

Everyone knows that the hit-and-run is on, even the spectators, nervously watching and getting more anxious with every pause by Dorfmann.

The next batter, a master of the swinging bunt by the name of Hunnicut, steps into the box. By putting just enough wood on the ball to push it down one of the lines, Hunnicut will force the ungainly Dorfmann to jump off the mound and make a play at second base.

Before setting up to make his pitch, Dorfmann steps off once again and sizes up McShea, who doesn't move an inch. McShea's steely gaze intimidates Dorfmann so much that he re-adjusts his tie and rubs the ball down even harder. The crowd stirs with exasperation.

Finally Dorfmann straightens himself up and faces home plate. Hunnicut stands with his feet wide apart and the bat out in front of his chest, ready to put the ball in play. Dorfmann peeks out of the corner of his eye at McShea.

As soon as the ball leaves his hands, McShea tears off for second.

The pitch is high in the zone but Hunnicut squares up and connects, dragging the ball down the third base line. Dorfmann springs off the mound and lunges for it, landing on his knees. He slings the ball to the shortstop covering second base, but the throw is low and hits the bag, ricocheting into shallow left.

McShea keeps running, rounding second and speeding to third. The third baseman chases the ball down, forcing Dorfmann to pick himself up and cover the base.

He squats down in front of the bag, readying himself for the ball and the onrushing McShea. They both arrive at the same time.

McShea, determined to do anything to beat the tag, slides feet first, sending a cloud of dust in the air. He strikes Dorfmann in the chest and legs with his feet, throwing him backward. The ball careens into foul territory without a play and the umpire calls him safe. The crowd erupts.

The dust subsides and everyone sees Dorfmann spread on the ground with his hands covering his face. He slowly gets to his knees and drops his hands. The crowd gasps at the sight of Dorfmann, his mouth wide open, his eyes wide with shock and trauma, and his nose crushed to one side gushing blood like a waterfall.

The Reading bench clears and converges upon the injured pitcher, aghast. Someone gets a towel and wraps it around his head, immediately soaking it red.

The diamond quickly fills with players on both sides. The terrified crowd in the stands becomes a muddled disarray of seersucker and brocade.

Shouts of protest trickle down, turning into a steady cascade. *"Outrageous! A felonious act of barbarism! Your man should not be allowed to don his uniform ever again. An attack on the moral standards of the game, if there ever was one! Savage beast! Ruffian!"*

Bent over with blood still streaming from his face, the maimed pitcher is helped off the field and slowly the cluster of players return to their positions, shocked over what they just witnessed.

Alone at third, McShea takes a lead off the base, bending down with his hands on his knees and grinding on his wad of tobacco. He glares forward as if nothing had happened. ■

VI.

Shoestring Huzzah!
(1874-1881)

Two quick, soft taps on the door to Sterne's office and Niedler tiptoes in to find the Governor preparing his tea behind his mahogany desk. The room is bigger than their entire previous office, with works of art hanging on all four walls and a bust in the corner. Daylight streams in from behind lace curtains.

Niedler pads across the floor and approaches the desk. Sterne, looking down at his steeping tea, beats Niedler to the punch. "Well, Henry, what can you tell me?"

"He just sent this telegram." He lifts up the tawny sheet of paper. "Read it."

Niedler clears his throat and reads the message.

```
"Dear sir as it is my obligation to inform
you of the ongoings of our joint venture and my
duty to uphold standard of excellence set forth
by your decree I must faithfully report I have
not personally witnessed any objectionable
```

```
behavior that would undermine any aspect of
core principles of our beloved game nor would
I condone or encourage any such unruly behav-
ior that may have been insinuated with past
query - yours truly G. Allistair"
```

Niedler peeks beyond the telegram.

"He's lying," Sterne says.

"Of course he is. He thinks he can protect himself by feigning ignorance from several hundred miles away, as if that's too great a distance for us to exercise our authority."

Sterne carries on with his tea. "It's a tactic becoming more and more effective, Henry. Every time I send out inquiries over players exhibiting intolerable conduct—excessive use of profanity, dishevelment, suspicion of drinking, belligerence—they come back and say they either hadn't seen such behavior or that the matter had already been settled."

"We're hearing more and more of these incidents as the weeks go by in the season. It's become fairly routine with these outlying clubs."

Sterne takes a sip of his tea. "I don't know who to hold more responsible: this new stock of ballplayers taking over these Western leagues or the owners who are supposed to keep things on the straight and narrow, the ones you suggested I install in the first place."

Niedler fidgets.

"What do you have to say about that?"

He clears his throat again. "We must impart a more firm message, something that will convince them to temper their players' actions."

"I've been thinking." He takes another sip. "What might be needed is something more rigorous. Perhaps I should send an envoy out there to act as a permanent intermediary on this office's behalf, a traveling liaison who would enforce our rules."

"A traveling liaison?" An odd look crosses Niedler's face.

"Yes. Someone willing to traverse the country where our game has lodged itself, from the most densely packed cities to the most far-flung specks on the map. Someone willing to hop from one coach to the next and sleep and eat like some wayward vagabond. All for the sake of upholding our principles."

"Vagabond?"

"Someone who knows the essence of this game inside and out. Someone so utterly dedicated that I can trust them to impose the will of this office without complaint."

"I…who?" His fidgeting increases.

Sterne sets the cup down on its saucer. His eyes finally meet Niedler's.

A short rasp escapes Niedler's throat. Then he straightens up. "The telegram! Yes! Must send a proper response to this fellow. Give him your concise retort." He jumps behind a leather chair and walks it to the front of the desk. He sits down with a legal pad and crosses his legs. "Shall we?"

Sterne carefully observes his associate. He puts his tea down, stands up, and walks over to the window. He stares out the window, clinging to his lapel.

Niedler's eyes are fixed on him, looking like an obedient dog waiting for a command from his master.

"Dear sir, stop," he begins. "My heartfelt appreciation for your timely response and sincerest honesty, stop. It is this office's highest priority to maintain the utmost standard of excellence of this great game of ours through the conduct and temperament of our gentlemen on the playing field, stop. Any threat to the integrity of this institution is a threat to its values that have been painstakingly cultivated to please the growing masses of devotees, stop. Without proper enforcement of our rules and regulations, a threat to its providence and long-term profitability is foreseeable, stop. Therefore, any such act or conduct that violates our principles shall not go unpunished, stop. All parties involved, including the steward presiding over said ballplayer or club, will be held accountable and subject to discipline set by this office."

Niedler finishes writing. "Perfect. I'll send this out on the wire to him immediately."

Sterne turns to Niedler. "Send it to everyone out there. Let them know any form of insubordination will not be tolerated. Anyone committing an offense against our principles will face my personal authority."

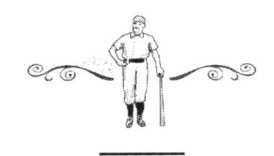

A NATIONAL CRAVING FOR PROSPERITY sweeps across the country. The pursuit to seize and claim, tread and trample, raze and flatten, tame and harness, is never greater. Industrialization is its boiler chamber and what springs up along its tracks are boomtowns and cities whose inhabitants thirst for American milk and honey.

Base-Ball is there to convert a new wave of enthusiasts looking for ways to spend some of their free time and money. Soon there are clubs established in places like Cleveland, Detroit and Chicago, and also in smaller towns as far west as St. Louis and as far south as Bowling Green, Kentucky.

The penetration of these new markets produces the potential for sudden wealth for its principals but also creates unforeseen complications. The breakneck speed of clubs popping up across the Midwest opens the door to a different kind of ballplayer, one unlike anything seen before.

Out of the dark and stale factories, mines and workshops come men—blackened, coarse, hardened men—looking to break free from their grueling restraints and find an escape. For those who are physically gifted and motivated enough to learn the game and play to win, Base-Ball is a godsend. They jump at the opportunity and play with a ferocious intensity, hell-bent on mastering the game and beating their opponents' brains in, determined not to go back to their previous livelihoods.

Their rugged style of play is a direct reflection of their

character—tough, physically demanding, win-at-all-costs-or-go-down-swinging. The public identifies with these players and soon flock to the games to see hard play, fierce competition and an occasional ruckus or two. Ticket sales skyrocket.

This development is a contrast to the styles and habits ingrained in the game back East where finesse, decorum and respectability still dominate. The game, they insist, should be a chess match between two astute clubs seeking an advantage through skillful calculation and strategy. They look down their noses at the grind-it-out, sweat-infused, dirt-and-grime boxing matches that soon define play in the West.

The scoffing and sneering do not change anything going on in the far reaches of the Base-Ball realm. The club owners have no incentive to tamper with their lucrative formula. The players might not be as refined or urbane as their Eastern counterparts, they think, but they sell tickets anyway and that's all that matters.

But as news reaches New York that these newcomers to the game are not at all the kind of gentlemen committed to preserving the integrity of the game, questions are raised. Suddenly a dilemma is at hand. As fast as the game grows across the developing West, so too do the chances of it devolving into something other than originally planned.

For the sake of conformity, an effort has to be made to keep the game from splintering. Its definitive authority has to step in and wield its power.

A lithograph of the club from Youngstown depicts seven portraits of mostly clean-shaven, solemn and unassuming faces. But that's hardly the case for these men who have come out of the blast furnaces of the Mahoning River Valley steel mills.

Well-muscled with wrists, arms and shoulders as strong as the steel they forge, they are one of the more formidable clubs assembled in the Ohio League. Having played together as a team for five years, the Workingmen Blue Collars, as they're nicknamed, are a cohesive lineup with a fondness for smashing the ball around the park with giant fifty-ounce hickory bats.

While short on pitching, they always come back with runs of their own and usually fall on the winning side of ballgames. Their rock-ribbed doggedness and confidence, bordering on arrogance, make them a favorite among spectators. As popular as they are, they've agreed to play two games every Saturday to accommodate the turnout in what has became known as the double-header.

And they hate losing. Every time the final score favors the other team, someone or something's going to pay for that outcome. A great many benches and drinking fountains have been destroyed as evidence of the team's volcanic nature.

On a day when the sun is high and beating down without relent, the Blue Collars are going for a team record twelfth straight win against their opponent from Stark County. But the game has entered its final inning and they are trailing by two runs. The stifling oven-like air crackles with an edginess that wafts into the stands.

Needing two runs to tie the game, a runner on second base and two outs, the anchor of their offense steps up to the plate. Chock Clodderman has already driven in five runs with his bat and is looking for more. Wielding the biggest bat in the league, a whopping fifty-seven-ounce behemoth that he nicknamed Ol' Booley Stagg, Clodderman digs his foot into the dirt and glares at the pitcher with menacing, bloodshot eyes, flaring his nostrils.

The pitcher stands motionless on the mound with the ball clasped tightly in his bare hands. Having already survived three turns of their batting order, he doesn't give in easily to any intimidation.

The first pitch is a fastball right down the middle of the plate. Clodderman takes the pitch without lifting his hunk of hickory off his shoulder.

The second pitch is high but Clodderman gets his Ol' Booley Stagg around it enough to foul it off sharply into the stands, beaning an old codger in the head, leaving him unconscious and bleeding away in the arms of three park attendants.

The third pitch is a flailing duck that Clodderman demolishes, sending the ball screaming into center field and beyond. The thick-bodied Blue Collar barrels down the line, careening around first. The runner on second scampers home.

The ball finally lands in a pasture next to the outfield. The fielder weaves his way through a herd of grazing cows before finding the ball.

Clodderman steps on second base and heads for third. The ball finally pops out of the pasture and lands in the hands of the first cutoff man. Without pause, Clodderman rounds third and hurtles home.

The second cutoff man fires the ball to the catcher. Expecting a train-wreck of a collision, the catcher drops to his knees and grips the ball with both hands up near his chest.

But Clodderman suddenly runs out of steam and stumbles to the plate. Instead of sliding in under the tag, he instead lunges at the catcher and jumps on him, hoping to crush him with his weight and free the ball. Clodderman flattens him right in front of home plate.

He bounces off and searches for the loose ball. The catcher, pounded six inches into the ground, stares up with the dark-leather ball stuffed firmly in his mouth.

Clodderman throws his arms straight in the air and clenches his fists, signaling to his benchmates that he's safe. But the umpire, seeing the ball lodged in the catcher's mouth, calls Clodderman out.

The third out, the game's over. The Blue Collars have lost.

The Youngstown bench leaps up and storms the diamond. Clodderman charges the umpire and bursts into a curse-laden tirade, jumping up and down in one spot and unleashing a vein-popping onslaught of abuse.

"Whaddy'a mean, out? He ain't got the ball in his hands! Don't ya' see that, ya' jackass!"

The umpire freezes, gaping at the ferocity blazing from Clodderman's mouth. The heated Youngstown players swarm in and surround the hapless umpire like some kind of trapped animal, closer and closer, until there is no more room for him to squirm.

The team from Stark County, sensing the rage in the air and fearing for the safety of the umpire, begin peeling players away from the tightening circle. His helpless voice makes one final gasp before being smothered by the snarling Youngstown players.

All the while, underneath the scrum and firmly embedded in the ground, the catcher desperately sucks air through his nostrils, terrified at the thought of somebody stepping on his throat.

Difficult Cheese

The Mule.

That's what everybody called him. Not Clifford the Mule or Mule Grumsley or even Clifford "Mule" Grumsley. Just the Mule.

The Mule took a beating year after year and never went down. Nearly every single day he climbed up the mound and faced batter after batter without the slightest hint of fatigue or complaint. Whether there was a downpour or one-hundred-percent humidity, whether he pitched thirteen innings the day before or finished the last six innings of the first game of a double-header, he always took the ball.

The Mule demanded to pitch time after time until he reached nearly a thousand innings by the end of the season. Then the next season he did the same thing. Then the next season and several more after that.

By then most pitchers had become sophisticated enough to carry a repertoire of special pitches to get batters out. There were off-speed pitches meant to disrupt the batters' timing, breaking balls that dove, looped and wobbled and ordinary fastballs that ranged in velocity.

Every year came different variations as pitchers tinkered with their grip and delivery in order to fool the hitter and gain the upper hand. A game within the game developed where each side tried to outguess the other as to what was coming. Good pitchers knew how to get outs through a combination of pitch selection, execution and sheer determination.

The Mule was not that sophisticated. His arsenal of pitches was an average fastball and a decent breaking ball that tailed away on right-handed hitters and cut in to left-handed hitters.

What made him successful were two things. One, to compensate for his lack of hard stuff, he consistently spotted his fastball over the plate with such precision that the opposing hitter rarely had a chance to square up and get a good piece of wood on it. The Mule was an expert on inducing weak groundballs and easy popups, much to the exasperation of hitters.

The second thing he did extraordinarily well was keeping batters off balance. Once the catcher threw the ball back, he quickly set himself up and delivered the next pitch. His lightning-quick pace never gave the hitter a chance to think. One pitch would be three inches off the plate then the next would plunge down off his shoestrings. Before the hitter knew it, a fastball would come sailing over the plate and he would flail at and pop out in foul territory.

As much as he had thrown, however, the Mule was not immune to bad stretches. Surely, at times, his arm must have been killing him. The stress his elbow and shoulder took was far greater than what any other pitcher endured. Thousands of pitches into a season, his arm must have been a throbbing, aching, swollen cut of meat. But he stubbornly refused to leave games when he didn't have his best stuff and was putting men on base at an alarming rate.

One summer, deep in the season, the Mule gave up runs like a preacher handing out Bibles. His pinpoint accuracy was not there, his fastball was even slower than usual, and his quick catch-and-throw delivery to the plate had slackened. Something was wrong.

After giving up six runs through three innings in one particular game, walking an astounding seven men, the club manager paced up and down the sideline, fretting over what to do about his workhorse. After the Mule served up a long home run that landed in a grove of beech trees, he decided to take the chance of removing him from the game.

The manager walked slowly to the mound. "What'ya say, Mule? It's lookin' like this ain't your day. How 'bout taking a break and giving the youngster O'Day over there a chance to get in some innings?"

The Mule's face cringed and his eyes narrowed. "I ain't no quitter so git yer ass back to that bench and lemme' get through this game."

"Mule, you can get 'em tomorrow. Why don't you save up yourself for then? Take the rest of the afternoon off, get back to the hotel. A good steak dinner and a good night's rest should do you some good and you'll be fresh for tomorrow."

"I said I ain't no quitter."

"Mule…" The manager went to reach for the ball and Grumsley, like a rabid dog gnawing at a bone, began to growl and show teeth.

"For chrissakes, Mule, your friggin' arm's gonna fall off one of these days!"

"Then I'll pitch with my other arm."

"Fine," the manager gave up, "but O'Day is in tomorrow. You're getting some time off."

"Like hell."

The manager walked back to the bench and the Mule went

on facing batters. He walked more men, gave up more hits and runs, and wound up pitching fifteen innings that day in a game that ended in a tie.

Later that season, when it became apparent that Grumsley was not rebounding from his rough patch, his manager did the impossible. He benched him for a stretch of five games and gave the ball to the young, inexperienced O'Day.

During that time, Grumsley either sat on the far end of the bench and stared off into space, speaking nary a word to anybody, or paced up and down the foul line like a caged animal.

Back at the hotel, Grumsley finally confronted his manager and threatened to leave the team if he wasn't put back on the mound.

"Fine," the manager said, "only if you do one thing for me."

"What?" the Mule said.

Then the manager did the unthinkable. He ordered a doctor to look at him and offer an opinion on the health of his workhorse. Grumsley capitulated.

The next morning the physician arrived with his black bag and ordered the Mule to strip off his shirt. He noticed his throwing arm hung lower than the other. He asked Grumsley to lift it over his head. He only got it a couple of inches above his waist. He took his arm and examined it.

"Does this hurt?" he asked, pressing hard against the back of his triceps.

"Does what hurt?"

He pressed harder.

"Don't feel a thing, doc."

The doctor started feeling around his elbow. "Hmmm…" His face turned quizzical.

"What is it, doc?" The manager asked.

"It's strange. I don't feel any ligaments in there."

After several more minutes, the doctor finished and declared Grumsley's arm dead.

"What do you mean 'dead'?" The manager asked. "He's just

got a tired arm, right? A bout of fatigue. A little more rest should do the trick."

"I'm afraid not. This man's arm is physically dead, from what I can tell. I don't think rest will help. He shouldn't be doing anything with this thing. It's useless."

After a long appeal, the manager convinced the doctor to prescribe to Grumsley a regimen to restore the function of his arm, including long treatments of ice water soakings, rubdowns with liniments and long spells of rest.

But when the time came for Grumsley to begin his treatment, the manager did not find him in his room. He found him instead on the mound warming up for the day's matchup. He pitched a complete game shutout.

Prickly, ornery and abrasive were the words most commonly used by those who described Grumsley's disposition. He never mingled or fraternized with his teammates. When they were on the road, Grumsley usually stayed in his room. Once in a while, to the amazement of his drinking teammates, he ventured out to the same saloon and sat quietly at the bar nursing a beer.

Many who played with him for several years had no idea who he was outside of the ballpark. He never talked about his personal life, where he came from or how he got to the big leagues. His acute hunger for the ball led some to believe he was out to prove something of himself. Others said they felt like he was running from something. Was he running from his past? The law?

Whatever it was, the Mule kept moving and never let up. When the season ended, he went off on a barnstorming tour and threw another three hundred innings. When early spring arrived, he was there at the ballpark pacing and brooding until he was able to get back on the mound once again and continue piling up pitches and innings.

After racking up thousands and thousands of innings, like all workhorses, the Mule's days finally came to an end and he disappeared just as mysteriously as he entered the game.

Many years later someone dug into his past and found that Grumsley was born on a farm in Southern Missouri to an impoverished family of thirteen. His father was an alcoholic with psychotic tendencies and constantly under threat of losing the farm to debtors.

Living in the most wretched conditions, Grumsley climbed out of his squalor through all sorts of backbreaking work that might have broken some other men. No one knew how he learned to pitch but by the time he was twenty-five Grumsley joined the Cleveland club and never looked back.

After the turn of the century, years after his glory days as the game's most durable pitcher, Grumsley was found to be working at a billiards parlor as a greeter and part-time vaudeville act known as "The Broken-Down Mule from Stumpsville, Missouri."

Chin Music to Soften the Senses

Tip Bullinger loved to intimidate opposing hitters. As one of the first southpaws to toss off the mound, possessing a complete lack of control, he warned opposing hitters that he had no idea where the next pitch was going.

Sometimes a fastball with extra kick pounded the hitter so far inside that he jumped back to avoid getting hit. The second pitch would sail over his head or even behind him. The startled hitter would gingerly step back in the box and cower ever so slightly, waiting for the next pitch.

Bullinger would smirk, shrug his shoulders, and then promptly strike him out with a ball slung from a sidearm motion that even baffled the catcher making the stop.

Those were the lucky ones. The ones less fortunate were the victims of balls coming straight at them, plunking them hard and frequently. Whenever Bullinger pitched, there was a good chance someone was going to have to be carted off due to a broken nose, jaw or hand.

Bullinger must have led the leagues every year in walks, wild pitches and hit batsmen. But he also led the league in strikeouts. If the batter didn't take his free base then he sulked back to the bench, the victim of a punchout. Bullinger had the capacity to get behind and then come back with something hard and fierce right down the middle of the plate.

One humid, sticky day when men were being carried off due to Bullinger's wildness, a slight, timid fellow by the name of Pudlow stepped up to the plate. Having already struck him out three times on nine pitches, Bullinger figured he had an easy out with this one if he managed to get the ball over the plate.

But on the first pitch, a blazing fastball that ran up on him, Pudlow flailed his bat and struck the ball, shooting it back up the middle of the plate. The ball cannoned right into Bullinger's face and knocked him off the mound.

The infielders rushed to the fallen pitcher and gasped. Bullinger's right eye had been knocked out.

Once he came to, he spent the next few minutes crawling around looking for his eye. He found it, looking like a squashed hard-boiled egg. It was mangled and completely useless.

Bullinger spent the next several seasons pitching with only one eye. As a lefty, he couldn't see the plate at all when he was in the wind-up position. But that didn't stop him. He turned into a different pitcher.

His bouts of wildness suddenly disappeared and he became a control artist, painting the plate with fastballs up and down, in and out, and forcing the opposing hitters to earn their way on base.

Still, he loved to intimidate the hitters.

On occasion, when a tough out stepped up to the plate, Bullinger would crouch down and stick his neck out toward the hitter. Giving him a wicked stare, the southpaw would take his thumb and index finger and slowly peel open his right eyelid, inviting the hitter to stare into his black chasm of emptiness.

The hitter would strike out looking on three pitches.

Dew-Drop Whimsy

Things were not going well for Kermit Givers. He couldn't hit enough to be an everyday lock in the lineup and his fielding skills were abysmal. So he gave pitching a try in one last attempt to stay in the big leagues.

Even his skills as a pitcher were not up to snuff. He couldn't locate his fastball. His breaking balls hung up in the air for the hitters to smash. Balls in the dirt became just as frequent as balls leaving the yard.

But he didn't give up. There was no way he was going back to the slums and putrid, blood-soaked killing floors of the slaughterhouse.

So he threw himself into the growing morass of trick pitches, hoping to pick up something that worked and got hitters out. He tried different types of fastballs with names like shooters, risers, short arms and whirlers to no effect. He tried breaking balls that hooked, dipped, spiraled and curled. Off-speed pitches tumbled, fluttered, faded and died. Nothing seemed to work.

Then he discovered the Wet Ball.

The Wet Ball moved in ways not seen before whenever he

applied something slippery to it. With diminished friction, the ball left his hand looking like a typical fastball but then suddenly dropped right before it reached the batter.

The first time Givers tried the Wet Ball, he licked his fingers and smudged the ball with his tobacco-cured saliva. It took a sharp turn downward and fooled the hitter so badly he took a mighty swing and lost grip of the bat, sending it sky-high into the stands.

Givers couldn't believe it. The ball plummeted like it was shot down in midair by some goose hunter's buckshot. He tried it again and again until the ball was completely lathered.

He became so good at it that the Wet Ball was soon one and only pitch he threw. Everyone knew what was coming, but they couldn't do anything about it.

He didn't know the reason for his own success. Was it the specific mix of his saliva and the right amount of tobacco juice? For a long time he refused to tinker with his special blend.

Since there was no rule prohibiting such practice, the rest of the leagues caught up with him, having varying levels of success with different substances—from cooking grease to petroleum jelly.

Feeling that he had to stay ahead in the quest for Wet Ball dominance, he searched for better applications and soon abandoned his saliva-and-tobacco-juice component. He tried things like candle wax, butter and camphor oil before moving on to more exotic elements like mucous off the skin of pond frogs. Nothing worked better than his original formula.

Then, one day, he became inspired when he saw a man walking down the middle of a street and slipped on a pile of horse manure. Givers thought he'd give it a try.

Through trial and error, Givers found his winning formula. With one part saliva, one part Choice Leaf tobacco juice, and one part Percheron dung, Givers' Wet Ball became the most dominant pitch at the time.

On his pitching days, Givers could be seen walking to the

mound carrying a bucket of his prized concoction. After every inning he would bend down, scoop up a dollop, and gently spread the blend across one side of the ball.

It wasn't too long before people complained. Not only did Givers benefit from an advantage he already had, he pushed it to the extreme until his opposition had no chance to adjust to the pitch. He also heard complaints from his own teammates who voiced their displeasure about handling the shit-lathered ball.

A backlash resulted and Givers was forced to give up the bucket. But he couldn't stop. Once he ditched the bucket, Givers found places on his body to conceal his magic blend, first hiding it behind his belt buckle, then underneath his cap and then finally under his woolly mustache.

The Manure Ball dominated the pitching world for years to come.

Yakker

On the first day of tryouts for the Akron Summit Cities club, manager Bill Gorsham could not believe his eyes at the level of play put forth by one Ralph "Sweet" Sweek.

He put him at third base and Sweek gobbled up balls and threw darts across the diamond every time. He put him in the outfield and he was like a gazelle chasing down flyballs with his scrawny legs. He put him behind the plate and he blocked every errant pitch.

The only problem for Gorsham, though, was Sweek couldn't hear or talk. Gorsham marveled at his oddity but decided to keep him on the team. He stayed there for twelve years.

It had been a long and improbable climb for the young Sweek. Born on the border between Oklahoma and Kansas, Sweek's hometown was devastated by a tornado and his family was killed, leaving him an orphan. Sometime before his fourth birthday he developed a double ear infection that cost him his hearing.

By the time he was twelve, Sweek had escaped his orphanage and gone to work at numerous low-paying menial jobs across the Midwest. His first taste of Base-Ball came when he was a traveling rodeo clown. In one small town, he befriended the local team's captain, who happened to be their manager. He gave Sweek a job as the club's mascot.

But once the player-manager noticed Sweek's athletic talent, he gave him a chance to play and Sweek took to the game like a fish to water. It didn't take long before he found his way north to the bigger clubs.

Gorsham had something special in the overachieving Sweek. Even though he couldn't hear a lick and could only communicate through the most primitive of means, he became a superb utility player who played everywhere on the field and perfected the skills of pinch-hitting and pinch-running.

His intense enthusiasm, bordering on hyperactivity, injected a healthy dose of energy late in games and helped the Summit Cities capture wins in tight games.

Despite his handicap, Sweek was one of the smartest players in the game. He played the role as the "deaf and dumb kid" to his advantage. Whenever Gorsham threw him out there, opposing teams treated him like a dimwitted imbecile who grunted and groaned like a quivering chimpanzee. They ignored him. It was a mistake.

Sweek silently studied the subtleties of the game—what the opposing pitcher was throwing, which outfielders were slack with their throws, which managers favored defensive setups, which opposing hitters were hot or cold—and took advantage of each one. He slapped weak fastballs past slow-footed shortstops.

He took the extra base on balls hit to careless outfielders. He stole bases whenever no one was paying attention to him.

And Sweek had a secret weapon. He knew how to read lips.

Whenever he occupied a base or caught behind the plate, he picked up on conversations between the manager and the players and between the pitcher and catcher. He reported back to Gorsham what the opposing team was up to by sneaking back behind the bench or underneath the stands and drawing a diagram in the dirt revealing their strategies.

Gorsham counteracted with moves of his own and handily beat the opposing team. Many described the team's success as simply dumb luck. Gorsham shrugged his shoulders and went on winning. Sweek held up his arms and shook his head in dumbstruck bafflement. When no one was looking, both men cracked a sideways smile.

There was nothing dumb about Sweet Sweek's guile.

After his playing career, Sweek became the dean of the Institute of Higher Learning for Deaf and Mute Citizens and received numerous honorary degrees from several universities. He retired on a full pension and spent the rest of his life giving "speaking" lectures on the art of listening and conversation.

DURING THIS TIME, a pivotal turn of events transpires that forever transforms the game of Base-Ball. What was once a game reserved for the affluent and neophile, Base-Ball quickly becomes embedded in the lives of everyday working folk, who are rising to prominence in what becomes the country's heartland.

No longer is Base-Ball just a part-time fancy for a few. It becomes a permanent fixture for people who are hungry to know what happened in a game every single day of the week.

These people attend games more frequently and are more emotionally invested in their team. Like the players on the field, they are boisterous and rough-hewn. They demand from their team optimal effort and a solid thrashing of their opponent.

They call themselves "cranks," a nod to their ability to whip up the crowds in the stands and get them rooting for their local heroes.

They do not sit passively and politely. If something is not to their liking they express their intense dissatisfaction. Booing enters the arena for the very first time.

Before the game spread westward, it was unthinkable for a spectator to raise their voice in such a vulgar manner. Now it becomes commonplace. If they hate the opposing team, if the umpire makes a bad call, or even if someone on their team is loafing it on the field, they are sure to rain down boos of utter dissatisfaction.

To accompany the growing segment of "cranks", ballparks grow in size and complexity. Crude wooden planks make way for multi-tiered platforms with roofs to cover their heads from the blazing sun and inevitable rain. Concessionaires have room to hawk their cotton candy, pink lemonade, hot pretzels and popcorn. Underneath it all are small, dank clubhouses and dressing rooms for the players to go before and after games.

The Cranks have an insatiable appetite for their sport. If they aren't at that day's game, they want to know what happened, down to the last detail. Word of mouth is too slow and unreliable. They demand accurate, dependable information.

Newspapers pick up the slack by posting the previous day's results in their morning edition. The box score becomes a valuable piece of information, telling them who did what and when.

But they want more. They want to read about the game as if they were there watching it at the venue. They want to know who was struggling at the plate, who made a great catch, who argued with the umpire and who scuffled with whom.

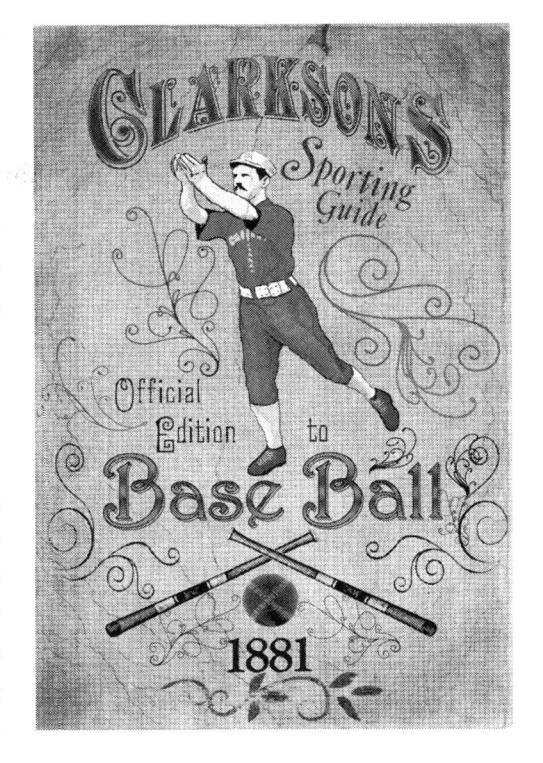

It isn't enough just to report the facts. Someone has to shape the story of the game, giving it color and drama.

Thus, the sportswriter is born, providing a written chronicle of each game's progress, taking liberties here and there to liven up the narrative.

But newspapers aren't the only forms of media to embrace the game. Gentlemens' sporting magazines had been around for years and many of them transform themselves into Base-Ball-only publications, joining the push to put the game to the highest pedestal.

Whiffed on Anti-Fogmatic

An upswell of cheering breaks out across the ballpark, celebrating the circus catch by Chicago's revered veteran outfielder, Flynt Doyle. The left fielder races into the corner and leaves his feet, making a diving catch that would have otherwise dropped and allowed the go-ahead run to score.

It would have been an ordinary catch just a few years before, but his nimble body has suffered a steep decline in recent years and now even the most routine of plays requires a Herculean effort.

But his diminishing agility isn't his only malady when he makes that catch. Doyle is also roaringly drunk.

He's more than just drunk. He's sloshed, plastered, soused. Hooched-up, pie-eyed. Inebriated. Much more so than the previous season when he could actually remember getting to the ballpark and putting on his uniform.

But this game, he can't remember a thing before the third inning.

In the past, he was convinced that a good belt or two didn't affect his playing. Better still, he thought he played better when he was a little tipsy, that it shook off the butterflies.

But those days are gone and now his drinking has gotten out of hand. He fears that the time will soon come when something will happen, revealing to the world that Doyle is nothing more than a rotting lush clinging to the one thing he knows how to do.

The circus catch is a close one. Lost in his own fog of semi-consciousness, he had no idea the ball was coming his way. He snapped to attention when he heard someone yell from the stands that the ball was hooking down the line.

Doyle ran to the corner before looking up to see where the ball was dropping. His aching legs felt like a pair of driving wheels failing to get good traction. His lungs seized up on him like steel hex nuts being tightened by a giant wrench. When he looked up to find the ball, the sun's rays pierced through the clouds and stabbed him in the eyes.

It came down in a hurry. He could have stayed on his feet and played it on a bounce, but his instincts took over and he launched himself. Parallel to the ground, Doyle stretched his arm out as far as he could and opened his glove, his palm as wide as possible.

The ball landed in his glove before he struck the ground. The impact was brutal, sending a bolt of intense pain down his spine. His shoulder exploded and then went numb. His ribs buckled. His head throttled.

After the catch, Doyle bounces to his feet and throws the ball back to the infield, saving a run. The deafening roar of the crowd stings his throbbing head but Doyle plays up to them with a tip of his cap. The crowd eats it up but Doyle wonders to himself just how much longer they will keep it up before realizing he's nothing more than a sopped-up bag of cheap gin.

Not too long before he would have glided under that ball with a Sunday-stroll ease. He would have patrolled the outfield like a general guarding his tract. Balls would never got beyond him no matter how shallow he played.

As great as he was with the glove, his bat was impressive as well. He sprayed balls all over the park and laid down bunts with such precision that, by the time the defender picked up the ball, he was already on the bag.

But what really made Doyle a crowd-pleaser, and one of the most popular players in the Midwest, was his workman's durability and teeth-gnashing determination to win. His perseverance was second to none. You may be more athletic and more talented, he said, but he was going to out-work and out-hustle you till the end. He wasn't going to stop until either you were beaten or he was left a bloody stump.

On one occasion, in his earlier days after Chicago's new owner relocated the team on the city's near-North Side, their had been an evenly-matched contest against their rivals from Joliet. The lead went back and forth for several innings before it came to a standstill late in the game. Tensions on both sides came to a head.

Both teams had a strong disliking for each other and took liberties in expressing their sentiments whenever possible. Dishing out pain became the norm. Runners slid hard into the defenders. Pitchers plunked hitters in the thighs. Balls were smashed hard on the ground and made dents in the bodies of the infielders.

Doyle wanted to beat them in the worst way. Joliet had a six-game winning streak over Doyle's club, which to Doyle felt like nails piercing his skin. Knowing his Chicago club was a far better team than their rival stung even more.

The Joliet crew was only good at one thing: aggravating their opponent. What they lacked in skill and talent, they made up for in a pain-in-the-ass style of play that annoyed and irritated everyone they faced.

They deliberately fouled off dozens of pitches in hopes of tiring the pitcher. They tripped over infielders, preventing them from completing a double play. They constantly poked and tugged at opposing baserunners in the attempt to break their concentration.

Their use of foul language was unequaled, offending even its worst practitioners. If it weren't enough to attack their opponent's personal pride with a barrage of cruel insults and scorn, they quickly expanded their target area to include most members of their family.

And they were filthy. They neither bathed nor washed their uniforms. When a Joliet hitter stepped up to the plate, the catcher sometimes bounced up from his crouch and walked away to avoid the revolting, fly-attracting stench.

Doyle was prepared to run through a wall in order to beat them.

The game was tied but Joliet was threatening to take the lead. A man stood at third base with only one out. Any sacrifice would score the go-ahead run. Chicago's pitcher was waning from fatigue and a merciless verbal attack from the Joliet runner.

The next batter stepped up. He plugged up one nostril with his finger and shot a load of green snot though the other. The glop missed the Chicago catcher but struck the umpire in the chest.

"You disgusting bastard!"

The Joliet batter retorted with a smile, opening his mouth wide like a hippo's, revealing a set of brown-tarnished, rotting teeth.

After the umpire wiped himself with a handkerchief, play resumed.

Two pitches into the count, the Joliet batter swung at a pitch inside and popped it up high, down the left-field line. Doyle raced along the foul territory, tracking it along the edges of the stands.

The runner at third braced himself, ready to run home if the ball was caught.

Doyle pressed himself hard against the base of the stands. One arm bent into the pack of men and women sitting in the front row. The other pointed straight up in the air, blocking the sun with his glove and gauging the downward path of the ball.

At the last second the ball moved further into the stands. Once it came down, Doyle leapt in between the spectators, sending up a scattering of popcorn. His arm popped up with the ball in his glove. As soon as the umpire called the batter out, the man on third tore off for home.

Doyle jumped up, his face bloodied from a deep gash on his forehead. He threw a bullet to home plate and nailed the runner by a foot and a half for the third out.

Now though, those game-saving heroics have deserted Doyle. What is left is a hollowed-out core replaced by drink and detachment.

Doyle always drank. It's what men of his kind did. But Doyle had the capacity to drink far more than others and function just the same. Tales of his alcoholic stamina and resilience to bounce back the next day were legendary.

As soon a game ended, Doyle left the park and headed for the nearest tavern, still in his game uniform, to spend the rest of the day—and most of the night—imbibing.

Whenever he didn't show up on time for the next day's game, the manager sent out a search party, which inevitably led back to the tavern and Doyle snoring away underneath a table. They'd get him back to the dressing room, splash some water on his face, and he'd be good as new, flashing his glove and beating out throws to first.

Many on the team tried to match his capacity for drink and failed. Often, when the club was on the road, they joined him at a nearby establishment to see who could outlast him. When the last teammate fell to the floor, Doyle cheerfully ordered another shot and beer.

One night, after countless rounds, Doyle's teammates surrendered and stumbled back to their hotel room. One teammate passed out and woke up several hours later to discover his wallet missing. Thinking he left it at the saloon, he went back and found Doyle standing at the bar enjoying another whiskey and yapping with the proprietor.

Eventually, Doyle's tolerance began to decline, but not his thirst.

More and more often on game day the Chicago manager, Mike Sweeney, had to go find him, carry him back to the dressing room and stretch him out on a table. Reviving him became harder and harder. Pitchers of ice water poured over his face did not work. Smacks on his bare skin with a piece of horsehide didn't do the trick, either.

Then someone offered a patent medicine called GunkWort's Rejuvenator, which promised to revitalize the bodily fluids of everyone from "enfeebled old ladies to the most sickly of draft animals." Sweeney was down to his last option.

He opened the bottle and poured its entire contents down Doyle's throat.

Several seconds later, Doyle's bloodshot eyes popped open and he sprang up on the table. Sweeney peered into his eyes and smacked his cheeks. "Doyle? Wake up. We got a game to play. Come on, let's go!"

A smile slowly formed on Doyle's face. "Yes, Hildy, my dear sugar plum!"

He then jumped off the table, grabbed his glove, and went two-for-four that day including a ringing shot up the middle for the game-winning hit.

Soon however, reviving Doyle proved to be near impossible.

One day, with Joliet back in town, Sweeney was desperate for a win and Doyle was laid on the table, completely unresponsive. Worse, they were out of GunkWort's Rejuvenator.

Already down two players with the mumps, Sweeney had to wake Doyle and get him out there. The rulebook explicitly stated that each team had to station nine men on the playing field at the start of each contest or forfeit the game.

In an act of desperation, Sweeney dressed up a cigar store wooden Indian in a Chicago uniform and rolled it out into deep left field, hoping no one would notice until they revived Doyle.

Teammates later started ribbing Sweeney that he should

have left the Indian out there instead of Doyle, whose defense continued to decline from bouts of lethargy and sheer delirium. Routine flyballs to left field kept Sweeney on the edge of the bench biting his fingernails.

Now, on days when he was half-conscious, Doyle struck out looking without lifting the bat off his shoulder. In one game the opposing pitcher had a touch of wildness and walked Doyle. Told to take his base, Doyle dragged himself down the line, barely lifting his feet off the ground. By the time he got to first he tripped over the bag and fell on his face. Laughter broke out across the park, but with it a murmur that something wasn't right with their outfielder.

In the middle of the season, the Joliet crew was back once again, and up to their old tricks. They managed to twist the Chicago Unions in a knot but Doyle's team maintained a slim lead in the ninth inning. All they had to do was hold Joliet off and they would take the season series.

With two outs, a Joliet runner advanced to second base on a wild pitch. Their shortstop came up to bat, a wiry, weak-hitting thing who had barely made contact his previous at-bats. Chicago took a collective, relaxed breath, thinking they had the game in the bag.

On the first pitch, he swung and sent a soft fly straight to Doyle. The home crowd roared and Sweeney jumped to his feet. Doyle was in perfect position to make the catch. He didn't have to move an inch. All he had to do was lift his hand up and let the ball fall into his glove.

But as the ball began its descent, Doyle didn't lift his glove. Sweeney knew they were in trouble. Doyle looked like a dumb farm animal grazing in the pasture.

"Doyle! Doyle!"

The ball plunked Doyle right on the top of his head. He dropped like a felled tree. The runner on second scored. By the time the center fielder got to the ball, Joliet's shortstop had rounded third and headed home to take the lead. Chicago didn't score in the bottom of the ninth and they lost the game and the season series.

Now, despite Doyle's diving catch, it is apparent to all but the most casual observer that he is used up. He sleepwalks through the last few innings and stumbles into the dugout, barely noticing if his team has won or lost. He takes a few swigs from his pocket flasks, drags himself into the dressing room and collapses on the table.

"Sweeney. Where is he?"

The voice startles Doyle. He opens one eye and see his manager and another man.

"Grover," Sweeney is caught off-guard. "What can I do for you?"

Grover Cleveland Griswold, owner of the Chicago team, is a roundish man with a walrus-style, silver-flecked mustache. His belly is like a barrel with a belt strapped across it. The cramped, dark dressing room suddenly gets even smaller.

Griswold pants. He pats himself with a handkerchief to absorb the beads of sweat forming on his reddened forehead. He sees Doyle spread out on the wooden table. "Well, Doyle, this time you did it, you *lunkard*. You really did it to the both of us!"

Doyle's opens the other eye.

Griswold reaches across his belly and pulls out a telegram from his suit pocket. He waves it in front of Doyle. "You had to go overboard with your antics and now look at what you've done. Getting the both of us in hot water when things were going swimmingly. Record ticket sales and now you go and get the Governor in on my heels. You *jack-scabber!*"

Doyle stares up at the ceiling. "Who?"

"Whaddy'a mean, *who?* The big cheese back East, that's who. The head honcho, the Governor. We were doing our thing out here, left alone, making gobs of money. But now he's pissed off and wants to see the both of us in person at his headquarters in New York."

Doyle eases himself up on the table. He rubs his face and strokes his hand across his sandpaper cheeks and thick, wavy hair. "What for?"

"'Cuz 'a your drunken buffoonery, that's what for. The man don't like it when you make an embarrassment of his game, and now we're gonna pay for it. You *pug-a-lug!*"

"What'd he say?"

"Here, read it." Griswold shoves the telegram in his face.

Doyle stares at it before laying his head back down.

"That's right, Doyle. You better get yourself sobered up. Next week you're gonna meet the real boss and you better pray he has an ounce of sympathy for you."

Doyle sits and waits outside the Governor's office. Behind the closed door he hears muffled voices and wonders how much longer it will be. His bladder pulsates harder against his trousers with every passing minute.

The hallway is something out of a museum. Still life paintings and ferns align the corridor on both sides. The white marble floor has a perfect sheen.

He takes a deep breath and clenches his teeth.

Finally the office door swings open and Griswold's portly frame hurries out in a manic, ruffled state. Muttering to himself, his face is lathered with sweat and stunned panic.

Griswold plods down the hall clasping a stack of papers in his hand. He loses his grip and leaves a trail of sheets, one by one, all the way to the elevator. The door opens and he steps in, continuing to mutter and twitch, blurting out gibberish. He cusses to himself, cracks a warped smile, then disappears.

An impeccably dressed man steps out of the office. "Mister Doyle?"

"Yeah?"

"H.H. Niedler, Mr. Sterne's executive assistant. Will you please step inside? He is ready to talk with you."

Doyle enters the office and steps on a carpeted walkway leading up to a dark, sturdy desk. Sitting behind it is a dapper figure neatly arranging things on his desktop. Seated on both sides are a pair of buttoned-up men wearing stiff, high collars and pince-nez spectacles. Like Doyle, their hair is slicked with pomade and parted down the middle. Each clutches a fountain pen and briefcase.

The nip of brandy Doyle took earlier has not subsided his butterflies. His tight-fitting dark suit and bow tie makes him feel claustrophobic. His bladder pounds. Standing there, he makes out a hint of pipe tobacco and wood polish.

"Please come in," Niedler says before withdrawing somewhere behind him.

Doyle pads closer to the desk.

Sterne stands up. "Mister Doyle, it's a pleasure to meet you. Thank you for coming all this way on such short notice." He points to the seated gentlemen. "These are my associates, Mister Sh—"

"So you're the Gov'nur, huh?" Doyle interrupts him. "The top dog in charge. I was told you like to keep things in order. Judging by the looks of things, I'd say you really got the knack for it. You got yourself quite a setup here. This room's bigger'n my whole flat back home."

Niedler wheels over a liquor cart. "Care for a drink, Mister Doyle?"

He sees the cart furnished with top-of-the-line bottles of alcohol and hesitates. "No thanks, considerin'."

"Oh, come now," Sterne says. "I've got the best Kentucky bourbon waiting to be opened. I stocked it especially for you."

"You don't say? Well, in that case, I don't want to disappoint you. I'll have one if you'll have one."

"Please sit down, Mister Doyle." Niedler pulls up a chair.

Sterne opens the bottle and splashes the bourbon into a rocks glass with ice. He hands it to Doyle.

"Nothing for you?" Doyle asks.

"Don't drink." Sterne sits down and slides on a pair of spectacles. "Why don't we get started, shall we?" He opens a folder and examines a piece of paper.

"Flynt Theodore Doyle. Veteran left fielder for the Chicago Unions. Ten years. Sterling reputation as one of the best players coming out of the Western leagues. Outstanding glovework. Good eye with the bat. A leader on the field. Plays to win. Work ethic second to none. Teammates and spectators love him."

Doyle takes a drink. The ice clinks in the glass.

Sterne's eyes flip up over his spectacles, stabbing at Doyle. "An imbiber."

Doyle moves the glass away from his lips.

Sterne motions his hand to one of the seated gentlemen, who pulls out a magazine from his briefcase and hands it to Sterne.

"Maxwell Brothers' Base Ball Sporting Guide and Journal. August, 1878. Page three. 'Randolph Sharm's Illustrious Giants of the Diamond' column. Headline: 'Flynt Doyle, Chicago's Once-Great Outfielder Befallen to Dipsomania.'"

Doyle swallows hard.

"It reads: 'Once the paradigm of hard-nosed, gritty determination on the field, Doyle's performance as of late has dwindled to the point of inertia. Loyal crowds have been spoiled by Doyle's relentless pluck and willingness to do whatever it took to win games—whether it was running through walls to make a catch or plowing through the catcher to score the winning run. Year after year, he did not disappoint; that is, until this season. As if someone pulled a cork out of Doyle, suddenly his zest and combativeness has evaporated. He no longer flashes fire in his eyes or feats of deftness. He's become a lifeless slug loitering in the outfield who erratically flops around the diamond in a deranged manner. Sadly, the effects of over-indulgence seem to have taken their toll. Doyle's legendary status as an accomplished tippler has made him an embarrassment for the game and his own legacy. Will this humiliating display continue? How much farther will Doyle fall? Is there a even a ghost of a chance he can reclaim his spot as one of the game's prominent statesmen?'"

Sterne lays the magazine down and eyes Doyle. "An embarrassment for the game."

Doyle balances the rocks glass on the arm of the chair and raises his hands as if he were about to launch into a long-winded explanation. Nothing comes out.

One of the other gentlemen hands Sterne a sheet of paper.

"It says here you've had to be carried off the field numerous times. You've relieved yourself in your own uniform in front of thousands of patrons. You once ran out into the field forgetting to wear pants. You once threw up on an opposing player. You were caught carrying a pail of beer into the outfield. Forgetting how many outs there were. Forgetting which inning it was. On and on this list goes."

"I can explain."

Sterne's eyes flare.

Doyle pulls out a torn-out page from an encyclopedia. He gives it to Sterne.

"Grogat's Dissociative Fugue Syndrome? What is this?"

"Temporary amnesia. It comes and goes. Had it since childhood. But I'm working on it and one day I'll beat this dreaded disease. By God, I'll lick it once and for all!"

"Mister Doyle, it's one thing to be intoxicated and completely cretinous but to be genuinely deceitful is another matter altogether. You've gone from being a model player to something betraying every mandate this office has issued. What do you have to say for yourself?"

"What's a Man-date?"

"To embarrass yourself time and time again and make a mockery out of our beloved institution is not only unacceptable but downright felonious. Acts that violate our principles laid down in the rulebook must be addressed with swift action."

"I ain't never seen no rulebook."

"Mandatory reading of the rules and regulations. Customary code of behavior for all players. Every club owner was required to give each player a copy and sign an agreement. Needless to say that hasn't happened, so here we are."

"Look," Doyle says, "I hear you're a stickler for all that stuff, but give me another chance and I'll turn myself around. No more boozin' before games. You got my word."

Sterne rises from his chair and dashes around his desk. "Disciplinary action has to be meted out."

"A slap on the wrist, I'll kick the hooch and we'll call it even. Whaddy'a say?"

"You're through, Doyle. Finished." His face reddens with anger.

"How's that?"

"I'm banning you from the game. Permanently."

A lightning strike runs down his spine. "W-what? What do you mean?"

"You're out of my leagues, Doyle. You've tarnished the game's image for too long and I will no longer tolerate any such transgression."

"You're kicking me out of the game?"

"Forever. As long as you're alive, you will no longer have the right to be a part of Base-Ball in any capacity. You cannot play. You cannot attend. You cannot even walk past a ballpark. You're now a pariah. A leper."

"You can't do that."

He chuckles. "Don't you know by now, Doyle? I own this game. I fostered it and I'll do as I please."

Doyle starts to shake. "But Base-Ball's my life. I don't know nothin' else but the game. What am I gonna do?" Shaking even more, he knocks the rocks glass off the chair and drops to his knees. "It's my life you're talking about here. Without this game, I'm a dead man, y'see? Give me another chance, Mister Sterne!"

Tears well up in his eyes.

Sterne stands above and coldly stares down at him.

"What do I gotta do, beg you? Please, give me another shot and I'll make good. I ain't a bad man. I'll be the player I once was. I promise!" He trembles.

"Can't you see, Doyle? Things have gotten a little out of hand out your way and an example needs to be set. I will not allow anyone to make a mockery out of our beloved pastime. You can crawl back and tell them yourself. If anyone dares get in between me and my game, there will be a price to pay." ∎

Tracy Tomkowiak

VII.

SCHNOCKERD
(1879-1883)

"I want to be a Captain of Industry."

Hubert Aloysius "Pete" Schnockerd IV watches his father across the table and waits for his response. The testing room bears the pungent infusion of steam, malted barley and hops.

His father gathers the mash bill in cheesecloth and leans in to smell the ingredients. He takes a long, deep inhalation and holds it in. Then he exhales through his nostrils, making a soft, whistling sound. He jots down a note in his ledger.

"Say again."

"A Captain of Industry. A Champion of Capitalism. You know, one of those guys with the art collection, the yacht, the private staff. I want the diamond-knobbed walking cane. All of it."

"Uh-huh." His father picks up the next cheesecloth and takes another deep inhalation. He writes again in the ledger before biting down on a pickle and piece of rye bread. He washes it down with a sampling of fresh beer in a chalice.

The younger Schnockerd continues. "I want to be at the helm

of a vast commercial empire, something new and innovative, and get really, really rich. Whaddy'a think, Pop?"

"Another moment of inspiration infiltrated your brain I see. What is it this time?"

"I think it's time for me to take over the brewery."

The elder Schnockerd gags and coughs out a chunk of pickle. "You what?"

"You know, hand over the keys to me, from one generation to the next. You took over after your dad, so why not me? Whaddy'a say?"

His father catches his breath. "Let me get this straight. You want to take over the family brewery?"

"Why not? Since Billy and Fred are off doing their own things I figured it'd be up to me to carry on the brewing tradition."

His father's face lights up. "Wilhelm and Frederick are on the board of executives. They are perfectly capable—"

"Yeah, but I've got tons of new ideas to really get this thing off the ground. Milwaukee and Chicago is just the start. I'll make us national. Breweries all over the country. New product lines, advertising, the works!"

A shock of disbelief and horror well up in his eyes. "You can't be serious?"

"Sure I am. Been thinking about it for some time. I think I know what it takes to become a business tycoon. Smarts, determination. Panache!"

His father wipes his mouth with a napkin and dabs it against his ivory-white vandyke beard. "He finally wants to take over the brewery," he murmurs to himself, "just like that."

His son beams a smile and sits up straight as if he just handed in a perfect term paper.

The elder Schnockerd closes the ledger and springs out of the chair. "You wouldn't last a month before shuttering the doors. Hell, you couldn't even manage the sausage press I set up for you last year before selling it back to Klotzenlutz. The brewery? Phh-yuh!" He dashes out onto the brewing floor and the younger Schnockerd follows on his heels.

His father stops in front of a copper brewkettle and faces his son. Junior and Senior Schnockerd are complete opposites. The elder is a tiny man, well-kept, tidy and snappily dressed. The younger is portly, oafish and disheveled.

"You see this?" His father points to the row of kettles. "Do you smell it in the air? Taste it? That's the culmination of decades of painstaking work, over the span of generations, striving for that perfect balance of flavor and ingredients. Do you really think I'd hand this over to you and screw it up?"

Pete Schnockerd rips off a cheeky grin.

"Look at you! You can't even keep your shirt tucked in your pants or your shoelaces tied!"

He follows his father downstairs to the fermenting room.

"Attention to the smallest details. Exactitude. Precision. What do you know about that? Oh, that's right. You once won a dart-throwing competition in college!"

His father busies himself all the way down to the coolery tunnels below street-level. He counts the barrels and enters the number in his ledger. Pete tags along behind him.

The diminutive beer magnate turns and runs smack into Pete's belly. "Jesus! Get out of my way!"

"Pop, I can do this. I really can! Just give me the opportunity and I'll prove it."

"You're nuts!" He pushes himself away from his son and stomps up the steps and through the ornate double doors.

Pete follows him outside, across the street, toward the Victorian house converted into the company's office. A light sprinkling of snow descends from the overcast sky.

"Pop!"

His father stops in the middle of the street and turns around. He grabs Pete and points to the top of the five-story brewhouse.

"You see those inlaid bricks? It says '1831.'" What started as your great-grandfather's recipe from the motherland, we now churn out at more than three thousand barrels a week. Just the thought of you being anywhere near this place sends shivers down my spine!"

"I'll double the production! Triple it!"

"Ain't no way, nohow!"

Inside, the elder Schnockerd's study is lined with red carpet and dark walnut.

"Why don't you leave me alone?"

"I can do this. I know I can. I have ideas. I'll turn this into an empire."

His father sifts through stacks of paperwork on his desk, trying to turn a deaf ear.

"I have vision. Backbone. I'll turn the family operation into the Standard Oil of breweries."

"*Mein Gotte!*"

"Just give me a chance to prove it."

"Prove?" His father stops and looks at his son. "All that you've proven to me is that you're a *pfuscher*—a fuck-up!

"Pop..."

"Son, you are not the working kind. You don't have an ounce of responsibility in you. How many schools have I sent you to, only to get kicked out of all of them? You drink and carouse more than anybody I know. You've stolen countless kegs, in clear daylight, right through our shipping doors! You've trashed our vacation homes. You've embezzled our family's purse and gambled it away. You can't even control your own body odor. I don't want you anywhere near this brewery, understand?"

Pete twirls his fingers. "How about a mid-level position?"

"No."

"Delivery man?"

"No."

"Taste tester?"

"No!"

"There's gotta be something for me, pop. I need to find something I'm good at. What can I do to prove myself?"

"Please." His father grows increasingly irritated.

After a moment, Pete snaps his fingers. "I know! I'll start from the bottom and work my way up. I'll clean out the kettles. I'll feed the dray horses. Give me something!"

"Listen to me. As long as I'm around, you will not be anywhere near the brewery in any capacity. Do you hear me? Now, please. I'm a busy man."

Pete gives him a minute. "How about this, a new position that's based on commission only? You know I can sell the hell out of anything. I'll be Chief Marketing Officer."

"Enough already!" His father slams down his fountain pen. "Just to get you out of my hair." He opens a drawer and rummages through a pile of files. He finds a folder and pulls out a piece of paper. "Here."

"What's this?"

"You want to run something? Start from the ground up? You can start with this."

The paper lists a number of businesses and addresses.

"A contract I signed off earlier in the year. When I swapped the waterway barges for the trunk line to Chicago I also received a bundle of smaller local properties as a throw-in. See anything you like?"

Pete scans the list.

"Take anything you like and do as you please. Just stay away from the brewery. Please, I beg you!"

"Hmmm. This sounds kind of cool. The White-Leggings."

"What the hell is that?"

"The local Base-Ball team."

"Base-Ball?"

"Yeah. Says here you're now the principal owner of the Milwaukee Moonlight White-Leggings of the Frontier League."

"Don't know anything about it."

Pete reads the finer print. "Interesting. Their ballpark's just a block from the Spring Street trolley stop."

"Take it! It's yours."

"What could I do with an actual professional ball club? It's not actually the big-time industry I had in mind."

"Take it from me, every business magnate started small and worked their way up. If you're such a marketing genius, what more could you ask for? The sky's the limit."

Pete thinks about it. "Pete Schnockerd, owner of the World Famous Milwaukee White-Leggings. Prime innovator. Pioneer. Millionaire Extraordinaire. *Captain of Industry*."

Pete's father closes the drawer. "Sounds perfect to me."

"Yeah," he says, dreamily. "I'd build it from the ground up and create an empire of my own. Maybe parlay it into something even bigger!"

"What could possibly stop you? Now please, take it and get out of my own business!"

Pete Schnockerd finds an opening in the wooden fence and peers into the ballpark. The playing field is a patchwork of dead grass and rock-hard earth. Tattered flags flap and paper wrappers twirl about in the gusty wind.

He walks around to the front gate and yanks down on the lock, then turns and sees a small brick building underneath the stands. He sticks his face up to the glass of the door and looks inside. A man sits back behind a desk with his feet up, dozing over a cup of coffee.

Schnockerd taps on the window. The man doesn't wake. He taps harder, then starts banging. The man jerks awake. He squints at the door. Schnockerd smiles and waves his hand.

The man finally gets to his feet and shuffles to the door. He's wrinkled, balding and scruffy. He's got nothing on but a natty red, one-piece union suit and black boots. A quilt hangs over his shoulders.

He shades his eyes from the sun's glare. "Whaddy'a want?" A lone tooth hangs from his mouth.

"The name's Schn—"

"Go away. I don't want any." He turns away.

"I'm the new owner of the ball club," Schnockerd calls out through the glass.

The old man stops and turns back, startled and annoyed. He unlocks the door and cracks open the flimsy door. "Who are you?"

"My name's Schnockerd, principal owner of this franchise from here on out. Care to let me in?"

"Schnockerd? The beer company? For chrissakes, not another rich family that don't know what to do with its fortune. Why don't you stick to the suds business an' stay out of this one?"

"Got it, pal. Now why don't you let me in and introduce yourself?"

The door swings open and the cold draft blasts into the tiny room.

"Name's Mustins. I'm the park superintendant, groundskeeper, equipment manager, clubhouse attendant, you name it. I do it all except write out the lineup card and play the game. Now close that damned door!"

Schnockerd shuts the door and looks around the room. Along the wall is a cork bulletin board with nothing on it, a drinking fountain and a cot. A small coal stove burns in the corner.

"Nice to meet you. I'm Pete. You're the first employee I've met so far. Anybody else around?"

"Nope. I'm the only one here, night and day, until the season starts." Mustins tends to the stove and pours some coffee.

"You live here?"

"Yep. Just me and the dog, whenever he shows up for some scraps."

"Where can I find the players?"

"Check the local saloons or lockup."

"How about the manager?"

"Ain't none. He quit two days before last season ended."

Schnockerd bends down at the drinking fountain.

"I wouldn't do that if I were you."

"Why not?"

"Be pissing iron for a week."

"So you manage the place year round? How's the ballpark?"

"The stands are falling apart and I'm down to my last coat of whitewash. I hope you're willing to spend money, mister."

"Not a problem. Gotta spend money to make money, right? I'm in this for the long haul. I'm looking to build this club into a winner."

Mustins chuckles.

"What?"

"That's what the previous owner said until he saw the daily attendance figures."

"What were they?"

"If you count out the drunks and hoboes trying to get out of the midday sun, you're a little south of full-capacity."

"We'll be packing 'em in before the season's out." Schnockerd starts looking through the desk.

Mustins chuckles again. "Yeah? Did'juh see how the club played last year? You might wanna reconsider."

"Why would I do that?"

"Cuz you rich folks are all the same. Buy something and dump it off at the first sign of trouble without the slightest clue how to operate a Base-Ball club."

"I'm not one of those types. We're going to make something

special out of this and become the envy of the league. Now where's the roster list?"

Mustins pulls out a clipboard and hands it to him. "You'll never get anything out of this motley bunch. They're the most stubbornest bastards you'll ever see. They don't like being told what to do. And plenty unpleasant."

"I don't mind stubborn. You want to see stubborn? Get a load of me. You'll need an elephant gun to put me down once I get to doing something."

"I bet you sell before the year is out."

"Ain't happening."

"You like to lose money?"

"Expert. Been bleeding the family's fortune since I turned eighteen."

"Why don't you go back to where you came from? Sit behind a cozy desk, light up a stogie, and count the barrels rolling out? Take it from me, save yourself the trouble and get out before you lose your shirt."

"Can't do that. There's no going back for me or for this sleepy, little shack you got here. Whether you like it or not, we're going to spin a cyclone out of this joint and become kings of the league."

Mustins bursts out laughing. "Good luck. I like your optimism but you have better odds finding sunken treasure in Lake Michigan than you do turning this around."

"I'll take those odds."

"Yeah? Who are you, the Great Waldini?"

"No, just the most tenacious little bugger you'll ever see. You?"

"Me? I'm just a tired old mutt looking for a comfortable spot on the front porch."

"Too bad. I'm looking for someone who's gonna get out there and find me these players," Schnockered taps on the clipboard with his finger. "I like the idea of a gang of hard-hittin' bastards who'll scare the shit out of folks."

"I know every watering hole, gaming house, cathouse and

flophouse from here to Chicago. Won't be a problem finding them."

"Great, then I'm keeping you on, Mustins my boy. Be looking forward to admiring that tiny, little tooth of yours."

"If it's winning ball you're looking for, though, I don't know how you're going to convince these roughnecks to play your style of game much less convince eight-thousand folks to come every day and watch these bums."

"It may take something more than that, but I'll work on it. You get me those players and I'll do the rest."

"You're either as gullible as hell or just downright crazy. I can't figure which one."

"I guess we'll find out, won't we?"

"Do you have any idea how to run a Base-Ball club?

Schnockerd grins. "Nope. But I've got a couple ideas."

Niedler studies the Governor from across the desk as he reads the latest cable. Behind Sterne's cool, composed veneer is an explosive rage quickly steaming to the surface.

Sterne's hand, holding the telegram, begins to quiver. As his eyes shift from left to right, his other hand reaches for the brass letter opener shaped like a dagger.

"This time an all-out brawl between the club and a group of hecklers in the stands. The local police had to be called in. Splendid."

Niedler nods.

"How many instances does it make this month alone?"

"Six."

Sterne reaches across the desk and gives him the telegram.

Niedler stuffs it into an accordion folder with the words "Schnockerd/Milwaukee" scrawled across the front.

"Read me the report again."

Niedler pulls out a sheet. "Milwaukee Moonlight White-Leggings. Frontier League. H.A. Schnockerd, owner and manager. Twenty-three—make that twenty-four—counts of illicit misconduct violating our standards of practice. Excessive rowdiness, hooliganism, drunkenness, fighting. One arrest for urinating on a public official."

Sterne's grip on the letter opener gets tighter and his face starts to twitch.

"Numerous claims of ongoing intimidation and thuggery against opposing clubs, managers, umpires and now spectators."

His forehead turns a splotchy red, as if the capillaries under his skin just burst.

"The game's sportsmanship is severely compromised by dirty-play tactics and out-and-out cheating on the field."

Something gurgles from his throat.

"Violence on a scale resembling barbaric savagery, on and off the field. Bloodshed."

The last word causes his arms and shoulders to quake. He braces himself.

"A total disregard for the values and principles we hold so dear in our beloved game. A blatant rejection for all things morally cherished."

"And that pissant?" Sterne strains to form a few words.

"He's allowed the ballpark to become a season's-long Oktoberfest complete with beer tents, polka bands, fireworks and odd promotions. Every aisle is awash in the foam of his family's pilsner lager. Besides drunken mayhem, he's also encouraged other intolerable offenses such as gambling and wagering. A real devil's den of degeneracy."

"That advertisement...once again..."

Niedler unfolds a broadsheet and reads it.

COME ALL!! This Week! An *Orgy* of Good Times, Fun & Pleasure. **SEE** Our Merry Moonlight Men Crush, Pummel & Cripple (balls & competition alike). ENJOY fresh **SCHNOCKERD BRAND** refreshments, pretzels, sausages, music, sunshine **AND MORE!** <u>LADIES DAY</u> every Tuesday & Wednesday—free entry for all women with purchase of beverage.

Niedler folds it up and crosses his legs. "All that and he's increased his season's attendance record by some four-hundred percent. His revenue is tops out there, even more than some clubs back here. He's like a regular P.T. Barnum."

Sterne stabs him with a look. "What have you done to stop this charlatan, this rogue?"

He clears his throat. "Threats of expulsion have been useless so far. Not once has he complied with our demands to come here and face punishment for these vile acts. Every time we order him to stop he goes off and does something even more defiant."

"And you're allowing him to besmirch my game?"

He starts to stutter.

"Goddamnit, Henry!" Sterne's rage finally bursts through.

He springs up and slams the letter opener down on his desk, impaling a stack of papers. Niedler jumps in his seat and falls back in his chair, tipping backwards and crashing to the floor.

"This madman is running loose and threatening to tear the whole thing down! Do something about it!"

Niedler picks himself up and scurries to gather his things.

"I want you to go out there and sack him if you have to. This monster's already caused irreparable damage. The Game is under threat! Do you hear me?"

"I don't even know how he seized ownership of that club. A backroom deal without our—"

"Get him! Whatever it takes to stop that sonofabitch from ruining everything. I want that man strapped and flogged!"

"Stopping him might take some extra coercion or creativity."

Sterne jams his fists into the desk and leans forward. "This ignoramus needs to be disposed of. Anything less than that, and I promise you there will be more than one person strung to the whipping post. Now get out of here!"

SCHNOCKERD'S WHITE-LEGGED MOONLIGHTS of Milwaukee, the bruisers of the outlying Frontier League, become the vanguards of an already-evolving style of Western Base-Ball. A win-at-all-costs attitude now pervades the leagues and destroying the opponent becomes the only objective of a game.

Led by a core of ferocious players, some of them ex-felons, the White-Leggings march across the Midwest and terrorize other ballclubs, securing a reputation as the most feared club roaming the diamond. They use the threat of violence to their advantage, much like a team deploying a pitcher with a devastating breaking ball.

They intimidate their opponents into submission. Opposing pitchers serve up soft tosses for them to crush instead of risking the prospect of plunking one of them and facing certain doom. The more timid teams facing the White-Leggings pray for a rainout. When the rain doesn't come, they simply forfeit.

While the members of the Milwaukee roster are good players in their own right, they prefer to dispense their brutality and secure an easy win. They love to fight. Brawling is deemed just as valuable a skill as the ability to draw walks or throw strikes. Bare-knuckled force trumps any talent with the bat. Pools of blood upstage speed and agility.

A fight is expected nearly every single game. They take it to their opponents at the slightest turn of events, whether it's a hard slide, the wrong slur uttered or even the wrong kind of glance given. If they don't like how they line up and sing The Star-Spangled Banner, they break out the fisticuffs.

Sometimes they start up even before they reach the park. One time, during the dog days of August when the Youngstown club is in town, the Milwaukee boys get antsy. The Blue Collars is a tough enough club to take a pounding all day long and aren't easily intimidated. Not wasting any time, the White-Leggings storm the hotel and conduct business there. After six players are sent to the hospital, along with four arrests, three broken bones and one defenestration, the Youngstown club forfeits.

But oftentimes the game is played without the courtesy of a full-blown riot and the contest is a constant parade of rough play and dirty tricks. The White-Leggings run the bases with the highest intent to inflict pain. Going from first to second on a slide means the infielder will sustain blows to the groin, gut, chest or face. One collision sends a player to the hospital with a punctured spleen and a mouth emptied of teeth.

When they aren't delivering blows, they're engaging in the practice of cheating. Sometimes they take the effort to hide their cheating, but most of the time they act in broad daylight and don't worry if anyone calls them out, especially the opposing teams and certainly not the umpire.

They master the art of stealing signs. Communication between the manager and players intensifies during games and the use of secret hand signals becomes commonplace. Determined to steal and decipher every single sign, Milwaukee plants spies all around their ballpark and concoct a method of communicating back to the bench. They become so successful at it that opposing teams have to abandon signs altogether.

The term "home field advantage" takes on another meaning at their ballpark. Milwaukee does everything they can to gain an advantage against their opponent. They place men in stands, trees and the scoreboard armed with small mirrors to reflect the sun's rays into the hitter's eyes and blind them when they are up to bat. On cloudy days they hang giant multi-colored sheets directly in the opposing batters' line of sight just to distract them. They hide extra balls all over the park and whenever they can't retrieve the original ball they simply pluck one out of a hiding spot and throw the runner out with it.

Their violent bullying and cheating make them favorites among the Cranks and die-hards who plunk down their dimes and quarters to consume this new brand of Base-Ball. The rough play, combined with Schnockerd's other innovations, including selling large quantities of his family's beer and allowing gambling, drives attendance to levels never before seen. Thousands and thousands of people flock the grounds and pack the ballpark every day to experience this new type of entertainment, fully engaging in debauchery and spending money. In short time, Schnockerd starts seeing his revenue triple and quadruple. Others around the leagues quickly take notice.

Like a bushfire raging out of control, Schnockerd's style of Base-Ball spreads across cities and towns, from one league to the other. Soon dozens of other clubs emulate his model, forgoing the antiquated, stale version of bland silliness in favor of gladiatorial matches between two hostile forces where the winner takes all. Like Milwaukee, they start drawing new hordes of converted Cranks and enjoy a dramatic surge in revenues.

Pete Schnockerd becomes a household name as the man who is ushering in a new, groundbreaking phase of the game enjoyed by millions of people across the heartland. They dub him the Great Innovator, the King of Base-Ball.

His grin stretches all the way to the East Coast.

Split-Fingered Muckler

Destined to be a small-time hoodlum and con man for the rest of his life, Mac Aintree snubbed fate and carved out a career in Base-Ball instead, spanning more than a decade.

A grifter in his early years, Aintree bounced around the country conning people by portraying himself as an honest, generous man with the unique fortune to be in the right places at the right time; but he was anything but an honorable man.

Aintree was highly adept at constructing false identities and convincing people he was the real deal. As soon as he gained their confidence, he would cheat them out of their money through bogus business deals and personal transactions. Through the years he foisted himself off as a wealthy diamond hunter from Miami, an archaeologist from Oxford, England, a steamship captain from Panama and an investment banker from Texas. The last one got him three years behind bars.

Winning over the trust of a bank manager in Rockford, Illinois, Aintree cracked open a safe and made off with a load of money. Making his way east, he made the fatal error of boasting about his windfall to a barber just outside of Chicago. The barber, suspicious of the supposed investment banker, notified his brother, the famous detective Allan Pinkerton. A tail was put on and Aintree was apprehended once he got to the city.

After his prison term, Aintree settled in Peoria, Illinois, and tried to live the straight life as a haberdasher. But the grifting bug finally got the better of him and he swindled his way back up to Chicago. Once there, he found a most opportune mark in the form of the rising meatpacking millionaire Phineas P. Calhoun.

At the time, Calhoun operated a lucrative processing plant at the Stock Yards and was one of the founding investors in the Unions and the ballpark on the West Side.

Aintree decided the easiest route to get to Calhoun was through the ball club and he cajoled his way on the team by posing as a veteran hitting ace from New Jersey.

But there was a huge problem. Aintree had never seen a game played in his life, let alone picked up a bat or tossed a ball. If he was going to pull off his charade, he needed to learn the game in a hurry and hit like the batsman he proclaimed himself to be.

With less than a week before the season started, Aintree plunged into an intense cramming session of hitting, fielding and game fundamentals. Incredibly, Aintree won a starting position as the second baseman and was punching balls into center field with regularity.

As unlikely as it seemed, Aintree discovered a hitting stroke that usually took normal players years to find. Aintree did it in a few days. With very little effort, he was able to drop the bat down and make solid contact. The ball always seemed to jump off his bat and shoot out like a bullet to all areas of the field. Teammates wondered out loud how he was able to do that with such ease.

Once on the club, Aintree turned his attention on Calhoun. His scheme to get closer to him started to take shape as the season wore on.

The wealthy meatpacker was an affable man who liked to watch games in his custom-made box seat and mingle with the team afterward in the clubhouse. One day Aintree struck up a conversation and soon gained the confidence of Calhoun, who dubbed Aintree his favorite player.

It wasn't too long before Aintree became a regular invitee to Calhoun's mansion on the city's South Side. It was then that Aintree decided to make his move on Calhoun and heist his entire collection of fine jewels right from under his nose.

Less than a week before Aintree planned to return to the mansion and steal the jewels, the Unions were at home playing the Milwaukee Moonlights. Aintree was riding an eleven-game hitting streak and catching the attention of beat writers for the local newspapers. All summer long they marveled at his hitting prowess and wired to the clubs back in New Jersey for more background information on the team's rising star. Those clubs replied back that none of them ever heard his name before.

Their curiosity aroused, they jumped on Aintree during the homestand, who spent an enormous amount of energy skirting questions and backtracking answers to get them off his back.

Then, during a game, Aintree stepped up to the plate looking to extend his hitting streak. After fouling off a number of pitches, he stepped out of the box and took a few practice swings. He looked into the stands and saw a man pointing his finger at him and hollering.

"That's him! That's the sonofabitch who stole my gold bullion!" The man stomped his feet. "Call the police! That man's a thief!"

Raving mad, the man tussled with the spectators around him before jumping down onto the field and charging the startled Aintree. The entire ballpark jumped up to its feet.

The man tackled Aintree and threw him to the ground, spitting profanities. Milwaukee's catcher, Ed Moynahan, threw his mask down and decked the man with one punch, knocking him out cold. Not wanting to feel left out, the rest of the Milwaukee infield piled on and pummeled the man into the dirt.

After the game, the newspaper writers swarmed Aintree. Who was that man? What was he accusing you of?

Aintree stiffened up. "Clearly, he was out of his mind or in a drunken stupor and had no idea what he was saying. That's all I can say on the matter."

But the incident was not forgotten. The day before Aintree was supposed to go to Calhoun's mansion, a newspaper ran an interview with the man from the stands. From his hospital bed, he swore that he had met Aintree when he was a clerk for a river port company on the Ohio River and that Aintree posed as a security officer, gaining access to a safe in the back office. He accused him of stealing thousands of dollars worth of gold.

Then the paper quoted Allan Pinkerton, who said that Aintree had served time for bank robbery a few years before.

Before the game, the writers returned and bombarded Aintree again with questions. He did his best to deflect and deny but by then the cat was out of the bag.

Was Aintree who he thought he claimed to be?

With all these suspicions flying, Aintree received the message that Calhoun had rescinded his invite to the mansion. His scheme to heist the jewels was foiled.

Fearing the whole thing would blow up in his face, Aintree abruptly quit the team and fled to Wisconsin. There he returned to the haberdashery business.

After a brief period of anonymity, a surprise visit shocked the one-time batting sensation. Pete Schnockerd entered his tiny store and offered Aintree a spot on his roster, provided that he shared his secret to his hitting success with the rest of the team

Aintree dashed behind a curtain and came out holding one of his bats. He laid it on the display case and sawed off the top half. Out of the bat poured a pile of sawdust and small bits of cork.

"Y'see? A hollowed-out bat makes hittin' things easier. I learn't that in prison when the guards were crackin' skulls with billy clubs stuffed with the same thing."

The next season the White-Leggings led the league in hits and Aintree was back playing, minus the accusations. Word had finally leaked about his tinkered bats, but instead of denying everything, he went public and published a book on how to cork bats. The book became a best seller and Aintree became a prominent celebrity in the Base-Ball world.

Aintree enjoyed a lengthy career with the White-Leggings, eventually publishing three more books on ways to cheat. After every season ended, Aintree boarded a train and made his way across the country doing what he loved best: pretending to be someone he wasn't and swindling innocent people out of money.

Caught Looking Like a Dilly-Dob

Having never spent a day in grade school, Jim Purfidies nonetheless knew how to put two and two together when he spotted the perfect match between Base-Ball and gambling. A journeyman outfielder for the White-Leggings, Purfidies started laying down bets on games and figured out a way to skew the odds in his favor and clean up on earnings.

Purfidies was no novice in the art of fixing games. Before

he arrived in Milwaukee, Purfidies was a professional gambler who won a fortune and lost it all by the time he was twenty-six. Journeying west of the Mississippi to places like Dodge City, Abilene and Leadville, Purfidies played high-stakes games of faro in saloons, brothels and gambling halls and cheated his way to an incredible winning streak that lasted nearly two years. But he met his match one day when he went up against a crooked dealer with a rigged deck box who drained him of his money before he knew what hit him.

Burnt out and broke, Purfidies returned to his home town of Decatur and operated a gambling parlor before bottoming out as a shoe salesman, living in a boarding room with six other men.

With nothing to lose, Purfidies traveled to Milwaukee and tried out for the team, winning a spot as a back-up outfielder. He managed to hang on a couple of seasons despite getting very little playing time. During this time he witnessed the frenzy going on in the stands when Schnockerd allowed gambling for the Cranks.

While Schnockerd frowned down upon players who gambled on their own games, he didn't prohibit it. Purfidies snuck in bets between games, winning a fair amount of earnings.

Then it occurred to him that he could earn even more winnings if he bet his team to lose. Since the team was usually favored to win everyday, the odds were always on their side. This is when Purfidies came up with a bold idea. If he found a way to affect the outcome of games and precipitate a loss, he could win big. But how was he going to do that riding the bench nearly every single day?

The longer he thought about it, the more determined he was to find a way for them to go on a lengthy losing streak. A method of sabotage had to be found, something effective enough for him to lay some real money down and buck the odds.

Perhaps a series of unfortunate injuries to a few key players would do the trick. During batting practice, he let a bat slip out of his hands and watched it tumble in the air, crashing into a huddle of players. The thick piece of wood bounced off the head of Ned Blackburn, the team's leader in home runs. The bat splintered in two but Blackburn didn't go down. He only suffered a small knot on his head.

Purfidies tried the bat trick several more times but only managed to kill a dog sitting near the stands.

Then he tried another tactic by taking out Bill Mumfries and getting him drunk. Mumfries was the team's anchor at first base and one of their top bruisers. Purfidies hoped to get him so inebriated the night before that he'd be worthless the next day game. But Mumfries proved to have a wooden leg and outlasted Purfidies at the saloon.

Realizing the need to step up his efforts, he got a little more creative. On a hot, sticky day Purfidies spiked the water cooler with an entire bottle of Ol' Gran'mams Bowel Shootin' Slippery Syrup, an elixir to cure constipation. He hoped to send the entire team running off the field and to the lavatory, but all it did was make them play extra innings in soiled pants. None of them budged.

Then he found his linchpin in pitcher Al Dunlop.

Dunlop was the staff ace on the mound who had taken on a heavier pitching load when two other pitchers went down with injuries, forcing Dunlop to pitch nearly every day. Purfidies targeted the hard-throwing righty, hoping to incapacitate the team of any serviceable pitching.

After several attempts to maim Dunlop, Purfidies was beginning to run out of ideas. Then, like an Edison light bulb going on, an idea flashed in his head. This brainstorm led to the incident that became known, as recounted by the sportswriters down through the years, as the Trenchcoat Peep Show Farce.

Purfidies knew that Dunlop had a very deviant palette for big, buxom ladies and sought out their company every minute he was away from the mound, visiting brothels, nightclubs and burlesque theaters. He could not keep his eyes off voluptuous women with large breasts, thick hips and pretty smiles. Purfidies decided to exploit that.

On the day Dunlop was about to begin a crucial string of ten starts in a row, Purfidies walked into the clubhouse with a shapely damsel next to him.

"Hiya, Al. I want you to meet a friend of mine, Miss Lucy Dandridge."

Dunlop was sitting on a bench with his elbow in a tub of ice water, wearing nothing but a towel draped over his lap. He looked up at the blonde-haired beauty, tightly wrapped in a revealing corset dress. She towered over both men, wearing black high-heeled boots. Her lips were red and full. Her breasts were tightly packed and protruding.

Dunlop's mouth dropped.

She smiled and extended her elbow-length, black satin-gloved hands.

Dunlop lifted his arm out of the water and took her hand. His eyes glued to hers. He couldn't speak.

"Yeah, our lady here, Miss Dandridge, is a huge admirer of yours, ain't you darling? She just loves the game. I got her tickets for the next two weeks."

Her face gleamed and her eyelashes fluttered. Dunlop shook her hand nervously.

"In fact, I got her a spot right behind home plate, center-left. You won't miss her," Purfidies boasted.

Locked onto her eyes, Dunlop refused to let go of her hand. As she stepped back, he slid off the bench and stood up. His towel dropped to the floor.

"Oh, my!" Miss Lucy looked down and blushed.

Purfidies put down a hundred dollars for the White-Leggings to lose the first game.

After three innings, Dunlop had already given up six runs. He looked flustered and unfocused. Schnockerd, playing the role as the club's manager, finally called a time-out and walked up to the mound. "What the hell's wrong with you? You look like you got something other than the game on your mind."

"I'm fine. Just let me go about my business." Sweat was pouring off him.

Dunlop returned to his set position and looked into the catcher for the next pitch selection. His eyes wandered again into the stands behind home plate. Lucy sat there like a lustrous gem. She stood up and flashed her curvy features before Dunlop delivered his pitch.

The ball was supposed to be a slider in the dirt. Instead it was a meaty fastball with no life, straight down the middle of the plate. The ball was tagged and two more runs scored. The final score was 11-2.

Miss Lucy was back behind home plate the next day, accompanied with her friend Miss Molly. Dunlop gave up a grand slam in the top of the first, on his way to a 14-6 trouncing. The White-Leggings were on their first losing streak of the season, much to the delight of Purfidies, who began upping his bets.

Then came Miss Virginia, Gimlet Rose and Lady Jane. Suddenly the team was mired in a five-game losing streak behind the scuffling Dunlop.

Schnockerd was beside himself. They never lost five in a row before, especially at home. He took Dunlop to the side and asked him if he was hiding an injury. Dunlop refused to say anything was wrong with him. Schnockerd threatened to bench him and go with his emergency back-up pitcher if Dunlop didn't get his act together.

The next game, his command improved but they still trailed 5-3 late in the contest. A ball booted by Mumfries extended their losing streak to six.

Getting increasingly hot under the collar for a win, the team was about to unleash a torrent of brutality if they didn't notch a victory soon. Purfidies sensed their urgency and knew he had to escalate his efforts if he was going to meet his target of ten losses in a row.

By the eighth game, he had seven women dotted around the stands flaunting their full-figured bodies in front of the much-agitated Dunlop. By then he was a shaking mess, but the pitcher bravely hunkered down to keep the game in reach.

Luckily for Purfidies, the opposing pitcher was riding a hot streak and blanked the White-Leggings 2-0. But he knew he needed more than luck if he was going to get to the ten losses in a row and collect the big payout.

For the ninth game, Purfidies reached down in his bag of tricks and came up with another creative remedy. As soon as Dunlop stepped atop the mound and began his warmups, he saw Lucy Dandridge bundled in a trench coat. Surprisingly, no one but Dunlop seemed to notice the stunning, curvaceous lady wrapped in a heavy raincoat in the middle of the hot summer.

As the game progressed with the teams trading the lead, Lucy finally stood up and slowly unloosened her belt. Her trench coat opened slightly at the top, revealing bare skin. Dunlop quivered.

Inning by inning, pitch after pitch, Lucy opened her trench coat a little more until it was obvious she was wearing nothing underneath. Her milky skin gave way to her plump, well-rounded breasts.

Dunlop froze in astonishment. Waiting for the next pitch, the catcher, Ed Moynahan, jumped out of his crouch and jogged up to the mound.

"You okay? You look like a bolt of lightning's hit you."

Dunlop shook his head.

"Snap out of it, will 'ya," he told himself, "and let's get this guy."

It was too late. Dunlop was completely mesmerized. He immediately walked the next three batters before giving up a long grand slam. The White-Leggings were trailing once again.

Purfidies sat at the end of the bench and smiled. His plan was working and his big payoff was in sight.

But then Schnockerd, pacing up and down in front of the bench, hopped onto the field and hurried to the mound. "That's it, Al," he said. "I don't know what the hell's wrong with you. You're supposed to be our workhorse but you look like your head's just taken a leave of absence."

"Leave me in. I'm fine." He continued staring into the crowd. Miss Dandridge closed her trench coat and slinked back down to her planked seat.

"I'm putting in Bailey."

"Bailey? That kid's got nothin'."

"Probably more than what you got right now."

Schnockerd held out his hand for the ball. Dunlop kept staring into the crowd.

"What the hell are you looking at, Al? You got a screw loose or something?"

That was it for Dunlop. Schnockerd's emergency pitcher came in and gave up another five runs for another loss. The team now faced an unprecedented ten-game losing streak.

The next day Purfidies went all in. He bet his entire pile of winnings on the last game of the homestand and now had all seven girls cloaked in trench coats. He wasn't taking any chances.

Schnockerd threw out Bailey to start the game and he promptly gave up four runs. The White-Leggings answered back with three of their own but it was plain to see that Bailey had no business being out there. Dunlop stood next to Schnockerd and urged him to put him back in.

"Are you crazy? We need to win this damn game before an all-out riot erupts. Get your ass back on the pine." But Schnockerd watched Bailey wobble on the mound.

Finally, Schnockerd relented and agreed to let Dunlop pitch. "But you better give me your damned word that your head's on straight or I'm gonna feed you to the wolves."

"Don't worry," Dunlop said. "I got me a secret weapon."

The score was tied entering the fifth inning when Schnockerd put Dunlop back in. The ace climbed up the mound with his cap tucked tightly over his eyes, wearing a makeshift pair of pop bottle eyeglasses that allowed him to see the catcher's mitt and not much else.

By then the crowd was stirring, seething for a win just as much as the rest of the team. Purfidies sat in his usual spot on the bench, sweating out the last five innings of the game.

In a reversal of fortune, Dunlop threw one fireball after another. Every pitch shot past the flailing batters. He quickly set down the side.

Purfidies began chewing his fingernails.

The next inning, Lucy Dandridge stood up and began peeling off her trench coat. But Dunlop wasn't the least perturbed. He struck out the side again.

Reinforcements came in. As Dunlop kept his head down, firing bullets, the rest of the girls stood up, one by one, and opened the tops of their trench coats. Nothing happened.

Entering the ninth inning, Milwaukee eked out a one-run lead behind Dunlop's stellar performance. He needed three more outs to end the ten-game losing streak. He got a quick groundout and then got a first-call strike on the next batter.

Purfidies jumped off the bench and waved his arms at the girls in the stands.

All seven girls stood up at once and untied their belts. In unison, they tore open their trench coats and revealed their naked bodies to the entire playing field.

Strike two.

Their trench coats completely off, the girls finally caught the attention of the surrounding Cranks, sparking a near-riot. A giant brouhaha broke out.

The Milwaukee players on the field turned their heads and saw the girls completely bare and bouncing up and down. Suddenly, the game ceased to exist.

Yet Dunlop, with his eyeglasses on and totally focused,

delivered the pitch. At the same time, the catcher, Moynahan, stood up and turned to see what was happening behind him. The ball struck Moynahan in the back of his leg, cutting him to the ground.

As the ballpark rippled at the sight of the seven nude girls, the ball ricocheted down the foul line and the astute runners in scoring position ran for home. No one, except Dunlop, saw them score the winning runs.

The White-Leggings lost their tenth in a row and Purfidies won his final bet, raking in a giant bonanza.

Asked by a sportswriter about the farce a week later, an unsuspecting Purfidies shrugged his shoulders and went about his business in the clubhouse.

"Don't you find it a little suspicious that something like that happened in the midst of the club's longest losing streak?" the writer asked. "In a place where gambling is so prevalent?"

"Don't know what you're talking about." He began to undress from his street clothes.

"C'mon, Jim. We know you guys slip in bets from time to time. Just how far would you be willing to go to make sure you cash in on those bets?"

Purfidies straightened up and brought his arm up to unbutton his cuff. The sun streaked through the window and caught his newly purchased gold wristwatch. Its glare blinded the writer.

"You got me, pal."

Soaplock Stinger

At five-foot, one-inch, Hughie O'Hallarhan was a keg of dynamite. Pound for pound, he was the White-Leggings' toughest brawler with a lightning-quick temper he unleashed on foes and umpires alike. O'Hallarhan fought like others breathed. It wasn't a question if he liked to fight—it was a necessity.

The seventh child of an impoverished family of fifteen, the feisty O'Hallarhan had to scrap, claw and grapple for the most basic necessities just to survive. Always competing against his older brothers, Hughie developed a wicked combative streak with a trace of vindictiveness on top.

In his first and only year in school, the pint-sized O'Hallarhan picked fights with older kids twice his size and got expelled for biting off the ear of one student. Fifteen years later, O'Hallarhan encountered that same student in a hotel lobby, now a grown man well over six feet tall. O'Hallarhan promptly bit off his other ear.

The only thing that seemed to curb his explosive temper was his love for Base-Ball. Playing every day in sandlots and open fields, O'Hallarhan became a very good middle infielder with good hands and quick feet. As a hitter, he drew plenty of walks since his strike zone was so low to the ground. But his combustible fury inevitably re-surfaced during the oppressively long, hot summers and he tussled with anybody who dared come near him.

He bristled at the notion of anyone getting the best of him. If he thought he was being shown up, serious payback was in order. Whenever the opposing team celebrated on the field after a victory, O'Hallarhan watched them carefully for any over-exuberant fist pump or backslap. It was just a matter of time before his temper would explode, sending O'Hallarhan blasting off the bench, throwing punches, banging heads and gouging eyes.

Another thing O'Hallarhan didn't put up with was teammates

who didn't give their best effort each and every day. Each game should be played, he insisted, with the same exertion one would expend running through a brick wall. If he didn't see that from a player, a clash was inevitable.

By the time he was nineteen he already was on his fourth team. The Joliet club, as foul and obscene as they were, brought him on to play shortstop but soon grew tired of his manic behavior.

On a train trip coming back from Fort Wayne, O'Hallarhan railed against his Joliet teammates in the lounge car, accusing them of being a bunch of slouches. After trading barbs, punches were thrown and a free-for-all ensued. Someone grabbed a whiskey bottle and smashed it against the back of his head, knocking him out cold.

Fed up with his antics, they carried the unconscious infielder into the mail car, stuffed him in a canvas parcel bag and threw him off the speeding train.

O'Hallarhan finally found a home with Schnockerd's Milwaukee White-Leggings. There, he found a band of teammates who shared his impulsive tendencies. They fell in love with their runty shortstop, who packed a wallop and never backed down. He quickly became one of their chief enforcers on the team.

They could count on him to terrorize the opposing teams and back it up with a set of fists that never surrendered. He specialized in instigating all-out brawls and could be seen on top of piles battering and kicking his way through or at the bottom with his teeth sunk in someone's face.

It didn't take much to set him off. Once, during a game, an opposing runner slid safely at second base without a throw from Ed Moynahan. The runner bounced up off the bag and dusted himself off. "Gotta love this hard-brick playing surface. I'm bound to break something if you guys keep letting me steal bases."

That's all it took. Without saying a word, O'Hallarhan dropped his glove and lunged at the guiltless runner. O'Hallarhan dove and clamped his teeth down on the runner's crotch.

The victim let out a blood-curdling scream and tried to spin the infielder off his groin, but O'Hallarhan was like a rabid pit bull terrier locked onto a rope, swinging in the air.

His contempt for his opposition was exceeded only by his absolute hatred for umpires. To him, they were a paramount evil who were at the forefront of a conspiracy to humiliate and defeat him.

Up until then, umpires were seen primarily as arbiters for the integrity of the game, upholding the sacred virtues of Base-Ball, keepers of order and formality. By the time the game reached the Midwest, though, they were delegated to the inconspicuous role of calling games and staying clear of any controversy.

Once O'Hallarhan joined the White-Leggings, he started a personal campaign to malign all umpires, accusing them of being corrupt egomaniacs who craved nothing but power and authority.

O'Hallarhan missed no opportunity to confront, berate, harass, attack and threaten them. Anything the umpire did led to a dust-up. If a call went the other way, he would charge at poor man, shouting every known curse word, kicking dirt on his shoes, bumping the guy's body and spitting on his chest.

O'Hallarhan's foaming-at-the-mouth outbursts even caused his most ill-tempered teammates to titter behind their gloves. His theatrical displays of hostility and defiance against the umpires became the source of his enduring legacy.

One particular game, the umpire's call led O'Hallarhan to unleash a blow-out of epic proportions. It was late in the contest and O'Hallarhan was up to bat. The White-Leggings were trailing by a run with a man at third and two out. Already five-for-five, he knew he was going to drive in the tying run. He just had to get a good enough pitch.

The umpire, Larry "Shithouse" Digby, looked up at the sky and saw black, swirling clouds. All day long the rain held up, but now drops started to fall, dotting the infield dirt.

O'Hallarhan stepped up to the plate and waved his bat. "Hurry up, 'yuh bastard!" He yelled at the pitcher, anticipating knocking in the run before Digby called the game.

The pitcher rubbed the ball down in his hands, bent forward and received the catcher's signal. The raindrops grew bigger and more frequent—Plip, Plip, PLIP-PLIP-PLIP!

"C'mon, goddamnit!"

The first two pitches were high and outside. "You better not walk me, asshole!" O'Hallarhan shouted.

The pitcher snapped up the throw back from the catcher, spit out a line of saliva and stomped his shoe on the mound to get a better footing. The next pitch sailed off the edge of the plate.

"Strike!" Digby bellowed.

"What!" O'Hallarhan jerked his head back at Digby. "That ball was six inches off the plate, you moron!"

Digby hitched up his pant legs and squatted down, staring past the fuming little batter. O'Hallarhan gnashed his teeth and growled. "Just give me one pitch to hit! Just one, 'an I'll nail it!"

The raindrops then turned into one continuous drum roll. The next pitch roared past him shoulder-high.

"Strike two!"

"Sonofabitch!" O'Hallarhan shook his bat, ready to pounce on the umpire. "One more like that and this bat's gonna be so far up your ass—"

Digby glanced up at the sky before giving O'Hallarhan a dismissive look.

"—you smug, mother-grabbin', piece of—"

The pitcher wasted no time. He unleashed his next pitch and hit the outer edge again, the exact spot from two pitches ago.

"Strike three!" Digby lifted his arm up and called O'Hallarhan out.

"COCK-SUCKER!!"

Suddenly, the rain turned into a hard downpour. A deluge of water flooded the ballpark and stands. Everyone started to run for cover.

Digby waved his arms to signal the game was over and turned

his back. O'Hallarhan jumped in his way.

"You no-good, rotten motherfuckin'—"

O'Hallarhan grabbed his arm. Digby saw in his eyes a raging ferocity and flinched.

"—sack'a dog shit!"

O'Hallarhan broke. He took the knob-end of his bat and rammed it into the stomach of Digby, immediately fell to his knees. The pitcher and catcher from the opposing team jumped on O'Hallarhan, pulling him back and wrestling the bat out of his hands.

But O'Hallarhan did not give in. He began throwing punches in all directions, landing blows on both players. They clamped down on him even harder, ripping him away from Digby.

The rain turned into a squall. O'Hallarhan burst through his captives' arms, spewing venom, turning purple with rage. Two more players jumped in to subdue the raving lunatic.

All four players tried to pull him down but he kept coming, tearing his clothes apart. They finally smothered him, but he broke free again, this time completely bare except for his shoes and socks. Eyes burning fire, he went after Digby.

"Jesus Christ!" The umpire scrambled for the bat.

Before O'Hallarhan got to him, the four players jumped on him and lifted him off his feet. They hauled him away, naked, covered in mud, stubby legs kicking, screaming like a demonic monster.

Bodacious Pluck

Adversity was a constant companion in Larry "Shithouse" Digby's life, like a black dog trailing him down a path toward bad luck and misfortune. Before becoming an umpire, Digby was a slick-fielding third baseman who was on a clear path to stardom. But a series of unfortunate events derailed his playing career and Digby spent his prime years desperately trying to get back in the game in any way possible.

As a player, he was a manager's dream, capable of doing anything on the field. He smoked line drives to the outfield all day long with a simple, easy batting stroke. He ran the bags with a compact efficiency and always took the extra base without a contested throw. At third, he threw bullets across the diamond and hit the fielder's glove with pinpoint accuracy.

But then his momentum as a rising star came to a screeching halt.

Riding the fortunes of a tremendous year, playing for his hometown of Cincinnati, Digby fouled off a ball right into his face, breaking his eye socket. He missed the remainder of the season.

The next year, the hungry Digby looked to bounce back in a big way. But ten games into the season he came down with tuberculosis and was bedridden for the next year and a half.

Undaunted, he nursed himself back to full health and donned his uniform once again. But by then Cincinnati had moved on without Digby, recruiting a hotshot youngster to take his place. For the first time, he was without a position and out of a job.

Scrambling, he landed a spot on the Cleveland roster and set out to prove he still had the talent and skills to be a superb player. But on his way to the ballpark, Digby was caught in the middle of a botched bank robbery and a stray bullet struck him in the ass. He was laid up for another eight weeks. When he returned, he fell into a horrible slump and spent the rest of the season trying to get out of it. The day after the season ended, Cleveland cut him from the team.

The next spring, Digby tried out with several clubs, finally winning a position with Pittsburgh. But the black dog caught up with him. One morning, while walking down Penn Avenue, a safe fell three stories and broke sixty-three bones.

The next year, he won a spot with Kalamazoo and started the season on a strong note, having gone ten-for-twenty and flashing some leather at third. But when he dug in for another at-bat, a thundercloud rolled in and a bolt of lightning struck him down right at home plate.

Charred, ravaged by illness, his bones brittle, Digby tried one more comeback but it was too late. By the age of thirty-two, his eyesight was bad, he couldn't run anymore and he couldn't bend down to field a ball without breaking in two. Digby's playing days were over.

Desperate to stay in the game, he tried his hand managing a small-town club but after one year they folded and he was out again looking for a job.

Then, in a stroke of bizarre luck, Digby was offered a job as an umpire. Having the reputation as a level-headed and an astute student of the game, Digby had the right attributes for being a fine game official. Without other options for getting back in the game, he accepted the offer. It was a seamless transition.

By then the perceptions of umpires had changed, thanks largely to players like O'Hallarhan. Once revered, umpires had become a despised enemy around the leagues.

Digby faced death threats, players with their blood up, prickly managers and inflamed crowds on a daily basis. But he plowed ahead and endured the rising storm of hate and hostility.

His biggest challenge came whenever he visited Milwaukee, the hornet's nest of animus and antagonism. Around the ballpark, Schnockerd allowed dummies to hang with nooses around their necks. Cranks brought in pitchforks and torches. Players stuffed their mouths with extra tobacco so they could generate ample saliva to spit at him.

From the very first pitch, Digby became the prime target for abuse from the players and the stands. O'Hallarhan usually broke out in a fit of rage before the second inning and a rain of debris fell from the stands, from food and rocks to old shoes and chairs.

The situation became so perilous that Digby constructed a three-sided wooden hovel behind home plate just to protect himself. Inside, he called balls and strikes and officiated the game. This unusual setup earned him the nickname, "Shithouse."

For the next twenty-five years, Digby endured the hazards of his job, never knuckling under to the constant barrage of cruelty. A writer once asked him why he never caved in to the adversity and he gave the same reply he'd given for years. "That old black dog, I shot that damned thing right square in the head a long time ago."

The door to the executive suite of the Pfister Hotel slams open and Pete Schnockerd enters the room with a twelve-dollar cigar stuffed in the corner of his mouth. Niedler, hunched over a desk, scribbling notes, jumps in his seat. On each side of the desk, Sterne's associates, in their high collars and pince-nez spectacles, cling to their briefcases.

"Mister Schnockerd, I presume?"

"You got it, bud. Are you Niederman?"

"Niedler. H.H. Niedler. It's a pleasure to finally meet you. Do you know how hard it's been to track you down? You're a slippery one." He extends his hand.

Schnockerd snatches it and shakes it so hard that Niedler's

entire upper body wobbles. "Call me Pete. Glad to meet 'ya. Can't say I've been dying to sit down with you New York fellas. Been busy doing my thing."

Niedler pulls his hand back and grabs his shoulder. "Yes, you've been doing quite a bit of that lately. I'm glad you finally agreed to meet with us, and none too soon. Though it took a little extra, shall we say, persuasion?"

"Yeah, thanks for the 4 a.m. knock on my door and the gifts of appreciation. Well done. Who are the bookends?"

"Please allow me introduce to you the Governor's personal counselors. This is Mister—"

"Hey!" Schnockerd points to their briefcases. "Nice satchels you two guys got there. By the way you're holding onto them, I'd say you fellas got a pretty good stash of money tucked in there."

The men stare, stone-faced, at the chirpy visitor.

Niedler continues. "We were just about finished preparing our indictment—"

"You guys can do a lot here in Milwaukee with that kind of dough. What are you up for? Wagering? Boozing? Women? Wink-wink!" He nudges Niedler with his elbow.

The silent men grimace.

"I assure you, Mister Schnockerd, these gentlemen are not here looking for a good time."

"Gee, that's too bad. But if you change your mind, just look me up. You guys like keno?"

They don't say anything.

"What's wrong with these two? I think their stiff collars are choking off the bloodstream to their heads."

"You can say they keep their emotions in check during a serious matter of punishment or termination."

"What's that?"

"Punishment, sir. We've been trying for months to corral you and mete out a suitable penalty on all the wrongdoings you've perpetrated. You've been a very naughty boy, I'm afraid."

Schnockerd inhales a hefty portion of his cigar and blows it out of the corner of his mouth. "What are you, some kind of cop or dick?"

The smoke blinds Niedler and induces a coughing fit. He takes a minute to gather himself. "The Governor pays enormous attention to the affairs of his game, with a keen eye for any wrongdoings."

"Who?"

"The Governor, J.B. Sterne."

"Sterne? Is he here?"

"No. He is back in New York patiently waiting on the outcome of this meeting. He has a great deal of interest in the severity of the charges we are about to press against you. Do you know how much stress you have inflicted on our office back East?"

"Nah."

Niedler shifts his eyes on the seated men, then back on Schnockerd. "Why don't you have a seat, Mister Schnockerd? There seems to be a lot to talk about. Apparently you didn't get our correspondence."

"Oh, I got them, all right. Pretty snippy letters from you guys, Neat-ler."

"Niedler."

"Right. Accusing me of destroying the integrity of the game and whatnot. As if I just set fire to the whole Roman Empire or something."

"Mister Sterne has a vested interest in the game, more so than anybody else, and you've become a direct threat to his investment. He'll do anything in his power to protect that investment."

"What's he gonna do, fire me?"

"Without question, Mister Schnockerd. Your list of exploits is extraordinary. Almost all of them are direct violations of the rules of engagement defined in our rulebook and all are subject to your immediate dismissal."

Schnockerd laughs. "Yeah, I got nearly half the clubs in the Midwest making more money than any of your highfalutin ninnies back home and you call it a crime."

One of the counselors pulls out a bound volume from his briefcase and hands it to Niedler. "We've got a hundred and fifty-seven pages of detailed information explaining all the rules you've broken. It's all here, fully laid out."

"Rules? What rules?"

"The rules you were supposed to abide by when you took over the Milwaukee club. Not only have you broken most of them, you've even exceeded our most wild imaginations. Congratulations."

"The only rule I've abided by is the only one that matters and that's making money. And I gotta hand it to myself, it's gone pretty good. Even your boss back East should appreciate that."

Niedler hands Schnockerd the volume. He eases into a chair, puts his feet up on the desk, and flips through the pages.

"The Governor abhors compromising the sanctity of the game in exchange for profiteering. You may have found a moneymaking formula but it's come at the expense of the purity of the game, the principles that the game was founded upon."

"Boo-hoo."

"Mister Schnockerd?"

"I don't see anybody out here complaining about the 'purity' of anything. I'm providing a product that people love, business is booming and my boys are stirring up a shitstorm. Everyone's having fun and the money's pouring in. What more could you want?" He blows out a line of smoke.

"I don't think you've grasped the severity of the damage you've inflicted upon this sport. You've created an air of devilry and lawlessness. This game was founded upon a strict set of rules and behavior each member of this fraternity had to comply with. You've totally ignored these rules. You're a miscreant."

"Here's one," Schnockerd points his finger on a page. "No participant may alter, modify or convert the playing field in order to gain a competitive advantage. On June 19th, the Milwaukee owner was accused of sneaking a herd of cattle onto the grounds of the Kansas City ballpark the previous night in order to damage the field and provoke a forfeiture from the home club." Schnockerd laughs. "That one was a doozy! The shit in some places was nine inches thick!"

"That's the sort of thing that is completely intolerable—"

"But they didn't forfeit. Those crazed bastards went ahead with the game and played in the cow shit. And then it rained!"

"Yes, well, the charges stand. And dozens of others."

"Yeah," Schnockerd leans his head back and pulls out his cigar between two fingers. "I'm all for playing the game but we all want to win. Your boss has got to appreciate that."

"You once diverted a local canal with sandbags and flooded an entire ballpark."

"Not one of my better moves. I didn't know the canal was a dumping area for a tannery. The stench!"

"You've caused irreparable harm to this institution."

"Really? Ask any one of those Cranks that have come pouring into those ballparks. I betcha' they have a different perspective."

"The virtues of the game—well-defined rules, honorable conduct from its players, respect and courtesy—have to be preserved at all costs. You've allowed insolence to sully these standards through fighting, cheating and gambling. They have to be eliminated."

"And whaddy'a get without it? A bunch of pansies running around chasing a ball. Where's the fun in that?"

"It's not about fun, Mister Schnockerd. It's about preserving integrity. There is no room in this sport for the improprieties you've permitted to seep into the Governor's game."

"*His* game? What is this guy, a king or something? He doesn't own this game any more than you and I do."

"No one's been more responsible for its inception and growth more than he."

"Give me more time. I'm working on it."

"No you won't."

Schnockerd blows out another line of smoke. "Stop me."

"We intend to do that."

"How're you gonna stop a train going seventy-miles an hour? I've got the momentum."

"Yes, but you see, Mister Schnockerd, we own the tracks. We can derail you at any time. We just need to find the best tactic."

"I ain't no pushover, Niedlebaum. I intend to be in this thing for the duration and reap in the bucks just like the next guy. I'm in it for the big haul."

"Everyone has a price and a weakness. We'll find it."

"Try me."

"Or we may already have found it. All league owners must sign an agreement to comply with our rules or face removal." Niedler glances at the stacks of paper on the desk.

Schnockerd stares at him. "You ain't got my signature and you know it. That's Slippery Pete for 'ya!"

Niedler glances at both counselors. His mouth twitches. "Rest assured you're going to have one hell of a fight on your hands."

"I think I can take it. I love a good fight."

"He won't back down until you're beaten, humiliated and possibly in the ground. Is that the kind of fight you want?"

Schnockerd stands up. "Sounds like fun. Count me in."

"He'll throw everything he has at you. He's got the resources to do it. Trust me."

"I guess I'm too damned dumb and stubborn to back down."

"You'll regret it. This game is something beyond just a typical asset for him. It's his legacy. He'll engage an entire legal army against you to bring you down just to protect it."

"Not if I get to him first."

"Others have gone up against him and lost everything. Men with more means and power than you. You'll just be another fly on the table. You won't get the best of him."

Schnockerd stamps out his cigar in an ashtray on the desk and grins. "Care to wager on that?"

Rhubarb

Everyone hated Sorley McGrady.

McGrady was regarded as the meanest, most sadistic son of a bitch to ever play the game. From rival clubs and managers to umpires and spectators, everyone detested him for possessing such a callous disposition and apparent contempt for any sense of restraint. Even his home crowd of Milwaukee, well-known for its admiration of goonery, wished him ill.

While there was no lack of foul-tempered players around the leagues, especially in the Frontier League, any acts of violence were confined strictly between the foul lines. McGrady changed all that when he ignored any boundaries and attacked anyone who crossed his path, on and off the field.

On good days his brusque temperament surfaced with just a grunt and a dirty look. But most of the time he exuded a sinister expression that can only be described as evil and inflicted such cold, calculated bodily harm that many thought him to be a genuine psychopath.

He stuck razor blades on the bottoms of his soles and dove feet first on steals, hoping to slash the infielder's jugular. He hid a set of brass knuckles in his glove and cracked the ribs of the opposing runners rounding the bases. He menaced everyone with his bat, his weapon of choice. He was said to carry a loaded revolver stuffed in the back of his uniform.

Going too far was in his blood. Once, after getting buzzed inside with a fastball, McGrady warned the pitcher that he was skating on thin ice. Unfortunately for the pitcher, the next fastball got away from him and sailed above McGrady's head. After picking himself up off the ground, McGrady tore off after him with his bat in his hand.

In a display of extreme brutality that sickened even the most hardened Cranks in the stands and his teammates on the field, McGrady chased down the pitcher and leveled several blows to his head, splitting it open. A burst of blood shot out. By the time the infielders ripped McGrady away, the pitcher's eyes were swollen shut, indentation marks riddled his deformed face and head, and blood oozed out of every orifice.

Soon the crowds voiced their displeasure over his bloodthirstiness. It was one thing to root for general roughhousing and brawling—broken knuckles and bloodied noses—but it was another to beat a man to within one breath from dying. Every time he stepped onto the field, fans showered him with boos and jeers. Instead of ignoring them, he inflamed their outrage by antagonizing them, taunting them, responding with his own venom. Games were often delayed because he climbed into the stands to spar with the patrons.

On the road, and even at home, McGrady was harassed by a constant barrage of vitriolic slurs. During a game when tensions were riding high, a heckler laid into McGrady for seven straight innings. In the eighth, the man finally stopped and left the game with his family. McGrady, sitting on the bench, pulled out his bat and slipped out of the ballpark.

He followed the man down the street and finally cornered him in an alley where he almost beat the man to death in front of his wife and young child. Leaving him unconscious and barely breathing, McGrady went back to the park and finished the game with another hit and stolen base.

But McGrady was not just another typical red-assed player with a severe violent streak. He also happened to be one of the game's most prolific hitters. McGrady was a hitting machine who smacked more singles and doubles than anybody else. His contact rates were off the charts, sometimes going an entire week before recording an out. It was common for him to go four-for-four in a game, or three-for-three with a couple of walks. He never struck out more than a dozen times over the stretch of a season.

His legs were just as potent as his bat, leading all Midwest leagues in steals for seven straight years. McGrady perfected the art of swiping bags, taking extra leads and evading tags. Oftentimes, however, the opposing team would simply let him take the extra base without a challenge for fear of risking a serious injury. They didn't want a punch in the groin from his brass knuckles or laceration from his blades.

Because he was such a dominant player—combining a superior skill set with the mastery of intimidation—McGrady won many games almost single-handedly and developed a love/hate relationship with Milwaukee's Cranks, despite being such a deplorable character.

In what can be considered one of the greatest individual performances in a game, McGrady snatched victory from the hands of one of Milwaukee's foes, the St. Louis Lamplighters, without a single act of violence.

St. Louis' pitcher, Fluke Wilcox, was a formidable force on the mound with a bag of tricks that shut down his opponents and kept him in games. The only trouble was he couldn't keep McGrady off the bases.

In the top of the first, Wilcox walked McGrady, who quickly

stole second, then third. McGrady took a few extra steps and then tore off for home. A startled Wilcox bungled the ball before throwing it to the plate. Instead of his usual feet-first slide, McGrady dove head first and snuck his hand in over the plate.

In the third inning, McGrady hit an inside-the-park home run. He slapped the ball down the third-base line and it skipped all the way down past the left fielder. McGrady burned past the first two bases and kicked into another gear when he spotted the fielder lofting the ball back to the infield. He touched the plate on a sprint before the catcher received the ball.

In the fifth and sixth innings, McGrady reached base again and scored both times on a hit and run. Despite McGrady's feats, Wilcox hunkered down and kept the rest of the White-Leggings from breaking the game open.

In the ninth, St. Louis mustered enough runs to take the lead; but with two out Wilcox walked McGrady. Bill Mumfries was next to bat, not having hit the ball past the mound during his previous at-bats.

Pete Schnockerd stepped forward and flashed a signal to McGrady and Mumfries. Something was going down. Was it another hit and run? A straight steal? Deke Clemmons, St. Louis' manager, yelled out to his team to keep on eye on McGrady while he encouraged Wilcox to go after Mumfries.

Wilcox fired the ball to home plate. Mumfries swung and missed. The catcher snapped a throw to first and almost caught McGrady too far off the bag. The next pitch was a blazing fastball and Mumfries missed again.

"Get him, Fluke! You got two strikes on him, don't worry about that runner on first!" Clemmons barked. But it was impossible not to keep his eyes off McGrady, dancing two or three steps off the bag and slapping his hands.

Wilcox was about to get in his wind-up when Schnockerd stepped back on the field and called time out. The entire ballpark watched him walk slowly across the diamond toward first base, taking tiny, deliberate steps.

"What's going on out here?" Clemmons shouted. "What are you up to, Pete?"

Finally, Schnockerd reached McGrady and stood beside him. He cupped his hand against McGrady's ear and leaned in. Then he drew back.

"What'd he say?"

Schnockerd then turned around and walked back to the bench the same way he came, taking his sweet time to cross the diamond.

The entire ballpark now had their eyes on McGrady.

"Don't worry about that guy. Pay attention to that batter. All you need is one more strike!" Clemmons shouted. Wilcox stared at McGrady for several seconds before he went back to his wind-up. Once he started his motion, McGrady took off for second.

"He's going!" The entire infield shouted in unison.

Mumfries hacked at the ball and popped it up, but no one seemed to notice — everyone watched McGrady instead. Clemmons jumped up and down. "The ball! Someone catch the goddamned ball!"

The ball hung up in the air and drifted past the infield into shallow center. Finally, the defenders looked up and saw it come down. The shortstop, second baseman and centerfielder broke for the ball and converged upon each other. Still keeping their eyes on McGrady, they collided and the ball dropped innocently in between them.

McGrady tore around the bases and sailed home. The game was tied.

Schnockerd gave a belly laugh. Someone asked him, "What did you say to McGrady?"

He grinned and crossed his arms. "Nothin'. Nothin' at all," he beamed. "But that was enough to scare the shit out of them, won't ya say?"

But the game was not over. It went into extra innings and stayed tied into the sixteenth inning. By then Wilcox had run out of steam. The last batter he faced was McGrady and he walked him on four pitches.

Clemmons had seen enough. He yanked Wilcox and replaced with his back-up reserve, a pudgy, soft-skinned rookie by the name of Wilbert Smithers. It was a mistake.

As soon as Smithers began his warm-ups on the mound, McGrady engaged in a dreadful act of terror, locking his eyes onto the knock-kneed, baby-faced milksop and intimidating him into submission.

Smithers froze as soon as his eyes met McGrady's, as if he were seeing pure evil for the first time. His jaw dropped and his shoulders sank as McGrady tore his soul out through his eye sockets.

Clemmons jumped up. "For chrissakes, Smithers, don't look into his eyes! Throw the goddamned ball!"

But Smithers couldn't do anything. He stood there petrified, unable to look away. McGrady nodded at him before tearing off for second base without a throw.

The second baseman walked up to the mound and tried to snap Smithers out of his trance, but as soon as he walked back to his position McGrady trotted to third base uncontested.

Both Clemmons and the crowd erupted. The rest of the infielders started yelling at Smithers, but McGrady's and Smithers' eyes remained locked. Amid the firestorm, McGrady kept him hypnotized. He nodded at Smithers and Smithers nodded back. Then he walked toward home plate.

"What're you doing! Get that bastard!"

The infielders raced to the mound to pry the ball out of Smithers' hands but it was too late. McGrady crossed the plate, scoring the winning run.

But all was not grandeur and glory for the contentious McGrady.

Late one season the White-Leggings were on the verge of having the best record in the Frontier League, aided by an unprecedented forty-five game hitting streak by McGrady. The ballpark was a cauldron of fervor—booing and cursing McGrady every time he walked up to the plate and cheering manically every time the White-Leggings scored. Even though he was most responsible for the team's success, they could not suppress their growing hatred of him. So they blasted him and hailed the team's success at the same time.

One afternoon, late in a game when the sun was setting below the tops of the stands, McGrady walked up for his final at-bat seeking his first hit in the contest. Having flown out twice and grounded out, all he needed to do was find a hole in the infield or hit a blooper and the hitting streak would be extended.

As soon as he stepped into the box, however, a man jumped out of the stands with a rifle and shot McGrady twice in the midsection. The shots echoed in the ballpark and McGrady dropped down on top of home plate. Chaos erupted. People in the stands ran in all directions. Everyone on the field scattered. Players on the Milwaukee bench jumped on the man with the rifle.

A crowd gathered around the plate. A giant circle formed to see if McGrady was dead. Some cried. Others cheered.

After several minutes, McGrady's body was lifted up onto the crowd's shoulders. Blood gushed from his torso and drenched his uniform. They carried him all the way to the local hospital. Surgeons managed to remove one slug but the other was lodged deep between his spleen and lung.

Despite his trauma, McGrady lived to see another day and came back to play the next season with the slug intact.

Everything was back to normal. He began another hitting streak and the ballpark patrons returned to their ways, pummeling the vastly talented and churlish player. McGrady stepped into the box among a deafening throng of boos and screams, waved his middle finger at the entire ballpark, and proceeded to smack a double in the gap.

Niedler sinks into the leather sofa and exhales a faint whisper of breath.

"A refreshment, sir?" Sterne's attendant stands over him.

"Yes, I would like some ginger water with a slice of mango."

"Yes, sir."

"And ice. Plenty of ice."

"Yes, sir."

"And Granville, please pour it in an extra-tall glass so I don't have to bend my head so."

"Yes sir."

Niedler's shirt collar is unbuttoned. Dark circles appear under his eyes. A slight trace of whiskers blooms on his cheeks and chin.

"I am so tired. Nearly two weeks of non-stop travel's done me in. That train throttled me about, I felt like a china doll in the back of a prairie schooner."

Sterne sits across from him, bent over a pile of paperwork. He flips off his reading glasses. "Your stamina's not what it used to be, eh Henry?"

"Six cities in ten days. More than two-thousand miles logged. It would have been nice if I were still riding in the *General Stockton* instead of a conventional passenger train. That berth nearly killed me!"

"Yes, a shame isn't it?"

"And not one decent cup of tea anywhere along the way."

"Tsk, tsk."

Niedler raises his head. "Are you mocking me?"

"I would never dream of such a thing, especially in light of your efforts."

Niedler settles back.

"Then again, what have you got to show for it?"

He raises his head again. "Depends on who or what you are talking about."

"I'm not talking about our drunken, mistaken friend from Chicago. You took care of that. Who else should I be talking about?"

Niedler knows exactly who he is talking about. "Just give me more time and I'll figure out a plan."

"I don't have time, Henry. Your failure to cap that barrel is costing us dear. Instead of getting him to capitulate, you've let him continue to run amok and now I can't wait on you anymore. I already got the gears in motion to stop him, once and for all."

"Behind that slow, dim-witted façade of his hides a sly fox with a lot of ambition. Proceed with caution."

"I have always been cautious, but now I've lost my patience. I've got my team downstairs implementing a double-front assault to finally do him in."

"What are you going to do?"

"Since the threat of disciplinary action and removal have failed, I'm going to do the next thing. I'm going to ruin that fat bastard."

Niedler sits up, his curiosity piqued. " A double front?"

"I'm going to choke off his money supply, then completely isolate him from the game. He'll have nowhere to go. He'll die on the vine like a like a withered grape."

"What money supply?"

"His family's business, the brewery. If I can't buy them out directly, I'll cut off their distribution network. And if that doesn't succeed—"

"But his father cut him out of having anything to do with the business. Why would you go after them?"

"—I'll go all out and start a lobbying effort for the prohibition of all alcoholic drinks. I've got friends in the temperance movement. We'll wipe out the entire industry."

"Sounds pretty extreme, even for you."

"If that's the price I have to pay to destroy that son of a bitch."

"What's the other front?"

"I'll take back the owners he's seduced. I'll buy them all out in one fell swoop. Their loyalties have been questioned ever since they began brushing us off. We'll remind them who really has the power in all this."

"That may take quite a bit of persuasion or force. Many of them have seen their profits double over the past year."

"There's nothing like a good, old-fashioned corporate takeover to scare the wits out of all the moles and rats, just like the old days when we cornered markets and devoured entire industries."

"But it's your industry you're devouring. You're eating your own foot."

"I'm just taking back what's mine. Either way, that potbellied lout is going to lose everything after I'm done with him."

"That's a pretty expensive and time-consuming endeavor, all for one lout."

"You're the one who's left me no choice, Henry. Your utter failure to terminate that corpulent fraudster has led me to take drastic steps to protect my game."

Someone knocks on the door.

"Come in, Granville."

The door opens and a deliveryman enters. "Special delivery."

"Excuse me, who are you?"

Without a word, he starts to squeeze something through the doorway, a monstrosity of an object.

"What the hell is this?"

The deliveryman wheels in a giant cake, triple-tiered with sparklers on top. He hands Sterne a clipboard. "Sign here."

Sterne and Niedler are appalled at the sight. On the side of the cake is a large, bulbous face, winking and grinning.

"What is the meaning of this? Granville, where are you!"

Suddenly, the top of the cake pops open and a burst of confetti shoots out. A woman, scantily dressed in a skin-tight outfit, jumps out and lands on the floor.

"A cake wench?" Niedler observes.

"Which one of you is the Governor?"

Niedler looks at Sterne.

"I have a message to give to you." She throws herself onto Sterne, wraps her arms around him, and plants a kiss on his lips.

Sterne throws her off. "Get off me, you trollop! What is the meaning of this nonsense? I demand an explanation. Granville!"

She then throws her arms up in the air and begins a song and dance routine.

"I've come all this way to say, 'How 'ya do?'
And give you this kiss as a mere 'Thank You,'
But please, Guv'nur, don't be mistaken
These bouncin' boobs ain't for your takin'
The cake's all yours, so please, stuff your face
Eat it all up but leave a lil' space
'Cuz the real treat's just a peek inside
Guaranteed to bruise your haughty pride
When I get my hands on your game
You'll be cursing my name
But please, sir, don't go throwin' a fit
Wait til I get done messin' with it!"

Sterne and Niedler look at each other.

Then another figure pops out of the cake, a man in a bow tie and vest, carrying a folio case. He climbs down and dusts himself off. "The things I get myself into!" He huffs.

"Who the devil are you?"

He squints through his wire-framed spectacles. "J. Barron Sterne? It really is you. I know who you are!" The man begins to unzip his case.

Sterne snatches the case and swings it to Niedler, then grabs the man by his collar. "I asked you a question, boy. What in the name of God is this thing doing in my office, with a harlot and a mouse like you doing inside it?"

The man is thunderstruck. "They told me I was going to your office but I didn't believe them. But it really is you in the flesh.

The greatest of all Captains of Industry, the Business Oligarch himself, the King of Capitalism!"

"Answer my question!"

"He's serving us." Niedler says, looking at the papers from the man's case.

"What?"

"We're being sued."

"Who?" Sterne burns a hole into the man with his glare.

"Don't know his name," the man confesses, "but he contacted us through our Chicago office. Some big shot from Milwaukee with a lot of money. And he's got a bunch of attorneys behind him. High-priced ones."

"He's challenging our claim of proprietorship over the game."

"That swine is challenging whether or not I hold dominion over the game that I single-handedly pioneered, nurtured and introduced to the world? Through my own inspiration, sweat and toil? The balls on him!"

Niedler flips through the papers. "Not only that, but he's motioning to form his own separate league without us having anything to do with it."

"He can't do that. I'll ruin him first. I'll strip him of everything's he's got! There won't be a club five hundred miles in his reach to employ. I'll buy all of them out!"

"Looks like he's beaten you at your own game."

"What!"

"He's already got the signatures of most of the owners from Pittsburgh all the way to Kansas City. They're a syndicate. They're going to call themselves 'The National Frontier League of Base-Ball Players.'"

The room goes silent and all eyes fix on Sterne, anticipating a furious response.

But nothing happens.

Taciturn, he straightens himself, adjusts his tie and walks out the office with his arms down and his chin jutting upward. ∎

Arthur J.
CHILLICOTHE
&CO.
CHICAGO, IL
U.S. PATENT
NO. 40134
A HEALTHY BLEND IN EVERY SPOONFUL
DELICIOUS!
Paddy Duggins - BaseBall Player
PRACTICAL GOODNESS &
EASILY DIGESTABLE.
SAVORY FLAVOR FOR ALL
YOUR COOKING NEEDS
PURE
LARD
C
OPEN KETTLE RENDERED. KEEP IN A COOL STORAGE PLACE

VIII.

STRETCH TIME
(1882-1887)

Duck Snorts & Greasy Doorknobs

No one had more fun at the old ballpark than Paddy Duggins. Cranks dubbed the portly outfielder The Jolly Joker of Base-Ball for good reason. He treated the game more like a vaudeville extravaganza than an actual competitive sport and folks in the stands delighted at his whimsical antics.

Duggins subscribed to the adage that entertainment trumped everything else and went straight for the cheap laugh by constantly making fun of himself and delighting the crowds packing the parks. He quickly became a top drawing card on his way to becoming a folkloric character who loved making hordes of people bust out laughing.

The unlikeliest of athletes, Duggins patrolled right field with a body more suited for the comic stage than the outfield. He constantly dropped balls and fell short of catches. But the crowd forgave him as long as he shrugged his shoulders and gave an "Oops!" gesture.

He cared less about the ball than he did of making a total idiot of himself. He bounced off the grass like a hippo flopping its giant mass into a bed of mud. He rammed himself through the walls of the stands like a rampaging elephant.

The crowd ate it up. A constant showman, Duggins always played up to them. He frolicked about in front of thousands, tipping his cap to waves of adoration.

However, Duggins was a powerful force with the bat. He always put his weight behind every swing and belted balls as far as the eye could see. Each blast could easily have been a home run except for the fact that Duggins couldn't run a lick. With his heavy girth and unusually tiny feet, he couldn't make it past second base before the ball made it back to the infield. Sometimes he tried to stretch it to third but fell woefully short, getting tagged out after stumbling to the dirt ten feet in front of the bag.

Everyone wanted to see the stout, paunchy Duggins finally succeed at a round-tripper and he lobbied the club owner to do something about it. In a creative solution that had far-reaching implications, a wall was erected in the outfield that stretched from foul-line to foul-line and a rule made that any ball hit over it was an automatic four-base hit. Bleacher stands were built behind the fence for more spectators.

The suspense of getting thrown out now eliminated, Duggins smashed home runs and slowly trotted around the bases. With his belly bouncing and his little feet dancing, he doffed his cap and waved it to the screaming spectators. His home run trots were always pretentious spectacles.

Never lacking the ability to amuse, Duggins did everything he could to go over the top. He sponsored eating contests before games, downing pies and hot dogs in a vomitous display of gluttony. He ran out to the field dressed in all sorts of costumes, for shock value. His favorite was dressing up like Falstaff and cavorting merrily about like the Shakespearean character. During rain delays, he would prance around the infield in nothing but his undergarments, slopping around in the mud like a pig, just to entertain the Cranks.

Duggins was well known for his hilarious pranks. Stunts involving his teammates, his opponents and even people in the stands became legendary. Even the much-maligned umpires became a target of Duggins' escapades, who were often on the receiving end of a bucket of water or pie thrown at their faces.

But Duggins went too far one day when he tried to give one of his teammates a hotfoot in the clubhouse and instead sent the entire ballpark up in flames. Luckily, no one was killed but the incident caused Duggins to slide into a crippling depression that he never recovered from, costing him his playing career.

The last time anyone ever heard of the plump mischief-maker, he planned to kill himself by eating himself to death. Duggins, who once entertained hundreds of thousands with his wacky pratfalls and feats of overwhelming power, had ballooned up to an enormous size and became a mound of blubber, permanently fixed to his bed and unable to squeeze through the doorway.

Melancholy Opine

Herman Nudbertiwald "Creepy" Crowley was one hell of an enigma, a man capable of exhibiting the most unpredictable, bizarre behavior seen in a grown man yet clever enough to fire a complete game shutout against some of the league's best hitters, making them look like fools.

During a five-year span, Crowley was one of the game's best pitchers, if not the best, baffling hitters with a top-of-the-line arsenal of pitches and a breaking ball slider that was virtually unhittable. A savant on the mound, Crowley knew exactly what pitch to throw and how to throw it in order to rack up outs and hang zeroes across the scoreboard.

However, as much time he spent being a pitching genius, he spent the remainder of his time being a complete screwball. Crowley was cuckoo. Nuts.

Competing against his identity as a sharp, crafty big league pitcher was a detached, child-like persona that bordered on psychosis and always led to bizarre antics and an eccentric demeanor on and off the field. This made for an interesting juxtaposition.

Crowley could set down five men in a row on strikeouts, each of them flailing away helplessly on his wipeout slider, and then spend the next ten minutes walking around the mound talking to himself, to the ball, or to an imaginary person next to him, laughing and engaging in real conversation. Then, as if nothing had happened, he'd get back on the mound and continue dominating the hitters.

He became infamous for his abrupt delays during games. One day, after zipping through the first five innings, Crowley suddenly walked off the mound and sauntered down the right field foul line, gazing into the stands. He stopped in front of a young woman sitting in the front row and began admiring the lady's charm bracelet, halting the game for fifteen minutes until a teammate convinced him to get back on the mound.

Crowley's combination of pitching prowess and unpredictability made him a crowd favorite. Every time he was scheduled to pitch, the ballparks would overflow with spectators trying to catch a glimpse of the pitcher and see whether he'd throw a shutout or go off the deep end.

One time, in front of a record-breaking crowd, Crowley dispatched eighteen of the first nineteen batters he faced. Then, before the twentieth batter stepped in the box, he plunked himself down on the mound, pulled out a dime novel, and began immersing himself in the book while twenty thousand Cranks screamed and hollered for a half an hour.

Crowley's managers were tolerant of his eccentricities, willing to see him cluck like a chicken or prattle about like a deranged lunatic, just as long as he provided them with a gem of a pitching performance and a win stuffed in their back pocket. But that became a risky proposition.

Sometimes Crowley would not show up at the park for a week and the manager would finally have to hunt him down at his apartment. Holed up behind the locked door, the manager would spend hours trying to cajole his prized pitcher just to open the door.

His behavior kept his teammates off-balance. They didn't know what they'd get out of him from day to day. One morning, Crowley would walk in the clubhouse and freely engage in small talk and camaraderie. The next day he'd come in completely shut off from the world, neither saying a word nor looking into anyone's eyes, staring lifelessly into his locker.

Crowley changed at the drop of a hat. He could be shooting the breeze one minute, then stop in mid-sentence and abruptly leave the room the next. No one knew what to expect out of him. Some had pondered that Crowley was a type of closeted crackpot, who could work his day job at the local bank, politely serving his customers, then go home and axe his family to bits.

Because of his extremes, some had begun to speculate that Crowley's antics were nothing more than a ploy to gain attention and fame, that deep down, underneath his thick guise of lunacy, was a cunning illusionist performing an act.

If that were the case, then his final curtain call came when he took the mound in front of eighteen thousand screaming people in St. Louis one steamy day.

From the get-go, Crowley was at the top of his game, mowing down one batter after another without the slightest hint of strangeness. Businesslike and methodical, Crowley set down eighteen straight hitters without giving up a baserunner.

The crowd began to stir. No one had ever pitched a complete game without allowing a single base runner. They knew they were about to witness history if Crowley could keep it up.

Suspense had filled the ballpark. After every pitch, every out, Crowley edged closer to perfection while everyone sat at the edge of their seats anticipating him going off his rocker at any second.

Yet Crowley remained straight-faced, almost vacant, as if someone had let all the emotional air out of his bag, and continued to humiliate his opponents with an array of pitches that defied simple physics — diving, bending and changing directions as if the ball had its own set of wings.

By the top of the ninth, the park was simmering with nervous energy, cheering and roaring. The last batter, the final out between Crowley and Base-Ball history, stepped up to the plate.

Crowley emptied his supply of trick pitches and the hitter bravely fought them off but found himself in the hole with two strikes. Just one more to get and Crowley would cap off the most flawless pitching performance ever.

The catcher tossed the ball back and Crowley stepped off the mound. Then something happened. He froze and began to stare at the ball in his hand, grasping it on the tips of his fingers, looking as if he were about to sink into some maniacal, Hamlet-esque, soliloquy.

The frenetic crowd gasped. Was Crowley about to implode with just one strike left to get? The suspense was too much. They stopped dead and watched Crowley ruminate over the dark leathery sphere.

He circled the mound once, twice, then three times. The manager popped up off the bench and stuck the nail on his thumb between his teeth. After every turn, the crowd groaned and his teammates behind him became deflated from their defensive stances.

But then Crowley snapped his head up, looked around the ballpark, and returned to the mound. The wild cheers and giddy anticipation resumed.

Without wasting another second, Crowley uncorked his wipe-out pitch, his devastating slider. The batter swung and missed the ball by a foot. The entire place broke out in pandemonium. Base-Ball had seen its first perfect game. History was his.

Cranks jumped down from the stands and swarmed the field. Crowley's teammates rushed him to congratulate him but stopped, not knowing what to do — either hug him and lift him up off his feet or keep their distance and only nod their heads in restrained awkwardness.

Crowley remained blank and empty the whole time while bedlam erupted all around him. Suddenly he turned around and started walking toward left field, past the swarm of Cranks storming the diamond, without the slightest hint of expression on his face.

His teammates watched him slowly course his way through the crowd, in a straight line, and disappear into a throng of people. That was the last they saw of him.

Without a trace, Herman "Creepy" Crowley had vanished forever.

Years after he pitched his perfect game, urban legends continued to spring up regarding his sudden disappearance. Theories were posited as to who he really was, why he disappeared and his possible whereabouts. For all his own weirdness, nothing would come close to the outlandish ideas floated about surrounding the mystery of one of the game's best pitchers and most paradoxical figures.

Across the country, people claimed to have spotted the enigmatic Crowley, from subway stations to post offices to the most run-down lunch counters in the middle of nowhere. Swearing that it was indeed him, they all said the same thing: that the man whom they recognized as Crowley winked at them and beamed a pranksterish grin.

'Tween Killing

A smash up the middle, a sure base hit, but the game's finest double play combo once again doomed the hitter's fortunes. Bill Whalen, the second baseman, and Irwin "Doc" Abercrombie, the shortstop, formed the best middle infield tandem in the big leagues, routinely stopping balls destined for the outfield and completing an acrobatic exchange that wiped out both advancing runners.

Their superior range on the diamond, excellent glovework and fluid agility made them excellent infielders, but it was their seemingly clairvoyant ability to know what the other was doing that made them defensive wizards.

They were two separate bodies running on the same brainwaves, functioning with one mind. When one snagged a grounder far to his left or right, all he had to do was toss it in the general area of second base, without even needing to look, and the other one would be in perfect position to snatch the ball in mid-air, step on the bag, and make a perfect throw to first to complete the double play. It was pure synchronization.

Their magical partnership was the product of more than fifteen years of playing side by side one another, grinding out thousands of innings together, growing more acclimated with each other with every groundball, chance and putout. Their long collaboration gave them a mutual familiarity that was comparable to a long-standing marriage, knowing everything there was to know about each other, right down to their smallest subtleties.

The Base-Ball community exalted the duo's feats and wherever Whalen and Abercrombie played, they were hailed as the 'Kings of the Infield, Thieves of the Base Hit.' They were acclaimed for being Base-Ball's best model for teamwork and coordination and were once presented with a special plaque, in front of the day's home crowd, honoring them for setting such a wonderful example for the rest of the world. They became luminaries and role models.

Inevitably, Base-Ball writers lionized them to the point of hyperbole, stating that their bond went beyond the Base-Ball diamond. They were best friends, an inseparable couple, who shared everything together from hotel rooms to meals on the train. It was indeed the perfect marriage.

However, it couldn't have been further from the truth. In reality, they hated each other.

They despised one another so much that their productive relationship on the field was a grueling test of nerves between the two that lasted for the entire duration of their playing careers.

Playing in games next to one another was like torture, and as soon as the day ended, they broke away with nary a word nor nod. That went on for eleven years, without one verbal exchange on the field or off.

Behind each double play was an incessant antagonism that always burned inside them, wanting to come out and make them tear each other's throats out. But somehow, someway, they subdued their loathing and continued making plays and maintaining their charade as the game's best and chummiest defensive twosome.

Their secret was hidden from the public until it became common knowledge after their playing days were over. But no one knew the reason for their shared hatred. Was their feud over something that happened early in their relationship and had festered for so long they couldn't patch things up? Was it something personal or trivial? Was it a woman, money or something so unusual that no one beyond them could comprehend?

Abercrombie was asked about their feud many times, long after Whalen had died. An old man, withered and senescent, Abercrombie still refused to answer. Perhaps even he forgot the real reason, lost in his fog of senility.

Perhaps there was no particular incident that sparked their antipathy in the first place. Perhaps it was just the result of playing together for too many years, side by side. Like an old married couple, they were trapped in a cage of convention and circumstance. Unwilling to give up the sport, they chose to hate each other instead, under a growing blanket of weariness.

Slanticular

The bane of superstition had begun to permeate throughout the big leagues, causing some of its most talented players to act like halfwits caught under a hoodoo spell, obsessed with the belief that they could become better ballplayers if they followed a set of ridiculous daily routines that had nothing to do with Base-Ball. It became an all-consuming neurosis for these men.

There was no one more compulsive than William B. "Twitchy Bill" Connell, who desperately tried to stave off curses and bad luck instead of allowing himself to be the serviceable journeyman he had been for a number of years. Connell was so engrossed in his habits and constraining beliefs that he eventually became consumed by them and succumbed to tragedy at an early age.

Instead of playing ball with a carefree, happy-go-lucky attitude, Connell was chained to a sequence of routines that inhibited him from enjoying the game. If any one part of his routine went askew, even by the slightest of measures, Connell felt cursed. Everything had to go right in order for him to have a chance at a productive day.

His pre-game rituals were exact and meticulous. In the clubhouse, Connell had a strict way of putting on his uniform. The first items on were always his socks and shoes, then the rest followed. If any one piece of the process didn't feel right, if anything felt loose or tight, he'd strip all the way down and start over again.

Once his uniform was on, he'd continue with his good luck charms. Every pocket of his uniform had to be filled with something. He put a rabbit's foot in his right front pocket and a dead cricket in his left. In his back pockets, he put a four-leaf clover and a small tin of chewed tobacco that was five years old, from the first game he ever played.

Then he stuffed his shoes with playing cards — a seven of diamonds and a three of spades. In one finger of his glove, he packed the shrunken head of a dormouse and the other fingers with birdseed.

After that he ate his daily meal, the same thing before every game, a bag of seven chicken wings and a cup of baked beans. He downed it with a glass of birch beer.

Running onto the field, Connell never touched the foul lines. He instead hopped over them. In the outfield, he picked two blades of grass and stuffed one up each nostril.

Then he was ready for the game.

At the plate, his bat had to be free from any dirt or dust. If he happened to go two for four or better, he considered himself to be in a lucky streak and refused to take off his uniform until his streak was snapped. He left the ballpark and ate and slept in his sweaty, filthy garments until his luck ran out.

On the flipside, if he went 0 for four the next game, his entire routine would start all over again, beginning by burying his bat in an undisclosed field and proceeding with a brand new one. If his hitless streak extended beyond four games, Connell burned his entire uniform.

Drastic and expensive though his superstitions were, Connell wholeheartedly believed they worked and he never dared waver from his routines.

But it all came crashing down when his teammates pulled a prank on him that led to a streak of bad luck with ultimately dire consequences. In the clubhouse one early afternoon, while getting dressed, he noticed someone had replaced his tin of five-year-old tobacco with a shiny new tin of baby powder. Connell called out for the perpetrator to hand over his old tin. But when he didn't come forward, Connell became irate. Even if the littlest things were out of order or misplaced, he became seriously distressed.

Connell lashed out and the entire clubhouse burst into laughter. No one returned his tobacco tin. He was now in a pickle. How could he perform without his tin? Connell feigned an injury in front of his manager, but his name was penciled on the lineup card anyway. He was going to have to play despite having his routine severely compromised.

Once the game started, he knew right away he was cursed. In the second inning alone, Connell lost the ball in the sun and was drilled in the back by an errant pitch, leaving a giant welt between his shoulder blades. He spent the rest of the game teetering on the edge of anxiety that quickly turned into a catastrophe.

The whole week, Connell was a nervous wreck, unable to hit or field. In a desperate attempt to reverse his bad luck, he bought a new tin of the same tobacco and chewed it non-stop for twelve hours until it looked like his five-year old chaw. It didn't work. His mind was still a bowl of mush and he slid further into a frozen pond.

Then, several days later, his old tin returned. Like a dense fog lifting, Connell was able to refocus again and get back to playing well with his routine back in place.

Connell played with an extra bounce in his step, no longer afraid of the bad luck that plagued him. Having gone almost two weeks without a hit, he looked forward to a new streak of good luck where the hits were coming and his uniform didn't leave his body.

He was well on his way, having gone two for three to start a game, when tragedy struck down "Twitchy Bill."

Making it to third base on a sacrifice fly, Connell dug in his heals and waited for the next batter to drive him home. On a two-and-two count, the batter swung at the next pitch and shattered his bat, sending the top half twirling in the air right toward Connell. With no time to react, the jagged, broken end struck Connell in the chest. A long, thin shard of hickory punctured his skin, plunging in between his ribs and severing his aorta.

It was a million-to-one shot. Connell slumped to the ground and bled to death.

He did not escape his bad luck after all, despite all his measures to fend it off. Perhaps Connell was, indeed, cursed, and no matter how desperately he tried to run away from it, it had finally caught up with him.

Bilious Brushback

A joke:
"Boy, George Williamson sure can play."
"Yeah, *they* sure can."

To understand the joke, one had to know the meaning behind the name George Williamson.

Quite a common name during the time, there were up to thirty-eight George Williamsons playing in the big leagues at the same time, scattered across multiple leagues. Sometimes there were two George Williamsons on the same team. It led to some confusion among the Base-Ball enthusiasts trying to track down which Williamson did what for whose team. And, as the years went along, more and more George Williamsons sprang up.

But, by all accounts, none of the players named George Williamson used their real names.

As ordinary as it was, George Williamson was a fake name, a pseudonym, for those players who didn't want their real names bandied about in certain circles for particular reasons. Some had been running away from their past or from somebody. Others were simply starting a new life.

But mostly, these players had played somewhere else on different teams under their real names. The problem was, they had signed contracts with their original teams that forbid them to sign anywhere else for a length of time. This was to protect the clubs from having players abruptly quit and hop from club to club in search of a higher payday.

Still, this did not stop them from abandoning their teams. To dodge the restrictions of their previous contracts, they found a loophole by signing with another team using a different name. By hiding behind the alias of George Williamson, they secretly colluded with their new team and continued playing scot-free.

So, on any given day, George Williamson hit a grand slam, stole two bases, struck out four times, pitched a two-hit shutout, made a diving catch in center field and sat on the bench without a chance of making it into the game.

But then, to confuse matters even more, a man whose real name was actually George Williamson entered the big leagues and bounced around from team to team for a few years, playing in relative obscurity.

Decades later, it took historians years to reconstruct the playing career of the real George Williamson. Since he moved around so frequently, just like the fake George Williamsons, it took an extraordinary amount of research to piece together his body of work, plucking it out with a pair of tweezers from the dozens of others who were playing.

Box scores were sometimes woefully inadequate, vague about crucial details such as how many at-bats the hitter ultimately had or how the scoring in the game transpired. Probably not aware of its enduring legacy, the people responsible for the early box scores sometimes failed to even record the players' first names. In one particular game, there were five anonymous Williamsons spread out with a total of thirty at-bats.

The historians did their best to record the real George Williamson's career. Within a reasonable degree of accuracy, they found:

He may or may not have played a total of six seasons with up to five different teams and three different leagues.

It is possible that he was an average hitter, at best, and played predominately outfield or infield.

His best season was either 1883, 1884 or 1886

His last appearance in the big leagues was either on September 30, 1887, or August 12, 1888, depending on which sporting guide listed the correct George Williamson (one had George A. Williamson and the other George P. Williamson).

His nickname was either "Hook," "Sourpuss," or "Old Turkey Neck."

After his playing days, the real George Williamson settled near Columbus, Ohio, and became an insurance salesman. Or a grocery clerk. Or a dentist. And he died in further obscurity, an exact date unknown (perhaps the late 1930s).

Phenominal

Mike Fowler had grown up dreaming about being a big league pitcher. Raised on a farm, the young lad slipped away from his daily chores to toss a crude, handmade ball against the side of his family's barn for hours. Practicing for years, the boy's arm developed into a thick, muscular hurling machine.

His father saw the gift of his son's arm and joined him in his wish to make it to the big leagues. After the harvest, he took him to a barnstorming exhibition traveling the West. For a fee of twenty-five cents, anyone could step up on a real mound and pitch to actual players. His father gladly plunked down the money and watched his son blow past the hitters with a fastball so hard and lively that they told him afterward they had never before seen anything so powerful and intimidating. Word quickly spread about the boy.

By his eighteenth birthday, the young Fowler was destined for the big leagues. Tall, strapping and solidly built out of the genes of hard labor and sweat, he was ticketed for the first train east after the next yield, assured of winning a slot on a pitching staff. He was on his way to becoming the next, great dominant pitcher for years to come.

But then, just as he and his father were finishing up the harvest, disaster struck. While feeding the combine, the junior Fowler slipped and fell into the threshing machine, whichbegan ripping his body to shreds. His father jumped off his perch on the harvester and lifted him away.

But it was too late. Mike Fowler's head had been almost completely severed.

His father quickly applied a tourniquet to his carotid artery and carried his body across several acres. He raced his son to the nearest hospital, twenty-five miles away, to try and save his life.

Miraculously, the boy survived.

In an extraordinary stroke of luck, the blades from the thresher missed his brain stem, which controlled his involuntary actions like breathing and heart functions. They were able to stabilize his wound and create pathways for oxygen and liquefied food for his stomach.

But his head was lost, completely churned up and obliterated.

However, to the shock and amazement of everyone, Fowler learned to function without his brain, able to walk and write. His doctors surmised that whatever was left of his brain stem on down must have taken up the slack.

His family worked out a system to communicate by tapping on his shoulders or chest using a method similar to Morse code. Once he was able to walk around freely, they tied a string around his torso and led him around, tugging at him and talking to him in code.

Determined to still be useful around the farm and not become some lowly sideshow freak, the plucky young man learned to do without the luxuries of a head. He got around well enough and was soon back on the combine collecting the harvest.

But deep down, Fowler did not lose sight of his dream of pitching in the big leagues.

He begun scrawling messages to his father pleading to let him get back in shape and try out for clubs in the spring. One little injury wasn't going to sideline him, Fowler wrote. He wasn't going to allow any setback to stop him from fulfilling his dream.

During the winter, his father set up a mound in the barn and devised a method for Fowler to pitch. He kept the string tied to his torso and tugged on him until he was able to locate his father's glove. It was a long, frustrating ordeal but the young Fowler eventually learned to spot the ball over the plate. His arm strength returned and the boy gurgled with confidence.

In the spring, Fowler and his father traveled to Kansas City to try out for the local club, the Zephyrs. The scouts were astonished to see the headless pitcher and told them to get lost. But his father was adamant. This is Mike Fowler, he said. The Boy with the Golden Arm.

The scouts remembered the name and his reputation. "Sorry," they said. "We, uh, didn't recognize him. Does he still have that cannon for an arm?"

"He sure does."

"But...how does he know where to throw the damn ball?"

"Leave that up to me."

The scouts watched the Fowlers set up. The son stepped up to the mound and the father squatted behind home plate with a glove and the string attached. He gave it a good tug and Mike began pounding the strike zone. The scouts let him face live hitters and he struck out all three on nine pitches. They offered him a contract on the spot and Mike Fowler agreed with only one stipulation. He demanded to have his own personal catcher, his father.

Six weeks later, Fowler made his debut in front of eight hundred people. With dust blowing everywhere and the ground as hard as clay, he struck out fifteen batters. The stunned crowd couldn't believe what they saw.

His next appearance drew three thousand spectators. Then seven thousand.

Fowler became a sensation and his name quickly spread across the Base-Ball landscape, as far east as New York. The Zephyrs travelled across the heartland trotting out their newest pitching battery and Fowler dominated everyone he faced. Thousands of people lined up to watch Base-Ball's latest marvel: The Noggin-less Flamethrowing Phenom.

As the season progressed, Fowler continued fanning hitters at an unbelievable pace. The farther east the club went, the more attention fell onto their shoulders. Newspapers and sports writers hounded the Fowlers for an interview. Biographers wanted to write the "The Life Story of Mike Fowler, a Tale of Misfortune and Determination." Companies wanted him to endorse their products. Everyone wanted to be associated with the tenacious pitcher.

The hype became too much. Showered with money, fame and

anything else he wanted, Mike Fowler took liberties with his instant celebrity. The long grind on the mound during the day ended with long nights out on the town. His father warned him of such distractions, reminding his son that the only thing he said he wanted to do was pitch, not bask in shallow glory.

The season ended in a whirlwind of publicity and exposure. Mike had broken the record for most strikeouts in a season and his arm still felt terrific. The Fowlers decided to join a barnstorming tour during the off-season and rake in huge wads of cash.

But the night before they were supposed to board the train for home, the elder Fowler walked into his son's hotel room and found him slumped over his bed, cold and lifeless.

Next to his bed was a 22-oz. cut of prime tenderloin. Mike Fowler had tried to eat the steak and mistakenly stuffed the filet in his trachea and choked. The kid with a cannon for an arm and the undying will to succeed had succumbed to hubris and suffocated.

"Where'd All the Fungo?"

The Baltimore Federals were the worst team to ever grace a Base-Ball diamond.

They were downright awful. Pathetic. Laughable.

How awful? In a season of historic futility and failure, the Baltimore team won only five games out of ninety, giving them the worst winning percentage for any club in any professional sport.

Not that they were a seedy bunch of rabble-rousers or a sauced-up hodgepodge of derelicts flopping around the diamond. Many on the team were actually quite intelligent, educated and well-intentioned. But when it came time to hunker down and compete, they fell miserably short.

At one time the Federals were a very respectable club, competing every day and drawing a large, loyal following. Their cozy ballpark, along the harbor at Fells Point, housed a team of hard-working, fundamentally sound players who gave it their all

Baltimore Club 1889

in front of a sellout audience.

Things were rosy for much of a decade. Devoted spectators packed their way in to see a hard-fought contest and got to see a real cohesive unit of sportsmen.

But things had changed once the game spread further westward. The demand for real players with a head screwed on tight and a solid set of playing skills had gone through the roof. Clubs like Pittsburgh, Cleveland and Cincinnati started to sniff around the established clubs in the Atlantic League and gauge the interests of the players. They wanted men of fine caliber willing to relocate and help get their clubs off the ground. And they were willing to pay.

Enter Baltimore club owner E. Charles Morrill-deNies, railroad executive, shipping magnate, Ice House King, Lord of the Frozen Water Industry and one-time close associate of J. Barron Sterne. For deNies, the Federals were just another investment property and he had no intention of ponying up raises to keep his players. He let them leave.

In a span of six months, twelve out of thirteen Baltimore

players had bolted for greener pastures and a mad scramble commenced to fill out the roster with warm bodies. The exodus of their favorite players deeply wounded the loyalty of the spectators who squeezed into every inch of the ballpark and fattened the wallet of the club's dyspeptic owner. Slowly, attendance levels began to wane.

Baltimore had to find players in a hurry. Insisting on keeping his payroll down, deNies did not look for experienced veterans. They would have cost too much. Instead, he searched for anybody willing to be paid the bare minimum, men who may or may not have had any big league experience. He convinced several men around town to abandon their secure occupations and join the club, men from all sorts of different backgrounds, like dentists, accountants, fishmongers, glassblowers, stationers and druggists.

None of them had big league experience. Only a few had actually played the game at all. But deNies forced them on the team's manager, who had no choice but to throw them out on the field. It was a disaster.

As if they were dumped in the middle of a gladiatorial arena, the new players were paralyzed with fear, not knowing what to do. Luckily, it was near the end of the season and they took solace in the prospect of practicing and learning the game during the off-season. They ended the year winning six of the last twenty games. That was the high-water mark for the crew.

The next season began and they brought with them a newfound sense of optimism, having practiced together over the course of the winter and studied the nuances of the game. They won two out of the first three games to open the season. It was downhill after that.

It became evident that they did not belong on the field with the rest of the league. Despite preparing themselves over the winter, they were overmatched in every capacity and were woefully deficient on simple Base-Ball intellect. They did not know the difference between a 1-2-3 inning and a 1-2-3 double play.

They kicked balls around the infield. They dropped soft, easy flyballs in the outfield. They couldn't catch up to fastballs. They barely got the ball over the plate.

The team quickly plunged into a losing streak, going the next eleven games without taking one lead. Instead of sulking or giving up, they cinched up their pants and lunged forward. They ended their streak when the opposing team, the Portsmouth Whalers, handed them a win when they committed a league-tying record seven errors in the game.

They managed two more wins before embarking on an unprecedented forty-five-game losing streak, almost doubling the previous record. As if everything they had learned had been completely discarded, they looked completely discombobulated.

Baltimore lost in every possible way. They gave up thirty runs in a game. They committed eighteen errors, eleven more than Portsmouth's previous record. Their pitchers could not locate the ball anywhere near the strike zone. They forgot the most basic rules of the game, such as how many outs there were in an inning. They couldn't run, throw, catch, swing or spit without making themselves look like complete idiots.

The Federals were the laughingstock of the big leagues and Baltimore's spectators, who were once some of the Atlantic League's most loyal and faithful supporters, had begun to abandon the team in droves and left the ballpark an empty chasm of wooden planks, with newsprints fluttering about and the wind whistling. Once a few thousand had shown up. Now they were lucky to get a few hundred.

They reached rock bottom when the players hit the field one blustery, rainy day and didn't see one person in the stands. The newspaper reported the attendance the next day as 1 after finding a man who had decided to sneak out of work and curl up underneath a tarpaulin to take a nap.

With no end in sight, the team went on a two-week road trip. They managed to play better but still came up short. Their manager had done everything he could to make them resemble a real professional club, but before they ended the trip, deNies sent him a telegram saying he was being relieved of his duties. The newspapers quoted deNies the next morning as saying he believed that all team needed was a shake-up to get them going. Before they departed for home, they were 5-82.

The first morning back, the team was shocked to discover every door and gate leading in to the ballpark had been padlocked. They were shut out from their own field. The city had finally disowned them and Sterne, acting as the league's eminent authority, forbid them from playing another game in Baltimore until they could prove they were worthy to compete with the rest of the league.

The Federals lasted three more games, all on the road. They lost all three by a combined total 45-3.

Monkey

It was a grand affair at the opening day ceremonies on the grounds of the new Detroit ballpark. People whisked themselves through the turnstiles and quickly filled the tiers of stands for a look at the latest jewel box. The grass was neatly trimmed and uniformly green. Freshly painted billboards and advertisements hung on the outfield walls. Ballplayers in chalk-white uniforms began to trickle out of their clubhouse and toss a ball around. A buzz of excitement crackled in the air.

Pete Schnockerd's White-Leggings were in town to kick off the season and the Detroit Brown Caps had prepared to duke it out with the mighty Milwaukee behemoth.

Before the singing of "The Star-Spangled Banner", both teams lined up along each foul line and the park's public address announcer stepped up to a megaphone and trumpeted out the day's lineup. A boy's choir delivered an alto rendition of "My Country, Tis of Thee," before making way for a marching band blaring a hyperkinetic Sousa piece. A back gate opened up and throngs of people spilled out onto the field—from the Wayne County Women's League of Bridge Players to the Swords and Sashes Michigan Civil War Veterans Committee—celebrating the day's events.

Then a Concord stagecoach wheeled in and stopped in front of the stands. Out popped a coterie of distinguished-looking dignitaries. One of them was the owner of the Detroit club, a white-haired, wrinkly codger in black, shuffling his feet and waving his shaking hands at the crowds in the stands.

Two men pulled out a wooden crate and dropped it on a dais. The owner stepped up and the public address announcer bellowed in his megaphone.

"Ladies and Gentlemen, on behalf of the esteemed owner of your mighty Detroit Brown Caps, and proud proprietor of this magnificent, new edifice of modern architecture, I hereby declare Base-Ball's first designated…CLUB MASCOT!"

The rows and rows of people in the stands shifted left and right to secure a view.

"I give you Mr. Buggles, the Brassy Chimp!"

The crate opened up and a chimpanzee hopped out, scared out of its mind.

Everyone went *Ooh!* and *Aah!* before breaking out into a courteous applause.

The chimp shook and bobbed in terror at the sight of the mass of people everywhere. Someone tugged at its collar and the creature snapped backward.

A photographer set his camera up in front of the platform, hoping to take a photo of the primate wearing a miniature Detroit cap with the owner and his entourage. They tried to wrangle the chimpanzee, but it darted off again. One of the men grabbed its chain and gave it a brutal yank.

They grabbed Mr. Buggles and threw him on the table like a sack of flour. The owner tried to place the miniature cap on its head. The chimp screeched and thrashed.

Another man plucked the hat out of the owner's hand. "Allow me, sir. This little wretch is a stubborn one!"

The man slowly closed in on the chimp but it screeched again and sunk its teeth into his hand. He screamed and jumped back. The frightened beast leapt up off the table and jumped over the owner, knocking him down. Mr. Buggles landed on the grass and tore down the left field foul line.

"Get that bastard!"

The crowd jumped to its feet. The men chased it down to the outfield wall. Cornered, the chimp turned and climbed up the foul pole, all the way to the top.

All eyes were now on the terrified creature. Everyone on the field, including both clubs, congregated in left field and looked up. A member of the owner's entourage put his hands on his hips and turned to him. "What are we going to do now, boss?"

Absolutely frightened, its teeth chattering in uncontrollable panic, the chimp dug into its rear end and began slinging feces all over the place. Shit flying everywhere, people ran and ducked for cover.

The man from the entourage picked up a stone and flung it the chimpanzee. "Take that, you filthy mongrel!" Mr. Buggles shot out a stream of urine, hitting one of the ladies from the bridge club in the face.

The game was already delayed for over an hour and still no one knew what to do. The chimp didn't budge. Schnockerd and some of his crew joined the fray.

"How we gonna get that sum'bitch down from there, Pete?"

"I don't know, Charlie. He ain't movin'."

"Maybe we can coax him down with some food or somethin'. We got that pie in the clubhouse. Maybe that'll do the trick?"

"Is it laced with bananas?"

"Nah. Rhubarb."

"Don't give him that!" Someone from behind shouted. "Or that damned thing'll be crappin' all over us again!"

Schnockerd crossed his arms and stood there, like the rest of them, perplexed.

People started exchanging ideas.

"Can anyone scoot up there and grab him?"

"Get the fire department over here and send up a ladder."

"Just cut the pole down."

"I know. Anyone have an ape suit? We'll trick him down, pretending to be his momma."

Mr. Buggles ripped out a piercing scream and inched up higher. Everyone shook their heads and began to talk all at once, arguing over what to do. Just as a melee was about to break out, the crowd parted in half and someone pushed his way through.

"McGrady!" Schnockerd looked at the tempestuous infielder. He was carrying a shotgun. "Where'd you get that thing?"

He stepped up and slung the firearm on his shoulders and aimed it up at the chimp.

"What are doing? McGrady…"

"Goddamned monkey!"

"Don't!"

He fired a shot at the screeching chimp and hit him square in the chest. Once the loud boom of the shotgun had subsided, there was shocked silence. Mr. Buggles fell lifeless off the top of the pole and landed in the stands. A woman screamed, then the rest of the park broke out in a clamor.

Schnockerd looked at Sorley McGrady and everyone around them froze. "McGrady, how in the hell…"

McGrady didn't look at him. He ejected the shells out of the shotgun and handed it to Schnockerd, barrel sides up. "Pheasants in Arkansas, on my grandaddy's farm. He taught me how to be a good shot."

Then he walked away past the stunned onlookers. ■

The Palace of the Cranks at Hillbottom Park

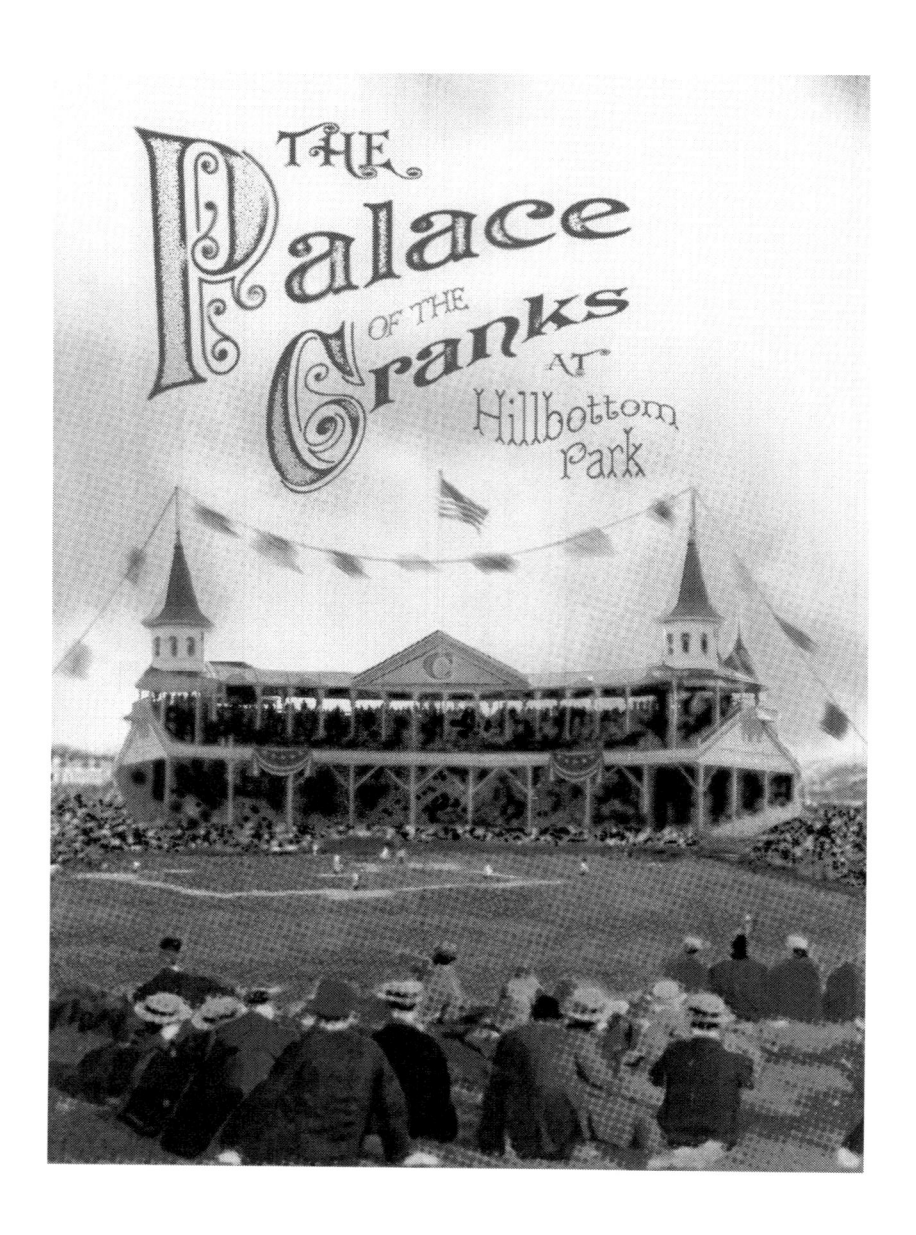

IX.

A Cut-Plug Can of Corn
(1883-1893)

The Governor's office has become uncharacteristically untidy. Law books and papers are stacked everywhere — on his desk, on tables, on the floor. Cups of cold, half-drunk tea are pushed aside. Crumbs of food dwell on serving trays and the carpet. The window blinds fail to let in enough light.

Sterne swivels his chair around and reads the headline from the *Wall Street Gazette* one more time:

"SUPREME COURT STRIKES DOWN J.B. STERNE'S EFFORTS TO RECLAIM GAME OF BASE-BALL"

He scans through the copy. "Three years of legal wrangling... No legitimate binding...False entitlement...Public domain... Finds Mr. Schnockerd to have every right to form his own league."

He snatches the speaking tube off its holder and blows into it. "It's me. Get up here."

Two minutes later, Niedler sidles in.

"Sit down, Henry."

"Did you want me to order the new carpet? This one's been

trampled on so much with foot traffic, back and forth with staffers, it's seen better days."

"No. That's not the reason why I called you up here."

Niedler's eyes widen. He straightens himself up. "I'll fix that horrible squeak in your chair. That dastardly Humbertus never answers my calls. I have a mind—"

"No, that's not it."

"That scratch on your ivory Waterman—"

"It's not my fountain pen, Henry."

"Then—"

"I need you to go back out there."

He shakes his head. "Out where?"

"You were successful at corralling him that one time. Maybe you can do it again. He may be willing to listen to you."

Niedler finally gets it. "Oh, yes, well—"

"The truth is, Henry, I've run into the proverbial dead end. The court's had their final say and after spending a great deal of my money and effort, that fattish clodknocker still stands, unscathed."

Niedler politely smiles. "The toughest nut to crack so far."

"Yes. I've used every trick in my book to ruin him. And yet, there he is, still deflowering my beloved game."

"Whatever happened to that mole who infiltrated the family's brewery?"

"He's now their Chief Accounting Officer. Quite happy living on a lakefront property."

Niedler waits a moment. "And what is it that you want me to...?"

"I'm sending you back out there. You're going to meet with him, get to know him a little more. And you're going to find out what he really wants, what his final price is."

"Buy him out?"

"The last resort. Every man has a price. Certainly, this slob has one. If I can't ruin him, I'll send him away a happy man."

Niedler clears his throat. "Pardon me for asking this, but after all you put him through, what else is there to offer him?"

Sterne leans back in his chair. "May I remind you about that dour fellow from Cleveland, the refinery man? There were supposed to be only three things exclusive in his life: oil, money and God. It took us a while, but we found a fourth, didn't we?"

Niedler snickers. "It took us almost a full year, but we finally got to him. Those were the days, weren't they?"

"I need your expertise once again, Henry. Can I count on you?"

He trips over his words. "I'd be honored."

"Good. This may increase your capital with me once again, Henry, if you get me a deal."

"What specific deal are you seeking, J.B.?"

"I want him to hand over the entire enterprise, in exchange for whatever he wants."

"I see."

Sterne leans forward. "Nothing less."

"And the price?" Niedler asks.

"Don't worry about a price. Keys to the kingdom depend on what lurks deep inside the soil. Will you discover an acorn or a truffle?"

"A cunning character, to say the least. One of the best ever."

"Yes, but he can't hide his truth forever. We'll find out what he really covets, either by cornering him through our predatory tactics or picking his pocket unknowingly. Either way, we'll finally expose the real reason why this lump of grease gets out of bed every morning."

"Are you sure you have what he really wants?"

"In the end, Henry, they all want the same thing. I'll give him that as long as he gives me back my game."

Niedler stands up. "I don't know what to say. Thank you for the opportunity."

"Strike a deal, Henry. You're my last option. I want my game back."

J. Barron Sterne comes face to face with a great dilemma. His version of Base-Ball has become irrelevant.

His remaining chattels quickly become stale and bland in comparison to the thrilling exploits going on out West. Spectators grow bored with the usual pomp and circumstance. They want something more dynamic and entertaining. They are still getting a game where its players favor cushy formality over bare-knuckled competition.

Attendance throughout his leagues plateaus, in some cases even declining. Even his prized jewel, the Elites, once the standard-bearer of excellence, begins to see its luster fade.

His attention focused on his war against Schnockerd, Sterne loses sight of what is happening to his own leagues. Aging players roam the diamonds, refusing to quit on a lucrative salary while contributing less and less. Whether they know it or not, the edge of competition has grown dull and many are just going through the motions. Even the ballparks start showing signs of age. Atrophy sweeps across Sterne's landscape and a feeling of banality begins to take hold.

A crisis is at hand. Like any other business skirting along a steep cliff, Sterne has to change his game or face death. He either has to allow for innovation or watch his empire crumble. Adapt or die. Having for years been reluctant to make serious changes, he now takes a hard look around and finally decides an overhaul is needed.

It isn't easy. He still clings to the values he first placed on the game at its very inception. The trick is to keep its sanctity while modernizing it to placate the spectators. He wants them to enjoy a new level of excitement, similar to the game out West, while rediscovering the purity that he first identified decades ago.

The key is to have better competition. Sterne has to find better players with more talent and athleticism who can flash their physical gifts while mastering the ever-growing complexities of the game. He wants players who are willing to eat a mouthful of dirt just to make a play and get plunked in the chest standing their ground at the plate.

It isn't enough anymore to hand over a position to a local fellow with a quick set of wrists and legs that can scurry down the line, hoping they'll turn into a decent ballplayer. Sterne insists on creating a better system of talent procurement. He soon installs a network of scouts and instructors who scour the region, plucking young, raw men out of the alleyways of inner cities and the pastures of backwaters and breeding them to be professional ballplayers.

One such ballplayer lands in Sterne's lap, a teenaged wunderkind by the name of Charlie "Fleet" Foote. At sixteen, he's already a phenomenal athlete who can catch the ball better than even the most seasoned veterans. Tall and rangy, he doesn't look like a typical shortstop, but when he mans the position for the very first time he immediately dazzles everyone.

His knack for the ball is remarkable, displaying a set of

instincts that can't be taught. He gets to every grounder hit his way and always throws the runner out. It doesn't matter if he's lying on his stomach in the dirt or spread out on the grass ten feet into the outfield. His arm strength, accuracy, balance and footwork are off the charts, especially for a such young shaver.

He quickly becomes Sterne's poster boy for his new-look Base-Ball. Foote is young, clean-cut, and full of energy. Some even describe him as an exuberant overachiever who doesn't know when to take it down a notch. If he isn't on the field, he paces up and down the bench area chewing nervously on sunflower seeds and shooting them out with his lips, leaving a trail behind.

Foote joins the Elites just weeks shy of turning seventeen and plays for them an astounding twenty years, becoming a cornerstone of the club synonymous with winning and playing with a new level of dexterity and energy.

Once his system to find better players is in place, Sterne goes about restructuring the leagues. Instead of several smaller leagues completely separate from one another, he consolidates his best clubs into one central division, The American Association League of Base-Ball Professionals, made up of ten clubs with the best players. The other clubs are relegated to 'minor' status, meaning they operate in the shadow of the sole "professional" league and have the duty of tutoring freshly chosen players destined for the top clubs.

A new, standardized rulebook is written, a streamlined delineation of every regulation and detail of the game, taking the place of the archaic rulebook Sterne had kept adding onto every year for the previous twenty-five years.

Still maintaining the highest emphasis on player conduct and appearance, Sterne doubles the number of pages on the subject and requires everyone signing a new contract at the start of the year to agree to its terms.

Then Sterne throws his money into two key assets: media and ballparks. He buys several newspapers in large markets in order to turn their sporting sections into a giant propaganda machine, lifting Base-Ball up onto a pedestal so high no one can ignore its presence anymore.

Sterne then replaces the wobbly and warped ballparks with new and improved structures. He adds steel to the mostly wooden framework of the stands and strengthens the load capacity to make room for more spectators.

The first park to be erected is the new home for the Elites. For years they played their games on the grounds of Central Park, but their surroundings had grown cramped and outdated and Sterne moves them into a residence of generous proportions just north in Washington Heights. Furnished with the latest technologies such as running water, urinal troughs and a giant scoreboard lit up with blazing light bulbs, spectators enjoy creature comforts never before experienced.

For an extra fee, spectators can buy a ticket and sit in new, individual luxury seats with velvet pads and supportive backings. He even provides each club with a new innovation to protect them from the forces of nature: the dugout.

In short time, a giant turnaround occurs. Sterne propels his league to the forefront of relevance once again and his brand of Base-Ball brings back a sense of superiority to the returning spectators. Their game is back, and better than ever.

A new era dawns, marked by the streamlining of Sterne's new League, focusing the attention on a new wave of ballplayers ingrained with better discipline and fundamentals and remaking the game's surrounding infrastructure. Sterne hopes to usher in a new generation of Base-Ball enthusiasts who are fixated on their local clubs and willing to spend their money rooting for them in die-hard fashion. He imagines them being fanatics of the game, or Fans for short.

Horsehide Indiscriminate

Philo Grogan was another one of J.B. Sterne's poster boys for his new Elites, a pitching ace and self-declared leader of the staff with God on his side. A teetotaler his entire life, Grogan led a virtuous path free from all vices including gambling, swearing, impure thoughts and soiled underwear.

Nonetheless, Grogan was a fierce competitor on the mound

who felt it was his moral duty to dispatch every single opponent he faced as if they were heathens falling under the axe.

Born into a life of privilege, Grogan spent his formative years transferring from one Ivy League school to the next playing in a variety of sports including fencing and rowing. When he reached Dartmouth, Base-Ball had become a regional craze and Grogan picked up the game like a natural. He quickly became the university's star pitcher. Upon graduation, Sterne persuaded the diligent student to join his club.

Grogan did not waste time in becoming the Elites' most upstanding player. Hard-working and dedicated to being the best, Grogan was always the first one at the park and the last to leave. When the rest of the team was still asleep, Grogan had already jumped out of his bed and attacked the day, having finished his drills before they showed up. He led a prayer group before each game and donated much of his salary to charity. Grogan quickly gained a reputation throughout the League for his unbending seriousness and rigid devotion to perfection.

On the mound, Grogan was a bona fide control artist. While not possessing a powerful arm, he was durable enough to last nine innings and get the most out of his performance by moving the ball up and down in the zone with pinpoint accuracy. Not afraid of contact, he was a master at inducing any type of ball to be put into play. If he needed a popout to shallow centerfield, he would run up a fastball in on the batter's hands. If he needed a groundball to the shortstop for an easy double play, he twirled a sinking slider away from the batter and had him reaching out in front of the pitch.

Sterne appointed him the club's disciplinary bulldog. If anyone on the team got out of line, he had the authority to straighten them out or report their indiscretions directly to Sterne, over the head of the Elites' manager, W.H. Pierce. Grogan proudly seized the responsibility, vocally expressing his detestation for insubordination and lack of discipline.

But sometimes he expanded his jurisdiction outside the Elites' clubhouse and into other clubs around the League. The Boston club was notorious for having players who played hard without incident on the field but were prone for the nightlife and all its seductions. Grogan was determined to weed out the perpetrators when New York visited Boston during a four-game, five-night road trip.

In just two nights, Grogan caught half the members of the Boston club gambling in halls and saloons, imbibing in the seediest establishments until they were completely flummoxed, and employing the services of several neighborhood brothels. Appalled, Grogan wired to Sterne the next day of their repulsive behavior, and the Governor promptly suspended them for a month without pay.

Grogan went on to have a stellar career as the Elites' top pitcher and continued to irk many players across the League with his priggish manners. But he ingratiated the Governor with his tenacity to win while upholding a high degree of propriety that most on the club failed to reach. Grogan never minimized his personal campaign to always be at his best while openly condemning those perceived to be dogging it. And he never lessened his contempt for sordidness and degeneracy.

Tree-Fingers

Stacks Bittner took a beating behind the plate before he revolutionized the sport by introducing protective gear for catchers, Bittner regularly caught hundreds of games a year with only his bare hands. His fingers were constantly broken and they never healed properly. Each digit became horribly disfigured, twisted and deformed. He couldn't shake hands anymore, nor write legibly.

But as the years went on, the game became harder to catch with fastballs edging upward in velocity and hitters fouling balls straight back at him. Squatting down in the dirt, popping up out of his crouch, chasing balls, blocking the plate and being a human backstop took a terrific toll on his body.

People joked that his body looked like it had been trampled by a circus elephant. He couldn't stand or walk straight anymore. He appeared to be in constant pain.

Yet, he always took his spot behind the plate and never complained. Despite the crippling punishment, his skills never diminished and he was always regarded as the game's best receiver. Not only did he exceed in the physical demands of the position, Bittner was an incredibly astute strategist of the game who was always involved in tactics to get the upper hand over the opponent.

Unlike any other catcher, he devised pitch selections customized against individual batters, taking advantage of their weaknesses. He knew the tendencies of base runners and either picked them off first base or easily threw them out heading for second. Instead of idly sitting back behind the plate receiving balls, Bittner took control of the game and dissected every single detail and possibility, effectively becoming a secondary manager.

It didn't take long before J.B. Sterne snapped him up. Already a veteran with thousands of innings under his belt, Bittner became the Elites' field general during games and was in the middle of the club's greatest runs of success, squeezing the best out of the pitching staff while keeping order on the diamond. No one came close to his combination of durability and in-game strategic maneuvers. Bittner, more than anybody else, transformed the position from an insignificant role to a major component to a club's day-to-day fortunes.

Bruised, battered and broken, Stacks Bittner surprised everyone with his sudden announcement that he was retiring from the game. As sharp as he was behind home plate, Bittner was just as shrewd with contract negotiations and when he signed with Sterne's Elites, he artfully slipped in language that gave him the right to terminate his contract at any time. Sterne could not stop him. By the time the 1894 season ended, Bittner had had enough and wanted to return home to the quiet life along the shores of the Chesapeake.

On the final day of the season, the club honored Bittner for his magnificent service and contributions to the game. They presented him with a plaque and handed out leaflets in the stands featuring his career highlights. The crowd caught their breath when the Fans read it. As they watched him lurch forward to accept the plaque—walking unevenly, his back slightly hunched, his hands permanently swollen and fingers looking like tree roots—they couldn't believe that he was only thirty-two years old.

Cork Tip of the Hat

For the very first time, there was a player who could damn near do it all and do it better than anybody else. Sterne's scouts described Gus "Fireplug" Johnson as a "tool shed crammed full of God-given talent, instincts and drive—a golden kernel sifted out from the rest of the bushel." They saw him as the game's most complete player, the prototype for near-perfection.

Johnson was deceptively short and stocky but he could hit a ball a mile and run like a greyhound. His hands and forearms were thick and sturdy, giving him the ability to explode his bat through the strike zone and belt balls all over the field. His legs were thick but he could take off like a speeding train at the drop of a hat, allowing him to track down balls anywhere in a sea of open grass. Some even claimed that he possessed an uncanny intuition, as if he knew what was going to happen on the field two or three plays ahead of everybody else.

He did everything needed to win the game. If his team was down three runs, he hit a grand slam. If a ball was in danger of splitting the gap, he closed in on it and made the catch, preventing the runner on third base from scoring. If they needed him to get in scoring position, he would steal second, third and sometimes home if needed. He even got up on the mound for an inning or two when they were in a pinch, holding his own until the next pitcher was properly stretched out.

Sterne's expansive scouting network discovered Johnson playing for the Louisville Generals, a lowly patchwork of a club hidden in the backwoods of Jefferson County, Kentucky. They saw his speed and not much else. They signed him to a contract, gave him five dollars and a ticket to one of their 'minor' clubs in Camden, New Jersey. There he flourished, flashing his entire cache of talent and skills, stunning the scouts. Without even knowing it, Sterne's fortunes took a dramatic leap forward.

And so did Johnson's when the Elites' centerfielder, a gentleman by the name of Wendell Crabtree, broke his foot in a freak croquet accident and forced the club to search for an emergency replacement. A scout urged Sterne to call up Johnson and have a look at him. He consented and Johnson made his debut in front of fifteen thousand people in Washington Heights.

In the very first inning, Johnson flagged down a fly ball hit to shallow center field, but he took his eye off of it for a split second and it popped off the heel of his glove. This allowed the runner on third base to score. The Fans in the stands, already conditioned to accept nothing but the very best, rained down a smattering of snooty jeers on Johnson. He stood there quietly and absorbed the criticism.

Throughout the game, they did not let up on him. Even when he was up to bat, they scoffed at him and stuck their noses up in the air. Yet Johnson kept his head down and stayed focused on the game.

Then the eighth inning came and Johnson stepped out of the dugout, looking for his first hit. The Elites were down by several runs and time was running out. With a runner on first, he walked up and clubbed a deep drive down the left field line. The ball kept going and going until it faded from view for a home run. Johnson circled the bases and slipped back into the dugout.

The Fans were quietly stunned by the newcomer's power.

In the ninth, with a man on and still trailing by a run, Johnson reappeared and smoked a line drive once again down the line. The crowd jumped up to its feet and roared, but the ball went foul. Two pitches later he crushed the ball deep to center field. He knew he had gotten all of it and started trotting around the bases. The ball landed about ten rows into the bleachers and the entire park erupted.

The Elites' bench jumped out of the dugout. Johnson still kept his head down while completing the circuit and got mobbed by his teammates when he reached home plate.

From there, the floodgates had opened. Johnson's brilliance was on display in front of the country's largest Base-Ball outlet.

Not too long after that, record-breaking crowds marveled every time he touched the ball or even stepped out onto the field. No matter what the situation was, Johnson found a way to win the game. That was his most valuable skill, his natural flair to do anything on the field to help the Elites win.

And win they did. In a span of three years, the Elites won more games than any club ever before, even outpacing their own achievements from a generation ago. Sterne's efforts to reshape the club had begun to pay off. Once again, they were the toast of the town and the preeminent club of the League, thanks to the additions of players like "Fleet" Foote, Stacks Bittner and Johnson, whose feats propelled the club back onto the national stage.

A newfound buzz charged the air. New riches were waiting to be made, glories to be met and legends forged. Base-Ball in the East was back on the map and people were hungry once again to feast on every little tidbit they could get their hands on.

But just as the return of the Elites was in full-stride, controversy erupted over their star centerfielder in the form of a shocking pronouncement.

Wick Lingstrom was a young and flashy newspaper columnist for the *New York Daily Herald* who took pride in being the first to break news stories and uncover scandals. In an early morning edition of the paper, the city woke up to the headline:

"BASE-BALL ELITES' CENTERFIELDER JOHNSON IS A NEGRO."

Lingstrom's article postulated that Johnson was a black man, despite any facts whatsoever to prove it except for the obvious appearance of his skin—which was a shade or two darker than any of the others on the team—and his admission that he came from the South. Lingstrom's allegation sent shockwaves across the entire city, sparking an entire backlash of emotions that ran from pure disbelief to absolute frenzy.

How could Base-Ball allow its integrity to be defiled, its purity desecrated, by permitting a lesser man of color to partake in its games? Fans were perturbed. It was heretical, they thought.

The firestorm of criticism struck lower Manhattan, where the Governor laid his eyes on the headline and called for an emergency meeting with the Elites' staff. Sterne sat them all down in his office. Could this really be true?

They replied that it never really crossed their minds. They always suspected the reason for his darker skin was that he simply stayed out in the sun longer and tanned better than anybody else.

Sterne pointed out the very brazen—and outrageous—specifics in Lingstrom's article, such as the reference to the shape of Johnson's nose and lips.

Could Johnson really be a black man?

Everyone went around the room giving their own opinion. No one could agree on what he was. A squabble ensued.

Sterne finally pounded his fist down on his desk like a gavel silencing the room and said, "Has anybody even ever asked the man?"

They all looked at each other.

"Get Johnson in here."

An hour later, the Elites' star player settled into a leather chair and stared into the Governor's eyes. "I dunno, sir. I grew up in an orphanage. I never knew my parents."

After several more questions, Sterne let his dusky-complexioned centerfielder go and gave his blessing to play in the day's game, convinced there was no proof to Lingstrom's claim.

But that didn't settle the matter for the Elites' Fans, who were up in arms over the idea of a black man playing in the big leagues. They couldn't fathom the idea. They wouldn't permit it happening to their precious game. To them, the wrong had to be rectified. Retribution had to be dispensed.

When the day's game was about to begin, Johnson ran to the outfield to man his position. The entire ballpark came crashing down upon him. Just the day before, he was their prized possession, the centerpiece in the imperial crown of Base-Ball. Now he was just another colored man with no business being on the field.

A verbal onslaught halted the beginning of the game. The crowd, once considered the game's finest and most sophisticated, could now be heard screaming, "Get off the field! Animal! Vermin!" But Johnson held his ground in center field and the game got underway.

Sterne was beside himself, incensed at what Lingstrom had written. Ironically, Sterne owned the very paper Lingstrom wrote for and his article was considered nothing short of an act of betrayal, breaking the ironclad edict that the Elites' prestige not be tainted in any way. That afternoon, Sterne ordered the paper's editors to fire Lingstrom. When they objected, citing his popularity, Sterne shut the entire paper down, terminating hundreds of workers.

But it was too late. In the eyes of the general public, Lingstrom's article was taken as literal fact and the blowback was tremendous. Over the course of the next several days, a tide of dissent washed over the ballpark, all the way down to Sterne's office. They did not want a colored man leading their beloved Elites. He had to go.

Amid the storm of protests, Sterne finally relented. He was not about to confront them on such a contentious subject such as this. No matter how great Johnson was, no one player was bigger than the club or the game itself. It was not worth the trouble or the risk of tarnishing the game's reputation. Johnson could not be part of the Elites any longer.

Instead of just releasing him or even sending him back to Louisville, Sterne demanded that they get something to replace Johnson's value. Then someone in the Elites' camp thought of a unique idea: why couldn't they trade Johnson off to another club and get something else in return, just like they do on the commodities markets? Sterne liked the idea, but opposed trading him to any of the clubs in his League.

Once word got out that Johnson could be had, people clamored for his services. But the 'minor' league clubs had nothing they could offer Sterne. That left only one other option, regrettably: Schnockerd's National Frontier League.

Sterne abhorred the idea of doing business with Schnockerd, but was determined to get something back for his centerfielder. His office sent telegrams proposing the idea and Schnockerd came back saying he'd love to have Johnson. But Sterne's initial demands were outrageous, requiring Schnockerd to relinquish several of his teams back to Sterne for Johnson. When that request was met with a hearty laugh on Schnockerd's end, Sterne lowered his demands. Knowing that Sterne had very little regard for his type of players, Schnockerd suggested a cash reimbursement. Figures went back and forth until a dollar amount was agreed upon. Finally, for the princely sum of $10,000, Gus "Fireplug" Johnson was now a member of Schnockerd's Frontier League.

The first-ever trade of a big league player had taken place. Milwaukee's Cranks were ecstatic they were getting the most dynamic and possibly the best player in all of Base-Ball.

While Sterne regretted the loss, he felt compelled to do something before his own base had broken out into full revolt. Once again, the game's integrity had to be preserved at any cost. Whether or not Johnson was truly a black man, the court of public opinion had to be placated.

Decades after the controversy, an ironic conclusion to the tale was reached. In the attempt to prove once and for all the exact ethnicity of Gus Johnson, a team of researchers conducted a painstaking investigation into the star centerfielder's background and published their findings exactly fifty years to the day after he first stepped onto the Elites' playing field. They concluded that Johnson was, at most, one-tenth African-American, to go along with several other bloodlines including Choctaw, Apache, Welsh, German, French and a nominal percentage of Southeast Asian.

Mustard Skedaddle

Holly McBride was nothing special. Having made the big leagues almost by accident, he spent several years trying to stay in Base-Ball despite being an unremarkable player. At best, he was an average hitter, an average defender, and an average base runner. Dozens of other men could have filled his shoes and done just as good a job, if not better.

However, he was good at one thing. He excelled at getting plunked by the ball when in the batter's box.

While no one took much notice, McBride consistently took the free base because of his skill at getting hit with the ball. While others ducked and jumped out of the way, McBride stood like a statue and endured the pain in order to be awarded the base. It was his only specialty and he took measures to get that skill officially recognized. It was his only redeeming quality.

McBride was a fledgling utility player for a minor league club in Binghamton, biding his time and eking out a living when a telegram appeared one day seeking his services for the major league club in Syracuse. He couldn't believe it, but he quickly packed his bags and headed north the next day.

When he arrived in Syracuse, the manager looked him over and said, "You're not McSwain. Who the hell are you?"

"McBride."

"McBride? Jesus Christ! I told that pencil-pushin' clerk of mine to send me for McSwain. My third baseman's down with a pulled groin and I need a replacement." He yelled across the clubhouse and his clerk walked over. "Feeney, who the hell is this?"

"Your new third baseman?"

"It ain't McSwain. I asked for McSwain, you got me Mc…mc…what's your name again?"

"McBride."

"Feeney, why the hell did you get me this guy?"

"All you said, skip, was to send you the 'Mick infielder from Binghamton'. You didn't get any more specific than that."

The Syracuse manager eyed McBride and wiped his mouth with his sleeve. "Can you play third, McBride?"

"Sure I can."

That was how McBride made the big leagues, but from that day on he fought to stay, never showing anything exceptional except for his penchant to get hit with the ball.

Already on his third club and running out of options, McBride made the bold decision to confront the Elites' manager, W.H. Pierce, about a job. Not known for his skills, McBride conjured up an unusual ploy. When he met Pierce in his office next to the clubhouse, McBride sat down with a ledger of typed numbers.

"What are these, McBride?"

"These are the statistics of your club from last year."

"Excuse me?"

"Statistics. Data. Numbers and figures for every one of the club's players. It shows in numerics what exactly they did during the season, production-wise."

"I know full well what my boys did over the course of the year. You don't have to tell me."

But McBride convinced Pierce to give him an opportunity to explain to him the merits of such new terms like batting average, on-base percentage and runs batted in. Pierce was intrigued. No one had ever broken down a player's performance quite like that until McBride walked in his office.

Then he showed the manager his own statistics. "As you can see, some of my numbers are better than the average, better than some of your regulars."

But Pierce wasn't entirely sold on the concept. He told McBride that he trusted his eyes more than raw numbers. He didn't offer McBride a spot on the roster.

Though he couldn't convince Pierce to give him a job, he still left an indelible impression on him. His use of numerical data sparked something in him. While newspapers and sporting journals always utilized some basic form of statistics, McBride opened Pierce's eyes.

One day, Pierce met with Sterne and described to him what McBride had done with the statistics. Sterne, ever the numbers-cruncher in the business world, was quietly impressed.

Always looking to implement a better method of finding the best players, Sterne created a new position on the club, Team Statistician, and hired McBride to collect and analyze statistics in hopes of assembling a better roster of players. Desperate to stay in the big leagues, McBride managed to exploit an unrealized resource and wound up creating a cottage industry.

Gallknipper

Securing his niche as one of Base-Ball's more popular players, and possessing the added advantages of rugged good looks and broad-shouldered charisma, Russell "Red" Cheatham's skewed sense of entitlement led him to demand his current contract be ripped up in favor of a more lucrative deal.

The trouble was, everyone in the game knew that Cheatham was not even worth his current contract as a bona fide Base-Ball player. He was more of a fraud and huckster who puffed himself up through hype and flair rather than proving his everyday value through solid play on the field.

Nonetheless, he was sure as hell going to get his money one way or another.

Cheatham was loud and brash. He took every opportunity to brag about every little thing he did on the field and never shied away from calling out his teammates when they made a blunder or missed a play. He was the ultimate show-off and the League's premier blowhard.

Already a five-year veteran for the Boston Pale Shirts, Cheatham climbed up the ladder through sheer cockiness and bluster. He was merely a one-dimensional player, having the sole ability to scorch the ball past diving infielders whenever he wasn't striking out. But that didn't stop him from proclaiming to be one of the best hitters in the League.

No one really believed it, but the longer and louder he boasted about himself the more he turned the tide of public opinion to his side. He mastered the art of self-promotion so well that he was able to hang his name on everything from chewing gum to a popular phonograph record, "Red Cheatham's Swingin' Base-Ball Blues," in order to boost his recognition.

Always the hawker, Cheatham never let up on selling himself. When he wasn't on the field needlessly showboating he was off to the saloons pretending to be the life of the party, buying everyone rounds of whiskey shots and seducing the local ladies. His self-made image as a larger-than-life superstar was a perfectly honed charade and the world fell for his deception despite his mundane numbers on the field.

The Boston newspapers also fell for his trickery and couldn't resist plastering his rare achievements on the front page, such as a game-winning home run or sliding catch. After all, they were in the business of selling newspapers and Cheatham's name had become a selling piece.

Always paid well by the club, Cheatham nevertheless wanted more. If he made a thousand dollars one year, he demanded double the next. If he made five thousand dollars, he wanted ten. During one year, and already the highest paid player on the team, Cheatham netted a whopping seven thousand dollars, all for a journeyman's production.

But that didn't matter. He was the biggest name out there, he declared, the top drawing card for the entire Boston outlet. He should be fairly compensated to match his true market value. According to Cheatham, a substantial raise was in order. At least double.

Boston's long-time owner, Archibald Erastus Bancroft, a self-made millionaire who had gone through plenty of negotiation ploys, had enough of Cheatham's ballyhoo. He had already given in to his contract demands too many times, giving him the best suite available when they were on the road, giving him his own private dressing room, giving him carte blanche on everything from his own choice of uniform to scheduling the start times of games. But enough was enough. Bancroft was not going to fall for Cheatham's horn-blowing anymore. He was prepared to let him go once his contract expired.

As soon as word reached Cheatham that Bancroft was not going to budge on his latest demands, he engaged in a full-blown smear campaign against Bancroft, using his newspaper contacts to pummel the club's owner in the press and portray himself as the unappreciated good soldier.

The tactic was short-lived, however, once word reached J.B. Sterne. Controlling many of the Boston newspapers, he put a stop to the public airing of dirty laundry and ordered both sides to come to an agreement.

When Bancroft objected to any new deal, noting that Cheatham was nothing more than a prima donna looking for a bigger payday, Sterne finally headed up to Boston to arbitrate a settlement for both sides.

As soon as Sterne arrived, Bancroft took advantage of the latest innovation of statistics and laid out reams of paperwork in front of him, arguing that Cheatham was not worth his salt, confirming that he was just an ordinary ballplayer. Sterne sided with Bancroft. A new deal was unlikely.

Cheatham lashed out like a sinking shipwreck survivor clinging to the side of a lifeboat. He wasn't going to drift away quietly into dark waters. Someone was going to hear his pleas.

Bypassing the press altogether, Cheatham still managed to get his voice heard and quickly secured a petition of five thousand signatures from loyal Fans who sided with the club's star attraction.

Backed by the Governor, Bancroft nevertheless remained silent. He watched in quiet delight as Cheatham squirmed to get his way.

Cheatham became desperate. First, he threatened to leave the League and bolt for Schnockerd's Frontier League. No reaction.

Then he threatened a lawsuit, claiming, of all things, that he was the victim of a vast conspiracy of perpetrators that led all the way up to Sterne. Still no reaction.

Finally, in a last-ditch twist of despair and dramatics, Cheatham stepped out onto a window ledge of an eight-story building and threatened to hurl himself down onto the growing throng of onlookers below if he didn't get a new deal before the end of the day.

The harrowing spectacle lasted nearly eight hours as hundreds of people packed the narrow street and watched Cheatham rave the whole time. Between bouts of comic lunacy and rambling monologues, someone finally grabbed Cheatham's ankles and yanked him back in the building. They smothered him in a straightjacket as he kept prattling on and rushed him off to the nearest asylum for a thorough examination.

No one could determine whether or not Cheatham was a certified loon or a master manipulator. So after spending a week in a padded cell, Cheatham was released. As soon as he was let out, he began rambling again about his contract and the newspapers once again jumped on his story.

Appalled by the negative publicity Cheatham was creating,

and limited in his influence to stifle the entire press corps, Sterne ordered Bancroft to do everything necessary to stop Cheatham from jeopardizing the Game's prestige.

Did this mean actually offering Cheatham a new contract and giving him what he wanted? Sterne waved his hand in the air, conceding. Whatever it took.

As if he were forced to swallow a bag full of thumb tacks, Bancroft reluctantly offered Cheatham a new deal with a substantial raise and just like that the whole thunderous dispute abruptly ended.

The wide-eyed world of Base-Ball resumed its daily affairs in relative tranquility and no one grumbled about their contract for a number of years. Not even "Red" Cheatham.

Some time later, though, Cheatham couldn't resist getting back on the bandwagon to complain about his contract. Groans and whispers of discontent were soon heard coming out of his mouth. But no one listened to him this time. The obvious reason was that Cheatham, never a good enough player to deserve such an exorbitant contract in the first place, saw his production on the field drop so much the last couple of years that everyone expected him to be out of the League after the end of the season. But that didn't stop him.

Nearing the end of the season, and with his contract soon expiring, Cheatham upped his theatrics to the point of silliness, ranting and bashing things around like a caged gorilla. Yet no one paid any attention to him, no matter how loud he got. Everyone around him had finally grown tired of his antics. He became a *persona non grata*.

Cheatham tried everything in his book to attract attention, but it was clear that his days were numbered. Screaming, raging, throwing tantrums and foaming at the mouth did nothing. Time was running out.

On the last day of the season Cheatham gave made one last attempt to create a scene and cause a stir. After the game, with writers mustering their last interviews and players gathering their things for the off-season, Cheatham chained himself to his locker and demanded his voice be heard one more time. Everyone stopped and looked at him for a second, then went about their business.

An hour later, the clubhouse emptied except for Cheatham, who continued blathering while pressed up against the steel lockers. Someone turned out the light and he heard the door slam behind him.

Cheatham finally stopped his ranting and immediately started crying for help. He squirmed and kicked in a futile effort to free himself from his chains. He had foolishly tossed the key to the lock down on the floor and couldn't get to it. He screamed at the top of his lungs but no one came. The clubhouse was an empty cellar.

He was stuck there for two days until he finally heard the door behind him jostle open.

"Oh, thank God! Someone help me!"

A fat, greasy, hairy man in a white undershirt and a cigar nub stuffed in the corner of his mouth shuffled in and saw Cheatham plastered against the locker.

"Thank Christ! Those bastards left me here to rot. Not only did they have the audacity not to listen to my appeal for a sensible wage increase, they also abandoned me in this dungeon along with its rats and spiders. Wait till they get their comeuppance when I secure my next financial windfall!"

The man in the undershirt stared silently at Cheatham.

"Right, my good man. Now will you kindly retrieve the key to these locks and free me so I can go about my business? It's on the floor, over there."

The man chewed on his cigar and shuffled away, out of view.

"What are you doing? Come back here! I demand to be unshackled. Do you hear me?"

The man came back, this time with a two-wheeled hand truck.

"What the hell is that?"

The man proceeded to disengage Cheatham's locker from the rest of the row, rocking it from side to side until it was in the middle of the floor, all the while keeping Cheatham chained to it.

"I appreciate the effort, whatever your name is, but I do believe an easier way out of my predicament is just to pick up the key on the floor there and unlock these chains."

The man took the hand truck and stepped behind Cheatham and his locker.

"A fine gratuity will be in order, I assure you, for freeing me. Once I secure my next contract, you won't be forgotten, I guarantee—"

There was a banging behind him and a violent jarring. Next thing he knew, Cheatham was tilted backwards.

"What the hell is going on?"

There was no response. Cheatham and the locker began to move.

"What are you doing? Unchain me! Do you hear me? I demand rationality!"

But he kept moving, across the clubhouse and to the steps leading up to the outside door. Slowly, the man lifted Cheatham up the steps, one at a time.

Cheatham began to prattle once again. "I'll have your neck once I'm free, you stinking bastard…they don't know who they're dealing with… I'm talking the most crippling of lawsuits…they're gonna pay for this!"

Once at the top of the stairs, the door flew open and daylight flooded the stairwell. Cheatham was wheeled across the walkway toward the street curb.

"They've done it this time… I'm going to get fifteen thousand, twenty thousand…the highest dollar amount… I'll be the highest paid player in history… No one will ever come close!"

The locker slammed down at the foot of the curb and Cheatham heard the clanking rustle of the hand truck behind him. Facing the street, he continued his delirious tirade, waiting for any passerby to notice his remonstration.

Effervescent Elixirol

Frank Horgan was known for his incredibly prodigious strength and ability to smash home runs farther and more frequently than anybody else. A genuine slugger in the truest sense, Horgan established himself as the game's first home run king, surpassing totals that not even entire teams could accomplish.

A giant of a man, standing six foot six, with hands and feet that dwarfed normal mens', Horgan could stand at the plate and launch towering shots over the fence time and again with ease. Wielding the largest bat ever seen, people paid to sneak into the ballpark early to witness the slugger's immense power during batting practice.

His feats with the long ball became legendary. Whenever he stepped up to the plate, everyone in the park stood up, anticipating something special. Horgan seldom disappointed. If he made solid contact, the ball shot off his bat like a round shot blasted into the sky, disappearing into the blue without a trace of descent.

Horgan's home runs became so celebrated that it created a subculture of enthusiasts who gathered behind the outfield fence just for the chance to fetch one of his balls and claim ownership. These enthusiasts later formed a semi-formal club and called themselves the Horgan Ball-Hawks, dedicated to retrieving every home run hit and recording how far the ball went and where it landed.

This became tricky in his home park of Boston. Since it

was located in the middle of a residential neighborhood, home run balls were frequently lost on the tops of apartment buildings or lodged in between crannies where they disappeared, sometimes taking years to be discovered. But the Ball-Hawks did their best to hunt them down and carefully document the end results. The club quickly grew in size and it became commonplace to see dozens of men chasing balls down the middle of the street as if they were running after a cable car.

Luckily for Horgan, his colossal strength was a tremendous asset. His other skills, such as fielding and running, were sub-par, to put it kindly. His Base-Ball acumen was quite poor; he usually failing to grasp even the most basic concepts of the game like force outs and sacrifices.

Some speculated that Horgan might have been a tad bit mentally challenged, a slow-witted simpleton, as evidenced by the molasses-speed, bewildering answers he gave to sportswriters whenever they asked him questions like, "Have you always been that strong?" or "Where in the world did you learn to hit a ball that far?" Inevitably, Horgan replied with incomprehensible gobbledygook unfit for print and left the writers scratching their heads, unable to figure him out.

For the most part, they left him alone and let him go about his business, crushing home runs and spawning the growing fascination surrounding his freakish might. The only trouble was finding a place for him on the field so he had the chance at getting four or five at-bats every game. After experimenting with him in the outfield, and where he failed to shag down the most routine fly balls with his pillar-like legs, they finally put him at first base where he was a lesser liability.

With a position finally secured, Horgan really took off. While the next home run leader after him averaged fifteen or eighteen home runs a season, Horgan entered a stretch of seasons when he hit thirty-five, thirty-eight, forty, then forty-four home runs. As the needle pointed north, so did the surrounding frenzy over his accomplishments. Everyone wanted a piece of Horgan. They wanted to know the secret to his prodigious slugging. They wanted to know his story.

The writers stepped up their efforts to get a decent interview out of him, but every time they approached him, Horgan stared confusingly at them and emitted a slow groan, as if he were an imbecilic oaf. They simply could not get anything out of him.

Then, one time during a road trip in New York, a traveling writer for one of the Boston papers spotted Horgan in a drinking establishment off the beaten path. Flashing a wad of cash and putting the charm on a few of the lady servers, Horgan looked anything but imbecilic. Instead of approaching him there, the stunned writer decided to secretly investigate the true identity behind the game's most prolific slugger.

Horgan went about his usual ways, shrugging off questions and maintaining his distance. In the meantime, his prowess for the long ball reached an all-time high, hitting an unprecedented ten home runs in twelve at-bats. The Base-Ball world went into a tizzy.

Yet the writer who spotted him in New York went to work trying to uncover the truth about the celebrated, yet enigmatic, home run king. At first, nothing odd seemed to turn up on him. Everyone willing to comment on Horgan said the same thing, that he was relatively quiet and reserved outside the ballpark and no one reported any suspicious behavior. To them, he was a gentle giant.

But the writer dug deeper, determined to get to the truth of who Horgan really was. Unafraid to bend the unwritten rules of ethics between sportswriters and the players and clubs they covered, he snuck into the clubhouse one day when they weren't playing and broke into Horgan's locker.

Stuffed deep inside the locker, hidden behind a tin of talcum powder and a jar of menthol rub, was a dark bottle with a fancy label: "Effervescent Elixirol."

A simple drawing of a man with his shirt off, contorting himself in a way to show off his vigorous upper body, adorned the label with the byline, "A Wondrous Potion to Restore Vitality and Promote Surplus Strength and Sturdiness to the Sinews."

Clearly, "Effervescent Elixirol" was a patent medicine Horgan used to build up his body. Judging by his recent power surge, the writer figured the nostrum actually worked on some level. There was only one way to get to the truth. The writer was going to confront Horgan.

After a game where Horgan blasted another home run, sending it crashing through a window three houses down the block, the writer and several of his colleagues surrounded Horgan, asking him the usual questions. He continued his usual routine, feigning dimwittedness. But after the other sportswriters gave up trying to secure a good quote and walked away, the writer held his ground. He stood in front of Horgan with his notebook and pencil and fired off questions.

"You must be doing something special to be in such a historic groove, hitting eleven homers in just as many at-bats. C'mon, Frank, what's your secret? Calisthenics? Vitamins? Eating more vegetables?"

Horgan kept his head down as he finished getting into his clothes.

The writer kept at him. "Or is it something else, something with a little more kick, eh, Frank? Nobody else has ever gotten close to what you're doing."

"I ain't got nothin' to say. Just good, old-fashioned country strength, I guess." Horgan tapped down his hat on his head, darted a look into the writer's eyes, and fled the locker room.

The writer chased after him, spouting off questions, trying to get Horgan to talk. Once outside, he took off down the street.

The writer kept pace. "What is it Frank? The world wants to know. How'd you become so big and strong? There's something else, isn't there?"

Horgan refused to take the bait. Instead, he started walking faster to keep away from the writer until he was in a full trot.

The writer stopped and yelled, "Effervescent Elixirol!"

Horgan stopped dead in his tracks and turned around. He stared a hole right through the writer. The writer walked up to Horgan and looked up at him.

"All right, pal. You got me. How the hell did you find out?"

"I wish I could say it was extrasensory perception," the writer said, "but it was much simpler than that. Why don't you tell me what that stuff is? Is it really behind your sudden spike in power?"

Horgan looked down at him. "It better goddamn well be. I mean, look at me. I'm Frankenstein's monster. Before downing hundreds of bottles of Elixirol, I was just a stick, a gangly mutt who could barely lift a bat much less hit a ball half a mile away. Now I'm a freak!"

"So this Effervescent Elixirol's given you the size and strength to perform—"

"Like a goddamn giant out of a folklore tale! They say it's nothing but a quack remedy, but they're wrong. The stuff's magical. I drink a few bottles a week and I feel like Paul Bunyan!"

"And what about your apparent lack of social skills?"

"Just a defensive strategy, to keep you nosy little pencil-pushers at a distance. I never wanted anybody to figure out my secret."

"I see. Aren't you worried about any side effects? Some parts of your body seem to have—"

"It ain't just the hands and feet that's gotten bigger, my friend," Horgan winked his eyes. "I'm like a hot-blooded stallion ready to explode each day. It's a bit challenging, but at the end of the day everything gets taken care of and all I have to worry about is getting my home runs. A nice tradeoff, I'd say."

The writer asked him more questions and Horgan went on to explain that he discovered the concoction while working in a traveling carnival during the off-season. He first saw a strongman drink it to build his muscles and increase his strength.

"That's when I thought I'd give it a try. I had nothing else to lose. I was such a bad ballplayer, I was on the verge of getting cut from the team. I was down to my last option, I had to do something to stay in the game."

He said the Elixirol gave him a boost of energy at first, but the power and strength came much later. That's when his home run totals started to rise.

"Suddenly, my body started to change and I could bash balls farther than anybody else. It was like a miracle. It felt like a blast of molten steel got poured into my insides. I became a one-man wrecking crew!"

The writer wondered what exactly in the Elixirol made him transform into a power-hitting beast.

"They say it's got all sorts of things in it, like mineral oil, turpentine, exotic spices and rattlesnake grease. But there's one key thing that makes the whole thing work, a secret ingredient."

"What's that?"

Horgan cupped his hands and bent down to whisper in the writer's ear. "Monkey jism."

"Excuse me?"

"Y'know. Stuff out of a monkey's balls, juice, test'arone, or whatever they call it. I'm telling you, whatever the hell it is, I'm a goddamn Goliath for it. I'm the king of home runs!"

The writer just stood there, unable to jot anything down on his notebook. He shook his head. "A bizarre quack medicine, made out of the bodily fluids of monkeys? Something that actually works? I got to look into this."

"Fair enough," Horgan said, "but do me a favor. Don't run with the story yet until I talk with the Elixirol folks."

"Why?"

"Maybe I can convince them to become a spokesman of theirs, touting its potency. We may be on the verge of something big here. Imagine that, a wonder drug that enhances the performance for ballplayers. Who wouldn't want to be part of that? I'd bet the League would welcome us with open arms and make this thing as common to the game as pine tar and chewing tobacco. It's a no-brainer!"

A Febrile Hankering

The body of George Malone lay in the doorway one hot and sticky afternoon in late September. Policemen and investigators were busy moving around the tiny apartment, trying to gather clues over the ballplayer's death. The fresh crime scene bore no evidence of a break-in, robbery or scuffle. Someone had shot him at close range, once in the chest and three times in the groin. Surprisingly, very little blood had spilled.

Malone was the star pitcher for the Philadelphia Robustos — debonair, sophisticated and urbane — and was, by all accounts, the club's biggest philanderer. As the investigation proceeded, it became known just how much a ladies man Malone really was. Just within the city limits alone, Malone was found to have up to thirteen girlfriends, all of them engaged in a relationship with the pitcher to some degree at the same time.

After an extensive interview process with all thirteen women, the profile on Malone came back with the same description: he was not at all the sleazy, lecherous man bent on getting as much carnal pleasure as one would imagine with thirteen girlfriends. Instead, they all depicted him as a faithful esquire-type who stopped at nothing to keep them happy. He showered them all with gifts of affection, adoration and love. In return, they loved him just as much.

Though no one knew the full extent of his affair-making, none of them revealed a motive to kill him and almost all of them had iron-clad alibis at the time of his murder. The team of investigators dug deep into their lives, looking to unearth anything remotely suspicious. They were not successful.

Surprisingly, most of the women seemed to have been cut from the same cloth. They were pretty but not knock-out gorgeous. They lived alone and were relatively independent. They worked as librarians, teachers, maids, seamstresses, nurses and office assistants. They were intelligent but not college educated. And they all had a deep love for the written word.

The investigators stayed on track. They couldn't believe that none of them ever demanded his hand in marriage. They couldn't believe that jealousy, rage or resentment never entered the picture at any time for any of the thirteen. Love was never made to be so neat and tidy. One of them surely must have cracked.

Yet, none of the ladies appeared to have had the wherewithal to do such a heinous act. Was there another person Malone was seeing? Perhaps someone from out of town? They doubled their efforts and still came up short. It was as if Malone was a victim of a random act of violence. The investigators were baffled.

By then, Malone's murder was national news. His mysterious death was only eclipsed by his seemingly impossible lifestyle of carrying on affairs with more than a dozen different women at the same time. His stamina must have been extraordinary.

As the story became a nationwide sensation, the investigators launched an unprecedented effort to uncover every detail in Malone's life all the way back to the beginning. Who was he? Why did he have such a fascination with women? Did he ever cross paths with anyone that could have led to his early demise? They were hoping to expose a sliver of light that might have led down a favorable path toward a suspect. Perhaps there was another lover in his life somewhere, sometime. Someone whose heart he may have inadvertently broken.

While they chased down every detail in Malone's love life, a small investigation ensued of his Base-Ball career. He pitched for Philadelphia for nine years, accumulating an impressive list of statistics while becoming the club's vocal leader and clubhouse mentor. Everyone on the team, and even the manager at times, looked to him for guidance and advice. His calm and confident demeanor went a long way with everybody associated with the club. Everyone on the team was devastated by the news of his murder.

How could he have pitched so well while leading such an extraordinary private life?

They said that he always showed up on time, always performed at the highest, most professional level, and never talked about his life outside the ballpark. He was an exemplary pitcher and teammate.

He never showed any signs of problems recently? Never once mentioned anything out of the ordinary?

Nope. Everyone knew Malone had a rather, well, busy social life. Ask any regular ticket-holder and they'd say the same thing. No matter what Malone did in his private life, he always showed up to pitch and compete. He was a pro's pro.

So, no outside incidents of trouble? Nothing out of the ordinary?

No, nothing that jumps out. The only thing out of the ordinary was his bad stretch of luck to end the season. Normally, he was our go-to guy in September, pushing us near the top of the standings. But this year he was off for some reason. I don't know if he was sick or something. He'd come into the clubhouse looking like he was up the whole night, yawning and rubbing his eyes.

No word of anything out of the ordinary?

Nah. He never mentioned anything. But he didn't look like his normal self. Sure, he jumped into his uniform and got up on the mound, but he lost every game he pitched the final month of the season. And for that, it cost us in the standings. We finished second from the bottom. A real shock. It never happened to us before. We always counted in him to pull us through.

I guess his life outside of Base-Ball finally caught up with him.

No one never dared to ask him. Sure, whispers always circled around. Especially outside the clubhouse. But he never let anything distract him from pitching.

Not as far as you could tell.

If he did have troubles, he was an expert at keeping things tightly sealed. He could have had fifty broads on the side and we wouldn't have known. He still would have been the same inside these walls and in between the white lines.

The case remained unsolved. Despite the national publicity, no one came forward with a helpful tip. Even Malone's girlfriends congregated together and floated a five hundred dollar reward for anybody who could provide any useful information that led to an arrest. Nothing came.

Over the next few months, the intense media frenzy had quieted down and the detectives resumed their investigation, running into one dead end after another. Then a letter arrived at the desk of the chief detective, with no return address.

He opened it and saw a handwritten note in bad penmanship.

Too bad the son-of-a-bitch couldn't pitch like he used to. It cost us dearly in the standings. Maybe he shouldn't have been chasing skirts around so much. It finally caught up with him. It messed up his brain and screwed up his delivery. Bastard got what he deserved. — A Disgruntled Fan.

The chief investigator felt something in the envelope. He reached in and pulled out a tiny metal key. It belonged to a small, antique wind-up toy, the exact kind found on Malone's kitchen table. No one ever reported that fact in the newspapers. No one on the ballclub knew about it. Not even any of Malone's thirteen girlfriends.

Out West, intense rivalries inflame the passions and tempers of competing clubs thanks to Pete Schnockerd's latest innovation: the pennant race.

Not content with the status quo, Schnockerd devises a playoff system at the end of every regular season where the top teams in the standings go on to play an extra series of games for a lucrative bonus. The last team standing gets the most money and wins a symbolic "pennant" to be hung in their ballpark.

While the pennant is a source of pride for the club owners, all the players really care about is the bonus money. Sometimes the payout is almost half the average salary. They compete like mongrels in a dogfight to get into the playoffs and win as much money as possible, sometimes going to great lengths to knock the other team out of the race and the playoffs.

It sets up to be an exciting finish to the season. Before, clubs ended the season not particularly concerned where they ended up in the standings. Some clubs with an overriding sense of pride felt it necessary to compete all the way till the end and finish as high in the standings as possible. But the majority of players rode the string out, collected their wages and bolted after the last game, either to go barnstorming across the Midwest or picking up a job over the winter. Some even departed their teams early just to get a head start on the off-season. There was no incentive to do anything more.

Schnockerd changes all that when he introduces the playoff system. Players now relish the thought of making a significant amount of extra money. And Cranks who indulge in gambling soon find a whole new reason to wager on games. A frenzy electrifies the National Frontier League and players and Cranks alike revel in the game's latest development.

Jockeying for position, teams fight like jackals just to get into the playoffs. Once in, teams really turn the screws to knock one another out. They do everything they can to defeat each other. Rivalries take on a whole new meaning. Things get heated, sometimes bloody. Genuine hatred and hostility foul the air. It is an awesome time.

Around this time, the term "Base-Ball lifer" enters the lexicon of the sport. Over the years, players who know nothing else but the game—those who clawed and scratched to stay in it in one way or the other—become known by that epithet. They are men who don't necessarily have the talent to stay in the game, but are crafty enough to hang around, bouncing around the Frontier League from one club to the next for years, finding ways to survive in the game they love.

Chester Deevers and Bill "Spit" Mullansky are two men who perfectly fit the mold of Base-Ball lifers. Both remain in the leagues for more years than they care to admit and become encrusted with hardened shells of experience that have tempered their perseverance. Each one is smart and intelligent, but also

DEEVERS – SCRANTON

MULLANSKY – PHILA.

savvy and cunning. For years, they battle each other in a duel of one-upmanship that further gains intensity when they find themselves in the middle of Schnockerd's playoff races.

Deevers comes from the old coal mining towns of Eastern Pennsylvania, where he worked in confined, filthy tunnels since the age of five. When Base-Ball enters the region, he jumps at the chance to play and vows never to leave the game. His hard-working ethic and zeal to learn everything there is to know about Base-Ball give Deevers a chance to do just that. He becomes a decent player, mostly at first base, but when he wrecks his knee while sliding at second base, he fears his career is over. However, Deevers then convinces the owner of the Scranton club to make him the everyday manager while continuing to play first base a couple of times a week. It is a brilliant move and Deevers manages to stay in the league.

Mullansky lives and breathes Base-Ball and isn't ashamed to

do anything necessary to keep playing. He once gets a fellow teammate drunk and stuffs him on a train to Baltimore just to win a competing spot on the team. Mullansky is as devious and conniving as Deevers is gritty and shrewd.

They face each other often and develop an instant disliking for one another. Call it bad blood or contentious friction, both men want nothing more than to beat the other one and do it convincingly. Deevers wants to outsmart Mullansky by pulling the wool over his eyes. Mullansky wants to bloody Deevers, abuse him, embarrass him.

Contests between the two become the stuff of legend, but when both players go west to play in the Frontier League and vie for a playoff spot, their rivalry enters a new phase of intensity as Deevers and Mullansky find ways to defeat each other, usually ending in ugly melees. Cheating, violence and unconventional strategic moves always play a part in their duels, much to the delight of the Cranks.

But before they can continue waging war in the playoffs, Mullansky loses his position to a younger player. Out of a job and looking in from the other side of the fence, Mullansky heads back East and finds a starting job in the American Association.

The heated rivalry between Deevers and Mullansky is cut short. But not for long.

"Hello, Central? I lost Milwaukee again. Can you please re-connect me? Hello?" The line to Niedler's telephone goes dead again. He cranks the box one more time and hears a garbled voice on the other end. "Yes, this is the Sterne office once again. Will you please connect me to Milwaukee? You've already wasted valuable time."

Niedler hunches over his desk with the handset pressed up against his face. He holds a small pad of paper with a jumble of words and numbers scratched all over it. His collar is opened and his skin is clammy. "You want me to hold? Hold what? What does that mean, HOLD? Connect me to Milwaukee at once, do you hear me!" Underneath the layers of his finely tailored attire, his heart races. "Goddamn newfangled machinery! What's it going to be next?"

A voice crackles in his ear. "You got him? Excellent. Put me on. Hello, Pete? Can you hear me? Yes, loud and clear. Yes, this gadgetry is something else. But, please, let's continue discussing our arrangement before we get disconnected one more time."

A long exchange follows. Niedler rapidly scribbles notes on his pad of paper, ripping off one piece after the next. "The general framework of the agreement is in place. The Governor's approved your stipulations, in exchange for the one specific requirement on his end. Now, if we can agree on a location for this engagement, we can iron out the details of the stock transfer."

He listens to the voice on the other end. "Chicago? He'd never approve that. Much too close to your city." Before Niedler interjects further, he is interrupted. "Yes, I understand. A grand opportunity to showcase the game in front of the world, a fantastic marketing ploy. I may be able to convince him with that level of reasoning. Let me get back to you."

Niedler disconnects himself from Milwaukee and dials a single number on his private line. He thinks he will have to push hard on the idea of Chicago, but, surprisingly, he doesn't have to. The conversation is brief. Relieved, he cranks the box and reaches the switchboard operator. "Central? Sterne's office. One more time with Milwaukee. What? I know it's long distance, but may I remind you that this office is one of the very few in the entire city who pay handsomely for this service? I'd watch it if I were you. Now, do it before I get the nerve to do something rash!"

He lets out an exhalation and rubs his temples while he waits. His hands tremble ever so slightly. Finally, a connection is made. "Pete? Henry. Thank God. Looks like we got ourselves a deal. No objections on his part. The last hurdle's cleared. Now we can move forward with the finer details, starting with your list of selected assets, again, cleared by the Governor. We just need to figure out the numbers."

A half an hour later, Niedler wraps up the negotiation. "We'll be sending you the paperwork, special delivery. Once we get your signature, we'll get the ball rolling, so to speak. In the meantime, any minutiae will be hammered out in the coming months. I guess the wink and nod will have to wait till October." Before hanging up, Niedler thanks him.

He disconnects and dials the number again. "Yes, everything's set. First week in October, right after the season ends. I don't see a problem, unless he reneges on his promise. I just can't imagine him doing that. He's got too much to lose if he tries to dupe us. We're giving him exactly what he wants, and in the end, you'll be getting yours." He listens. "No. Just the fine particulars need to be worked out. I can probably hand that off to an underling with no problem."

Niedler hangs up the phone. He collapses back in his chair. After months of traveling, cajoling and persuading, an agreement has finally been reached. What was once impossible to fathom is now a reality. J.B. Sterne was going to confront Schnockerd once and for all and decide who was going to be Base-Ball's sole master of the game.

Exhaustion takes hold of his body. The months-long ordeal has taken its toll, but his brokering of the deal is his best and most significant one in a very long time. He knows how personal the stakes are, and for the first time, allows himself to think of the ensuing rewards that are likely to follow, perhaps even regaining the confidence of his boss.

While he reflects, the phone rings. He picks it up. "Yes?

Absolutely. I'll be right up." The Governor wants to see him. He stashes his notes in a brown folder and heads upstairs with a newfound bounce in his step.

Niedler knocks on the door.

"Come in."

He opens the door and sees the Governor sitting behind his desk. Then he sees Sterne's associates on opposite sides, buttoned up in their high collars and clutching their briefcases. A shock blasts through Niedler, who knows immediately why he was called into his office.

"Henry," Sterne's voice is steely.

Niedler stares at the two men. "Shadrach. Toplitz."

Both men stare back through their pince-nez spectacles.

"You've seen this many times before over the years, so I'll spare you the histrionics," Sterne commences. "Henry, you've done your deed with the Schnockerd situation. Now, I'm afraid, I have no need for you here anymore. So I'm giving you one of two choices."

Niedler is paralyzed, barely registering what Sterne is saying. Just like everyone else who has dealt with the Governor over the decades, his end has finally arrived.

"I'm building a rail route across South America. I need someone there to help in matters. You'd be reporting to my number two man there. Are you with me?"

Niedler whispers to himself, "All we've been through together, what we've accomplished. Poof! Just like that and it's over. I guess I should have known better."

"Business, Henry. The first order of business is —"

"What about Schnockerd? Who's going to guide this thing until the very end?"

"You said it yourself. The hard work is over. I'll put someone on it to see it through." Sterne turns his attention to Shadrach and Toplitz, who busy themselves with paperwork and signatures.

A current of emotions charges through Niedler. He is left

standing in front of the desk, deflated and empty.

"Anything else, Henry?" Sterne throws his bifocals on and inspects a ledger. He doesn't look up.

Niedler cannot bring himself to speak. It doesn't matter. He knows that the other choice has already been accepted without the need to say another word. In a matter of seconds, decades worth of loyalty and sacrifice vanish into thin air. Niedler has now become a blurry memory in the eyes of his former feudal lord.

The deal is finalized. Emulating Schnockerd's original idea of a playoff series, Sterne approaches his nemesis with the idea of matching up his brand of Base-Ball against Schnockerd's — the Frontier League with its raucous and unruly players versus the refined, honorable nobility of the American Association's — fielding their best men on both sides in a best-of-five series to see which is the superior league.

It is hailed as the preeminent clash of Base-Ball ideals, a winner-take-all duel for supremacy. The upcoming engagement is quickly touted as the biggest sporting event ever, bigger than anything ever seen. It is a match of immense consequence.

The stakes are enormous. The winner of the series gets to declare victory and pronounce dominion over the entire Base-Ball realm. Besides enjoying the bragging rights, a giant pot of money is there for the taking. Everyone knows the future of the game hangs in the balance. Does Schnockerd have another ace up his sleeve or is Sterne finally going to reclaim his cherished empire? It makes for high drama.

The venue and time for the series can't be more opportune. It is the year Chicago hosts the World's Columbian Exposition, the World's Fair that had been held all over the globe since the middle of the century. The city erects an extravagant diorama of magnificent neoclassical buildings along the lakefront on the South Side, with mammoth pavilions housing the latest triumphs of industry, technology, culture and the humanities. Canals and lagoons spread across the expanse of the exhibition, giving the Fair a sense of grandeur and opulence. Millions of people are expected to attend.

Sterne has no complaints over the location for the momentous event. Besides inaugurating the first-ever Championship Series, the Exposition is the perfect setting to lift his game onto the world stage and introduce the whole globe to America's National Pastime.

Once Schnockerd signs off on the deal, they scramble to find a location to build the ballpark. Luckily, there is a plot of unused land along a stretch west of the main fairground. Sterne puts up all the money to secure enough acreage to build a park to house as many as a hundred thousand spectators. The cost is enormous but the potential payoff is worth it. Folks can walk the promenade of the Midway, soak in the worldly displays of international flavor before taking in the main attraction of their country's very own cultural achievement.

Everything comes together for one final act of kismet. It's just a matter of time before everything is settled. While the rest of the world braces for the upcoming extravaganza, J.B. Sterne and Pete Schnockerd prepare themselves to finally get what each has always wanted. ■

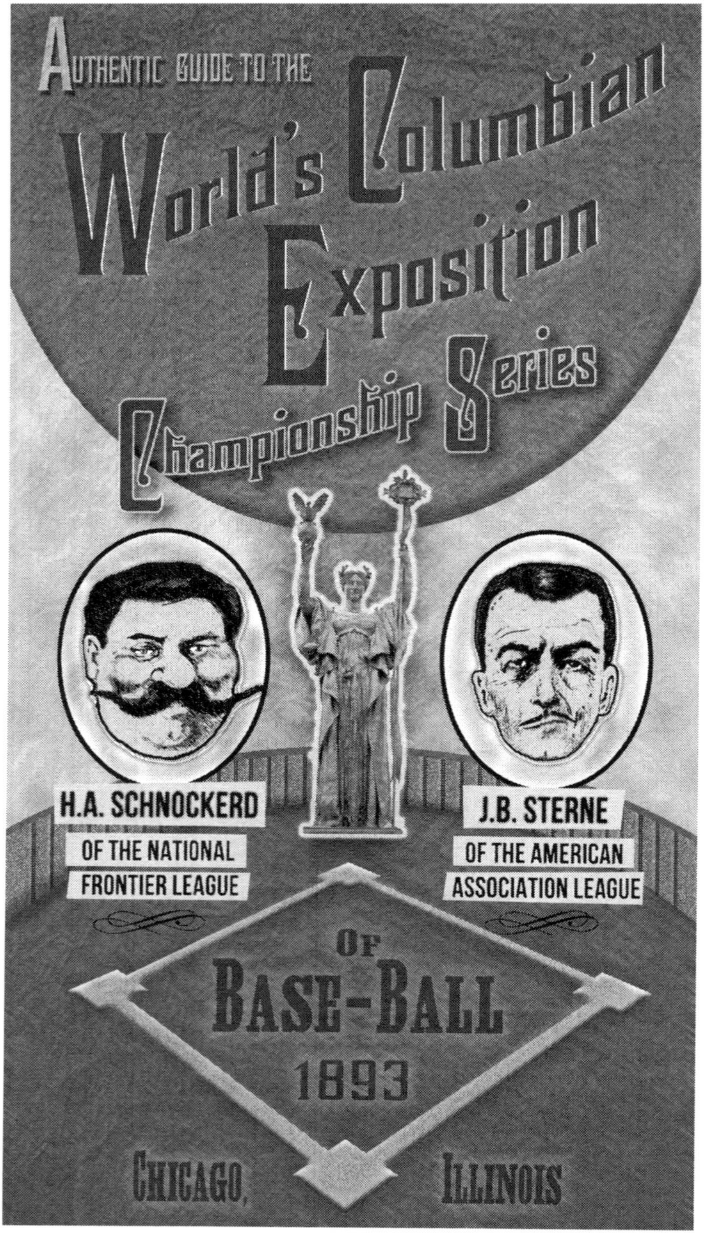
Authentic Guide to the
World's Columbian
Exposition
Championship Series
H.A. SCHNOCKERD
OF THE NATIONAL
FRONTIER LEAGUE
J.B. STERNE
OF THE AMERICAN
ASSOCIATION LEAGUE
Of
BASE-BALL
1893
Chicago, Illinois

X.

GUMMER OF THE CENTURY
(1893)

The *General Stockton II* pulls into Union Depot between Madison and Adams Streets, plugged into the heart of the Midwest's burgeoning metropolis. The morning is crisp and shafts of sunlight streak past steel beams and into the station. The knotty air is already thick with tense, vibrant energy.

Herds of people bustle their way on and off the platform. Hiding in the shadows of the headhouse is a cluster of reporters wearing flat caps and brown pinstriped vests and sack coats, carrying notebooks.

A release of steam, then a door slides open to one of the twin passenger cars. A couple of well-dressed men hop out and begin unloading luggage and cabin trunks. After several minutes, J.B. Sterne steps out into the light wearing his usual top hat and Paddock coat.

"That's him!" The reporters dash into the morass of moving bodies and form a blockade in front of the Governor. They immediately start firing off questions.

"What are your real chances against Schnockerd?"

"Do you really think you can beat him in a best-of-five series?"

"How are you going to win even one game with a lineup like that?"

"Thoughts of grandeur aside, aren't you worried about getting thoroughly embarrassed?"

"When will you admit that this was a very bad mistake on your part?"

Clearly, Sterne is not home anymore. The local beat writers are free to ask him anything, and in any manner, without the fear of a lethal backlash or threat of reprisal. Since he doesn't own any of the newspapers, and has very little influence in this part of the country, he is free game to them. And they take liberties in bombarding the prominent figure from New York with questions tainted with an unsavory bias and a smattering of rudeness.

Sterne puts on a good face. He steps off and slowly pushes his way through the crush of reporters, beaming and smiling. They continue their barrage.

"What will happen to your men at first sign of blood?"

"Who's going to cry foul first—you, your manager, or one of the players—when things don't go your way?"

"What about the Gus Johnson fiasco? Was that your biggest mistake, shipping him over here, right into Schnockerd's breadbasket? Some consider it a gift since he's been the best player in all of Base-Ball."

The last question stops Sterne. He snaps his head and glowers at the reporter who asked the question. His eyes turn into daggers. "Look here, my good man." Sterne is about to lay into him but at the last second stops himself. He gathers his composure. "My men have solid constitutions and can play with anybody. I expect a good series. You may be surprised by how well we'll compete. Now, good day gentlemen. See you all at the ballpark!"

Sterne weaves his way through the station and ducks into a hansom cab for the nine-mile journey directly to the ballpark.

The rest of his entourage continues unloading the contents of the passenger car for eventual delivery to a penthouse suite on Michigan Avenue. The reporters make a mad dash to their own transportation, hoping to follow the Governor.

Along the shores of the lakefront, the World's Columbian Exposition's White City unfolds its magnificence with massive, neoclassic structures. The Grand Basin and its surrounding lagoons gently accommodate Venetian gondolas and replica galleys. Majestic rotundas extend high in the sky with only the imposing Ferris Wheel making a more impactful mark on the skyline. Men, women and their families stroll the grounds in their best attire.

The Midway, the passage heading west of the main fairgrounds, hosts foreign attractions and Buffalo Bill Cody's Wild West Show. Further along, the largest banner ever seen towers over the thoroughfare:

"COME ALL: OUR NATIONAL PASTIME ON DISPLAY. BASE-BALL GAME at 1P.M."

The ballpark is an edifice of freshly ripped wood and iron girders. A sea of planks rises like a tide in the grandstands. The upper deck alone is so massive that it could out-number the total capacities of any of the newer ballparks back East. A formidable fence lines the perimeter, forcing gatecrashers to find a serviceable knothole to sneak a view of the game.

Hoopla is everywhere outside the park. People stand in line, waiting to be the first to enter the premises. Vendors hawk their possessions, from hot dogs and game programs to the latest invention in snackery — the fusion of molasses, popcorn and nuts called Cracker Jack.

Men wrapped in trenchcoats scramble to the opposite side of the walkway to shanty-like booths hastily built to act as temporary bookmaking parlors. Since Sterne banned the practice within the ballpark, gamblers rushed to find a way to continue their feverish practice.

Sterne's cab finally arrives at the front entrance. He steps out and makes a beeline for the gate, hoping to avoid another onrush of reporters. But someone recognizes him from the gathering crowd. "Hey, *Sternes*, why don't you go back to New York with your pansies before we paste your lily-white asses to the ground?"

His private box sits atop the stadium, with a perfect view of the field, pristine with clean-cut, manicured grass, finely dredged infield dirt and foul lines painted white and straight like rules on a chalkboard.

The gates open and an infusion of frenzied Cranks search for good seats. Although gambling has been forbidden, the sale and consumption of alcohol has been allowed. The Cranks guzzle copious amounts of Milwaukee's finest beer, leaving them properly intoxicated well before the start of the game.

But the Cranks are not the only ones in the park rooting for their team. Fans from back East, mostly from New York, have made the trip in loyal support of their League and the Governor. Wearing dark, three-piece suits, spat boots and high hats, they try their best to blend in with the crowd but stick out like dandelions in a grassy field. The Cranks eagerly and shamelessly tease, taunt, harass and throw popcorn at them. The Fans sit in quiet restraint, too timid to do anything about it.

The sun is high and the park already near capacity. Huddled and boisterous, the upper deck begins chanting out loud to get the game started. Even the outfield bleachers, seemingly a half-mile away, drum up a clamor.

Finally, a scattering of uniformed bodies jump out of the dugouts and dash out onto the field. A loud thunderclap goes up. The players stretch, warm up, toss balls around and take batting practice before the pre-game ceremonies commence.

Schnockerd's renowned belly inches its way out of the dugout, followed by the rest of him. The Frontier League's ringmaster engages in lively banter with everyone, jawing with players, Cranks in the stands and even the chief umpire for the series, Larry "Shithouse" Digby, wearing a metal facemask for protection.

While chewing the fat with Digby, Schnockerd's eyes wander across the upper deck and spot's Sterne's private box, decked out with red, white and blue bunting. He sees the Governor sitting like a Roman Emperor overlooking the arena of the Coliseum.

Sterne glances down and sees Schnockerd. Their eyes meet for the very first time.

Both men slightly nod their heads in awkward recognition, not knowing what else to do, until Schnockerd reaches into the dugout and pulls out a half-empty mug of beer. He lifts it into the air, pretending to salute Sterne. Then he raises his other arm and cheerfully waves it like a giddy adolescent who just made eye contact with his best friend across a crowded auditorium.

Sterne glares at the man who's been at the core of his years-long nightmare, the sole source of aggravation, anger, loathing and rage—the one man whom he hadn't yet conquered and destroyed. He'd like nothing more than take the mug of beer and smash it over his head and then giggle like a schoolboy bully, watching his sworn enemy slump to the ground and roll his barrel-shaped body over in a bleeding mess.

Instead, Sterne can only grimace with revulsion.

It is already half-past noon with no sign of the game getting underway. The expanse of spectators in the stands grows increasingly impatient.

Finally, the public address announcer slips into a tiny booth in the upper deck and shoves his face into an oversized megaphone. "Ladies and gentlemen, may I have your attention please? Today's historical festivities will now get underway." A thunderous roar ripples throughout the ballpark.

The first order of pre-game ceremony is the announcement of the lineups, starting with the managers. For the American Association, Sterne's skipper for his Elites, W.H. Pierce, steps out and waves to a tepid chorus of applause, mostly from the minority of Elites Fans.

Then it's Schnockerd's turn. The rest of the ballpark erupts when he walks out and approaches Pierce. The managers shake hands over home plate and pose for a photographer. Smiles abound, but a slight tint of aversion seeps into Pierce's face, as if he just clasped hands with someone who used his own hand as a slobber rag.

Next, Pierce's team is introduced, many of them straight off the Elites' roster. A flood of boos rains down on the field. Philo Grogan, anchoring the pitching squad, races out and lines up along the foul line. The rest of the team is called out, one by one, including Grogan's battery mate, Stacks Bittner, and the slick-fielding teenager, Fleet Foote, who can't control his excitement enough to quell his visible jitters.

Though the team is mostly comprised of the League's best players and most upstanding individuals, a mild shock runs through the stands when the next two men are called: Frank Horgan, still the home run king but embroiled in controversy over his alleged use of the nostrum Effervescent Elixirol, and Bill Mullansky, who barely made it on a regular roster the last couple of years but must have used his clever guile one more time to get on the series team.

Then the National team is called. Chester Deevers steps out, playing first base and assisting Schnockerd in the dugout, followed by the Mule, Cliff Grumsley, who insists on delivering every single pitch of the series. The rest of the crew includes Sorley McGrady and Hughie O'Hallarhan defending the middle of the infield and, lastly, "Fireplug" Johnson patrolling the outfield. The Cranks let out a loud, riotous cheer that lasts a full minute while pummeling Sterne and his fans with more insults and taunts.

Though both teams are assembled and ready to go, the pregame ceremonies have just begun. What follows is an extensive and seemingly endless circus of people tromping on the field—from marching bands, singers and dancers to Egyptian snake charmers and even Buffalo Bill's Wild West Show, complete with bison, whooping Indians and screaming cowboys. The overblown spectacle further exasperates the crowd.

Already nearing two o'clock, the field clears, replaced by a long progression of dignitaries who step onto a dais in front of home plate to dedicate the day's events to everything from divine providence to the lowliest of administration officials of the Fair commission. The city's mayor—crusty, rumpled and hunched over—slowly walks over to the podium and presents the keys to the city to none other than J. Barron Sterne for his efforts to bring the game of Base-Ball to the Exposition, though he fails to mention his greater achievement, that of being the principal architect of the Game itself.

Sterne rises in his box and acknowledges the mayor and waves at the Fans who applaud vigorously until Sterne grows uncomfortable with the attention. The mayor then rolls out a sheet of paper that's almost as tall as he is, intending to deliver a tortuous, long-winded speech.

Before he has a chance to fasten his bifocals on the tip of his nose, the crowd disperses a vehement, deafening boom of protest. They have had enough. They want the game to begin. The demonstration drowns out the mayor's words, and before someone jumps out of the stands and throws a canvas sack over his head, he rolls up the paper and steps away in defeat.

At long last, after the singing of the National Anthem, the game can begin. The Championship Series deciding the fate of so much finally gets underway.

"Play ball!"

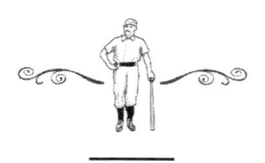

Through the first five innings, no one has scored. It's become a pitcher's duel between Grumsley and Grogan, though the Mule has allowed his share of baserunners.

Schnockerd nervously chews on sunflower seeds, leaving a pile of shells at his feet. Deevers stands next to him in the dugout, his eyes locked on the infield. He leans against the metal railing, toying with a toothpick in his mouth.

"I can't do this any longer. Something's gonna give," Schnockerd says.

"It always does," Deevers surveys the field. "Don't get too

nervous. It's not like we're getting our brains bashed in."

"No, not that."

"What?" Deevers looks behind him and sees Schnockerd bobbing forward and back with his legs closed.

"I gotta pee."

"For chrissakes, go find yer'self the pisser. I got 'er covered."

Having downed his twelfth mug of beer, Schnockerd's bladder is about to burst, but he refuses to leave the dugout. He doesn't want to miss anything.

Deevers turns around and searches for something. He finds a couple of mason jars and hands them to Schnockerd. "Here, use these. Hide next to the beer barrel."

Schnockerd empties himself and lets out a long sigh of relief. He buttons up and rejoins Deevers. "What'd I miss?"

"Still nothin'. He just notched his seventh strikeout. This Grogan fella's really one tough hombre."

"What are we gonna do? Can't we come up with something? What's in our bag of tricks?"

"We can't even get on base to do anything like that." Deevers twiddles his toothpick.

"Why don't we scare the pants off him then? Throw him off?"

"McGrady's been giving him the staredown all day but he ain't moved an inch. Stubborn bastard."

"What about O'Hallarhan? Something's got to work." Schnockerd paces.

Deevers notices his uneasiness. "What's gotten into you, Chief?"

"I don't know. Nerves, I guess. If I had it my way, it'd sure be nice to steal the first game. You know what I mean?"

Grogan is a marksman taking pleasure at dispatching each of his Western adversaries. Each pitch is perfectly placed. No one can square him up. Through the first seventeen men he's faced, he's only given up a flair to right field and one walk. He ends the inning by inducing a weak groundball to second.

Schnockerd throws up his arms. "Do something, will ya?"

Deevers grabs his glove and runs out to the field. "I'm working on it."

As tough as Grogan is, the Mule keeps pace with him despite flashing less-than-stellar stuff. Something isn't right with him. His usual pinpoint accuracy is off and his catch-it-and-throw rapidity has tapered off. All day, the hitters have waited for him to make a mistake.

Grumsley's shirt and cap are drenched with sweat but he keeps fighting. He loads the bases but battles back to get the third out before a run crosses the plate.

Deevers returns to the dugout.

"What the hell's wrong with him?" Schnockerd grumbles.

"Why don't you ask him yourself?"

Schnockerd shrugs his shoulders, knowing it's fruitless to question the Mule's performance.

Grogan returns to the mound and keeps firing bullets. The first two batters go down quickly on strikeouts. Then it's O'Hallarhan's turn at the plate. Deevers turns to Schnockerd, "Let's see if the little guy can start something."

O'Hallarhan kicks up a huge cloud of dust in the batters box, choking up on a bat that is just as big as he is. Already 0-for-3 with three strikeouts, he's determined to make contact with the ball.

Digby, O'Hallarhan's favorite target of abuse, snickers. "Hey, Hughie, better watch it or that stick might fall on you and pin you to the ground."

He blasts back. "Don't you fuckin' call one against me you prick, or else I'll shatter this bat over your goddamned head!"

"Shaddup, ya shit-ass pipsqueak. My stitches from last time haven't gotten out yet and I ain't in the mood for any of your bellyachin'." Digby squats down and readies himself for the first pitch.

O'Hallarhan turns toward the mound and scowls at Grogan, baring his rotten teeth. He hoists the bat above his shoulders.

Grogan's first pitch is high and inside.

"Steeer-rike!"

"Sonofabitch!!" O'Hallarhan drops the unwieldy piece of lumber and spins toward Digby, jumping into his face.

Digby throws off his mask and slams himself into his antagonist. Both men fire obscenities at one another like Gatling guns in full bore. Their faces turn blood red and their eyes pop. Their bodies quake in an exchange of rage.

Bittner tries to get in between them but fails. Pierce jumps out of the dugout and attempts to do the same before blows are thrown. The crowd in the stands jumps to their feet. Even Sterne, high up in his box, stands up to observe the troubling fracas.

Deevers and Schnockerd stay in the dugout, watching O'Hallarhan's infamous rage veer out of control. "Why couldn't he do that to Grogan? Just once I'd love to see him use his intensity in a productive manner."

Both men are finally separated and pivot away like boxers in a ring returning to their corners. After a cooling off, Digby pulls his mask over his face and O'Hallarhan lifts up his massive bat in his hands.

Grogan settles back on the mound and continues his assault. O'Hallarhan bravely fights off a bombardment of nasty pitches before flying out to deep center. Jogging back to the dugout, O'Hallarhan lets fly a glob of spit halfway across the diamond and smacks Digby square on his mask, splattering in between its metal bars and into his eye.

Deevers stands motionless next to Schnockerd. "Hmm. Did you see that?"

"Yeah, he got him real good, didn't he?"

"I meant Grogan."

"What?"

"The way he holds his glove. See how close he kept it to his chest before throwing that last pitch? And the previous two, it was lower and farther away, at least an inch or two."

"Yeah. So what?"

"He's tipping his pitches."

"What do you mean?"

"Watch." The next batter steps up to the plate and Grogan sets himself up before winding up. "He's gonna throw a fastball," Deevers says out of the corner of his mouth. Grogan fires a ball and hits the outside corner.

Schnockerd turns his head to Deevers and gives him a puzzled look. "How'd you know that? Do it again."

Deevers correctly calls the next four pitches. "You see?" He whispers. "When his glove is up and tight to his chest, it's a fastball. If the glove's down and away, it's a breaking ball."

"Good eye, professor."

"Quick," Deevers nudges him, "stand in front of me and give out some hand signals to the next batter. I'll stand behind you and tell you which ones to give."

Deevers hides behind Schnockerd and peeks out at the mound, watching Grogan's glove. "Breaking ball," he whispers.

Schnockerd signals to the batter what's coming. He lays off the pitch and watches it dive into the dirt. Two pitches later, the batter drills a fastball past a diving third baseman.

"I think we got him."

The ninth inning rolls around and still no score. In the absence of runs, an air of suspense hangs in the air. McGrady comes out to face Grogan, looking for his first knock of the game.

Deevers peeks out again at Grogan. "First pitch fastball. Quick, give the signal."

Schnockerd dances his hands across his chest and arms. McGrady catches the hidden signal out of the corner of his eyes and waits for the pitch. Grogan delivers the ball right down the middle of the plate and McGrady smashes it down the line for a double. The ballpark erupts.

Grogan is beside himself, furious that he let the potential game-winning run get on base. He gathers himself and wipes out the next two batters.

"Chrissakes," Schnockerd whispers back at Deevers. "They

knew what was coming and he still struck them out."

"Looks like it's up to me." With two out, it's Deevers' chance to bring home McGrady, still stuck on second base.

The public address announcer calls out his name and the Cranks cheer him on. Not known for his bat, Deevers nevertheless has the ace up his sleeve.

Grogan's glove brushes up against his chest before gripping the ball and making the pitch. The fastball paints the outside corner.

"Steeer-rike!" Digby blares.

He takes the next two pitches, breaking balls low and away, before swinging at the next fastball, barely making enough contact to foul it off. Grogan's pitches have more kick than before, as if he's emptying the tank of whatever he's got left.

At the last second, Deevers steps out of the box right before Grogan's next pitch and calls time out, a trick he's learned over the years to disrupt the pitcher's timing. He takes a few practice swings before Digby orders him back in the box. By now the crowd is in a state of frenzy.

Deevers already knows what's coming next: a wipeout slider that crosses the plate at the very last moment before darting away. At the very least, he has to foul it off to stay alive.

Sure enough, Grogan's slider starts out high before sweeping down across his knees. Deevers drops his bat in the zone and gets the slightest knick on the ball.

"Foul ball!"

He guesses that Grogan will stay with the slider until he strikes out. The next four pitches are identical, sweeping over the plate at the very last moment. Deevers again manages to get a splinter of wood on the ball.

Then he sees Grogan's glove up high again and he gears up for the fastball. This is the pitch he has to do something with or else face another barrage of deadly sliders.

The crowd is deafening. McGrady takes a lead off second base. Grogan delivers the pitch.

The fastball comes in on him. Deevers swings, getting enough of the barrel to make solid contact. He bounces the ball right up the middle.

McGrady tears off for third.

Fleet Foote, the best infielder in the world, dives to his left to make the stop but at the last second the ball takes a funny bounce and skips over his glove, sputtering into shallow center field.

McGrady could coast home for the game-winning run. Instead, he rounds third and ratchets up his speed on a collision course with Bittner. The catcher sees McGrady and steps out of the way, but McGrady leans forward with both forearms out and nails Bittner in the throat and chest, knocking him off his feet and slamming his body backwards into the ground. McGrady jumps up, stomps Bittner in the chest again with his spikes, then taps home plate.

McGrady scores the winning run. The Cranks go nuts. The stadium rocks and shakes.

With the final score 1-0, Schnockerd's team takes Game 1.

The hotel bar is loud and lively. The player piano has been going non-stop for three hours. Rounds of drinks for the players keep coming. The man of the hour swivels his stool around to face the bartender.

"Another Old Fashioned, Charlie."

Deevers finally gets the chance to sit alone and ruminate about the day's game and the next. He wonders if Grogan caught on to their discovery that he was tipping his pitches. Next time they shouldn't be so lucky.

While he mulls over the game, two men in derbies and red

bow ties approach the bar. They nod at the bartender but don't order anything. Finally, the one closest to Deevers looks down at him.

"Hey, aren't you the fella with the game-winning knock at the championship game today?"

Deevers nods and sips his drink.

"Congratulations. You beat that pitcher from New York. What's his name?"

"Grogan," the other man with him says.

"Yeah, that's right, Philo Grogan. He's supposed to be their number one pitcher. A real…what do they call him? Oh yeah, a real *professional*. And you got the best of him today."

Deevers flashes a quick smile but stares straight ahead with his Old Fashioned. The man keeps looking down at him.

"Say, I didn't get your name. What's it again?"

"It's Deevers."

"That's right, Chester Deevers. The seasoned vet who's been playing ever since the Game began, or so it seems. Bounced around every which way just to stay in it. What's the word they call you, a *lifer?*"

Deevers doesn't answer.

"Or just an old-timer who either refuses to quit the game or doesn't know when to hang it up?"

The other man cuts in. "Too stubborn I suppose."

"Or too damned ignorant or uneducated to take a real job in the world."

Deevers looks at them out of the corner of his eyes and takes another sip.

"But I suppose once the sun burns through your eyes and fries your brains you fail to accept the inevitable, like a goddamned dray horse bound for the glue factory. Am I right, Pops?"

Deevers turns his head half way. "Just who the hell you think you're talking to? Why don't you boys get the hell out of here before I sick my dog after you two?"

"We're just talking here, Chester. Just a couple of gents shooting the breeze with one of the game's—"

The other man leans in. "An old coot with no business being out there on the field any longer, who needs to be shown the door once and for all."

Deevers slams his glass down. "Charlie, go get me Hughie. We got a couple of wise cracks here who need to be taught a lesson in manners."

The man next to Deevers straightens up and reaches into his pocket. He tosses a few dollar bills on the counter. "Now, now. No need to get so belligerent. Like I said, we're just shootin' the breeze—"

"Bullshit. Charlie—"

The man looks at the bartender and points to the money. He puts his hand on Deevers' shoulder. "Look, we don't want to make a scene. We just wanted to congratulate you on your fine performance today."

"Thanks, now beat it."

The man persists. "They're lucky to have you on the squad. They say you know the game inside and out, better than anybody else. You may be a little long in the tooth, but you don't miss a thing. You can spot a fly taking a dump from ninety feet. Am I right?"

Deevers takes another sip.

The man drops down closer to Devers. "And that fat ass in the dugout, he's leaning on you pretty good for some advice, isn't he?"

Deevers shrugs his shoulders.

The man gets even closer and whispers. "You're the one who spotted the kink in Grogan's setup, weren't you?"

"Don't know what the hell you're talkin' about."

"Sure you do, Chester. You're the brains behind the team. Everyone knows it. If the fat slob doesn't cheat his way to a series victory, he'll use your know-how to get the job done."

"Who the hell are you two clowns?"

The man looks closely into Deevers' eyes. "You're looking at a pretty good payday if you win it all, aren't you Chester? How'd you like to double that pot for yourself, guaranteed?"

Deevers finally turns and looks at him. "What do you want from me?"

"We want you to help us out in any which way you can. You see, it's in our best interests if your team comes up on the short end of the stick."

"You want me to lose the series? Are you off your rocker? Fuck off!"

The man's eyes narrow. "Think about it, Chester. We're talking about a lot of money here. More than you've ever seen at one time. Think about your future. Be honest, how long have you got before the wheels finally come off?"

"If I can't play, I'll manage. I'll find something to do in the game."

"Yeah? And how long you think before that dries up? There are no guarantees in Base-Ball, Chester. Especially if we have something to say about it."

"You? A couple of bookies looking to rig the series? I don't throw games, mister. It's not in my blood. I may have bent the rules a few times in my day just to win a game, but I ain't no double-crossin' conniver."

The man wraps his arm tighter around Deevers. "We're not bookmakers, Chester. If you don't take the deal, we can make life hard on you. Real hard. We can see to it that you never step onto a Base-Ball field again."

"You're just bluffin'. If you're so damned serious and can pull it off, why don't you work over some other chump?"

"We already are, Chester. Someone who can directly affect the outcome of the game, but he's a bit squirrelly. We'd rather not put all our eggs in this one basket. That's why we're coming to you. You're our insurance policy."

"And you're full of shit."

"Maybe." He pauses. "But I'd sure as hell wouldn't take the

chance of heading back home jobless with the burden of taking care of a family with half its members dying from Black Lung, would I? And that little girl of yours. Think about her, too."

A shock runs through Deevers. "How did you—"

"Are you with us, Chester?"

He finishes his drink and drops the glass on the counter, clasping it with both hands. He stares straight ahead. Something starts to well up inside him.

"Good. Now listen up."

A dribbler down the first base line and Deevers shuffles his body to his left to make the stop. He bends down but doesn't get his glove down far enough. The ball squirts through his legs and trickles into right field.

The fifth run for the East squad rounds third and trots home. Deevers straightens himself up and tilts his head up toward the sky in disbelief. The Cranks in the stands rumble with displeasure.

Barely into the third inning, Deevers already has two costly errors and a baserunning mistake. Normally sharp as a tack, he's playing the field as if someone turned out the lights in his head.

Schnockerd paces in the dugout and runs his fingers through his hair, stunned by his captain's gaffes. The inning ends and Deevers slow-foots it back in the dugout. Schnockerd grabs his sleeve. "What the hell's going on out there, Chester?"

"Nothin'. I'll be fine. That ball should'a bounced up into my glove and it didn't. That's Base-Ball for you."

"That's Base-Ball for you? Jesus Christ, you looked like an old coot with a bout of lumbago going after that ball. What's the matter with you?"

"We'll get it back. It's just the third inning. Plenty of time."

"Get your head out of your ass, Chester, or else there won't be any more time left to get back in the game. Can't you see I got enough to worry about with Grumsley? His arm looks like it's hanging by a thread."

Two innings later, Deevers fails to cover first base on a bunt attempt, leading to a two-run homer served up by Grumsley. For the first time, the Cranks rain down a hail of boos.

Schnockerd rips off his cap and pounds it into the ground. After the third out, he goes after Grumsley. "I've never seen such a shitty pitching performance in all my life!"

Grumsley sits at the far end of the dugout and ignores him.

"You heard me, Mule. What kind of lackadaisical effort are you giving me?"

The Mule stuffs a fresh wad of tobacco in his mouth.

"From now on, anyone not pulling their weight is gonna have a seat and that starts with you, Grumsley. I'm pulling you out of the game."

Grumsley finally jumps off the bench and faces his manager. "You ain't doin' nothin'."

"You're done. I gotta go find myself another pitcher somewhere who's worth a damn."

"Bullshit."

"Bullshit? You know what bullshit is? It's when a pitcher who's so damned stubborn won't admit when he's got nothing left! Look at you out there. I'm surprised the ball still has its cover on it."

"You spineless jackass—"

Both men bear down on each other, about to come to blows, before several teammates get in their way. Amid an upheaval of shouts and shoves, they get wrestled back to opposite ends of the dugout.

Deevers edges up to Schnockerd. "You're not really thinking of pulling him are you?"

Schnockerd pours himself a beer and blows off the head. "Nah. Just riling him up. Riling everyone up."

"Good. For a second there I thought you lost your marbles. We don't have another pitcher on the staff."

"Don't worry about me. Worry about yourself, *Cappy*. That was a message to you, too. I don't know what the hell happened to you. Somebody get into your head or something?"

"The hell does that mean?"

"Look, I ain't no dummy, Chester."

Deevers stares down at him.

"You got something to tell me?"

Deevers motions his head to the door leading into the clubhouse. They sneak inside.

"What are you getting at, Chief?" Deevers asks him.

"I haven't been around nearly half as long as you, Chester, but I've seen it when a player's got something on his mind and it always has something to do with the green stuff."

"Money? Listen, Chief, I didn't—"

"You don't have to tell me. I know the situation you're in."

"You do? What situation is that?"

"The one that's racing through your mind right now, the one where you're asking yourself the questions, 'What's the best thing I can do to help me get where I need to be?' and 'Did I make the right decision?'"

"That's nothing new. I've been asking myself that question for thirty years."

Schnockerd knocks down his beer. "We all have. The other question is, 'Can I pull it off while still saving face, or will I look like a big, fat turd in the mirror every day for the rest of my life?'"

Deevers looks at him. "What would you have done?"

He smiles. "Just get me to five games and you'll find out. Play your ass off and don't worry about anything else. I'll take care of the rest."

Deevers thinks about it. "What do you mean by that? Why

five games?"

"I mean, let's give them one helluva fight till the last game and then let's see who's left standing. Anything can happen. Like you said, that's Base-Ball for you."

"What's going to happen, Chief?"

Schnockerd laughs. "Hell, I don't know. Either way, I'll make it worth your while. Trust me. Five games."

"What if it doesn't last five games?"

"It's gotta, or else this whole thing's a giant waste of everyone's time. Look how many people are out there screaming their heads off? They want a hotly contested series. Can you do that for me?" Schnockerd slaps him on the shoulder.

They get to the door leading out to the field and Deevers turns to him. "Just for the record, I never gave them an answer. But it's been eating at me all day."

Schnockerd winks at him. "You're a better man than me, Chester. I'm sure you'll do the right thing."

As soon as they step out, one of his teammates grabs him. "There you are. You're up next, Cap." Deevers sees two men on base. He grabs his bat and jumps into the on-deck circle. He takes a few warm-up swings and peers out into the stands, hoping to find a couple of red bow ties in the sea of tweed and corduroy.

With two on and two out, Deevers steps up to the plate, facing a different pitcher. The Cranks begin to chant in the dim hopes of rallying their bats for some runs.

The first pitch is a fastball in on him. He swings and misses. The torque on his back produces a sharp pain that slices up and down his spine. Deevers steps out of the box and takes a couple more practice swings before stepping back in.

He fouls off the next pitch, weakly chopping it down the third base line. He steps out again and spits into both hands. He rubs them together and grips his bat. By now, the Cranks are at full decibel.

Back in the box, Deevers waits for the next pitch. The pitcher winds up and delivers a breaking ball. Fortunately for Deevers, it hangs in the air and fails to break. He lunges at the pitch and smashes it deep to right-center. Both runners take off and don't stop. The ball is hit so hard that it ricochets off the fence away from the outfielders.

The baserunners score easily and Deevers scampers to second on a stand-up double. The Cranks leap out of their seats and go wild, giving him an ear-splitting ovation. He turns to face them and claps his hands as if to say, "Let's go."

In the dugout, Schnockerd raises his mug to his captain, sensing a comeback is at hand.

Down 7-2, Schnockerd's team belts out three more runs and forces Pierce out of the dugout to make a pitching change. Philo Grogan tries to convince him to put him in so he can shut the door on the comeback. Instead, Pierce puts in another pitcher.

It proves to be a bust, as two more runs score to tie the game in the ninth inning. By now, the Cranks are out of control.

Pierce finally gives the ball to Grogan, who is more than happy to shut down his Western foes. Grumsley, still fired up after his altercation with Schnockerd and closing in on his three-hundredth pitch of the game, keeps both teams at a standstill without the slightest hint of fatigue or strain.

The innings roll on but a growing threat to the game emerges. Already half-past five o'clock, the sun is quickly setting in the west and twilight begins to descend. The field turns into a darkening cavern. Ironically, most of the Exposition was wired for electric illumination, but not the ballpark.

Everyone plays on, but it becomes increasingly difficult to see the ball. Both pitchers easily strike out the side.

As soon as the fifteenth inning is over, Digby peels off his mask and visits both dugouts, entertaining the notion of postponing the game till the next day. Schnockerd wants to keep going and Pierce suggests playing one more inning before calling it off. Fully empowered, Digby agrees and declares the sixteenth inning the last of the day. The next run scored likely wins the second game.

In the top of the sixteenth, Schnockerd's men go down quietly on only ten pitches. It's up to the Mule to finish the bottom half before suspending the game till tomorrow.

Before ascending the mound, Grumsley pauses to windmill his arm several times and stretch his shoulder. He does it for a solid minute.

"Uh-oh." Schnockerd gets alarmed.

The Mule's first pitch wobbles and flutters.

"Shit. Ain't no coals left in the firebox." Schnockerd mutters to himself under his breath.

The next pitch tumbles into the dirt five feet in front of the plate. Schnockerd races out of the dugout and yells time out to Digby. He makes a beeline toward Grumsley.

"Get back in the dugout, fat man."

Schnockerd walks up and sticks his hands in his back pockets. "I know it'll take an act of God to get you off this mole hill, so I'm not gonna say a damned thing."

"Then why don't you just turn around and head back to the bench?"

He smiles. "Man, sure is dark out here. Getting darker by the second."

"Come on, Pete." Digby walks up to the mound. "Don't be wastin' no more time. I know what you're up to."

"Five…four…three…two…one."

A hand slaps down on Schnockerd's shoulder. "Let's go."

"I'm considering a pitching change, 'House,"

"Like hell you are!" The Mule blares.

"Hmmm…maybe I'll stick in Johnson. He's always good to give me a couple of good innings. Let me think about it."

The crowd groans. Digby lifts his arms up in a gesture of anticipation. Grumsley, getting hot under the collar, grabs his manager by the shoulders and ushers him off the mound and back to the dugout.

The Mule, his blood up, coaxes a soft grounder to second for the first out. But then Frank Horgan steps out of the dugout brandishing a bat the size of a tree trunk. Everyone in the stadium knows with one swing of that thing the game will be over. A collective moan of anxiety rustles throughout the stands.

Grumsley wastes no time. Whatever he has left, he uses for this one moment. He wrenches his thick wad of tobacco out of his mouth and discards it off to the side. He hurls his body forward, slings his slackened arm, and drives the first pitch forward.

Horgan, towering over everyone else, steers his massive hunk of wood and makes contact. A loud crack resonates throughout the whole ballpark. The crowd jumps to their feet. Grumsley immediately looks up. Digby throws his mask off and springs forward to scan the field.

Everyone looks at one another. *Where did it go?*

"Foul ball back in the seats, eagle eyes." Horgan says. He steps back in the batter's box and digs his front foot in the dirt.

They return to their positions and Grumsley delivers his next pitch. This time, Horgan crushes it and watches it sail through the indigo sky. The crowd jumps to their feet again. Everyone thinks it's long gone.

But it stays in the park.

Johnson, the best outfielder in all of Base-Ball, leaps up against the fence but misses catching it by a couple of inches. The ball bounces off the top of the fence and lands at Johnson's feet.

"Oh, shit!" Horgan yells and starts lumbering down the line. He reaches first base and decides to chance it. He goes for second.

Pierce and the rest of the dugout, already on their feet, scream in unison, "No! Don't do it!"

But Horgan commits to the extra base. He should have been out by twenty feet, but the relay throw back to the infield is muffed by O'Hallarhan and Horgan crashes down on top of the bag, safe at second.

"Son of a—!" Schnockerd pours himself another beer and downs it in three seconds.

McGrady, at short, turns to the home run king. "What's the matter, didn't get that last drop of Elixirol down that throat of yours, freak?"

Horgan dusts himself off. "That would have been long gone in any other park."

"I bet you never hustled like that in your entire life. You looked like a giraffe with a piano strapped to its back."

"Give me another crack at it and you'd be heading back to your hotel looking to pick a fight with some doormat."

"Hey, Hughie, sounds like we got ourselves a smart-ass standing here."

O'Hallarhan walks over and looks up at Horgan. "What, you think you're better than us, carny-boy?"

"Careful. I don't mind stepping on annoying little bugs."

"Watch it, asshole. I'll have your leg chewed off before the pain reaches your brain."

"I'll flick you off like a dust mote on my sleeve. And you, McGrady, I heard you get your kicks beating the stuffings out of namby-pambies in front of their families. What a tough guy!"

Both infielders drop their gloves in the dirt and charge the long-limbed slugger.

Hoping to stave off an all-out bloodbath, Digby bolts across the infield and tackles all three men. Everybody else on the field rushes up to them. Both benches clear. Players on both sides crash into one another, pushing and shoving. The entire ballpark breaks out in hysteria.

Amazingly, Digby quickly restores order without a single punch thrown. The game resumes amid the growing darkness.

The gangly Fleet Foote, his socks hiked up to reveal his spindly calves, is next to bat. Grumsley fires the first pitch and pounds the strike zone before Foote even knows it's coming.

"Time out!" Pierce runs out of the dugout.

"Now what?" Digby jumps out of his stance.

"It's obvious the kid can't see a damned thing, Larry. Why don't you call the game now and let's resume tomorrow?" Pierce pleads.

Schnockerd jumps out. "Aw no, Pierce! We agreed on sixteen full innings. What's fair is fair. It doesn't matter if the kid can't see his own two feet let alone see an incoming fastball."

"This is getting ridiculous," Digby says. "Will you two get back to your holes and shut up? We got two more outs to get, or less."

But Pierce is adamant, knowing his precious game-winning run sits at the mercy of his light-hitting infielder, who can't see a thing. Both managers get into a heated argument in front of home plate.

"Stop!" Digby yells at the top of his lungs.

Digby proposes a compromise between the two managers: keep on playing but find a way to color the ball so it can be seen in the dark. They look at each other and consent. Someone quickly locates a bucket of paint and splashes a coat of white over its existing dark brown leathery shade.

"There, are we happy?"

They nod.

"Good. Let's get this over with."

Grumsley stretches his shoulder again and takes to the mound. He continues to pound the strike zone against the raw-boned teenager.

But Foote doesn't give in. Able to see the white ball, he fouls off the next five pitches before stepping out of the box to take a quick breather.

Grumsley winds his arm around one more time to stay loose.

Schnockerd's eyes widen. "Come on, Mule! Get after it!"

The pitch comes in and this time Foote keeps the ball fair, shooting a line drive toward left field. It carries, sending the left fielder dancing back toward the fence until he runs out of room.

Everyone in the park jumps up. The ball streaks in the dark and lands in the very front row of the bleachers for a two-run shot.

A couple of seconds pass before everyone realizes what has just happened. A chain reaction of cheers and boos starts in the bleachers and quickly makes its way throughout the rest of the dusk-enshrouded ballpark. Foote, the unlikeliest of sluggers, wins it for his East team.

The series is tied 1-1.

The next morning, a heavy downpour penetrates the city and a cold, dreary pallor blankets the area. The ball field becomes a marsh filled with pools of water and bogs of mud.

People who arrive early at the stadium huddle under the grandstands. Cranks hitch up their coat collars and nip on their hip flasks. East Coast Fans seek protection under umbrellas, biding their time smoking pipes and conversing with one another. It's too miserable to engage in ribbing or goading between rival contingents.

Luckily, the rain eases and hope arises that the game will start on time.

Digby is the first one out on the field and is covered up to his ankles in slop. He has the authority to call off the game, but knows better. Instead, he delays it by an hour to let the water wash away before calling out the teams to take batting practice and drills.

The park quickly fills with bodies. High above, Sterne enters his box wrapped in his coat and a cashmere wool scarf.

The game finally gets underway and by the third inning it's become evident that the East's pitcher has something special going for him.

"Who is this fella?" Schnockerd grumbles to Deevers.

"Somebody named Smith. Straight from the universities to their minor league breeding grounds."

"Whoever he is, he knows how to shut the door on our guys. Once he gets behind on someone, he comes back with a real zinger. See how that ball drops off the table?"

"Yep. And the best we can do is pound it into the ground."

A pattern emerges with Smith on the mound. Once he gets behind on the count to the first batter, he either walks him or gives up a base hit. But then he comes back with a nasty, sharp breaking ball on the next hitter and gets both men out on a groundball double play.

"Spit" Mullansky, the East's first baseman and Deevers' bitter rival, gives Smith a pep talk every time he gets in a jam. Once a runner reaches first base, Mullanksy calls time out and walks up to the mound. Whatever he says works, because on the next pitch Smith reaches in and delivers a devastating sinker ball that befuddles the hitter, tapping the ball back to the infield and wiping out the scoring threat.

Schnockerd starts to get antsy. Deevers folds his arms over the dugout's railing and carefully observes the pitcher.

This time, two men reach base and "Fireplug" Johnson walks up. Smith's first pitch is a softy right down the middle of the plate. Johnson gets all of it, slamming the pitch down the right field line before hooking foul at the last second, drawing an uproar from the stands.

"Time out!" Mullansky hollers and heads to the mound. He leans into Smith and has a word with the pitcher. Smith, his eyes fixed on the first baseman, nods and Mullansky plunks the ball back into the pitcher's glove.

Deevers locks his own eyes on the mound and doesn't blink.

Mullansky pats Smith in the seat of his pants and walks back to first.

Johnson steps back in the box and Smith starts his wind-up.

The ball is just like the previous pitch, right down the middle of the plate for Johnson to smash, but drops off a ledge at the very last instant. Johnson takes a whack and beats it into the mud. It sloshes straight to Foote who steps on the bag at second and throws to Mullansky for the easy double play.

"Goddamnit!" Schnockerd yells.

Deevers shakes his head. "I don't get it."

"What?"

"That was virtually the same pitch as before but this one dropped straight down right at the last second. Whenever this Smith fellow needs to get out of a jam, he pulls out a pitch like this every time. Unreal."

"Maybe he's scuffing the ball?"

"I'm not seeing it. This kid's pretty straight and narrow. Haven't seen him fiddle with the ball yet."

By the sixth inning, the East takes a 4-0 lead in the game and both Schnockerd and Deevers grow more frustrated.

"Spot anything yet?" Schnockerd begins chewing on his sunflower seeds.

"Nope."

"Come on, Chester. It's getting late. Find something."

"I ain't finding anything off this kid, Skip. What do you want me to do?"

"Look harder. Nobody shuts out this team. Something's up, I tell you."

"I just can't figure it out."

"We lose this game, we'll be in the hole."

Deevers turns to him. "Isn't that what you want, anyway? A tight series?"

Schnockerd shrugs his shoulders.

The next inning, Smith gets into another jam. He loads the bases with no one out and McGrady walks up looking to clear the bases. Again, Mullansky calls time and heads to the mound. Deevers watches carefully.

"See anything?" Schnockerd whispers.

Deevers doesn't say anything.

McGrady, already 0-for-3 with two punchouts, is looking to settle the score. He grits his teeth and grips the bat like he's wringing a chicken's neck.

Smith's first pitch sails in and dives right before crossing the plate. McGrady smashes the ball into the soggy grass and bounces it in the hole to Foote's right. It would be a clean single if not for the gifted shortstop, who dives to make the stop, springs up and tags out the runner heading to third. Then he slings the ball to the other infielder at second who fires the ball to first.

McGrady, splashing through the mud like a plodding thoroughbred, cannot beat the throw. He's a victim of a rare triple play. Smith gets out of the inning unharmed.

Schnockerd rips off his cap and throws it across the dugout. "Piss-shit!"

McGrady turns around, picks up his bat, and shatters it over his leg.

Deevers shakes his head again. "He's never done that."

"What? Break his bat over something? Sure, I've seen it. But usually over someone's head."

"No, I mean McGrady's always been able to square up on breaking pitches. He's the best in the league. No one is that good to fool him. Especially not this Smith character."

Deevers keeps his eyes on Smith. The pitcher trots back to the dugout with his chest held high. He takes a seat on the bench. Mullansky slides up next to him and gives him a different ball. The first baseman keeps clutching the one used to initiate the triple play. He hides it behind his glove. Then it disappears.

"Son of a bitch."

"Did you find something?" Schnockerd springs up.

"Why didn't I see that before?"

"What? What?"

"I think that bastard's using a Lead Ball."

"A what?"

"Lead Ball."

"The hell's that? I thought I knew every trick in the book."

"A Lead Ball's a regular ball but with something stuffed inside it, something heavy enough to weigh it down and cause it to do some really funny things, like drop down right before it crosses the plate. I should'a realized he was doing something like that."

"You mean that kid's cheating? I told you!"

"It's not the pitcher, Skip. It's Mullansky."

"Mullansky? How the hell—?"

"He's hiding the damn thing on him and when Smith gets in a jam he comes up to him and switches the ball without the poor kid even knowing it."

"You've seen him do it?"

"I don't know where he's hiding it and I can't spot the transfer, but I'm sure he's doing it. Once Smith gets out of his mess, he switches back to a regular ball."

"Are you sure?"

"Me and him's got history. I wouldn't expect anything less from that rotten dirtbag. He's the trickiest sum'bitch I ever laid eyes on. He'll do anything to get one up on you."

"That's it," Schnockerd says. "If they're cheating then we'll oblige them. Send a note to the boys in the stands to get ready to start stealing signs."

"We can't do that."

"Why the hell not?"

"I'm sure that Sterne fellow has dozens of spotters all over the place lookin' for that kind of thing. If he catches us, we'll have to forfeit the game."

"The hell we will. If they're gonna cheat, so will we. We'll pull out a Gentlemen's Fog on them or a Rusty Belt Switch. Pierce ain't gonna get the best of me, especially when it comes to cheating!"

"I don't think he knows. Pierce is too straight-laced to tolerate that kind of thing."

Deevers and the rest of the players run out to the field. They give up another run. Luckily, Bittner chases a bad one low and away and strands two runners on base. Deevers returns to the dugout.

"Do something for chrissakes!"

Deevers finally yells out. "Hey, Spit! Wat'cha got up those sleeves a yours?"

Mullansky smooths out the infield dirt in front of him and shoots out a dart of tobacco. His shadowy eyes make contact with Deevers.

"Where 'ya hiding it, Spit?"

Mullansky cracks a small, ever so detectable.

"Pummy bastard!" Deevers grabs Schnockerd. "Go out there and complain to Digby. Tell him we think he's got a Lead Ball."

Schnockerd calls time out and runs out to Digby. He tells him.

Pierce runs out. "What's the problem?"

"We think your first baseman's hiding a Lead Ball."

"A what?"

"A Lead Ball. He's using it to cheat."

"Cheat? All my men have honorable dispositions, Mr. Schnockerd. None are capable of lowering themselves to such distasteful levels as you lot. What effrontery!"

"Yeah, why don't you ask him?"

Digby calls Mullansky over. "You doing anything shady, Spit?"

He peers into the dugout at Deevers. "I don't know what you're talking about."

"Check his uniform." Deevers yells from the dugout.

"They're pointing the finger at you for hiding a rigged ball. Come clean, Mullansky."

"I ain't got nothin' on me. Go ahead and check me."

Digby searches his uniform. He finds nothing.

Pierce boasts. "There, I told you my players are respectable men. Now let's get on with it!"

"Check up his ass!" Schnockerd demands.

But Digby is satisfied and orders everyone back in their places. Deevers is emphatic. "I know that wily prick has it!"

"Whaddy'a want him to do, strip down to his long handles in front of a hundred-thousand people?"

"He's gonna hornswaggle us out of this third game, Skip! We can't let him get away with that."

But they can't get near Smith and the East wins it decidedly to take a one game lead.

In the clubhouse, Deevers stews in front of his locker. A couple of teammates next to him ask him what's the matter.

He pounds his fist on the metal lattice. "Damnit, what's fair is fair. If we can't cheat, then we gotta level the playin' field. That's all there is to it."

"What happened, Cap?"

He tells them and the clubhouse flashes with a burst of rage. "We can't let that sonofabitch get away with it!"

Deevers leads the men, half-dressed and some armed with bats, underneath the stands to the East's clubhouse. They pound on the door. Someone opens it. "*Magubber's Uncle!* What in blue blazes?"

"Get him out here!"

"Who?"

"That snake, Mullansky. That no-good, hustlin'—" The men behind Deevers push forward, cursing and swearing.

Pierce rushes into the doorway and is startled to see the raw animus brewing in front of him. "Pacify your savages, Deevers, or else I'll have you forced to forfeit the rest of the series. I can make it happen!"

"Mullansky! He's a cheatin', lyin' cracker-crook. Where is he?"

"The ump checked him, Deevers. He was clean."

"Bullshit! I've known him for years. The man is as crooked as your catcher's fingers. He's hoodwinked us out of this game and he's doing the same to you."

"You better have proof, old man."

Someone throws a bat against the wall and Pierce ducks for cover. Deevers and the rest push through into the clubhouse. They find half the East team with towels wrapped around their waists and thick layers of shaving soap on their faces. They run and hide at the sight of the storming ruffians.

The other half, already in their clothes, defiantly stands their grounds, ready to engage in an epic bout of fisticuffs. Before they converge, Deevers gets in between them and finds Mullansky's locker.

Mullansky, dressed in trousers, suspenders and a white undershirt, turns the corner. "What the hell are you doing?"

Deevers rummages through his locker and pulls out a ball. "It's time you fessed up, Spit."

Mullansky points to the ball. "Fess up to what? That's not mine. You planted that thing."

"Feels kind of heavy." Deevers reaches into his back pocket and pulls out a pocketknife. Like digging into a citrus fruit, he jabs into the ball and peels back the leather skin. He picks through the inside's twine and opens up the center. There he finds a dark, lopsided hunk of something. "Whoa, what's this I find? I don't think this belongs in a standard issue ball."

Deevers lifts the ball high in the air to show everybody its suspicious contents. Everyone's anger now turns to Mullansky. "What do you got to say for yourself now, Spit?"

"*Fuggin' muzzlewort!*" Mullansky lunges at Deevers and punches him in the face.

Both sides swarm in and engulf the two men. After some jostling, several men rip Mullansky away. Deevers gets to one knee and wipes blood from his mouth.

"He's a deceiving scoundrel! A *cockdolloger!*" Mullansky spews.

Pierce jumps into the broiling fray. "Says the pot to the kettle!" The rabble splits into two. "Look, Mullansky, he's got you cold, right before our eyes. I'm afraid your masterful deception has finally reached its end."

"You're going after me, right in front of this dusty, old *pick'aroon?* How 'bout you, Deevers? Don't tell me you're all harps and flappin' wings."

"I've done nothin' dastardly out of bounds in this series."

"You're a two-bit liar!"

Someone opens the door to his locker and a heap of balls spill out on the floor, making a heavy, thudding sound.

"We have no tolerance for cheaters," Pierce says. "Get him out of here!"

Before they have a chance to grab him, Mullansky dives to the floor and tries to gather as many tampered balls as he can. Then he makes a mad dash through the crowd of players and heads for the door. They follow him out.

Mullansky races out from under the stands and stumbles onto the playing field. By now, heavy rain is falling. He trips and splashes down into the mud, covering every inch of his body. Players from both sides run out and pelt him with the remainder of balls left from his locker.

Deevers bumps into Pierce. "I meant what I said in there."

"There better not be any funny business going on, Deevers. Not on your side!"

"We want a level playing field, that's all. Play by the rules!"

"Do I have your word?"

"You can count on me. What's fair is fair. No surprises. What about you?"

"No surprises…within the rules of engagement. Now what about Schnockerd?"

"As far as I know, he's all right. I'll keep an eye on him."

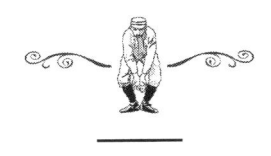

Like the clouds that have held back the sun, the series cannot hold back "Fireplug" Johnson any longer. For Game 4, he leaves no doubt to anyone that he's the game's best player by a wide margin.

From the outset, Johnson straps the team on his back and completely dominates every aspect of the game. Everyone within the confines of the stadium gapes at his ability to play the game. He's a man among boys.

He runs faster and chases balls down that no other player can get close to. He's already three-quarters of the way from stealing a base before Bittner has a chance to leap up out of his crouch and make a throw. At the plate, he crushes balls out of the park just as effortlessly as laying down a bunt single. He masters the game with a natural, fluid ease.

Out of the eleven runs scored by the West team, Johnson has a hand in ten of them. And it's only the fifth inning.

Philo Grogan, the stalwart of the League and Sterne's highest example of polish and vainglory, is reduced to a hollow shell of himself at the hands of the dark-skinned dynamo. On the mound, he is almost completely stripped of the pride and resolve that made him such a fierce competitor.

What's left of him is a residue of hate and acidity.

No matter what Grogan does, no matter how hard he rears back and delivers his best, Johnson has an answer for him. It's as if he's toying with him.

With another couple of men on base, Johnson enters the box. Grogan had feared this potential situation even before he put the two men on. It is like that the whole game, as if he is self-fulfilling his worst destiny.

The profusion of Cranks stand up to cheer their squat, compact powerhouse.

Grogan, beaten inside and out and now barren of any sense of propriety, can't control his anger any longer. A torrent of words gushes from his mouth.

"You're the lowest of vermin to crawl out of the mudbanks of sewage trenches. Worthless excrement shot out of the ass of our great Union. What gives you the right to think you can trudge in the same footprints as those entitled to preserve the merits of decency? You're nothing but cud!"

Johnson lowers his bat and stares at the pitcher as he spews forth a deranged tangle of racial slurs and epithets. His defenders behind him look at each other, growing uneasy and becoming more and more embarrassed by the pitcher's sudden meltdown. Finally, Bittner calls time out and trots out to the mound.

"What the hell's the matter with you, Philo?"

"He can't do this to us…to me…" He mutters.

"You're sounding like a pickled herring. Now gather your wits, for God's sake, and get us out of this inning!"

But Grogan's too far gone and Johnson takes him to task, belting a screaming line drive to the deepest part of the park. Both runs jog home and Johnson slides in to third base.

A tremendous squall of noise inundates the field and reverberates upward. Johnson gets to his feet and hikes up his uniform to release some dirt. He doesn't respond to the crowd. Instead, he keeps his foot on the bag, puts both hands on his hips and stares straight ahead.

Even the loyalist Fans from New York can't help but stand and give Johnson a standing ovation, all the while keeping one eye on the Governor's box.

Once the roaring finally subsides, Pierce's head pops out of the dugout. As soon as Grogan retrieves the ball, he heads out to pull his headstrong pitcher.

"No." Grogan shakes his head.

"I'm sorry, Philo, but enough's enough."

"I can't let that uncultured mongoloid get the best of me. Give me one more shot at him so I can teach him some respect."

"School's out, I'm afraid, and your backside's pretty tender. Let's say you hand me the ball over so you can make a dignified retreat to the dugout."

Grogan's eyes intensify. "No, sir. I just can't do that."

"Grogan, please. Don't make a fool out of yourself." Pierce sticks his hand out. Grogan's face clenches. "Philo, I beg you."

But the pitcher will not give in. He clings to the ball like a child smothering a treasured knickknack. Pierce keeps his hand out and then leans forward.

"You're embarrassing all of us, Grogan. Everyone's looking down at us. *He's* looking. Now, stop being an ass!"

Grogan stands firm. Pierce tries to wrench the ball out of his hands but the pitcher pulls back with a violent jerk. The manager turns toward the stands and smiles, as if to say, "Everything's all right." Then he makes another jab for the ball. Grogan rips himself away from Pierce and runs off the mound.

"Grogan, get back here!" Pierce orders his players to fetch their teammate.

A spectacle soon breaks out in the outfield as the entire East team tries to chase Grogan down. He proves to be slippery. Thinking they have him cornered, Grogan kicks, punches and squirms his way past them. By now, everyone in the stands is laughing.

Sterne sits in his box with an look of embarrassment on his face.

Some teammates get hold of a large net and finally subdue the pitcher. They wrap a white sheet around him and escort him off the field. All the while, Johnson doesn't move off third.

The game mercifully ends by the score 15-2. The West team evens the series due to the total domination by Johnson.

Sterne hurriedly exits his box. At the gate, the same throng of reporters who have been hounding him all series surge upon him. They assault him with questions, namely about Johnson's feats. He pushes through toward his cab without saying a word. They close in tighter but Sterne forces his way through, shoving bodies aside.

"Would you describe that as the most dominating performance you've ever seen by one player?"

"What's it feel like to be so thoroughly whipped?"

"Johnson....Johnson....Johnson..."

He makes it to his cab. A scowl never before seen in public marks his face. He struggles to open the door. He tries to push them back.

"Hey, Guv'ner. Did you ever know that Johnson was this good, or were you so overwhelmed by the man's skin color that it made you blind to everything else about the man?"

Halfway in, Sterne stops and lifts his head up. "Who the hell said that?"

"I did." A smallish man pressing a pencil against a notebook listens for a response.

Sterne's eyes flare with rage. He lifts his closed umbrella and bops the reporter over the head with it. He does it two more times with greater force, battering the man down, then slams his door.

Game 5 arrives, the final match to decide the series winner and set the course for the game of Base-Ball for years to come.

Grumsley, the West's sole pitcher, opens his eyes in bed. Sunlight fills the hotel room, making the air stuffy and smell like the insides of a spittoon. The sounds of voices and footsteps in the hallway have awakened him. It must already be mid-morning, he thinks.

He stares up at the ceiling, trying to recall last night's events. His mind is foggy. He remembers going out by himself, having dinner, then drinks. But there's a haze floating in his head, suggesting he may have overdone it.

He rolls over onto his right side and immediately realizes something's not right. He sits up in bed and reaches to feel for his right arm. It's not there.

A sharp, tingling coldness zaps through his body. If he wasn't already awake, he certainly is now. He reaches again and slides his hand all the way up near his shoulder joint. Nothing.

His pitching arm is completely gone.

He throws the sheets off his body and jumps out of bed. He bangs into the dresser and looks at himself in the mirror. Still wearing his white dress shirt from last night, his white sleeve is limp and empty.

"What the *fuck?*"

He stares at himself as if expecting his mirror image to explain the disappearance of his arm. His hair is disheveled. A thick growth of whiskers smears his face. His eyes look disoriented and panic-stricken.

What the hell happened last night?

He undoes the first several buttons and pulls back his shirt. At his shoulder is now a stump of skin, callused and ashen.

A couple of footsteps approach the door. Then a knock. "Hey, Mule. You in there?"

"Yeah, I'm comin'." His voice carries.

He grabs the water pitcher off the dresser and pours it into the basin. He splashes his face, hoping that he's just suffering from a weird hangover after a rough night of drinking. His eyes slit open and he looks again.

Another knock on the door, harder and forceful. "Let's go, Mule. We got a series to win!" He hears the march of several footsteps in the hallway and the boisterous chatter of his teammates.

His heart begins to pound. He turns and ransacks the room, hoping to find his arm. He checks under the bed, between his sheets, underneath piles of clothes and rubbish. He even checks the fire escape. There's no trace of it.

Grumsley stands in the middle of the room, completely befuddled. His mind races.

Two taps on the door.

"I said I'm comin', for chrissakes!"
"Mule? It's Deevers. You okay in there? Let's get movin'."
"C-Cap?"

Grumsley, Deevers and Schnockerd sit in a circle.
"Let me see it again," Schnockerd says.
Grumsley shows him the stump of hardened skin at his shoulder.
"It's like the goddamned thing just fell off like an infected, dead toenail. I told you this was bound to happen!"
Deevers puts his elbows on his knees. "Tell us again what you did last night."
Grumsley takes a deep breath. "Like I said, I came back here after the game, changed, then came down for a drink or two. Then I went out by myself, as per my usual, and got a steak dinner. Had a few more drinks, then…."
"Yeah?"
"That's all I can remember."
"Jesus, Mule," Schnockerd says, "I knew you weren't that big of a drinker but, c'mon, that's just an opening teaser for some dudes I know. You really got smashed?"
"You didn't go anywhere else?" Deevers asks.
"Not up until that point."
"And you didn't run into anybody? No tussles, no bar fight? No one approached you?"
"Nope."
Deevers sits back, completely flummoxed. "Un-*friggin*'-believable. There goes the series."
"It couldn't wait till *after* you pitched the final game? Bad timing." Schnockerd crosses his arms and rests his foot on his knee.
"We were *this* close," Deevers concedes. "All up in smoke!"
"Whoa, whoa, whoa. You're sounding like we don't have a shot at all. What's the matter with you?"
"What's the matter with me, Chief? Our workhouse here just lost his pitching arm and he's all we got on the staff. We got a

little problem on our hands."

"Okay, okay. Mule can't find his arm, we have no other pitcher and we got three hours before the game starts. Big deal. We'll come up with something."

"Are 'ya kiddin' me?" Deevers gives him a look. "You're the one who's been the basket case all series. I'm surprised you're not running for the beer keg."

"There's no time to panic, Cap. We'll put a few calls in, see if his arm shows up."

"Oh, and if it does, we'll just sew it back on?"

They sit in silence. Then Schnockerd snaps his fingers and looks at Grumsley. "Can you pitch with your left arm?"

They sneak out the back of the hotel and race to the park. Grumsley gets on the mound and picks up the ball.

Deevers squats down at the plate and pounds on his catcher's mitt. "Put 'er right there, Mule."

Grumsley starts his wind-up, an awkward inverse to his natural delivery. The ball shoots out of his hand and sails to his extreme left, closer to first base than the plate.

"Just the first pitch," Schnockerd says. "Gotta get used to a new delivery. Try again."

Grumsley tries again. He falls off the mound and stumbles to the ground.

Deevers looks at Schnockerd.

After several more tries, Deevers stands up. "This dog ain't gonna hunt. Time for Plan B."

"Plan B?"

"We need a Plan B. Quick." Deevers pulls out his timepiece.

"Hell, I don't have a Plan B. That was my lone idea for the day."

"C'mon, Chief. We gotta come up with somethin' else. We need somebody who can pitch for us in a tight pinch."

They stare at each other for the longest time, then blurt out the same answer simultaneously: "Fireplug!"

Johnson squeezes into Schnockerd's office in the clubhouse, with Deevers and Grumsley. "Show him your arm, Mule."

He peels back his shirt.

"So as you can see, we're in a bit of a pickle, Gus. Whaddy'a say? Are you up to giving us some innings?"

"I'm always up to playin', Chief."

"Good! Just grab your mitt and be ready for us on the mound."

"Problem is, I don't remember the last time I pitched in a game. I'm bettin' I'm as rusty as an old steel trestle."

"You can stretch out underneath the stands. We're counting on you, Gus."

Johnson fidgets in his chair. "Look, you all know who I am. I'll do anything to win the game, short of maiming or bamboozling somebody. I'll take the ball, except…"

"Yeah?"

"I don't know how long I can go. If you're smart, you'll find yourself a decent backup in case I run out of steam."

"Sure, no problem, Gus. We're on it!"

"I mean what I say, Chief. I can run around the outfield and the bases all day. But with pitchin', you only got so many bullets. Unless you're the Mule." He winks at Grumsley.

Deevers eyes Johnson. "How many innings we talkin' about?"

"A few. Four, maybe five."

"That's good enough," Schnockerd. "We'll piece together the rest."

Johnson and Grumsley leave Schnockerd's office.

"Okay, we bought ourselves a couple of innings. What now?" Deevers asks.

"What do you mean?"

"Who else are we gonna get who can pitch?"

Schnockerd laughs. "Nobody. We'll stretch Johnson out the whole game. Once he gets his competitive juices flowing, we won't be able to yank him off the mound."

"I don't know, Chief. You heard him. He won't go the whole

game. We'll need a backup."

"Anybody else on the team who's thrown a pitch before? How about you?"

"I'm not even going to answer that."

"With a pot of money on the line, I'm sure we can find somebody who's still in town." Schnockerd turns his telephone around. "Look around."

Several calls later, Deevers hangs up. He scratches off the last name on his sheet of paper. "Greeley. Still in town but he's face down in his own vomit after a three-day bender."

"Shit, I remember he tossed a two-hitter."

"Anybody else?"

"How about any of those Joliet fleabags?"

A disgusted look crosses Deevers' face. "Ain't worth a damn."

"Not even for a couple of innings?"

He thinks about it, then shakes his head. "I wouldn't be surprised that two out of their three pitchers are back at the Elgin psyche ward. We need someone in town fast."

Schnockerd leans back in his chair, folds his hands together over his lap and looks up.

"Well?"

He snaps his fingers. "Say, remember that old judge down in Indiana? What town was that?"

"Indiana town? What, that business with the Clabber Girl promotion gone bad?"

"Yeah, that thing. He got me off the hook for that."

"Terre Haute."

"Right. I still owe him a favor."

"What?"

"He had a son, a pitcher, trying to make it to the big leagues. Remember his name?"

"We can't get him. We don't have enough time."

"No, no. Last time I heard, the kid's up here going to school."

Deevers shrugs his shoulders. "Is he any good?"

"We got any other choice?"

Twenty minutes before the game is scheduled to begin, Schnockerd enters the clubhouse with his arm around a young man. They approach Deevers, who's lacing his shoes.

"Cap, I'd like you to meet our newest member of the pitching staff. This is Gerald Wheatley."

Deevers looks up and sees a wide face with soft, lamblike features. Wheatley's eyes are spread apart and his lips are narrow and slight. His immediate thought: *This kid is going to get murdered.*

He stands up and shakes his hand. "Howdy. Chester Deevers. Glad to meet you."

Wheatley is tall and gawky with a thin waist and oversized hands and feet. His shirt is buttoned all the way to the top. His pants are up too high on him, causing a gap between the leg bottoms and his shoes, exposing his socks.

Wheatley's mouth opens but no one hears a sound come out.

G. Wheatley — *Pitcher*

He makes an attempt at eye contact, but quickly drifts off toward a neutral space.

An awkward pause, then Schnockerd continues. "Yep. This boy's one heck of a pitching prospect. Got a real lively arm. Real strong too, ain't you, son?"

Wheatley doffs his ivy cap. His mussed-up hair sticks close to his prominent forehead. "Yessir." Finally, audible words. He wedges his cap underneath his arm and sticks both hands in his pockets.

"That's good to know," Deevers says. "What regional clubs have you pitched for?"

"The Maroons."

"The Maroons? Never heard of 'em. Are they out of Peoria?"

Schnockerd cuts in. "No, that's, uh, the nickname for his university's athletics department."

"Come again?"

"Y'see, Chester, Wheatley here's been studying real hard at school just down the street and hasn't gotten picked up by any club yet. But it's just a matter of time, ain't that right, boy?"

Wheatley nods.

"Pete…"

"Yep, just a matter of time. Got a real good arm, strong as an ox. He'll do fine. Not a problem!" Schnockerd guides Wheatley toward an empty locker to get dressed and comes back.

"Pete, for chrissakes, he's gonna get eaten alive."

"Don't you go worrying about that, Chester. Odds are, we probably won't even need the kid."

"How do you suppose?"

"As long as we got Johnson, we'll ride him as long as we have to."

"He said it himself, he can only go a few innings. What are we gonna do after that?"

Schnockerd brushes away the thought. "When's the last time ol' Fireplug disappointed? If the game's on the line, who better to count on?"

"Yeah, but what if, Pete?" Deevers lowers his voice and whispers. "Are you willing to count on a timid schoolboy with no experience in the pros? Try to explain that to everybody in this clubhouse."

"Trust me, he'll be fine."

"In front of a hundred thousand screaming folks? The biggest game possibly in the history of the sport? Yeah, I think he'll do fine."

"Oh, just one more thing. The kid, he's got a bit of an issue. I'm told he doesn't like to be in pressure situations. Sometimes his body reacts adversely."

"What do you mean? He breaks out into hives or something?"

"I don't know. His dad didn't say."

"Great. Hope to Christ we don't have to find out."

Word quickly spreads outside the stadium that Grumsley's out for the final game, further stirring the swelling number of bodies gathering at the gates. Gamblers in their trenchcoats make a mad dash to the wagering booths across the street.

The gates finally open and the biggest crowd of the series jams the park, occupying every inch of seating plank in the stands. And more keep coming. Not to be turned away, they pay to get in just to stand somewhere and be witness to the monumental game.

Sterne's cab pulls up in front of the gate. Just before he gets out, someone runs up and delivers a note on the news of Grumsley's plight. He spends an extra minute inside before opening the door and stepping out. The ever-present reporters mob him. But Sterne, his chin up and chest out, pays no attention. He slices through them like a confident general charging a battlefield.

On the field, both teams finish up their batting practice and warm-up drills. Schnockerd and Pierce come out of their dugouts and exchange lineup cards with Digby.

"So sorry to hear about your pitcher. An unfortunate loss." Pierce sounds apologetic.

"Can it, Pierce. Everyone knows you probably wee-wee'd your silk undies when you heard the news."

"Schnockerd, you've got to be the most churlish mudsill to ever grace the grounds of a—"

"So I'm forced to make a substitution." He hands a card to Digby and a copy to Pierce.

"Johnson? He can pitch, too? You're reaching, Schnockerd."

"Maybe, but I'll happily take my chances with the game's best player and the series on the line. He won't allow us to lose. That's what champions are made of."

A photographer snaps a picture of both managers shaking hands in front of home plate.

"Got any more surprises up your sleeve, fat man?"

"No. You?"

"I guess you'll have to wait and see." Pierce snaps off a quick, brief smirk before returning to the dugout.

The East team takes their defensive positions and Digby calls out, "PLAY BALL!"

After a one-two-three top of the first, Johnson runs out and picks up the ball. A giant wave of cheers rises from the stands.

After a few warm-up tosses, Johnson faces his first hitter and gets him out on a pop-out. Not sporting any tricks or specialty pitches, Johnson's all force and maximum effort. He strikes out the next two batters. The wild cheering does not let up.

Schnockerd pumps his fist.

In the bottom of the third inning, the West takes a lead on a sacrifice fly that scores the game's first run.

Johnson then steps up to the plate and smacks a single, driving in the second run. He tries to stretch the single into a double, racing for second. Foote squats down, defending the base, waiting for the incoming throw. He bends his knee, extending it in front of the bag.

Johnson slides just as the ball reaches Foote and a collision occurs. A cloud of dust kicks up. As the dust clears, everyone sees Johnson writhing in pain.

"Holy crap!" Schnockerd jumps out and calls time. He races to Johnson and bends over him. "Hey, 'Plug, you all right?"

He grabs the inside of his leg, near his groin. "Skinny little punk, damn near kneed me in the balls!"

Schnockerd turns to Foote. "What the hell do you think

you're doing, Beanpole?"

"Hey, it's a fair play. Ask the ump."

Schnockerd helps Johnson to his feet. "You've got to be careful, Gus. Next time, take it easy around the bases. We need you on the mound."

"That's not my game, Chief, and you know it."

The next couple of innings, everyone watches nervously every time Johnson makes a play. His next at-bat, he swats a ball into the gap between outfielders. He rounds first just as hard as before. Schnockerd, chewing maniacally on a mouthful of sunflower seeds, watches him slide again at second. He swallows the entire wad of seeds.

"This is getting to be too much."

"This is what you wanted, Chief," Deevers smiles. "Game 5, for all the marbles. And we're almost halfway home."

By the sixth inning, the West clings to a slim lead before breaking the game wide open. For the first time, Johnson has nothing to do with scoring the runs.

With two men on, and already up by two runs, McGrady rips an extra-base hit down the left field line. The ball skips all the way to the corner. Both men on base trot home. Eyeing a triple, McGrady kicks it up a notch.

Frank Horgan, manning left field for the first time, lumbers his body to retrieve the ball. He kicks it around, opening the door for McGrady to try for an inside-the-park round-tripper. By the time he flings the ball to the cut-off man, McGrady is past third.

Expecting another brutal collision at home, Bittner keeps his mask on and guards the plate. The cut-off man spins and throws a bullet. Instead of barreling over Bittner, McGrady dives head first, his arms and hands fully extended, his body parallel to the ground.

Right when Bittner catches the ball, McGrady lands and sneaks the tips of his fingers over the edge of the plate.

"Safe! Safe!" Digby hollers.

The Cranks jump out of their seats. The dugout goes nuts. A five-run lead sends everyone in a giddy lather.

Up in his box, Sterne sits stone-faced.

As much there is to get excited about, Deevers knows there's plenty of Base-Ball left to be played. Anything could happen.

Into the bottom of the seventh, Johnson appears to be sailing along. No one bothers him to ask if he's okay. They assume he's doing his usual duty of hoisting the game on his back and assuring victory.

He gets the first out on two pitches. But then the next two batters get on base, one on a hard-hit single, the other on a four-pitch walk. Johnson steps off the mound to take a breather before serving up another ball, which is crushed deep in the outfield. The East scores their first run.

The crazed exuberance in the stands fizzles like air let out of a balloon.

Deevers calls time out and heads to the mound. "You holdin' up?" He finally asks.

"I'm swell. Let's get after it."

"You sure?"

Johnson nods emphatically but won't look at him in the eyes. Deevers turns his head and looks at Schnockerd in the dugout. "Remember what you said about bullets." He slaps him on the back and returns to first.

With two men on, the next man up smashes a grounder to Deevers' left. The first baseman topples to the ground, trapping the ball with his glove. Everyone is safe.

He slowly gets up and takes several steps toward the mound. "Easy does it, Gus." He tosses him the ball.

Johnson takes a deep breath and gets back on the mound. Facing the next batter, he unwinds a fastball that sails straight for the batter's head. Luckily, he ducks just in time. The crowd erupts.

Pierce runs out toward Digby. "Just what in the hell does he think he's doing? He almost decapitated my man! That should warrant condemnation, at the very least."

Digby points his finger at him. "Get back in the dugout, Pierce. I'll call the game as I see it!"

Before turning back, he barks at Schnockerd. "Better watch your pitcher, Schnockerd. He's either blatantly trying to injure my players or he's starting to slip."

Schnockerd blows him a raspberry.

Johnson's next pitch nails the batter in the thigh, forcing in the second run.

What was smooth sailing just a few minutes before quickly turns into a nail-biter. Everyone inches closer to the edge of their seats, hoping for Johnson to get out of the inning. His overpowering fastballs have quickly petered out.

Foote enters the box. Johnson rears back and delivers his next pitch. It's right down the middle of the plate, but Foote can't catch up to it. Johnson does the same thing again on the next two pitches and Foote strikes out.

With only one more out to get, Johnson coaxes a lazy fly ball for the third out. Everyone breathes a sigh of relief.

Deevers returns to the dugout. "I don't know how much he's got left." He warns Schnockerd.

"Just two more innings. That's all we need from him."

"The steam's just about run out. They're starting to square him up pretty good."

They look down and see Johnson, sitting on the edge of the bench, glowering. Past him, sitting alone at the very end of the dugout, Wheatley stares straight ahead.

The eighth inning is even more ominous. Johnson starts off by giving up a ringing double, then another walk. Horgan and his monstrous bat are up next. Schnockerd rushes out and calls time out.

"How's it going, 'Plug? Whatever's left in the boiler, now's the time."

Johnson keeps his head down and nods. Schnockerd pats him on the shoulder and walks off.

Horgan waves his tree trunk bat. The crowd stirs.

Johnson goes right after him. His first pitch flutters in and Horgan sits back and waits for it. He swings and drives the ball deep, straightaway to center field.

Everyone thinks it's gone, but the backup to Johnson at center field tracks it all the way to the fence. At the last second, he leaps up to make the catch but it clanks off his glove.

"Damnit!" Horgan slams his bat to the ground, forced to hustle his giant frame down the base path.

Both men on base cross the plate, narrowing the lead to 5-4.

As if taking Schnockerd's words to heart, Johnson gathers himself and gives it all he's got. He strikes out the side. An ear-splitting thunderclap bursts from the stands.

Johnson staggers back to the dugout and collapses on the bench.

"Atta boy, 'Plug! I knew you could do it!" Schnockerd sits down next to him and rubs his shoulders. Johnson can barely keep his eyes open. "Just one more inning to go!"

"I don't know, Chief." Deevers looks down at the both of them.

"What don't you know, Chester? Gus here's doin' just fine! Just three more outs to go and you'll all be swimming in green!" His voice is loud and overly confident.

"We gotta get the kid up, just in case, Chief."

"Hog-Nuts! You still got something left, don't you, 'Plug?"

Johnson's head slumps down.

"I think the holster's empty, Pete. Time to get Wheatley up."

But Schnockerd won't hear any of it. "Our man won't let us down, will you, Gus?" He shakes his shoulder and Johnson slides off the bench and hits the floor.

"Gus! Gus! Come on, buddy, snap out of it!" Schnockerd pats him on the face with the back of his hand.

"That's it, Pete. We gotta go with Wheatley."

They both look at the tender-faced pitcher at the far end of the bench, clinging to his glove.

"Bullshit! I got him to go this far. Just three more outs, for chrissakes!" Schnockerd splashes water from a jug on Johnson's face and gets him back on his feet. He walks him back and forth in the dugout like a tavern patron trying to restore the senses of a drinking buddy.

Deevers pulls out a small vial of something. "Here, try this."

"What's this?"

"Smelling salts."

Schnockerd sticks it right under Johnson's nose. "Okay, Gus, big inhale!" Johnson breathes the fumes and his eyes bug out. "One more time!"

Johnson comes to.

"Atta boy!"

"What happened?"

"Nothin'. Just took a little nappy-poo. Now you're ready to shut the door on these clowns."

Johnson shakes his head. "I don't know, Chief. Like I told you, I don't think I have the staying power to pitch a whole game. My body's not used to it. I spent my last bullet."

"I told you, Pete." Deevers says.

Schnockerd grabs Johnson by his shoulders. "Look at me, Gus. You got us this far. Now you gotta reach down and pull up whatever's left in the barrel and get us through the last three outs. Can you do it for us?" Schnockerd grins. "Can you do it for me?"

The bottom of the ninth. A runner on second with two outs.

The entire stadium is permeated with a wild, deafening noise. All Johnson has to do is get one more out. Just one measly fly ball. A grounder hit right at somebody. A pop-up. Anything.

But Johnson is beyond exhaustion. Schnockerd paces. Even he realizes that Johnson is at the end of his tracks. Deevers keeps his eyes locked on him. Everyone in the stands is on their feet. Even Sterne gets out of his chair.

Stacks Bittner approaches the plate, looking for a good pitch to smash. Johnson circles the mound with his head down, mustering any last bit of energy and concentration. He climbs up the mound and stares blankly at Bittner. He slowly winds up and fires the first pitch.

"Strike one!"

The shrill bedlam from the stands gets even louder.

Bittner fouls off the next pitch.

Strike two.

Bittner steps out of the box, releases a dollop of saliva, and chokes up on the bat.

Johnson closes his eyes, takes a deep breath, and delivers the pitch. The ball sails over the outer corner of the plate. Bittner reaches out for it and hits it down the first base line. Deevers crashes to the ground but the ball shoots past him.

The runner on second races home, tying the game.

The ball hugs the foul line all the way to the fence. Bittner, never graced with speed, eyes a double. But once it reaches the fence, the ball gets stuck in a knothole and the right fielder can't dislodge it. Seeing what happens, Bittner hauls his broken-down body all the way to third, thinking about heading for home.

Fortunately for the West, the backup centerfielder rushes up and helps pry the ball loose. He whips himself around and throws a dart to the cut-off man, forcing Bittner to stay at third.

A cacophony of cheers and anxious moans clash in the stands.

Schnockerd rips out the sunflower seeds from his mouth and sprays them across the dugout floor. Deevers slowly pulls himself up off the dirt. Both men see Johnson crumple to the mound, looking like a marionette having lost its strings.

"Shit," Schnockerd mutters.

On his feet, Deevers calls time and gestures to the catcher to meet him at the mound. He bends down to check on Johnson, then looks over to Schnockerd.

Schnockerd turns toward the end of the dugout. "Wheatley!"

The young pitcher jumps in his seat.

"Get ready." Schnockerd make his way to the mound.

Johnson sits up. "I'm sorry, Chief."

Schnockerd puts his hand on his shoulder. "Don't worry about it, Gus. You gave it everything you got. What more could I ask for?"

Deevers straightens himself. "Is the kid ready?"

"Ready as he'll ever be."

Schnockerd turns and points to Wheatley, then announces the pitching change to Digby.

The public address announcer calls out Wheatley's name and the young pitcher trots out to a sweeping murmur across the stadium: "WHO??" The distinct feeling of imminent doom ripples like a wave.

Schnockerd greets Wheatley with a forced smile. "There he is. Ready to save the day, kid?"

Wheatley nods. His cap is pulled down tightly across his brow, concealing his eyes.

Deevers gets up close to him. "Okay, Wheatley, here's what I want you to do. The next hitter's a real free swinger. I want you to pump a fastball right down the middle of the plate, then work your way out. Make him chase the ball. Got it?"

Wheatley nods again.

"Okay, good. Remember," he looks at him straight in the eye, "don't pay attention to the runner on third. Just concentrate on the hitter."

Schnockerd hitches up his belt. His belly jiggles. "Are you nervous, Wheatley?"

"Pete…"

"Like Deevers said, just concentrate on the hitter. Don't worry about the hundred-thousand screaming people all around you."

Wheatley's eyes shift away from Schnockerd to the sea of bodies beyond the dugout.

"Don't get him nervous, Pete."

"Try and buck up as best you can, kid. Just one little mistake will cost us—"

"Pete, for chrissakes!" Deevers grabs Wheatley by his shoulders. "Just listen to me, Wheatley. Just one more out. Nice and easy. We got your back."

"Show 'em all what you're made of!"

Wheatley keeps nodding, but doesn't say anything.

"Cool as a cucumber!" Schnockerd heads back.

Poise. Wheatley keeps repeating the word in his head. *Don't think. Just throw.* He can't control the thoughts racing in his head.

But the moment hits him anyway.

His heart begins to pound against his chest. The anxiety that he's been able to tame for so long rises underneath his skin. He pulls off his cap and wipes a torrent of sweat cascading off his forehead.

Not now. You will not do this to me. I am in control.

Schnockerd claps his hands and showers Wheatley with encouragement.

Deevers smoothes some dirt with his foot and slaps the inside of his mitt. He looks across the diamond at Bittner standing on third, knowing that just one little bloop single, wild pitch or errant throw will be enough to dash all their hopes.

The next batter is absent. Everyone looks into the East's dugout and sees a shuffling of bodies. Pierce then hops out with his lineup card in hand and approaches Digby.

"What's this?" Schnockerd says, suspecting a pinch-hitter to be called. He scans his lineup card hanging on the dugout wall and tries to guess who it will be.

Pierce and Digby exchange words. The umpire nods, scratching something on the card. He shows the card to somebody in the stands, who passes the name to the public address announcer.

The crowd anxiously stirs.

Digby walks toward Schnockerd and motions to him. "Pinch-hitter, Pete."

"Who is it?"

The public address announcer blares through his megaphone. "Ladies and gentlemen, now hitting in place of Dunkle—"

The noise from the crowd suddenly escalates and drowns out Digby's voice.

"—GRANTHAM WENTWORTH!"

It takes about a second for the name to register a response from the crowd. When the legendary player for the New York Elites steps out, the Eastern Fans cannot contain themselves. Euphoria blazes across the stadium.

Their superstar hero from the glorious, halcyon days of yesterday has gallantly returned to seize this critical moment of the series.

Wentworth slowly makes his way to the batter's box. Though gaunt and worn, he manages to manifest a veneer of swagger and vanity, deliberately basking in the limelight he had commanded so long ago.

Recognizing the significance of the moment, a photographer runs up and snaps a picture of the enduring demigod.

"Wait a second." Wentworth stops and poses for another shot. He elevates his bat, cranes his neck and peers out toward the outfield, looking like a bronze statue from the days when his immortal mystique was a national phenomenon.

The Fans jump out of their seats, unable to contain their excitement. Sterne, standing in his perch, leans forward against his box and steeps in the fervor of his creation.

Schnockerd throws up his hands and looks incredulously at Deevers. Time is called once again and they converge at the mound.

"Who the hell is this guy? He's not on the roster list. What's Pierce cooking up?"

Deevers' eyes light up. "You mean you don't know who Grantham Wentworth is? He's the legend beyond all legends."

"How can that old shoe be a legend? He looks more beat up

than you, Chester. No offense."

"He single-handedly put the game on the map back in the day. No one was bigger than him. An American icon!"

Wheatley's heart pounds even harder. The anxiety ravages his legs.

"Yeah? So what do we do now? We could just plunk him and put him on base. Face the next guy."

Deevers shakes his head, unsure what to do. "I'd say yes, but we can't afford to risk facing the next batter. We'll have to pitch to him."

Schnockerd shrugs his shoulders. "How bad could that be? I mean, look at him."

Deevers rubs his fingers over is whiskery chin. "They wouldn't run him out there unless he's still got something left. I have no clue what to throw him."

Schnockerd yells at the East's dugout. "Hey, Pierce! Looks like you got yourself a ringer. Congratulations. Ha, ha! You really pulled one over us, didn't you?"

Pierce crosses his arms and smiles smugly.

Deevers grabs Wheatley by his uniform collar. "Kid, this is what you're gonna do." A surge of adrenaline jolts the pitcher's body. "You're gonna go right after him, *mano a mano*, get it? Throw him everything you got. Don't hold back!"

"Yeah, so what if this guy was the King of All Base-Ball," Schnockerd adds. Who cares? Just get him out, Wheatley. Let 'er rip!"

Before leaving the mound, Deevers pulls the pitcher close. "Again, nice and easy. Stay poised."

Keep your composure. Make your pitch. Nothing else but the pitch. Block out everything else.

Wentworth takes a couple of practice swings and enters the box. He glares right at Wheatley. The pitcher stands erect and still, keeping his glove up near his chest, looking like a poker player hiding his cards. The entire stadium is now in complete pandemonium.

Just look at the catcher. No one else. Breathe.

But Wheatley steals a peek at Wentworth. Their eyes lock, and the mythical hero curls his lips sideways — his immaculately tailored mustache skewing in the same direction — forming a devilish grin.

Whatever amount of self-control Wheatley had immediately vanishes. His anxiety breaks through his skin and overwhelms his entire body. He begins to shake.

No! Don't pay attention to him. Focus. Got to stay —

Before he tries delivering the first pitch, Wentworth suddenly relaxes his grip from his bat and steps out of the box. He points his finger at his opponent, as if he were sapping whatever energy Wheatley had left in him. Then he taps his finger on the end of his bat and points it again straight outward beyond the confines of the ballpark.

The crowd sees this and roars.

The hand gesture renders Wheatley powerless. Having nothing left to hold his anxiety back, it rips through his body and triggers a full-blown seizure, turning his shakes into a complete epileptic fit.

Everyone watches him convulse as if he were plugged into the Fair's AC generators. The ball falls out of his mitt. Wheatley drops to the mound.

The alarming spectacle causes everyone to stop and stare at Wheatley. But then Pierce jumps and hollers at Bittner on third base. "Run home, Stacks! Run!"

Bittner takes his eyes off Wheatley and sees his manager waving him in. For a second he doesn't know what to do.

Deevers immediately realizes what is about to happen and rushes to the mound to retrieve the ball and fire it to home plate.

Schnockerd thrusts his belly into the railing and throws his arms out. "Get that ball!"

Deevers pounces on Wheatley and tries to pry the ball out from underneath him. But it's too late.

Bittner hustles home. Before reaching the plate, the East's dugout empties and a trickle of Fans jump onto the field. They surge upon him right when he steps on the plate for the series-winning run.

Digby calls him safe and throws his arms up, declaring the game over. The East wins the series, three games to two.

Like a cannon shot, an explosion of noise rocks the stadium. Absolute chaos engulfs the field as throngs of people spill out onto the dirt and grass, running amok.

The Eastern Fans, rejoicing in the win, swarm the field and hoist their champion players on their shoulders. They parade them around, crowing loudly for everyone to hear that victory is theirs.

The mound quickly becomes a submerged island. Deevers can only take Wheatley—semi-conscious and tears streaming down his cheeks—and rest him on his lap.

Schnockerd finally comes out of the dugout and tries to wind his way through the onrush of spectators. Unable to move, he looks around and peers up into the stands.

High above, Sterne watches the celebration. His face shines with a glow of elation. His eyes beam. He grins with a smile never before seen in public.

Their eyes meet again.

Sterne snaps the brim of his tophat with his fingers and joyfully tips it in the direction of his nemesis.

Schnockerd nods back to him, mustering his own grin.

"WORLD'S" SERIES WINNER!

Champions & Goat

Sterne Group Defeats Schnockerd Team on Blunder

Local Player's Gaffe Costs Game

The field finally clears and the dignitaries who inaugurated the series return to their dais to deliver some closing remarks and present a trophy—garish and resplendent—to the East victors. But they know there is only one true recipient of the trophy and they convince the Governor to come down and accept it.

Ecstatic and overjoyed, Sterne, nevertheless, gives a short speech, thanking his players and manager for the fine effort in the fierce battle for control of the Game.

Someone pops a champagne cork and the sparkling bubbly just misses him.

He slips away just as the players and their Fans begin celebrating.

Sterne exits the stadium with the trophy in hand. The reporters hound him for one final charge, battering him with questions. He ducks into his cab and rides back to the train station without saying a word. They doggedly follow him, hell-bent on getting a quote.

At the station, Sterne finally steps out onto the rear platform of his car and looks down at them.

"Like inhaling a breathe of fresh air, I once again taste the sparkling purity of the sport that had been encumbered by the sullied waters of corruption, debauchery and immorality. Under my aegis, Base-Ball will no longer suffer from these afflictions. I guarantee that the Game will never again be infected by these pernicious forces. It will forever be wholesome and virtuous!"

With that, the *General Stockton II* triumphantly pulls away. ■

EPILOGUE

Honey Fuggle Tailpiece
(1976)

The staffers on the eighth floor of the *Times* empty out, looking for a bite to eat or lunchtime cocktail, but Jack Mullen sits in front of his Underwood typing away furiously with a pencil lodged in between his teeth.

Chuck, the beat writer, plops down in his chair and sticks his hand in a grease-stained paper bag, pulling out something wrapped in aluminum foil. He lobs a question over to the sports columnist. "Hey, Jack. How's the story coming?"

Punching away, Jack doesn't hear him.

Chuck wheels himself closer, biting down on a limp french fry. "Guess you won't be forced to answer dumb readers' letters in the column anytime soon."

"Hmm?" He pulls out the pencil. "Sweet Mary, I got more than enough material here to last a year's worth of Sunday columns. Maybe even a book down the road." He stops and chomps down on his liverwurst and cheese sandwich.

"The old man downstate really opened up something for you."

"Like a gold mine. I just had to deal with his occasional nodding off and the smell, of course."

"And you got it all checked out?"

"Yep. My man Leonid downstairs is lending me a hand." Mullen adjusts a new sheet of paper through the typewriter guide.

"You mean Leonard?"

"Yeah. Whatever."

Chuck stuffs his mouth with several more french fries. "He's still filling in the blanks? What about that Schnockerd guy? Did he find out about him, yet?"

"Not yet. He's still digging."

Chuck twists open a bottle of pop. "I bet you that pitcher's arm's been hanging on Schnockerd's wall in his den for years, like some kind of mounted trophy."

Mullen keeps fidgeting with the sheet of paper.

"He must have thrown the series, didn't he?"

Mullen lifts his finger. "Ah, the question du jour. Did he or didn't he? The old man always thought something fishy had happened, but had no definitive proof to back it up."

"I say yes. Why else would Schnockerd disappear soon after that, selling everything he had to do with baseball? He was bought off by that New York dude, found a way to lose the series, then went bye-bye."

"We'll just have to wait and see if ol' Lenny down in the dungeon can unearth something. In the meantime, I can't finish my story without a kicker. And without a kicker, I got no lede. No lede, no story. Right?"

"That's what they keep telling us." Chuck leans back in his chair. "So, he's working on the Schnockerd angle. What about the New York guy?"

"Sterne? I think we got him covered. He got his cherished game back through whatever means and returned to rule over it like a king and his empire until he finally kicked the bucket."

"An impressive reign, don't you say? Built the game from the ground up and took it all the way into this century."

"It's funny, Chuck, but if he could've hung on for another year or two he would've seen a championship for both sides of this town. Here we are and it's been diddly squat ever since."

Chuck takes a swig from his bottle. "And yet, ask any baseball nut about him and they'll say the same thing, '*Who?*'"

"Not one word in today's books. Not one mention in the Hall of Fame. Not even a plaque somewhere. Totally forgotten."

"That's hard to believe. If what the old man said was true, they should've named the damned building after him."

"So it goes, Chuck. Here today, gone tomorrow. Luckily, the world has Jack Mullen and his storytelling wizardry to revive the past."

"What did you find out about Sterne's family?"

"They petitioned the Hall of Fame for years, but no dice. They couldn't get him in. So he's buried in some fancy-schmancy mausoleum or tomb in upstate New York with all these inscriptions telling the world what he did for the game. That's all there is."

"Some legacy. At least he died a super-rich guy."

Mullen smiles. "In the end, that's all that matters. Don't let anybody else tell you differently. Legacies are for saps."

The phone rings. "Sports desk. Mullen." He listens. "Yeah? I'll be right down." He grabs a notebook.

"Leonard?" Chuck asks.

"Yep." He slaps his palms together. "Time for ol' Jack to cash in on some history. My basement rat's got me my kicker!"

"Ten bucks says Schnockerd did it." Chuck says. "He got paid off and ran away with the Mule's arm!"

"Ten bucks and drinks at O'Rourke's." Mullen winks at him.

Mullen bursts through the door of the Archives and Collections Department and glides across the darkened, musty room to Leonard's cage.

"Lenny, my boy! What's the poop?"

Leonard, wearing his heavy cardigan, is bent over a very old newspaper spread out over the counter. He peers over his bifocals and sees Mullen.

"Did you finally take my advice and escape this dungeon for some real oxygen and sunlight? Lennn-yyy? Watch'a got for me?"

He straightens up and removes his bifocals. "I've been giving it some thought about Schnockerd. I couldn't figure out why he suddenly disappeared after the series and never showed his faced ever again."

"'Cuz he got bought out and was forced to hand everything over, right? Tell me you found a letter or something. Tell me you have proof that he threw the series."

"Well, no. But I found it peculiar that his name never came up after that. But then I got this funny feeling in my head that I saw it somewhere before."

"He changed his name? Moved to Brazil? Someone killed him!"

Leonard shakes his head and points to the newspaper. "Sunday advertisements, 1897. Here." He hands Mullen a magnifying glass and points to a spot on the page crammed with blocks of tiny text, bold headings with decorative typefaces and crude line drawings of everything from soap to calligraphy services.

"What is it?" Mullen looks down.

"The microfilm never picked it up, but I remembered something. Really teeny-tiny. So I searched through the real things and finally found it."

Mullen bends down and hovers the magnifying glass over Leonard's finger. He sees an ad for an early automobile with the headline: "FORGO THE HORSE!"

Beneath the headline is an illustration of a couple riding in an open carriage. He scans through the text: "Save the expense of caring for the beast…our motors are the best of their kind…ride in comfort…pneumatic tires."

"What am I looking for?"

"Look at the name," Leonard says.

"The Rambling House Motor Carriage Company, Cleveland,

Ohio. So what?"

"Beneath that, the very last line, in the smallest font size. Do you see it?"

Mullen looks closely. "A Boorsley/Schnockerd Motor Manufacturing Company, LLC." He looks up. "Yeah?"

"It's an advertisement for one of the very first car companies, before the rise of the giant corporations."

"No shit, Sherlock."

"Do you get it? Schnockerd got out of the baseball business and into the car business, right at the very beginning of the auto industry."

"Okay, good for him. We know where he went after the series. But did he take a payoff from Sterne? Did he throw the series or not?"

"That's the interesting part," Leonard says. "I did my usual digging and came up with this." He lays a blotchy Photostat down on top of the newspaper filled with lines of signatures and handwritten numbers.

"What's this?"

"An old record of stock transferrals. Don't ask me where I got it."

Mullen looks down at the piece of paper.

"If you look closely, you'll see two names you're familiar with and a particular date."

Mullen looks up at Leonard. "Where are you going with this?"

"Don't you see? A controlling interest in this motor company was transferred over to Schnockerd right around the time of the series. They really had some sort of secret deal going on between them."

"Great. Sterne pays off Schnockerd by giving him ownership of this auto company. In turn, Schnockerd dumps the series and loses it for him. Where's the evidence that corroborates this? A nice, juicy letter between them that nails Schnockerd to the wall."

"Well, no, I didn't find any actual proof that Schnockerd threw the series. Just this record of them conducting a business transaction."

"Come on, Leonard. There's gotta be something out there, an actual document saying, 'I, so-and-so Schnockerd, will accept this stock transfer in exchange for throwing the 1893 Series.'"

"There's nothing out there that proves Schnockerd did anything to fix the series."

"Look some more, damnit."

Leonard shakes his head. "Did it ever occur to you that maybe the agreement was for the two of them to simply play against each other?"

"No way. Sterne went all the way to guarantee victory. He paid him off to lose the series any which way he could."

Leonard shrugs his shoulders. "Maybe so, but there's no evidence."

Mullen slaps his hand down against the counter. "I need the proof, Leonard. Without it I don't have my kicker. I don't want to be forced to start making shit up. Dig some more."

"I did. I found out more about this company, The Rambling House Motor Carriage Company. Sterne definitely had a controlling interest in this small company and signed it all over to Schnockerd. He operated it until after the turn of the century when General Motors gobbled him up. He made a tidy profit."

"Big whoop."

"But there's a kicker in all of this."

"Yeah?"

"There were patents involved that Schnockerd was allowed to keep, something to do with the design of the motor he was selling. Real technical, detailed stuff."

"That's not the kind of kicker I'm looking for."

"Yeah, well, Schnockerd retained the rights to those patents and GM integrated his design into their motors. One thing led to another, the auto industry exploded and he became a *gazillion*-aire. Nice, huh?"

"Real nice, Leonard. That still doesn't help me. Where's the kicker?"

"The kicker is that Schnockerd snatched that business away from Sterne. Took it right out from under his nose without him knowing the full ramifications. Perhaps he had the foresight and Sterne didn't. It was just a throwaway to him in exchange for the chance to get his game back."

"He got it all right." Mullen closes his notebook and stuffs his pen in his shirt pocket.

"Yeah, Sterne got what he wanted and Schnockerd got his, at the enormous expense of his rival. Kind of ironic they both lived out their lives in obscurity."

"Maybe Schnockerd did move to Brazil and lived a tycoon's life on the fruits of the auto revolution?"

"The next, great industry took off and he capitalized on it."

"I'd say. Right time, right place and he scored big time."

"Just like any good Captain of Industry." ■

About the Author

Tracy Tomkowiak is a graphic designer who lives in the Chicago suburbs with his wife and two sons. His interests include history, biographies and...wait for it...baseball.

Made in the USA
Lexington, KY
30 March 2014